BETRAYAL

Center Point
Large Print

Also by Christina Dodd and available from
Center Point Large Print:

The Bella Terra Deception Series
Secrets of Bella Terra
Revenge at Bella Terra

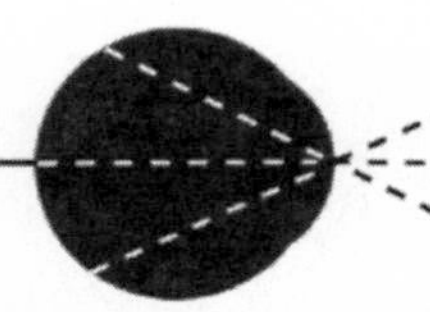

This Large Print Book carries the Seal of Approval of N.A.V.H.

BETRAYAL

A BELLA TERRA DECEPTION NOVEL

CHRISTINA DODD

CENTER POINT LARGE PRINT
THORNDIKE, MAINE

This Center Point Large Print edition
is published in the year 2012 by arrangement with
NAL Signet, a member of Penguin Group (USA) Inc.

This is a work of fiction. Names, characters, places,
and incidents either are the product of the author's
imagination or are used fictitiously, and any
resemblance to actual persons, living or dead,
business establishments, events,
or locales is entirely coincidental.
The text of this Large Print edition is unabridged.
In other aspects, this book may vary
from the original edition.
Printed in the United States of America
on permanent paper.
Set in 16-point Times New Roman type.

ISBN: 978-1-61173-387-7

Library of Congress Cataloging-in-Publication Data

Dodd, Christina.
Betrayal : a Bella Terra deception novel / Christina Dodd. — Large print
ed.
p. cm. — (Center Point large print edition) (A Scarlet Deception novel
series; 3)
ISBN 978-1-61173-387-7 (lib. bdg.)
1. Large type books. I. Title.
PS3554.O3175B48 2012
813′.54—dc23

2012005407

For Joyce,
thank you for so many years of
sharp critiquing and true friendship.
Cilantro will always burn in our firepit
on the summer solstice
in remembrance.

Acknowledgments

Leslie Gelbman, Kara Welsh, and Kerry Donovan, my appreciation for your support. Thanks to NAL's art department led by Anthony Ramondo. To Rick Pascocello, head of marketing, and the publicity department with my special people, Craig Burke and Jodi Rosoff, thank you. My thanks to the production department and, of course, a special thank-you to the spectacular Penguin sales department: Norman Lidofsky, Don Redpath, Sharon Gamboa, Don Rieck, and Trish Weyenberg. You are the best!

Thank you to Roger Bell for reading *Betrayal*, and always being so kind in your critiques.

Chapter 1

For Penelope Alonso Caldwell, the distance between Portland, Oregon, and Bella Terra, California, was five hundred miles and nine years.

She hadn't expected to remember the way. As she and her mother left Bella Terra, Penelope had been crying so hard. . . . Her eyes had been swollen; every breath had hurt; her eighteen-year-old self had thought she would die of agony.

But she must have soaked it all in: the scent of pine, the asphalt slashed by sun and shadow, the sudden descent into the valley, where grapevines stretched in unending rows, where boutique wineries nestled in groves of trees, where here and there an old-fashioned farmhouse sat sometimes ramshackle and abandoned, and sometimes . . . sometimes it was tended lovingly by the descendants of the very family that had built it.

The highway plunged from the mountains to the flats created by the wanderings of the Bella River and took a turn to the south.

Then she knew she was close to her destination. She knew by the strength of the sunshine against her knuckles on the steering wheel, by the breeze against the arm she rested through the car's open window, by the intoxicating scents of sunshine on fresh-turned earth, of ripening peaches and wine-scented oak barrels. Here in Bella Terra, spring hung on the cusp of summer, and the air smelled like broad green leaves, like freshly mown grass, like breathless first love and young hope dashed.

What a fool she'd been.

So why did this place smell like home?

It did not. Could not. She would not let it.

Penelope had been raised in Los Angeles and Portland, and she'd lived most of her adult life in Cincinnati. Hot pavement defined the smell of home, so she concentrated on the odor of asphalt baking beneath the California sun, and watched for her destination.

She'd been afraid she wouldn't recognize the Sweet Dreams Hotel, but there it was on the right, twenty-five rooms of ramshackle inn glowing with the same violent turquoise paint that had graced it nine years ago.

She turned into the parking lot and noted the changes: The doors had been replaced; a new sign pointed the way to the office; the trim had been changed from vibrant peach to staid white, as if that change made any difference to the overall tackiness of the place.

The Beaver Inn was next door, a rough-and-tumble bar that used to be the hangout for the farmworkers in the valley, a place where fights were a nightly occurrence and everyone carried knives. Nothing about it said the bar was anything different today: A variety of fluorescent beer signs blinked in the windows, the smudged door had a high, diamond-shaped window, and a flatbed truck was pulled into the shade with the hood open and two guys armed with wrenches staring disgustedly into the engine compartment.

Right now, with her finances iffy, she could afford this place.

She parked her mother's aging yellow Volvo C70 in front of the motel office and walked in.

A large man with massive shoulders and no neck sat reading something on an e-reader.

He looked like a football player. He looked like a *familiar* football player.

She delved into the depths of her memory for his name. *Primo Marino*.

When she'd lived here, he'd been the town's pride and joy, a running back for UCLA and one of the NFL's most dazzling candidates for the draft. Apparently his bright career had ended here, working behind the counter at his family's dilapidated motor inn.

She wondered what had happened to dash his bright future . . . but mostly she hoped he didn't remember her.

From the bored way he surveyed her, she would guess he didn't.

"I'd like a room for a week," she said.

"A week?" He looked her up and down, then

glanced around at the worn office and raised his eyebrows. "Really? A week?"

"Yes. I've got business in Bella Terra and I need a room for a week." He scrutinized her with more interest, as if she were an anomaly in this place—she was wearing flip-flops and jeans and a T-shirt that said, LORD OF THE ONION RINGS, so she wasn't overdressed. But maybe she was overclean.

As intently as he viewed her, she feared some of his brain synapses would start to fire. So she handed him her credit card.

Money always claimed people's attention.

He held the silver plastic between two massive fingers and studied it, his brow wrinkled. "Don't you want to see the room first?"

"Is this still Arianna Marino's property?"

"Yeah. Aunt Arianna. You know her?" He handed Penelope a clipboard with a form to fill out.

She took it gratefully and wrote down her name, home address, and her car's license plate number. "The motel gets good ratings on Yelp, and she's cited as the reason." Which was true. It was also true Penelope knew her, and intended to stay out of her way. "As long as the room is clean, I'll be happy." And it would be. She'd stayed here with her mother that whole long, lovely summer, and she knew that with Arianna Marino in charge, the place might be shabby, but it would be spotless. And quiet. And there would be no renting of the next room for an hour.

Arianna Marino was a force to be reckoned with.

Not to mention that Penelope found a measure of comfort in the memory of that time with her mother, and these days Penelope took comfort where she could.

"Okay," Primo said. "I need a photo ID before I run this credit card."

She passed her Oregon driver's license over the counter.

"Penelope Caldwell," he read aloud, then compared the two and held the license up to compare the photo with her face. "Looks good."

She sighed in relief. Her last name had changed, but her first name was fairly uncommon. If Primo was going to remember, he would have when he looked at her license. He really wasn't the brightest bulb in the box.

"No one else in your party?" He looked at her car, searching for another guest.

"I'm alone." An understatement.

"Okay, I'll put you in number fourteen. It's far enough away from the bar to be quiet, but not so far you couldn't yell for help if you got into trouble."

She didn't like that comment. "What kind of trouble would I get into?"

"Sometimes the guys at the bar misunderstand

about a single woman at the motel, especially after a hard night of drinking. Don't worry. You'll be safe." Primo shrugged his massive shoulders. "I do security. Aunt Arianna says it keeps me off the streets."

Penelope relaxed. "I'm sure you do a good job, too." She couldn't imagine any man going up against a behemoth like Primo.

"I've had a few guys who thought they could take me," he said.

"What happened?"

"They lived."

She laughed.

He didn't.

He handed her a key card. "The ice machine's in here. We had to move it inside when the drunks started peeing in it. But you can always get ice—we keep the office manned at all times. No cooking in your room." He spread a map out on the counter, then got an envelope and stuffed a bunch of slips of paper inside. "Present one of these tokens at any of these fine eateries in town"—his big finger moved from one mark to another—"and they'll give you breakfast, a value of up to ten dollars."

Since the room was sixty-two fifty a day, she thought that was a pretty good deal. "Thank you."

"You can always ask us for recommendations—wineries, restaurants, activities. The Marinos have lived here for over a hundred years. We know the valley inside and out. We won't steer you wrong." He pointed toward his right. "Number fourteen is that way. Park in front. Welcome to Bella Terra." In a none-too-subtle invitation to buzz off, he picked up his e-reader, flipped it on, and stared at the screen.

He was probably "reading" the swimsuit edition of *Sports Illustrated*.

"Thank you," she said again, and backed out the door, immeasurably cheered to have the first hurdle of her visit to Bella Terra successfully leaped.

She might just pull this off after all.

Primo waited until Penelope had moved her car into the parking space in front of her room. Putting aside his e-reader and the open file of *Dante's Inferno*, he picked up the chipped pink princess phone—Aunt Arianna didn't believe in replacing perfectly working equipment, even if it was fifty years out of date—and placed the call. "Aunt Arianna, you aren't going to believe who just pulled into the motel and booked a room."

Chapter 2

At the Di Luca family home, the pounding of hammers and the sound of nails being wrenched from old wood echoed through the open front door screen and down the hall to the kitchen. There Sarah Di Luca placed a King Ranch casserole into the three-hundred-fifty-degree oven. The chicken dish was loaded with fat and sodium, cheese, sour cream, and canned cream soups, but the boys—her grandsons, Eli, Rafe, and Noah—loved it, and working as they were in the heat, they'd burn off the calories.

Her bodyguard, Bao Le, stuck close most of the time, but right now Bao had gone to check on the security guards who patrolled the perimeter of the Di Luca property.

Her granddaughters-in-law, Brooke and Chloë, had left to pick up a flat of strawberries for shortcake.

So Sarah was alone in the kitchen, and these days that was a rare thing.

Wiping her hands on her apron, Sarah listened as, with well-controlled violence, the boys—she never thought of them as her grandsons—tore apart her front steps. But she heard no voices, no banter, and they worked with an unceasing urgency, as if the stairs that had stood with the house for a hundred and twenty years needed to be demolished *now*.

The boys said the steps were too steep for her. Which wasn't true. She'd lived sixty years in this house, since she'd come here as Anthony Di Luca's bride, and she'd never once fallen down those stairs.

But ever since she'd been attacked here in her home, the boys had been anxious, solicitous, and *bossy*. That didn't surprise her; in her life she'd learned a lot of things about men, and number one was, when they were scared for someone they loved, they didn't say they were scared. They didn't express affection. They didn't give solicitous cards or boxes of candy.

Darn it.

Instead, they *fixed* things. Things like the stairs. Her security system. They had even provided her with a nurse and a bodyguard. Putting things to rights made men feel better. Made them feel in control.

Which was great for them, but she could stand only so much of their fixing before she wanted to knock their stubborn heads together. Because they hadn't solved anything. Instead . . . now they were angry at each other. Furious.

She hated that.

It wasn't as if they had never fought before. They'd grown up together (mostly) in her house (mostly) and had always made Sarah's life interesting. But when they were boys, their fights had resulted in scrapes and bruises and the occasional black eye. This time . . . this time they nursed a corrosive fury that, if not resolved, could dissolve the sense of family and affection they felt for one another.

Taking three bottles of water from the refrigerator, she walked down the hall, past the second bedroom and the bathroom and the dining room, past her bedroom and the front room. She bumped her hip against the screen door. It swung open, and she walked out onto the high front porch.

The house was old, built at the turn of the twentieth century by Ippolito Di Luca for his bride. At the time, the farmhouse had been the height of style and comfort, with two bedrooms, a spacious kitchen, and even an indoor toilet. By modern standards, it was tiny and worn, but every time Sarah stepped out onto her porch, she knew she had the best view in the world.

Her home sat perched high on the south end of long, narrow Bella Valley, and from here the vista spread out in a glorious, constantly changing array of browns and greens and golds. With a glance, she could see the lush bottomlands and the silver trickle of the Bella River that had, through thousands of years, carved the basin.

Outside of the town of Bella Terra, swaths of

orchards rustled with leaves that protected the burgeoning fruit from California's sun, and long stripes of grapevines rose from the valley and crested the neighboring hills. Beyond that, the mountains cradled the valley in rocky arms, protecting it from the harshest ocean storms and the blustery winds that swept down the Sierras.

Throughout Sarah's eighty years, she'd watched as Bella Terra grew from a tiny country town to a bustling urban area; right now, she could almost hear summer's influx of tourists buzzing like bees as they set out from the hive to tour the vineyards and sip their finest wines.

Much of the land she could see was Di Luca land. The family was a kind of nobility here, first among the Italian families to realize the potential of the soil and take it as their own. Sarah supposed it wasn't a gracious thing to exult in the Di Luca possessions. But she did. She loved it all: their acres of grapes, their illustrious winery, their luxurious resort. . . . More than all of it put together, though, she loved her grandsons.

She stood staring down at Rafe and Eli, at the tops of their heads, hair matted with sweat and exertion. Rafe attacked her steps with a pry bar. Eli, hampered by one cast on his arm and another on his foot, tossed the splintered wood into a pile.

Noah was nowhere in sight.

She viewed the two oldest sternly. "Where's Noah? Did he leave?"

Rafe and Eli scowled, lowered their tools, and reached up to her for their water.

She held the bottles out of their reach. "Well?"

Eli wiped his forehead on the arm of his blue denim shirt. "We buried him under the hydrangea."

Sarah wouldn't have minded the sarcasm . . . but beneath his mockery lay that wealth of anger. "Where is he?" she insisted.

Rafe raised his voice and called, "Hey, Noah! Come out; Nonna thinks we've killed you."

Using the tall hole where the stairs used to be, Noah ducked out from beneath the porch. He grinned up at her, a half-cocked grin she recognized from his childhood. Whenever he looked like that, it meant he was in trouble and hoped to charm his way out.

She didn't think he could charm his way out of this.

"I'm okay. But I need to get you some mouse killer for under the porch. When one ran across my foot, I jumped so hard I about knocked myself out." He rubbed his head.

His brothers laughed, and Rafe smacked him on the place he rubbed.

Noah socked Rafe in the belly, and for good measure smacked Eli on his fit arm.

For a moment, things were almost normal.

Then the laughter died and Eli and Rafe

stepped away from Noah as if he sported a suspicious rash.

"Drink some water," Sarah said hastily. "I don't want you boys getting dehydrated." She handed out the bottles, and though she was upset with her grandsons . . . pride swelled in her.

Even covered with dirt and sweaty with exertion, they were long limbed and healthy, filling out their T-shirts and jeans in a way that made young women watch with profound appreciation.

Of course, how could these boys be anything but attractive? Their father was a movie star, as charismatic as the full moon and with just about as much parenting sense. Gavino, her only son, careless, unfaithful, selfish and her greatest failure. But he'd produced sons, and these boys were everything for which a grandmother could hope.

Eliseo—Eli—was the oldest, thirty-four, with the Di Luca family's dark hair and his beauty-queen mother's big brown eyes. He was tall and lanky, muscled by long hours working in the vineyards. At the same time, he had the rare and exquisite sensibilities of a man who produced wines that tasted of green grass and spring, of red ripe berries and summer, of warm spice and autumn. He was a genius with the grapes, and for that, he was venerated, adored, and feted.

Luckily for him, he'd recently met the love of

his life, and Chloë had cut him down to size and made him human again.

Raffaelo—Rafe—was thirty-one, with dark hair and electric blue eyes. His mother, one of the world's foremost Italian movie stars, and his father had created a young man so handsome that before the age of ten, he'd been a star himself. But he'd hated the phony emotions that his parents portrayed so convincingly, and as an adult he'd become a real hero. He'd joined the military, then created his own security firm and done everything he could to protect Sarah and everyone he loved from harm.

But he had almost lost the woman he loved. He'd almost lost Brooke. That had broken his false pride, given him new perspective, and now he treasured his wife in a way that made Sarah proud.

If only . . . if only she understood what madness drove Noah.

Genoah—Noah—at twenty-eight was the youngest of Gavino's boys. His dark hair was his father's. His guileless green eyes . . . Sarah didn't know whom he'd inherited his eyes from. She didn't know his mother. She'd never met his mother. As far as she knew, no one had ever met Noah's mother—except Gavino, of course. Sarah had never doubted Noah was Gavino's child; he possessed the arrogant Di Luca bone structure as well as the Di Luca allure.

When Gavino brought Noah home and placed the red-faced, squalling baby in Sarah's arms, Gavino had no longer sported his usual bland, uncaring, movie-star charm. He had been angry, embarrassed, and defiant, and he had refused to say how he came by the child—and that was unlike the Gavino she knew, who enjoyed hugely public marriages and affairs with a parade of gorgeous women.

Yet for all that Sarah wanted to unravel the mystery of Noah's parentage, to raise the child without interference from his parents was easy. Noah had been the golden child, raised in Nonna's home, a loving, happy, laughing boy. She and her beloved Anthony had been his parents, and she loved Noah so much, her second-chance child, the one she hoped to raise to be a good man.

She had never expressed her hopes to him; looking back, she was sure she had never burdened him with her expectations.

But ten years ago, after Noah graduated from high school, he'd taken a year off to travel the world, and when he came home . . . she no longer recognized him as the boy she had known. Something dreadful had happened, and no matter how carefully she questioned, he refused to talk. He shrugged and smiled and told her he was fine, and went to college, and excelled in his studies.

Of course, Rafe and Eli were oblivious.

They were such *guys,* Noah's older siblings. When Sarah mourned the changes in Noah's behavior, they patted her shoulder and told her their little brother had become a man. They'd believed it was cool that Noah's personality had changed, that he'd suddenly become reckless, riding his motorcycle up steep mountain slopes in Colorado, breaking bones in international karate tournaments, handling every kind of firearm with ease . . . as if his life depended on it. . . .

Eli and Rafe had been oblivious, as all men were, to emotions and nuances, and the fact that Noah behaved like someone who feared nothing, not even death . . . and he could no longer quite meet anyone's eyes. For a decade, she had feared for her youngest grandson.

It had taken this crisis to peel back the truth. Not the whole truth, though, merely a single layer of truth. When Sarah's nurse had been murdered, Noah had said in a burst of ill-considered grief and passion, "I'm right in the middle of this. These people . . . they're ruthless, and they are going to find Massimo's pink diamonds any way they can."

Too late, he had reined himself in.

Now Rafe and Eli, Brooke and Chloë—and Sarah—wanted to know it all. Needed to know it all. They had worked out that there could be priceless stolen diamonds hidden in the family's oldest, missing bottle of wine, but *who* were these people he spoke of?

Yet Noah refused to talk. He shook his head and said he'd take care of it, and nothing they had said had changed his mind.

Eli and Rafe were furious that they'd been deceived, that their brother knew something he wouldn't divulge, while if they'd been willing to simply open their eyes, they would have known, as Sarah did, that something horrific had happened ten years ago, something that changed Noah, hurt him, made him afraid. . . .

Sarah's unbidden tears splashed on the dusty white-painted railing.

She hastily wiped them away.

How had everything gone so bad so quickly?

Chapter 3

Noah didn't need the furious glares of his brothers to know the truth.

He was the biggest shit in the world.

Nonna was crying. He'd made Nonna cry.

And they were going to have to do something about it.

Noah vaulted onto the porch first, then Rafe; then they both helped Eli heave himself and his casts up and over.

Nonna watched them, tears welling in her big brown eyes, splashing down her wrinkled, tanned cheeks, painful sobs racking her shoulders.

Noah felt sick with guilt.

Maybe the other guys did, too, because without discussion or discord, they put their arms around her, surrounding her with love. Her boys. She called them her boys, and they owed her more than they had given her lately.

Eli was the oldest, so he said, “Nonna, it’s okay. We’ll get this mess figured out somehow.”

That didn’t help at all. Instead, she put her head on his chest and cried harder.

Nonna wasn’t a woman given to outbursts of emotion. She was strong, had been strong all her life. But there had been too much turmoil lately.

She’d been attacked by a robber in her own home.

She’d been hospitalized with a concussion and a broken arm.

She’d come home with Bao, her bodyguard, and Olivia, her nurse, and the three of them had formed a tight and loving circle . . . or so it had seemed.

She’d been betrayed. His sweet, loving grandmother had been deceived by someone she trusted.

In between her sobs, Nonna said, “Poor, stupid, dishonest Olivia. It’s . . . my fault . . . she’s dead.”

“What?” Rafe shook his head as if he couldn’t

quite believe he'd heard her correctly. "How is it your fault?"

"I knew it was either Bao or . . . or Olivia who searched my room. I'm the one who . . . who set the trap. When she fled . . ." Nonna took a long, quivering breath. Her crying calmed. She lifted her tearstained face. "In those last minutes of her life, that poor girl must have been so afraid. When I think of her, shot in the back of the head, execution-style."

Eli, Rafe, and Noah exchanged glances.

They should never have told Nonna how she'd been killed. They should have known that knowledge would haunt her.

"So much trouble has come to Bella Terra. So much pain. So much suffering. So many victims," Sarah lamented. "And for what? A bottle of wine. A few diamonds. They're only *things*."

Eli, Rafe, and Noah had come here today to rebuild Sarah's stairs—but actually, they were here so she wouldn't be left alone to grieve.

She had lost a little of the faith and trust that made her who she was. They could not bear that.

"Nonna, Olivia was in league with thieves and murderers. She drugged you. You could have died." Eli hugged her more tightly against him.

"She drugged Bao. You had no protection. My God, you could have been kidnapped. You could have been killed." Noah's hand convulsed on Nonna's shoulder.

His fault. All of this was his *fault.*

Since the year he was nineteen, Noah Di Luca had known he towed death along behind him with an unbreakable chain and he had forged that chain himself.

His family called him the carefree one, the one who had escaped unscathed from the angst that drove his brothers through hell. That was fine; he took care to maintain that lighthearted facade.

Because he wasn't like his brothers, tortured by an unkind fate. He and he alone had screwed up his life.

Once he had faced that fact, he made choices. Some had been easy, some difficult.

He played hard: raced his motorcycle, skied the black slopes, flew a glider.

He worked hard, maintaining tight control over the family-owned Bella Terra resort, constantly improving the service, the setting, the restaurant.

He loved deeply. But only his grandmother, his brothers . . . even his fickle, thoughtless father.

Noah's crime was old, but like Jacob Marley's chains, he'd dragged it behind him into the present.

He wanted to say something, do something that would make it all better. But the last time he'd opened his mouth, he'd said too much. For the first time in ten years, a smidgen of the truth had come bursting out of him. If he had told them the entire truth . . . their deaths would be on his hands. It was too dangerous to confide in his family.

Now he remained resolutely silent, totally ineffectual, doing nothing more than standing close, with his hand on Nonna's shoulder.

She sniffled. "Do any of you boys have a handkerchief?"

"No. Here." Rafe offered Nonna the hem of his T-shirt. "Olivia got tangled up with the wrong people, and she paid the price."

"Of her life!" Nonna's eyes flashed, and she used the hem of her apron to wipe her cheeks.

"A very wise woman once told me that life ain't fair," Eli said.

"Once?" Rafe said.

When they were growing up and they complained about getting picked last in baseball or a teacher who didn't like them, "Life ain't fair," had been Nonna's response.

Noah had come to think that was the truest piece of wisdom she had taught them.

From the open screen door, Bao Le spoke. "Olivia's death is my fault." Slowly she opened the door, and with the fluid ease of a martial artist, she moved out to join them. Petite and slender, the daughter of Vietnamese immigrants, she was one of Rafe's most trusted employees. Although Noah would have said it wasn't possible, with Olivia's betrayal Bao's protection of Nonna had escalated. Bao had always been intense; now her large brown eyes glowed with fervor. Three times a day and, as far as he knew, five times a night, she left the house and stalked the grounds, checking with the other guards, looking for any sign an intruder had crept through their net of security. "It's my fault," she repeated. "She had a clean background check, but I should have seen the truth." She offered Nonna a box of tissues.

"No, Bao." Nonna broke away from her grandsons. She took a tissue and wiped her nose. "I should have questioned Olivia more. Instead, I thought I should respect her privacy. She never told me about herself."

The ultimate damnation. Nonna had a way of listening, as if she was really interested, and everyone talked to her. They confessed everything in their pasts, happiness or sorrow or guilt or self-satisfaction. Sooner or later, Nonna knew all of everyone's hopes, ambitions . . . and sins.

Nonna hugged Bao.

Bao stood stiff and unresponsive. Finally she gave in, bowed her head, and put it on Nonna's shoulder. For just a second. Then she sprang back to attention, as if afraid that even a moment's daydreaming would once more result in disaster. "Someone offered her money," Bao said, "either before she came to Bella Terra or after she came to work in your house, and she took the bribe. I don't understand why you cry for her, Mrs. Di Luca. She was the worst kind of person, one who betrays all that is good and honorable in this world."

"You're right, dear. And yet I cry." Sarah smiled at Bao, but that smile wavered.

Bao scowled. "I will check your casserole." She went in and slammed the door behind her.

"She's angry that she failed you," Rafe said.

"I know. Yet I failed, too. I should have seen that Olivia could betray us." Nonna dabbed at her red nose.

As much as it pained Noah to see his grandmother cry, he felt an even deeper sorrow. Sooner or later, she would know Noah's secrets and sins, and when she did, she would ache for him as she ached for Olivia.

For like Olivia, he would be dead.

Chapter 4

We were all fools." Eli collapsed back into the porch swing. With his good hand, he lifted his broken foot onto the seat and grimaced as if it ached from the heat and the work. "How could we not have investigated *why* someone so desperately wanted that bottle of wine?"

So true. They had simply assumed someone—Joseph Bianchin, a longtime enemy of the Di

Lucas—had wanted the bottle for the prestige of owning the last bottle created by famed winemaker Massimo Bruno.

Rafe leaned against the porch railing and in a pontifical, mocking tone, he said, "I have a brother . . . who's an authority on wine . . . and he told me that any bottle of wine made by Massimo Bruno during Prohibition had the potential to be worth many thousands of dollars."

Eli, the aforementioned brother, turned sideways, rested his casted arm on the back of the swing, and said, "Well, it has. It is! And once Nonna told us Joseph Bianchin wanted the bottle, I figured that was the whole"—he gestured—"mystery. He *was* behind the attack on Nonna. Nasty old bastard."

Everyone on the porch nodded.

Nonna said, "He tried to kill your grandfather on our wedding day. That makes him more than a nasty old bastard. That makes him a—"

Noah's arm shot out, and he hugged her to him hard. "Nonna, speaking as one of your grandsons, I gotta tell you—you can't say stuff like that. It makes us duck and run while we wait for the lightning to strike."

She chuckled drily against his shirt and hugged him around the waist. "All right, dear, but I've heard all the words. I've even used them in Scrabble with Annie and June."

Annie and June were Nonna's sisters-in-law and best friends, Noah's great-aunts, women who lived at the Di Luca family's resorts on California's romantic Far Island and on the wild Washington coast. "But you haven't seen them in a year," Noah objected.

Nonna dismissed his objection with a wave. "Oh, please. We play online."

"Foolish me. Of course you do." Because Nonna would use every means at hand to keep in touch with those she loved.

"I still believe Bianchin was behind it all," Nonna said.

"It was definitely him who started the trouble. Noah's done one thing right." Rafe looked at Noah. "He chased Joseph Bianchin out of town."

Noah inclined his head. "I wish he was back in town. I want to know what he knows, now that we figured out what was in that bottle—"

"*We* figured it out?" Eli smirked.

"Okay, *you*." Security guy that Rafe was, he liked to be the one who figured stuff out.

"Me and Chloë," Eli said.

"She was the real brains behind the whole pink-diamond discovery, wasn't she?" Rafe asked.

Eli stretched and grinned. "What do you think? She's a writer. She plots mysteries for a living."

Noah watched his brothers, amused by Rafe's chagrin, by Eli's newlywed complacency.

Rafe must have seen, for he turned on him and snapped, "Noah! Did you know something about Olivia?"

"What? No! Why?" He'd spent so many years practicing a casual expression—had he looked guilty? Or were Rafe and Eli suspicious of his every expression now?

"You were interested in her," Rafe said. "Then you weren't. Did you suspect her?"

Noah relaxed infinitesimally. "I was interested in her. She was interested in me. We shared a few kisses, but she wanted more than I was willing to give."

"You mean like marriage?" Eli asked.

"Yup."

"And you won't marry," Nonna said.

He looked away, discomfited by her steady gaze. "No. I won't marry."

Nonna lowered herself into the red-painted rocking chair, moving slowly, painfully, like an old lady.

She wasn't an old lady. She was eighty, but until this ordeal had started Noah and his brothers had bragged about her, how active she was, how astute, how cool she was, a fan of Australian football, a proud, sharp-voiced liberal, a volunteer at the food kitchen, and when she dispensed advice about business or finances or personal matters, the Di Luca boys listened.

For God's sake, she drove a 1967 titty pink Ford

Mustang convertible with original upholstery. And she drove it *fast*.

Now she looked tired and red eyed, and as if she ached with sorrow.

Noah spoke hastily, waving the mystery of Olivia like a shiny toy to distract her. "Anyway, Olivia tried to put pressure on me, then suddenly . . . boom! She shrugged me off. I suppose she wanted money—my money. I suppose when *they* contacted her, she decided she didn't need me."

"They?" Rafe's blue eyes lit with triumph, and he pounced. "Why *they?* Why not *him?* For a job like this, I always suspect a man."

"Okay. *Him*." Noah let his very real annoyance sound in his voice. "You know the ropes *in a job like this*. In my business, *as head of the family's resort,* the real pains in the ass are women, especially in large groups. I swear to God, I am never letting another romance writers' conference in my hotel."

Rafe and Eli exchanged glances.

"When you had your little reveal, you said, 'I'm in the middle of it. These people are ruthless, and they are going to find Massimo's pink diamonds any way they can.' " Eli pointed his cast at Noah. "So what the hell am I supposed to believe? What you say now? Or what you said then?"

"I'm a congenital liar." Noah shrugged.

"You little shit," Rafe said in a low voice. "Tell us."

"Look, I got suspicious about all that fuss about a bottle of wine, so I looked up information about Massimo. I figured stuff out, got too involved in the process, and when I said I was in the middle of it, I meant I was in the middle of looking into the case. I didn't realize everyone was going to take me so literally." Noah checked his brothers for their reaction.

They weren't buying it.

Tempers sizzled. The emotional temperature on the front porch rose. If Nonna hadn't been there, Eli and Rafe would have reverted to childhood, sat on Noah, and punched him until he gave up the information—or lost consciousness.

He *would* have lost consciousness before he told them the truth.

Thank God, the low-throated roar of a powerful motor sounded in the distance.

Heads turned.

"The girls are back!" Nonna said, and smiled.

She loved her new granddaughters-in-law.

She loved seeing Eli and Rafe married at last.

Noah had hoped those two marriages would satisfy her, but obviously she still had hopes for him. And in the normal run of things, he would be married, with a string of kids.

Hey. No regrets. He'd made himself a good life.

Eli stood and limped over to join Rafe at the rail. Both men watched the long, winding drive to the Di Luca farmhouse with an intensity that all too plainly expressed their anxiety. They knew they had to let the women go to town. They couldn't confine Brooke and Chloë for their safety. But with the violence that had happened in Bella Terra, they feared every moment Brooke and Chloë were out of their sight.

Nonna joined them at the rail and watched the cognac metallic Porsche Panamera 4S with palpable lust. "I have to talk to Chloë about letting me drive that bad boy," she said.

Noah grinned.

Eli wore the pained expression of a man whose wife had bought herself a treat, a grossly expensive sports car, for finishing her second book.

"I can't believe you haven't already driven it, Nonna," Noah said. "Aren't you the one who urged her to buy it?"

"I didn't *urge* her to," Nonna said primly. "When she saw my Mustang, she said I *inspired* her."

With a sigh, Eli put his arm around Nonna. "Thanks, Nonna. I owe you for a lot of gray hairs."

"It's payback," Nonna said tartly.

With a wave at the porch, Brooke unfolded her tall frame from the passenger seat. She had her

Nordic father's fair skin and her Irish/Native American mother's glossy dark hair, and she blew a kiss to Rafe as she walked around the car. "Everything's fine, honey," she called.

Leaning into the driver's seat, she helped Chloë out.

Chloë was the exact opposite of Brooke. She was shortish, too thin, sported white-blond hair with pomegranate red streaks over one temple . . . and she hadn't finished her part of the recent fight for the Di Luca bottle of wine in good health. The break in her breastbone had needed further repair, and her surgeon had recommended a light, abbreviated body cast until healing was confirmed. Her dislocated shoulder and the necklace of bruises that had not quite faded from around her throat made her seem even more fragile.

At the sight of her slow, painful motions, Eli clutched the horizontal rail so tightly his knuckles turned white. But he sounded calm and confident as he called, "Hi, Chloë. How was the drive?"

Chloë looked up at him and grinned. "Great drive. *Great* car. Want to come down and help with the groceries?"

Eli hit the ground so fast the casts on his foot and arm might have been imaginary.

Rafe followed, looking grim and trying to smile at the same time.

His brothers wanted their wives to feel safe, and at the same time, they feared for them so much.

Noah shook his head. He couldn't stand to watch; his big brothers, Eli and Rafe, stripped of confidence by the love of a woman.

But Noah had never loved a woman as much as his brothers loved their wives.

He enjoyed women, of course. He enjoyed everything about them: their scents, their smiles, the curves of their bodies, the way they moaned as they moved beneath him in bed. Or on top of him. The first time, the last time . . . it was all good.

But once he realized death would follow him at every turn, he also realized he could never settle down, marry, have children. He could never grow old with that one special woman he had imagined he would someday find. Because a man who loved a woman, knowing that in his untimely dying he would cruelly desert her, knowing that his disgrace would haunt her and their children forever . . . he deserved to burn in hell.

So his relationships were fun, joyous, short-term, and trivial. He fell a little in love with each woman. He thought they all fell a little in love with him. But his lovers knew the score, and they were never surprised when he smiled and kissed them good-bye.

He had broken his own rule only once.

Now, as he watched his brothers, he envied them fiercely. They had what he would never have.

Eli, always solemn, always mature, laughed and tried to wrap Chloë in his sweaty, dirty arms while she edged away, screaming, "No! No! You're yucky!"

But she didn't scamper very fast, and when he caught her, she didn't seem worried about his yuck.

Rafe willingly made a fool of himself by flexing his muscles while Brooke made cooing noises and ran her fingertips over his pecs.

Nonna laughed aloud.

And an image rose unbidden in Noah's brain. Penelope Alonso, her heavy, long black hair hanging in a braid down her back, her exotic brown eyes peeking from beneath the sweep of long, thick, dark lashes, her full lips smiling as she watched him make a fool of himself . . . for her . . .

He told himself it wasn't surprising he had broken his rule for Penelope. He had been almost twenty, and still grieving over his broken future and the inevitable loss of his own life.

More important, she had been everything he'd ever wanted: tough, proud, joyous, ambitious, hardworking, smart, and brash. He supposed she hadn't been technically beautiful: a little short, very curvy, a quarter white, a quarter Hispanic, and half something else—she didn't know who her father was. Not that she'd cared. Nor had Noah. Because he'd seen her, and he'd loved her, and she'd loved him back.

At the end of that summer, he'd realized what a bastard he'd been to start a relationship with her, and he'd sent her away.

Noah promptly put the image out of his mind.

He saw no point in remembering her. In a moment of weakness three years ago, he'd looked her up on the Internet and come across photos of her wedding.

He was glad she'd moved on. Because no woman deserved a man who kept secrets, a man doomed to die for his misdeeds.

Thank God Penelope Alonso was the only woman who had ever tempted him, and thank God she had moved forever beyond his reach. . . .

Chapter 5

Penelope arrived at Joseph Bianchin's estate at precisely nine a.m. Thursday morning—late enough that she couldn't possibly be rude, but early enough to catch Bianchin before he left to run errands, or go to work, or go golfing, whatever eighty-one-year-old extremely wealthy men did with their time.

But no matter how many times she rang the

electronic buzzer placed outside the closed gates, no one answered.

Stone lions glared down at her from atop limestone pillars, their claws raised and threatening, while she stood like a beggar, her hands gripping the cold metal bars blocking the wide driveway. She stared across the wide swath of grass at Joseph Bianchin's house, stared so hard her eyes hurt.

House?

No, it wasn't a house. It was a mansion, built in the style of a formal Italian villa. Its pale yellow stucco walls rose two stories to a flat roof. Along the top, a balustrade ran like a series of stone teeth, and in the forward left corner a narrow watchtower rose, surveying the countryside with cold authority.

Penelope was an interior designer; architectural classes had been a requirement for her degree, but she so loved the craft she'd taken extra credits. So she knew her stuff. She knew the building before her was perfectly designed, perfectly proportioned, a monument to good taste. But its perfection repelled rather than attracted . . . or maybe it was simply that she had stood here for ten minutes, fruitlessly pushing the electronic buzzer and getting no response, and so she hated the place.

She supposed she shouldn't have expected Joseph Bianchin to open the door to her so easily.

She'd thoroughly investigated him, reading every biography she found online and following up every rumor.

The verdict was unanimous: The man was like the house that stood before her: arrogant, cold, friendless, and uncaring. His wealth had been handed to him by his family and he had ruthlessly increased it by fair means and foul.

The dense shade of the live oak trees that dotted the lawn increased the gloom that hung over the place, and although at a distance she could see a single, tall, thin, aging Asian gardener who clipped the spent blooms off the rhododendrons, she had to admit the house had an air of abandonment.

Joseph Bianchin wasn't home. From the looks of things, he had been away for a while.

But in her life, she'd been rejected so many times . . . and to have come so far, to be standing at this gate and have to leave without saying what she'd come to say . . .

A dreadful thought brought her up short.

Oh, God. What if he was dead? She'd packed and loaded the car and made the drive from Oregon without allowing herself to think too much about what she meant to do. Because if she really thought about it, she was afraid she would chicken out.

But she knew the facts. Joseph Bianchin was eighty-one years old. He could have died yesterday, or the day before, or while she visited her mother's grave and tried to express her frustration and unhappiness in a manner both respectful and firm. Because somewhere, she knew, her mother was listening.

Pulling out her phone, Penelope checked the local obituaries.

No. There was no death notice for Joseph Bianchin. He might not be *here*. But he was alive somewhere.

She sighed with relief, then brushed at her wet eyes. She shouldn't be surprised that her mind had jumped in that fatal direction. For far too long, she'd been surrounded by death in all its forms.

It was hard to be alone.

Squaring her shoulders, she made a new plan.

The thing was . . . all those years ago, when she left Bella Terra, she hadn't truly understood how she had come to be there in the first place. Now she knew.

Now she wondered whether she could ever forgive her mother. For anything. For everything.

Bella Terra wasn't huge. About forty thousand people—and in the wine-growing season, a whole lot of tourists—so Penelope would be able to find someone who could tell her where Joseph Bianchin was hiding.

As she turned away, she cast a last wistful, resentful glance toward the house—and saw a flash at the upstairs window.

She turned back and stared.

Was someone watching her?

But nothing stirred, not even the leaves on the live oak trees.

Maybe it had been the reflection of a bird's white wing.

Maybe she had imagined it.

Maybe Joseph Bianchin was skulking in his house and refusing to speak to her.

But that made no sense at all. He had no idea who she was—why wouldn't he at least answer his intercom, if only to tell her to go away?

Resolutely, she turned away, made her way to her car, and drove into Bella Terra.

Chapter 6

Who was that girl at the gate?"

Joseph Bianchin sat in his leather club chair in the master bedroom and glared resentfully up at his kidnapper, that cruel, damned blond giantess—his jailer.

He didn't dare call her a giantess to her face. He called her that only in his mind, because like it or not, he was afraid of her.

She called herself Liesbeth Smit. When they were both standing, she was tall enough to look him in the eyes, and although he'd lost two inches of height since he turned seventy-five, he was still six feet tall. Liesbeth played up her athletic figure, her long blond hair, and beautiful green eyes as part of her carefully cultivated Nordic aspect.

After his confrontation with that little upstart Noah Di Luca, Joseph had decided it was best to revisit the European sights he'd enjoyed before. In Amsterdam, he met Liesbeth, but she wasn't Nordic; he would swear to that. He didn't for a minute believe her true hair color was blond. As old as she was, it was probably gray. Or white. But hell, he didn't even believe her eyes were green. Or that her name was Liesbeth Smit. Nothing about her was real. Nothing.

He did believe she was athletic. When he'd gotten suspicious of her intentions—he'd thought she was a chance-met whore, then realized she had stalked him—and he refused to go with her to her hotel, she had taken him down as if he were a weak old man.

He was not. He was in excellent health.

"Who is she?" Liesbeth stood over him, asking questions. Always asking questions, interrogating him as if she had the right.

He hated her. He resented her for overpowering him. "I don't know."

"She rang the bell for ten minutes."

"I don't know her."

"She wanted to see you badly."

Liesbeth was a woman, younger than him, but

not young. He didn't know her exact age, but he guessed she was at least sixty-five. Yet she controlled him with the use of some goddamn fancy karate moves that made him buckle from the pain. He was pretty sure she used pressure points. He needed to learn them ASAP.

"She probably wanted a job as a maid." He didn't give a crap who the girl at the gate was. She couldn't help him out of this mess, so she was useless to him.

"She was dressed awfully nice for wanting a job as a maid."

When Joseph had met Liesbeth, her English had made him think she was from London. As soon as the private plane he'd hired had landed in the States, her accent changed, became purely American English.

He didn't know how she did it, but it was spooky to watch her move from one environment to another and adapt so smoothly that everyone in the vicinity thought she was a native.

"Khakis and a button-down shirt?" He raked Liesbeth with his gaze. "You've got low standards."

Unfazed by his condemnation of her denim capris and tight T-shirt, Liesbeth asked, "Is she your current lover?"

"No. I told you. I've never seen her before." Although there was something vaguely familiar about her. . . .

He stared into space, trying to remember. Whom did she look like? A business associate? One of the damned Di Lucas? Or some movie star he'd seen on the Internet?

Liesbeth studied him, knew every nuance of his expressions. "You do know her."

"Let me use the phone, and I'll call around and see what I can find out."

"If I did that, and you called the wrong person, I'd just have to kill you." She smiled kindly and without an ounce of compassion.

And he believed her. "Look. The trouble with being our age is, there aren't that many different kinds of faces. Everyone looks like someone I've already met."

Liesbeth waggled her head as if admitting he had a point.

"I don't understand what you want with me. Why me?" he asked, not for the first time. "I've offered you money. And yet you refuse and continue to keep me prisoner here. What was your reason for kidnapping me?"

"You're the one who put that ad on the Internet and made it necessary for me to move on this job before I was ready." Her green eyes gleamed like an icy glacial stream. "So you might as well provide us room and board while we take care of the matter, and keeping you here—well, it's easy to ensure that you don't get your hands on our little prize."

It's not your little prize. But according to her, it was.

He simply didn't give a crap what she thought.

Liesbeth glanced up a split second before one of her young male cohorts wandered in. "What do you want, Hendrik?"

In his singsong Dutch accent, Hendrik said, "This is a very nice bedroom. I think I should take it."

Joseph growled like a lone wolf who had been challenged. "And do what with it? Spit on the floor?" As far as Joseph could tell, Hendrik was Liesbeth's enforcer: big, ugly, and mean. He seemed to have no sophistication, no manners at all, and the lustful way he eyed Joseph's possessions made Joseph want to slap him. Hard.

"I would sleep here, of course." Hendrik strolled over to Joseph's seventeenth-century baroque Italian antique bed and caressed the wood with covetous fingers. "You must imagine yourself to be a king, lolling around in such a valuable piece of furniture."

"I do not loll," Joseph said coldly. His designer had created this room as a reverent homage to Joseph's importance in the world, with a fireplace, a sitting area, and that bed, raised on a dais and enfolded with velvet bed curtains. To be here, insulted and disdained, cut off from the world, his privacy stolen by gangsters who wanted a place to stay and the bottle of wine he so deservedly coveted—it was almost more than he could bear.

"Enough, Hendrik," Liesbeth said. "What do you want?"

"To find out what you want on your pizza." Hendrik grinned like a half-wit and rubbed his stomach in a crude imitation of hunger.

Joseph snapped in bitter irritation. "I don't want pizza again. My God, how often can you eat that crap?"

Hendrik's grin widened. "Why shouldn't I, old man? And in fact, why shouldn't you? You're Italian. Don't all Italians like pizza?"

The cold rage of helplessness burned in Joseph's gut. "No wonder *you* work for *her*." He pointed a shaking finger at Liesbeth. "You are so *stupid*."

Big, bulky, mean, and so fast Joseph never saw him move, Hendrik lunged.

Liesbeth punched her elbow hard in his chest, and the move made a sound like thumping a ripe watermelon. "No, Hendrik. We need him."

Hendrik lunged again, trying to get around her, snapping like a junkyard dog.

She stiff-armed him, knocking him against the wall. One of Joseph's finest pieces of art, an original Klimt art nouveau painting, rattled and turned sideways on its hook.

Joseph gasped in horror, and snapped, "Be careful, you careless fool."

Liesbeth stilled.

Joseph had been an only child, one of the privileged Bianchins of Bella Valley, and he said whatever he wanted whenever he wanted, and never worried who was hurt.

But now, as Hendrik pushed off from the wall and stood staring at him, chin thrust forward, hands in loosely balled fists, looking like a bull about to charge and gore him, it occurred to Joseph that *he* was the fool. Perhaps this time he should have held his tongue.

Liesbeth stepped back. "He's an old man," she said. "Don't hurt him too much."

Hendrik's eyes narrowed. He straightened. He grinned into Joseph's face.

For the first time Joseph saw a cunning intelligence there.

Turning slowly, Hendrik faced the wall. He cocked his head at the same angle as the painting.

An icy, incredulous thought trickled into Joseph's mind. He fumbled to place his gnarled hands on the arms of his chair, to lift himself from his seat, to stop Hendrik before he dared to . . .

Hendrik's big fist rose.

"No!" Joseph's left palm, sweaty with anxiety, slipped off the leather. "No!"

Hendrik slammed his knuckles through the canvas, splitting the art from top to bottom, destroying its value, stealing it from Joseph with a single blow. Then he tore it from the wall and smashed it to the floor.

While Joseph sat gasping, holding his chest, Hendrik turned to face him. Blood dripped from his split knuckles, but he still wore that offensive grin, and in a genial tone he said, "I'll order Canadian bacon with pineapple, and a thick crust. Hope you like it, old man. It's my favorite." He swaggered out of the room, his big feet clomping in his black leather boots.

Liesbeth watched him leave, anxiety and love clear on her face.

Something about the two of them tugged at Joseph's mind, a thought struggling to escape. It burst from his brain and into words. "He's your son!"

She laughed, laughed long and hard and spitefully, until Joseph shriveled in embarrassment. "No, he's my nephew." She waved a hand toward the interior of the house, where three men and two women lounged with their feet on Joseph's furniture, eating and dropping crumbs wherever they wished, drinking and putting their cans down on his polished wood tables, scratching themselves and laughing—at him. "They are all cousins or nephews or nieces."

"Your gang is all family?"

"Of course. Who else could I trust?"

"They're thugs!"

"Don't be silly." She airily waved Joseph's insult away. "We are not thugs. We contract for a job and we do it well. Each of us has a specialty. Each of us is highly trained."

Information. Information could help him. "Who hired you for this job?"

Her smile faded. "This is personal."

"Personal? What do you mean? Why do you care about a bottle of wine?"

"You know perfectly well why. Don't pretend you don't." Her smile was back. "I care for the same reason you care."

He didn't want to discuss what he knew or why he cared. They weren't partners. By all that was holy, the bottle was *his*. "So you have a gang, and each of you has a specialty. What are *you* trained in?"

"I'm the leader. I make the decisions. I make the plans."

"Lousy plans."

"Oh, I think this one is working out very well. Brigetta is our munitions specialist—she knows weapons. Grieta is our computer programmer—she can break through any security system in less than five minutes. Klaas does disguises." Liesbeth laughed. "He transforms himself and us, and not even facial recognition software can tag us. Rutger knows the worth of every piece of art and every precious stone, and he can spot a fake from a distance of one hundred yards."

Liesbeth gave up the information so easily, Joseph knew she considered him no threat. And that infuriated him more. But he was descended from the Borgias, and his legacy of shrewd cruelty would overcome this upstart. "Who's the Incredible Hulk?" he asked.

"Hendrik? Hendrik took his father's place as my right-hand man."

"He's the muscle."

"A good way of putting it." She gestured at Joseph's ruined painting. "His father had a terrible temper, too, and I'm proud of Hendrik for his restraint."

"His restraint?" Rage bubbled like acid in the pit of Joseph's stomach. "He destroyed a priceless painting!"

"Not priceless. Everything has a price. That painting is small, an early, lesser Klimt, a simple ink drawing without gold ornamentation, and unless a bidding war set up, at auction it would have gone for no more than one hundred thousand dollars, one hundred and twenty-five at the most."

At that cool, precise appraisal of his art, Joseph's mouth opened and closed in silent shock. Fifty years ago he'd bought it from an Englishwoman. He'd paid a mere five thousand pounds and laughed at her ignorance. He'd had it appraised every year since, gloating as it gained value. He knew what it was worth, what he had it insured for—but how did this brute of a woman know? Know that it was genuine? Know with a single glance? How was it possible that this Amazon warrior possessed the eye to successfully evaluate art from the turn of the twentieth century?

Maybe she was telling the truth. Maybe she was the brains of the operation because . . . because she deserved to be.

"You know"—she leaned over him, put her hands on the arms of his chair—"you're old, and your bones are brittle. If you're going to infuriate one of my people, it would be wise to choose one of the others. Hendrik is a throwback—more Russian than the others, demanding the respect owed a man of his noble ancestry."

Joseph seized on that shred of information. "You're Russian?"

"Aristocrats who oppressed the peasants for centuries until they rose in revolt and killed us. Not all of us—some of us escaped and have since made our living on our wits."

"That was a hundred years ago," he said spitefully. "So don't tell me you're anything but a washed-out version of a failed aristocratic system."

"So true." She caressed his hand. "And yet I rule you with a tyrant's touch." She straightened. "Hendrik says we don't need you. That we can kill you, stay here and use your credit card, and not put up with your sour face while we search for that bottle of wine. My heart is soft and sweet; I tell him there's no need to commit murder unnecessarily. But you're convincing me Hendrik might be right. Remember *that* next time we want to order pizza."

Chapter 7

Penelope drove toward town like a woman who feared nothing.

And she didn't. Not really. Running into Noah would be uncomfortable, but she'd faced more daunting challenges. Really, what were the chances she would see him?

Well. Possibly good, since he managed the Di Luca family's resort, it fronted on Bella Terra's main street right on the square, and she intended to look around at the changes that had been made in the last nine years. She would not, of course, reminisce at all. Because, yeah, she'd spent the most memorable summer of her life in Bella Terra, but she wasn't here to remember.

She was here on a whole different business.

Penelope had taken a circuitous route from the Sweet Dreams Hotel (north and west of town) to Joseph Bianchin's estate (on the southeast), around the outskirts that stretched to encompass mansions and subdivisions where people who worshiped the California wine country lifestyle had built homes. Now she drove to Bella Terra's main street and into the compact, vibrant downtown.

She stopped at the red light, two cars back from the crosswalk, and peered through the hustle of tourists and locals. She wanted to see the town square, a park of grass and a gazebo, where benches rested in the shade of tall trees.

The square hadn't changed a bit. It was still quaint, a carefully preserved early-twentieth-century square, still Bella Terra's beating heart. Restaurants and art galleries lined the streets around it, and those had changed names and possibly owners, but the buildings hadn't changed, and neither had Penny's Bookstore, where Noah and Penelope had spent many a pleasant afternoon browsing the titles on the shelves.

For her birthday in that long-ago August, Noah had bought her a picture book about the history of Bella Valley.

She had kept it. It was packed in a box in a storage area with most of her furniture and knickknacks from Cincinnati. When she got back to Portland, she had to go through it all and . . .

But she couldn't think about that now. There was too much to see here, too many memories to confront.

The Bella Terra resort's stucco exterior faced Main Street. It had been washed a light gold, and guests strolled out of the breezeway holding icy bottles of water and wearing good-humored smiles.

Yes, the resort had that effect on people. She knew; nine years ago she'd been an intern to the interior designer hired to freshen the interior of the main building, and the Di Luca family had made their desires clear. Their first directive had been to make the lobby, the breakfast area, and the lounge as relaxing as possible. Although Penelope had worked on the project for only two and a half months and left before it was finished, obviously the design had been successful.

Or perhaps by now they'd done another redesign. She would love to go in, see whether she could spot Noah's influence on the resort, sit and have a glass of wine in the Luna Grande Lounge.

Not that she'd done that before; in those days, she hadn't been old enough to drink.

It would be good to see whether Tom Chan was still behind the bar. He'd been an influence on the design of the lounge, and such a trusted friend of the Di Lucas, she thought he must still be there.

She wished she could linger, observe every little detail of the resort, but the light turned green, and resolutely she refused to drive around the block for another look.

She needed to remember her mission. She was

here to use one of the Marinos' breakfast coupons. To see whether she could find out anything about Bianchin, where he was, what he was doing, when he'd be back.

But first, she had to eat, because no matter what the crisis, her body demanded sustenance. It seemed so shallow to face tragedy, disease, and death and still need to eat, but there it was—her stomach growled in demand, and she had learned to listen.

Rhodes Café sat three streets off the square, narrow, unassuming, and outside of the main tourist flow, but even at nine thirty in the morning it was busy. She took a chair at the counter between a guy who never needed to eat again and yet was shoveling in scrambled eggs and sausage as if it were his last meal, and a young woman with chin-length dark hair who stared with such revulsion at her toasted bagel Penelope checked to make sure it wasn't crawling across her plate.

The bagel looked fine to her.

She glanced again at the young woman, noted her complexion, pasty pale under what normally would have been a healthy color, and hoped that whatever she had wasn't contagious. Stomach flu while staying at the Sweet Dreams Hotel would be an ordeal Penelope did not wish to face.

Plucking the menu from between the napkin holder and the saltshaker, she studied it, made her decision, and ordered a Denver omelet, crisp bacon, and wheat toast. She tried hard not to look around, but the woman next to her reminded Penelope of her mother during the worst of her chemo, and she couldn't stand it. With the intention of distracting her from her misery, Penelope asked, "I've never been here before. Is the food that bad?"

The woman turned her head slowly, as if afraid a quick movement would set off disaster, and gazed at her. "No, it's pretty good. I just don't feel too well this morning. . . ." Something sparked in her blue eyes. She leaned back, scrutinized Penelope, and asked, "Aren't you Penelope Alonso?"

Bingo. First time out of the gate, someone knew her.

Penelope wet her lips and scrutinized the woman in return.

She was pretty, fit, and a little less pale than she had been a moment ago. Her jeans and black T-shirt looked expensive, and rather incongruously, she wore a lightweight camouflage vest zipped up halfway.

Penelope didn't have the foggiest who she was. "I am Penelope Alonso—or rather, I was. Now I'm Penelope Alonso Caldwell."

"You're married!" The woman beamed.

"Widowed."

Her face fell. "Oh, no! I'm so sorry."

"Thank you. It's been over a year. The first shock is over." Penelope recited the usual soothing phrases, then changed the subject. "I'm sorry, but I can't place *you*."

"Brooke . . . Brooke Petersson. It's been years, and we really barely brushed shoulders." Brooke's eyes narrowed intently. "You were here that summer after your freshman year, an intern at Bella Terra resort in . . . Wait. I almost have it . . . interior design."

"That's right." Penelope was seriously impressed. "You have a great memory."

"I've had to have. I'm the head concierge at Bella Terra resort and we're expected to remember everything about everybody. Although actually—I recently got married and quit."

Penelope lifted her brows. She had barely known Brooke before, but somehow this woman didn't seem the type to leave a job she loved for a man.

Brooke launched into an explanation. "I quit before I married him. I was going to work in Sweden. He persuaded me to stay." She half smiled. "Anyway, I remember you because you and I were roadkill in the Di Luca love caravan, and I felt such a kinship with you!"

Remembrance jolted through Penelope. "That's right! I remember now. Gossip said you and one of the Di Lucas had had a thing in high school and then split when you both left for college.

Something about he wanted to join the military and you didn't like it?"

"You have a pretty good memory yourself." Brooke picked up her bagel and nibbled on the edge. "What are you doing in Bella Terra? I never would have thought you would return."

Here it was. Penelope's chance to get the scoop, and from the former concierge of Bella Terra resort. "I have business with Joseph Bianchin. Do you know him? Do you know if he's in town?"

Brooke's eyes went flat and cool. "No, he's not. I don't know when he's coming back—if ever."

Penelope's fork stopped halfway to her mouth. She stared at Brooke.

Her horror must have shown on her face, for Brooke said, "What? What did you want to see him for?" A thought seemed to jolt through her. "He didn't get you pregnant, did he?"

Shock rocked Penelope backward on her stool. "No. Ew. No! He's past eighty!"

"He's a nasty old man," Brooke said, "and I wouldn't put it past him to promise the world to a young woman and then betray her. But I've insulted you by insinuating you'd sleep with the old fart. Forgive me."

"It's all right." What an eye-opening revelation of how Joseph Bianchin was viewed in the community.

"I'm bitter about him," Brooke said. "We've had a lot of problems here in Bella Terra and he started them all."

Penelope sighed. "I know he has a challenging personality."

"That's one way of putting it."

"I researched him. He's a jerk. But I need to talk to him and I really don't have the funds to sit around here and wait until he—"

"Slinks back into town? Really, I don't think that will be very soon." Brooke studied Penelope and nibbled the bagel, studied and nibbled the bagel. "Did you become an interior designer? Finish the courses and everything?"

"I had a full-ride scholarship to the University of Cincinnati and finished their five-year interior design program. Best studies program in the country." Maybe Penelope was a little too emphatic, but she had the baggage to justify a little bragging.

"Very cool. My husband and I just bought a house. Our first house. Here in town. It's an old Victorian built in 1913. It's thirty-nine hundred square feet in three stories, built on half a city block, really a great house, but it needs work. I've been going there every day since we closed on the deal, making sketches and stuff—"

Penelope listened with rising excitement.

"—but I've realized that looking through architectural magazines and watching HGTV doesn't qualify me to redesign this monstrosity. Would you be willing to take a look . . . ?"

Penelope tried very hard not to jump up and down and squeal. Because this wasn't why she was here, but—what an opportunity!

Instead she concentrated on presenting a reassuring, professional image. "I've got my résumé and references on my computer. I can shoot them right to you. I worked in Cincinnati for a design firm—we did office interiors. It was great money, and my husband and I were trying to start a family, so I kept at it, but what I always wanted to do was work with older homes—"

"This was meant to be!" Brooke put her hand on Penelope's forearm.

Penelope observed the contrast of Brooke's pale skin against Penelope's own warmly tanned flesh, and thought how nice it was to have someone touch her in kindness. It had been so long since Keith had died, since life had been lived in sunshine, since she'd been able to concentrate on the mundane bits that made up the days she imagined she wanted to live. . . . She was so tired of being melancholy. More than anything in the world, she wanted not to be alone.

"I think you're right." Penelope knew she was going to make things worse, but that after that they would be better, easier for Brooke, who she hoped could be a friend, and really, no one needed to know the whole truth. "I know it seems dramatic, but after Keith died, I kept working at my firm for a while, but when I discovered my mother's cancer had metastasized, I quit my job and returned to Portland to stay with my mom until the end"—she was leaving out a huge, heavy chunk of grief, but who would blame her?—"so I'm unemployed and short on funds. I am glad to have you check my credentials—they're impeccable, I promise—and you can show me your house, and I hope we can come to an agreement."

Brooke scribbled an address on half a napkin, then used the other half to wrap up what was left of her bagel and drop it in her purse. "Are you finished eating?"

"Pretty much." Penelope crunched her last bite of bacon. "How do you eat so little?"

"This was my second breakfast." Brooke put a five on the counter and waved to the waitress, who waved back and kept pouring coffee.

Outside, she handed Penelope the napkin. "Follow me, and if you get lost, there's the address. It's the three-story white Victorian with two huge oaks in the front and an overgrown blackberry thicket on one side."

"Okay. I'll meet you there." This was it. Penelope followed Brooke, determined not to lose her.

This offer of a job is an omen. I am in the right place at the right time. I am doing the right thing.

At last.

Chapter 8

A mere five blocks later, Brooke turned into an old neighborhood filled with a mixture of grand Victorian homes and small fifties bungalows. She pulled up before one of the largest houses.

Penelope parked behind her, turned off the motor, stepped out onto the sidewalk, and studied the project with slowly rising excitement.

From the top of the tall, narrow cupola to the place where the foundation sank its sturdy concrete footings into the brown dirt, the home was a jumble of classic styles, with irregular, steeply sloping roofs, a round turret on the left front, a wraparound porch with turned posts and a pediment above the steps, and massive double doors with cut-glass panels at the sides and above.

This Victorian was a noble monument to bygone days. Yet the wide swath of wood shingles that circled the second story showed signs of rot, the decorative porch railing sagged, and plywood covered an upstairs window.

"Isn't she a beauty?" Penelope murmured in awe.

"Yes!" Brooke turned and hugged her. "I knew you'd see it, too! The bones are there. All we have to do is a face-lift to the outside, maybe some Botox to stop the rot, some filler to smooth out the wrinkles—"

Penelope laughed. "You've given this a lot of thought."

"My mother-in-law is a movie star, and right now she's practicing for her first Broadway role. She's growing old gracefully . . . with the aid of her dearest plastic surgeon." Brooke gestured to the porch. "My mother suffers from rheumatoid arthritis, and one of my husband's great-aunts is in a wheelchair, so on the side of the porch, we have to construct a handicapped ramp."

"That's always a wise idea, and with the right design, it'll fit right in." As they walked up the steps, Penelope's fingers itched for a sketch pad.

"Come inside. Don't worry about falling through the porch. It's not original construction. About fifty years ago, someone replaced the boards and they're still in pretty good shape." Brooke waved a hand at the peeling paint. "At least, structurally speaking." Pulling a keyless fob from her purse, she clicked it. She typed in a code on the keypad beside the door. Only then did she turn the knob. At Penelope's raised eyebrows, she said, "My husband's in security. As soon as we closed on the house, and before he would let me set foot inside, he replaced all the locks with electronic sensors. It's not traditional, but it's reliable, and like I said, lately we've had a few problems in Bella Terra."

"Must be some impressive problems."

"Oh, yeah." Brooke sounded disgusted.

Penelope meant to inquire further, but as they stepped into the two-story entry hall, the prospect of working on this project took her breath away.

A few broken pieces of furniture remained scattered throughout the visible rooms, but for the most part, the place was, as Brooke had said, stripped down to its bones.

Yet what glorious bones those were.

The solid wood floor swept into the parlor at the left and the grand room on the right, toward the curving sweep of the staircase and into the shadows beyond. The plaster walls met the wainscoting of the ceiling, and at each corner a carved wooden ribbon held a spray of plaster flowers. A mirror, mottled with age, decorated the wall over a broken, listing entry table. The crystal chandelier hung in front of the transom window atop the door.

Brooke flipped the switch; the massive chandelier lit, but half of the thirty candle-shaped bulbs were burned out. Cobwebs and dust obscured the rest of the illumination, leaving the entry still in shadow.

Yet Penelope could see what had put that

hopeful expression on Brooke's face. "The house faces west, doesn't it?"

"Yes."

"And as the sun sets, the rays strike the prisms and rainbows dance up the stairs?"

"Yes!" Brooke beamed.

"When it's cleaned, it will be magnificent." Penelope tossed her soft leather purse into the corner of the entry, knelt, and ran her hand over the floor, scratched and worn, yet glowing with ambers and with a distinctive grain pattern she thought she recognized. "Is this heart pine?" She had to ask. It was so rare, she'd seen it used only once before, in a historical mansion in Virginia.

Brooke leaned against the doorframe, tense with excitement. "They told us that's what it is, but I don't know what that means."

"It means that it is cut from the heart of first-growth pine trees that stood before the first settlers arrived on these shores, trees so old and so large that their straight-grained heartwood could be used for flooring. Even if there were such trees now, they'd be preserved, and rightfully not cut for such vanities as heart pine flooring." In theory, Penelope mourned the trees that gave their lives for such a frivolous vanity, but that had happened long before she was born. And to have a chance to work with such beauty . . .

"Now I know what it means. It means we scored big-time," Brooke said.

"Exactly, because this wood is known for its resilience, and once you have it sanded and refinished, it will last you and your children and your grandchildren." Penelope watched as Brooke passed a betraying hand over her belly. "I haven't seen the whole house yet, but if the rest of it has these kinds of accoutrements . . . restoration will bring it back to magnificence."

"I know!" Alive with eagerness, Brooke stepped away from the door and slammed it shut.

Standing, Penelope asked, "Where shall we start?"

Two trips to the drugstore and a food delivery later, the two women sat on the bottom step in the entry, picking the toppings off the remains of a large cheese-and-pesto pizza.

As the day progressed, Brooke seemed to have recovered her appetite.

Penelope propped her brand-new grid-paper pad on her knees and sketched her ideas for the remodel of the main floor. "We've got the kitchen at the back of the house—it's going to have to be gutted. There's a good-size pantry and a large porch we can incorporate into the house as a breakfast nook. We've got the dining room between the kitchen and the parlor. Now, I'm pretty sure this is a load-bearing wall"—she pointed at the wall that divided the parlor from the dining room—"which means it supports the structure of the second floor. We can't remove it without consulting an engineer to design a load-bearing substitute."

"But it can be done?" Brooke asked.

"With enough money, anything can be done."

"My husband's rich."

Penelope had already figured that out. "Cool."

"Yes, it's one of the traits I like about him." Brooke smiled. "Also, he wants a home with me. This time he's determined that everything is going to work between us. Plus he negotiated a really good deal on this place and gave me an outrageous budget to get it into shape as soon as possible."

Envy tasted bitter on Penelope's tongue, but if anyone deserved happiness, it was this woman, so generous, so kind to an almost-total stranger. "So he's not only rich, he's got the right priorities."

"I will love him forever." The words were dramatic, but so simply spoken Penelope suffered a pang in the region of her heart.

She struggled with loneliness, with the prospect of long days to fill and no one with whom to share her trials and her triumphs. She would work, of course, and make friends, but to never speak with her mother again, to never go home to the one man who loved her, to never hold her child in her arms . . .

Maybe it wasn't envy she tasted. Maybe it was sorrow.

Tears pressed against the backs of her eyes. She picked up her water and drank, trying to wet her suddenly dry mouth; then in a flurry of activity, she came to her feet and strode into the parlor. It was even dimmer in here than in the entry, an echoing room that needed a fringed Persian carpet on the floor, a Queen Anne sofa artfully angled with a large easy chair on the side, and a fire burning in the hand-carved rose marble fireplace that dominated the room. She kept her voice hearty and forceful. "Yes, I think this would make a lovely room for entertaining. We'll break through to the dining room, then create a supporting arch, or even possibly install a pocket door so you could feed your guests, then leave the dirty dishes and close off the dining room—"

She must not have been convincing, for Brooke rose to her feet and in a gentle voice said, "Penelope . . ."

An overload of emotion rolled over Penelope—months after her mother's death, fifteen months since the phone call about Keith, it still sometimes happened—and she knew she hadn't fooled anyone. Not Brooke. And not herself. She took a quivering breath, held out her hand in a stop gesture. *No sympathy,* she meant.

Brooke nodded, understanding without words.

And Penelope knew she'd found more than a job. She'd found a friend.

Thank God. This was surely the first sign that she had moved on beyond the tangle of pain and sorrow. Now, at last, she could successfully rebuild her life.

As she struggled to subdue her unruly sentiments, the front door lock made a clicking sound.

Both women turned to look.

Two men, tall and broad shouldered, stood silhouetted and unrecognizable through the cut glass.

The knob turned. The double doors swung wide.

Brooke's face lit up, and she cried with rapturous pleasure, "Rafe!"

A distant memory stirred in Penelope's brain, an ominous rumble of trouble.

Rafe? A rare name. A distinctive name. She'd heard it years before. . . .

All day, Brooke had never said her husband's name. Why? What was she hiding?

The men stepped into the foyer, both handsome, dark haired, obviously brothers.

Brooke looked between them and Penelope and deflated like a balloon. Her whisper sounded loud in the silence. "Oh, no."

The truth, and the horror, struck Penelope through the heart.

Brooke's husband had arrived, and he was Rafe Di Luca. And the other guy . . .

The other guy was Rafe's brother.

He was Noah Di Luca.

Her Noah Di Luca.

Chapter 9

Time shifted. Motion froze. Penelope saw the tableau etched with such clarity, each one of them might have been a figure in an artfully lit wax museum.

Rafe, in a dark suit, white shirt, and tie, walking toward his wife, his hands outstretched, saying, "What's wrong, honey?"

Brooke staring at Penelope in wide-eyed dismay.

Noah, in blue jeans, a blue T-shirt, and a linen jacket, glancing around as if assessing the house, catching his first glimpse of Penelope.

And the shock of meeting his eyes flung Penelope ten thousand feet up into the atmosphere.

The air was thin; she couldn't breathe. Her ears were plugged; she couldn't hear. All her concentration narrowed down to a single focus: Noah's face, his chin, his lips, his lips, his lips. And his eyes, as deep and as green as the ocean, and just as unfeeling and faithless . . .

She was cold, frozen; she couldn't move, couldn't feel. . . .

Then, abruptly, he moved and the ice snapped.

She was back with her feet on the heart pine floor . . . and she could feel. Her skin was icy, her fingers trembled, and the pressure in her chest made her wish she could sink to the floor in a nineteenth-century faint.

He started toward her.

She stiffened her spine. She was not a Victorian maiden. She was not a coward. She had faced far worse than this confrontation. She would get through the experience with the courtesy and poise life had taught her.

Noah extended his hand.

Good. It was to be a businesslike meeting.

She extended hers. "Noah, how good to see you again." A lie, but for a good cause.

"Penelope, I had no idea you were in town." His voice wrapped her in the remnants of the old, dark, rich depths of remembered passion. He took her hand.

And Penelope was flung once more into space. Everything was in that one touch: all the joy of first love, all the pain of his rejection, all the years of being apart. . . .

This time Penelope didn't wait for release. She took time by the throat, slammed herself down to earth.

She breathed.

She smiled.

She made herself look pleasant and *normal*.

She spoke. "I arrived yesterday. I hadn't told anyone I was coming, but Brooke and I met at the diner and we discovered a mutual appreciation for turn-of-the-century architecture."

"You always did love old houses," he said.

She tried to think how a person behaved when meeting another person in business circumstances. She should know this. She *did* know this.

First, get your hand out of his.

She freed herself.

He let her go.

She rubbed her palm against her jeans, trying to wipe off the sensation of his touch.

She couldn't. He was here, exuding the warmth of the California sun, the scent of bergamot orange clinging close to his skin, the structure of his face as striking as ever, but refined, matured. . . . After nine long years, one marriage, and too many devastating losses, she hadn't been able to erase the memory of his touch. Why would she succeed now?

When Brooke picked up the thread of conversation, Penelope deliberately looked at her rather than at Noah.

Brooke chatted nervously, brightly. "Rafe, dear, I don't know if you ever met Penelope when she lived here before—"

"I did. I remember her." Rafe looked right at her. "Penelope Alonso. You've changed."

Noah spoke. "I don't think she's changed at all."

Like his presence, like his touch, his warm, rough voice raised goose bumps all the way to the top of her head. But this time she was able to respond at once, meeting his gaze, smiling that same smile that stretched across her lips like a tight rubber band. "I have changed. Nine years is a long time."

"Your hair is shorter," he said.

"After I graduated, I worked for an interior design firm in Cincinnati. A braid down my back seemed unprofessional." She turned to Rafe—or rather, she turned away from Noah. "I remember you also. You were home from the service." She walked toward him, offered her hand. "I'm now Penelope Alonso Caldwell."

He shook it briefly. "You're married."

"Widowed," she countered.

"What happened to your husband?" he asked.

"He was killed in a car wreck over a year ago." Brooke had said Rafe was in security; Penelope could almost see him storing away the information to check on it later.

"I thought you were going to say divorced," Rafe said.

She recognized the tone of his voice, like an L.A. cop arresting a young, foolish, frightened shoplifter. How ironic. He wanted to protect his baby brother from his wicked seductress—and she would rather be anywhere but here.

“I’m sorry for your loss.” Noah said the words, and sounded sincere.

“Thank you.” She’d learned that was the easiest thing to say. Because really, what else was there? *Keith was a nice guy; I loved him for his kindness, and in the pain and anguish that followed, I forgot him too easily.*

That had been the worst: looking back in shock and realizing that his passing had barely made a ripple in the emotional tenor of her life.

When she did think of him, she wondered . . . was it that first bright, heated love for Noah that had cast Keith into the shade? Or was it the tragedy that followed that made him a thin, transparent memory in her mind?

Blaming Noah was too easy, too convenient. Dwelling on what had happened after . . . what good would that do her?

She didn’t want to discuss her marriage or her husband with Noah. It was none of his business. Pushing the subject aside, Penelope said, “I told Brooke that this house looks like a good, solid acquisition.”

Noah glanced impatiently around. “Yes.”

“With good planning and the Di Luca connections, the remodel should not take long. Don’t you agree?” she insisted.

He looked around again, seeing his surroundings for the first time, scrutinizing the entry, the stairs, the visible rooms. Turning to

Brooke, he asked, "How soon do you plan to move in?"

"Six months," she said.

He gave a bark of laughter. "Six months for a remodel of this magnitude? You were the concierge at the resort. You know what contractors are like. *Schedule* is just a word they like to use."

She considered him, then announced, "We have to move in six months. I'm having a baby in seven."

Chapter 10

As if he'd been smacked between the eyes with a pole, Noah rocked back on his heels. "A baby?" he croaked.

Penelope shook her head in wonder. How could Noah be so oblivious? She hadn't had to be told. Five minutes in Brooke's presence and Penelope had had her suspicions. An hour and she was certain.

Right before her eyes, Noah transformed into the Italian family man. He hurried to Brooke and pulled her into his arms. Crushing her in a massive hug, he kissed the top of her head. "I've got to go buy a baseball glove."

"What for?" Rafe was clueless now.

"For my nephew!" Noah grinned.

"Or your niece," Brooke said.

"Or my niece," Noah agreed.

"There's plenty of time for that," Brooke said.

Noah's grin faded. "Yeah. Plenty of time."

Surprised, Penelope scrutinized him. For the merest moment, he looked like an older caricature of himself, haunted by the deeds of his past.

Then his expression became once more smiling and cocky. "Who else knows?"

"Nonna guessed. We told my mother right before she flew to New York to visit Rafe's mother while she rehearses for her Broadway debut, and we told Francesca while Mom was in the air. We were going to wait until Sunday to tell everyone else, but now that you know . . ." Brooke turned to Rafe. "We're going to have to drop by to see Eli and Chloë tonight."

"Ha! You told me before you told Eli," Noah said.

"You are so mature." Brooke's sarcasm was crushing.

Noah just grinned as he set Brooke aside, very carefully, as if she were fragile. "So we have to get this remodel going. I assume we need floor plans drawn?"

"We most certainly do," Penelope agreed.

"I'll get the guys in here to take measurements right away." He extended his hand to Rafe. They shook, all manly congratulations, and then, like brothers raised in affection, they hugged and laughed.

The way they acted, it looked to Penelope almost like a reconciliation.

"You didn't waste any time." Noah stepped away from Rafe and pounded him on the back.

"We didn't plan it." Brooke watched them, smiling. "After the last couple of months' trouble, we just . . . weren't very careful."

"Let me think." Noah puckered his mouth like an elderly lady. "What did Mrs. Burns teach us in junior high? Oh, yeah. It only takes once."

"Shut up, Noah. You've made your share of mistakes." With a glance at Penelope, Rafe stopped abruptly.

"Not that mistake," Noah said coolly.

No. It was true. That summer Noah had been very, very careful about contraception. At the time, Penelope had been relieved to have a boyfriend who meticulously took all the responsibility. When he later tossed her aside with casual disdain, she realized it hadn't been for her, but for him—he hadn't wanted the possible entanglement of a child with her.

Now she knew a little more about the stats concerning condoms—they were ninety-eight percent effective in preventing pregnancy. That meant that in one year's time, two couples out of one hundred who used condoms would have an unintended pregnancy.

When she looked back on that summer, on the urgency of their passion and the pleasure of spending every possible moment in each other's arms . . . Well, it was lucky she hadn't conceived.

And her own mother, who had raised a daughter on her own with no help from Penelope's father or her own family . . . her mother would have *killed* her.

Before the pause could grow awkward—more awkward—Brooke said, "It's true, Rafe. Penelope is an interior designer, and we are so lucky I found her! As soon as we met I knew we were simpatico."

"Where did you meet?" Rafe didn't sound nervous or overly cheerful. In fact, he scrutinized Penelope as if he knew she had stolen the family silver.

"At Rhodes Café." Brooke put her hand on Rafe's arm and squeezed hard. "I knew she was the exact right person to help me make this house our home."

Rafe looked at his wife as if trying to curb her enthusiasm. "First we'll want to check her credentials, of course."

"I've already forwarded my résumé and references to your wife," Penelope answered.

"And darned if I'm not capable of checking and approving those credentials myself, seein' as how I used to be the head concierge of a large resort and hired hundreds of employees in my time." Brooke smacked her husband hard with the sarcasm stick.

Noah laughed.

Rafe was clearly unmoved. "Of course you're capable. I would never insinuate you're not. But I'm in charge of security now, and all employees are vetted by me."

Startled by Rafe's inexorable tone, Penelope lifted her brows at Brooke.

"It's a long story," Brooke said to her, hands rising and falling in uncharacteristic vulnerability.

Noah stepped in with a swift change of subject. "Rafe, you're lucky. Penelope's degree is from the University of Cincinnati. Isn't that right?" Noah smiled at her.

My God. That smile. It used to make Penelope's heart stop. "I don't remember sending you a graduation announcement," she said. Which sounded surly. But she felt surly. Had he been spying on her?

"Nonna told me." Still Noah smiled at her.

That smile used to make her world go around.

He said, "You know how my grandmother is—no matter where you go, she'll always be your friend."

Oh, great. Now Penelope felt surly *and* guilty.

"Nonna would love to see you again."

When Penelope left Bella Terra, she had been eighteen and Mrs. Di Luca had been ancient, at least seventy years old. Of course, she had been vital and busy, kind to the young woman who had managed to land a job as an intern to a thriving design business in Bella Terra.

"While you're here, I hope you'll visit her." Noah sounded winsome and appealing.

It was a little late for him to appeal to her. "I can't imagine she remembers me."

"Nonna remembers everyone, but she remembers you with particular affection. She liked you very much, and she never understood why I broke it off with you."

That makes two of us, buster. "My plans right now are rather . . . confusing, but I would love to see Mrs. Di Luca again." Which was the truth—that summer, Penelope and Sarah had become fast friends, and when Penelope and her mother left town, Sarah sent a lovely note expressing her hope that Penelope would keep in touch.

Penelope had not responded. She meant to, but she didn't know what to say, how to revisit that pain and heartache, and in the end it was easier to walk away and never look back.

Now Penelope wondered . . . had Mrs. Di Luca suspected the real reason Penelope and her mother were in town?

No, probably not. As far as Penelope knew, no one had suspected the truth—including the youthful Penelope.

She looked at herself in the mottled entryway mirror. She resembled her mother. . . .

Behind her in the mirror, a figure moved out of

the dark reaches of the corridor down by the kitchen.

Alarmed, she swung around to face the stranger as he emerged from the shadows.

Simultaneously, Rafe pulled a pistol from beneath his jacket.

Smoothly, Brooke plucked a pistol from beneath her vest.

And suddenly, Noah held an eight-inch-long knife in his grip.

Chapter 11

Penelope stared in openmouthed shock at the weapons—and at the grim-faced people who wielded them so handily.

Her heart sprang into a thundering beat. As fast as she could she backed up, slammed her spine against the wall, and . . . well . . . cowered.

The shadowy figure flung his arms into the air and said, "It's me—Bryan DuPey. Put the firearms away!" He moved slowly into the light, revealing himself to be a wiry man of medium height with thinning brown hair and bloodshot eyes—and he was wearing a police uniform.

"Damn it, DuPey, what the hell are you doing sneaking in like that?" With a glance at Penelope, Noah slid his knife beneath his jacket.

Brooke's pistol disappeared into the holster hidden beneath her vest.

Rafe continued to hold his gun, but he pointed it toward the floor.

Apparently they knew this policeman.

Cautiously, DuPey lowered his hands. "I parked in the alley and came through the backyard. I thought I'd come around the front; then I saw the back door was open a few inches and I—"

Rafe interrupted. "It was open a few inches?" Turning to Brooke, he asked in an overly polite tone, "Honey, did you leave the back door open?"

"No." She couldn't have sounded surer—or more steely. "We went back there, Penelope and I. We paced out the covered porch and talked about our plans for the backyard, and when we came back in, I distinctly remember shutting the door and setting the alarm. Didn't I, Penelope?"

Penelope nodded and whispered, "Yes, and we've been together ever since."

Rafe's cool gaze swept Penelope, judged her, and he nodded. "All right. Let's check things out. Noah, come with me. DuPey, check the house. Brooke, you stay here with Penelope." He looked at his wife as if expecting her to argue.

She nodded and unzipped her vest to reveal the holster strapped to her ribs.

DuPey drew his pistol.

Noah's knife reappeared.

The men headed toward the kitchen.

Penelope stared at Brooke, quivering with aftershocks as sharp and nasty as after an earthquake. "Why is everyone armed?"

"I told you. We've had problems." The answer wasn't so much curt as brief; Brooke appeared to be listening.

So Penelope listened, too. Listened to the sound of the men's shoes on the floorboards, listened as the back door opened and closed, listened as the house creaked and moaned. "Problems? Like vandalism?"

"Problems." Brooke shot a sympathetic sideways glance at Penelope. "Like murder."

Penelope took a quivering breath. "Oh."

"Things have been happening here. Ugly stuff. It's not the same small, quiet town you left nine years ago. But listen." Brooke glanced toward the back of the house, then spoke quickly. "I want to talk to you. Explain . . . I swear to you I didn't set you up. About Noah, I mean."

"Oh." Yes. First Noah, then weapons, then a search for someone who had broken through the Di Lucas' security while she and Brooke were actually *in* the house . . . maybe taking this job was not such a bright idea.

Brooke continued. "I've been asking Noah to come and look over the house for weeks. He knows a lot about remodeling, about building. He has to, because of the resort. But he's been busy, and I'd given up on him. His showing up while you were here—that was pure bad luck."

"I never thought you . . . It didn't occur to me that you had set me up." It didn't matter right now, either. What mattered was this almost casual acceptance by a seemingly normal woman of that most heinous crime—murder.

The old house, formerly so welcoming, now felt cold, haunted. Penelope bunched up her shoulders and sidled closer to Brooke.

Still in that urgent, quiet tone, Brooke said, "I didn't tell you my husband's name because I thought you'd hesitate to take the job, and I've interviewed so many interior decorators, and you wouldn't believe how unwilling they are to listen. I want my house to be done my way, not theirs, and you . . . you have exactly the same instincts I do, and I really want you to work with me. I should have told you about Rafe. I *did* intend to, but just not yet."

"He's going to investigate me, isn't he?" Penelope had secrets. Probably nothing Rafe would care about, but she hated that sense of exposure.

"He's jumpy." Brooke excused him. "Everybody is these days, but a couple of months ago I was almost murdered—"

"You . . . you . . ." *Brooke* was almost murdered? "When you said murder, I thought—"

"Yes, we've had real dead bodies, too." Brooke looked down at her hands with a grimace. "If you don't mind, I don't want to talk about it. I urp easily these days."

"Sure. No problem." Although Penelope probably needed to know some details before she signed a contract. "But you're okay now?"

"I'm fine. I fight back." Brooke smiled tightly. "You'd think I should be the one having nightmares, but no. Rafe is. He's so afraid of losing me."

Everything about this conversation was surreal. "I thought . . . Wasn't it Rafe who broke your heart all those years ago?"

"We're the proverbial star-crossed lovers. But this time, we got it right." Brooke passed her hand over her belly again. "We were supposed to move to Sweden. Then we found out we're having this baby."

Penelope wavered between joy at a new arrival and envy . . . and a surge of sorrow. Concentrating on the joy, she said, "Congratulations."

"We didn't mean to, not yet, but you know what? Mess up one time . . ." Brooke's mood turned in a moment; her laughter was a lighthearted trill of amusement. "I can't believe it. It's such a miracle. My mom is so excited, and Nonna—so we're staying in Bella Terra, and we bought this house, and we've only got six months, maybe a little more, to get it in shape. I want to make the little bedroom into a nursery—"

"And the attic into a playroom."

"Yes!" Brooke took Penelope's hands. "See? I told you. You have the same vision for the house I do. Please stay and work with me. I know what the rates are for interior decorators"—she named a price that took Penelope's breath away—"and I could help you get more work. There's demand here. You could move to Bella Terra."

Penelope shook her head. "No, I couldn't." Because no matter what she told herself, she couldn't live every day knowing she might run into Noah.

Brooke started to speak, then turned her head toward the back of the house.

DuPey appeared, pistol in his hand.

He walked quietly for a man in boots.

He focused his nondescript gaze on Penelope, for the first time really observing her. "Who are you?" he asked bluntly.

Brooke introduced them. "Penelope Alonso Caldwell, chief of police Bryan DuPey."

"Welcome to Bella Terra." He nodded with a little more sociability. "I hope to see you soon in better circumstances."

But Penelope noted his pistol never wavered, and she would bet a second investigation of her background would be conducted before the day was out. She didn't like being treated like a felon when her worst crime was a shoplifting charge at the age of fourteen. She didn't like this whole setup.

"I've got to finish looking around." DuPey entered each ground-floor room with his pistol at the ready, clearly anticipating trouble hiding behind every door.

Could Penelope stay here when people she thought seemed perfectly normal pulled guns and knives and handled them competently, as if they'd had far too much experience in their use?

"Brooke."

Brooke turned back to Penelope. She must have read Penelope's wariness, for she said in despair, "You're going to quit before we even start, aren't you?"

Penelope was going to back off. She really was. But Brooke's pleading eyes reminded her how much they'd enjoyed their time together.

Brooke waved a hand around. "Look at this place! It needs us. It needs *you*. Just from the few hours we've been together, I know how much you would enjoy seeing the house come back to life. Things aren't as bad as they look. . . ." She hesitated, then corrected herself. "That is, they are, but you're not involved. The trouble won't touch you. We'll keep you safe."

"I'd like to work with you on the house," Penelope admitted. "But—"

Still in high-alert mode, DuPey walked through the entry again and started up the stairs.

Penelope's gaze followed him as he disappeared into the dim light above. She needed to remember that she had no stake in the Di Lucas and their lives. She needed to recall what happened the last time she was in Bella Terra, and act with caution.

On the other hand, she had to remain here until she saw Joseph Bianchin, and God knew when he would be back in town.

Was meeting him at last worth the worry of working with a family that had already caused her so much pain? Was meeting Joseph Bianchin worth seeing Noah again?

She straightened her shoulders.

She'd already made that decision. Yes, she could deal with the Di Lucas and with Noah. The unexpected element was . . . murder. "Let me think about it before I agree."

Chapter 12

The back door opened and closed again.

Brooke reached for her pistol.

Rafe called, "It's us!"

Penelope realized she had been holding her breath, and let it out with a sigh.

The men tromped back from the kitchen, weapons stowed but, Penelope suspected, still easily accessible.

Brooke looked at Rafe grimly. "Well?"

"No footprints in the dirt in the back, but the porch has been swept," Noah said.

"I didn't do it," Brooke said.

"I told him that," Noah answered. "I said, 'Brooke doesn't do housework. As soon as she came to work for me at the resort, she established that very clearly and loudly.' But Rafe is still under the delusion that his wife can be trained with firmness and affection to shake, sit up, and beg—and clean house."

Rafe smacked him in the chest. "Shut up, you idiot."

"I was trying to help!" Noah protested.

"God protect me from your kind of help." But in the first bit of humor Penelope had seen in Rafe, one corner of his mouth kicked up in a crooked grin.

Brooke chuckled and shook the hair back from her face, and when Rafe pulled her into his embrace, she went willingly.

Noah's glance touched Penelope, but for her he didn't seem to feel the good humor he felt for his brother and his brother's wife. For her, his gaze was grave, considering, and she looked back steadily. She wanted to speak up, to tell him that if she fled Bella Terra, it wasn't because of him. He meant nothing to her now; all that mattered was finding her place in a world that had become cold and lonely.

Oh—and staying alive.

But she didn't speak. Of course not. To start that discussion would be perilous in the extreme.

"So who swept the back porch, and why?" Brooke asked Rafe. "Are you sure it wasn't the neighbors trying to be social?"

"I'm sure." Penelope noted that although Rafe held Brooke close to his side, he kept his shooting hand free. "The lock contains a computer chip that records all the activity at that door, and is supposed to send the record to my security team. The door was not only opened from the outside, but the electronics in the lock were scrambled in such a way that the alarm didn't go off and the report was not sent."

"If the lock was scrambled, how did you get that information?" Penelope asked.

Every eye turned to her with varying degrees of suspicion.

DuPey replied from the head of the stairs. "Rafe always has a backup system." Slowly he descended and he, too, kept Penelope locked in his gaze. "Everything's fine upstairs. You might do a sweep for monitoring equipment, though, Rafe."

"Oh, believe me, I intend to."

Penelope had never felt so awkward, so embarrassed, as if she were guilty of some heinous crime, of distracting Brooke while these people, these criminals, slipped in and did . . . nothing.

"What about the video? Surely you can see who broke in," Brooke said.

"It's been wiped," Rafe said. "This is my best system. Or was. It's about to be upgraded."

Penelope still struggled to understand. "Why would someone do that? Break in and do no damage?"

"It's a warning." Rafe gazed pointedly at Noah.

Noah stood still and silent, and that did seem . . . odd. But now he turned to DuPey, and in a quiet voice, he asked, "What are *you* doing here? Is this a social call?"

"Hardly. With all the crap that's been happening in Bella Terra, I don't have time for social calls." In the flash of an eye, DuPey assumed a different attitude, one of a sheriff questioning suspects. "I was going to call you Di Lucas and have a little chat about this guy who's currently in the hospital with ten broken fingers."

"Ten broken fingers." Noah's voice was very quiet. "Sounds like we have a gang in town."

"Yeah, what Noah said. So why do you want to talk to us?" Rafe asked cautiously.

Brooke's mouth tightened into a thin, grim line. "Why would you assume we're involved?"

As far as Penelope was concerned, no one was asking the right questions. Shouldn't they be asking how a guy got ten broken fingers? Or why? Why were they acting like ten broken fingers were a usual circumstance in Bella Terra?

"I know you're not involved, Brooke. Not

Chloë or Mrs. Di Luca, either. It wasn't a youth gang, if that's what you mean, Noah. Just possibly the Di Luca brothers. The hospital called when this guy showed up at the emergency room with his hands looking like someone took a crowbar to them. We don't see stuff like that here." DuPey pushed his hat toward the back of his head and scratched his forehead. "Or we didn't used to. It took a while to dig the story out of him, especially since he's got a record dating back twelve years: breaking and entering, vandalism, suspected murder."

"An upstanding citizen, then," Rafe said sardonically.

"This is a bad son of a bitch," DuPey said.

Brooke stirred in Rafe's arms. "Let me guess. He stumbled across the job posting on the Internet about someone being willing to pay good money to find and retrieve a bottle of wine."

DuPey's worn bloodhound eyes looked like they were barely open, but his gaze touched every one of them with screened acuity.

Noah stood apart, in the shadows by the stairs, his face turned away, but his very immobility made Penelope think he was listening intently.

No one asked about the wine, so they knew something Penelope did not, and she wasn't about to interject herself into the conversation. Every time she did, someone viewed her with suspicion.

"That's about it, Brooke," DuPey said. "He

said there was word out that the matter was being handled, and no one was to interfere. But he's belligerent and not too bright—"

"And greedy," Brooke said.

DuPey nodded. "As soon as he heard about the money, he was on his way. According to him, he got here, dropped into the Beaver Inn, had a couple of beers, asked some questions, mouthed off, and the next morning headed out to recover the bottle from Mrs. Di Luca."

Sarah? Criminals were chasing Sarah? Penelope's head was spinning.

DuPey continued. "But before he got very far, three guys, older men, he said, pulled him over and told him to get the hell out of town. Apparently he doesn't have a strong protective instinct, because he threatened to bring his cousins in to battle for turf."

"And?" Noah's voice was quiet, pitched to reach each person and no farther.

"They got his tire iron out of his trunk and broke all his fingers. Broke"—DuPey's mouth twisted in disgust—"hell, they pounded them."

Penelope protectively closed her hands into fists.

"He'll be lucky to ever use his hands again." DuPey pulled his hat low on his forehead.

No one else seemed as distressed as Penelope. It was almost as if they'd all seen worse and were inured to the horror.

Murder. Brooke said there was murder. More than one? And violence of a most horrific kind . . .

"What has this to do with us?" Rafe asked.

DuPey hitched up his belt. "Actually, trouble is . . . he said the three men were brothers. They looked alike. And the men he described sound like Di Lucas."

Rafe and Noah looked incredulously at DuPey.

"You really think we'd do that?" Noah asked.

"No . . ." DuPey sounded doubtful. "Seems excessive. But I do think you'd do anything to keep your grandmother safe, and if this guy said the right stuff—and he's got quite a mouth on him—I think things might get heated."

Rafe and Noah exchanged glances.

"When did it happen?" Rafe asked.

"This morning around eight," DuPey answered.

"I was on a conference call with my people on the East Coast." Rafe looked and sounded sure of himself. "I've got witnesses to that."

"You employ a computer hacker who could fake the time and your presence," DuPey retorted.

"Darren is good," Rafe acknowledged.

DuPey finished, "And your people are loyal enough to lie."

Rafe didn't argue. Instead, he inclined his head.

Penelope swallowed. These guys were spooky.

DuPey looked at Noah.

"I was in the shower. Alone. No witnesses." Noah put his hands on his hips. "And no, I don't know where Eli was, but I'd guess Chloë does. They're together . . . a lot."

The guys smirked.

Brooke rolled her eyes.

Apparently Eli and Chloë were an item.

"I'll check with him. Chloë's no better as an alibi than Rafe's people, but maybe Eli was working in the vines or in the barrels. All we need is one valid alibi, and all of you are off the hook." DuPey touched his hat. "Okay, I gotta run."

Noah grinned. "Doughnuts just come out of the fryer at Binkies?"

"Yeah," DuPey drawled. "You want to come and get your usual dozen?"

Penelope noted that DuPey and Noah sniped at each other like old friends. . . . How interesting that she didn't get the same feeling of camaraderie between Rafe and Noah.

A few more jabs, and Noah escorted DuPey to the back door to make sure it was properly closed.

With a great deal more intensity and less cordiality, Rafe turned once more to Penelope. "*What* are you doing in town?"

"Come on." Brooke pulled on his arm. "I'll fill you in while I show you what Penelope and I decided to do upstairs."

He hesitated, clearly wanting to argue with his wife . . . and *not* wanting to argue with his wife.

Brooke patted his shoulder and murmured softly, and, with a final hard glance at Penelope, he let Brooke lead him up the stairs—leaving Penelope alone to face Noah.

Chapter 13

Facing Noah might be no big deal—was no big deal—but until Penelope made a final decision about this job, she had no business sticking around here. She could go back to the motel and . . . well, read a book or something. She had no responsibilities. . . .

But leaving felt awkward and childish and as if she were running away, and she couldn't bear for Noah to think she couldn't face him. So she stayed, alone in the tall entry, listening to the echo of the footsteps on the floors above and hoping to hell that Joseph Bianchin turned out to be worth all this trouble.

When she heard the back door open and close, an unexpected chill ran up her spine. Noah and Rafe and Brooke kept weapons at the ready. Brooke used words like *trouble* and *murder*. The way they acted made Penelope wonder all of a sudden who had come in.

Then Noah came around the corner and walked toward her through the afternoon's downward-slanting light, and a different sort of chill ran up her spine. Because, oh, God, he was handsome.

She assured herself that there wasn't a woman in the world who could remain unmoved by the sight of him. He had the kind of beauty that came from centuries of wealthy Italian families breeding their sons and daughters for the choicest lands and sums of money. His arms were too long, his hands too big, his shoulders impressively broad, his hips dangerously narrow. But it was the way he stepped that made her gaze cling to him; his strides were long and smooth, centered on his being. He moved like a dark-browed pirate king in command of his ship, his crew, the very elements that raged around him.

"Rafe and Brooke bought this place, and Rafe wanted me to see the house." He was close.

She was skittish. "I know. Brooke thinks a lot of your opinion. We were discussing whether this is a bearing wall." Penelope walked into the parlor and rested her hand on the peeling plaster.

"It is," he said with assurance.

"You didn't even look or tap or . . . whatever."

"In older homes, assume every wall is a bearing wall. When you go in for the permit, it's easier." His peculiar green eyes observed his world with good-humored interest—and Bella Terra was his world in every way.

Yet she remembered the way his eyes changed

to the angry gray of a stormy sea . . . or the rich gold of a great passion.

"I've learned a fair amount about remodeling. I'm the manager of Bella Terra resort, you know, a job I got by shrewdly being born into the Di Luca family." He smiled at her, inviting her to smile back.

She did not. Instead she stared like a rodent enthralled by a snake.

He continued. "The resort has grown since it was built in the thirties, and I've had to deal with every electrical upgrade and plumbing disaster."

Charming. My God, he was as charming as ever.

"The resort keeps me busy most of the time, and by most of the time I mean I'm on call twenty-four hours a day. So when I vacation, I leave town, ski, or go to Hawaii for the Iron Man competition or hike. . . . Last summer I went to Nepal and tackled a couple of pretty impressive peaks. Nonna said that was stupid." He chuckled. "But it's one more item off my bucket list."

"I'll have to agree with your grandmother."

"I've done it now. I can go to my grave knowing I've conquered K2."

He could have died. Plenty of people had fallen to their deaths on that mountain, their bodies never recovered. And Penelope shouldn't care, but she did. Too much death . . .

She folded her hands at her waist and, to hide

her expression, looked down at them. "I would say it's more important to go to your grave later than earlier. But . . . that's just me."

"How's your mother?" he asked. "Is she visiting Bella Terra with you?" He must have seen something in the way she stood, or heard something in her voice . . . or maybe he had simply moved on to another topic of conversation.

"No." Penelope gained control, looked up at him. "I lost her a few months ago."

She had caught him by surprise. "L-lost? She died? Your mother? But she seemed so vibrant!"

"Yes. Always." Until the very end.

"What happened?" He added hastily, "If it's not too painful."

"I came to Bella Terra the summer after my freshman year in college."

He nodded. "To serve an internship for the interior designer who was updating the resort."

"The summer *before* my freshman year, Mama discovered a lump in her breast. But we had a lot to do to get me ready to go to college. Plus she was working for Mrs. Walters."

"Your mother was her . . . nurse?"

"Nurse/companion, I guess. We lived with her, you know, and Mama was at her beck and call." Penelope looked down again, remembering how her shoplifting in L.A. had precipitated the move to Portland, how she had been flung into an all-girls Catholic school with no more chances to screw up . . . and how she had realized she could never stand to disappoint her mother like that again.

The two of them were on their own.

"Mrs. Walters did a lot for us—I would never have been able to afford Cincinnati if it hadn't been for her. But she was always demanding. Cincinnati was a long way away, so Mama didn't say anything about the lump to me or Mrs. Walters. She didn't do anything about the lump." Penelope put her back against the wall, slid down, and sat on the floor, arms on her knees, eyes staring straight ahead. "Once she got me settled and returned to Portland, she had it checked out. They removed it. It was malignant. She underwent chemotherapy, and by the time I came home for Christmas, she was . . . She looked thin, but her hair was growing back in, and when I asked her, she didn't tell me she'd had breast cancer. She said she was fine." If only Penelope had questioned her further. If only she'd been less selfish and more concerned for her mother. If only . . .

If only.

Noah joined her on the floor, staring straight ahead, not looking at her . . . but listening. He might be her enemy, but he knew her and he knew her mother, and he remembered. . . . "It's not your fault," he said. "If your mother had told me lies, I would have never questioned her. She was a force of nature."

"And I was selfish, happy to be home, to see my friends. Mrs. Walters might have told me if I'd asked, but I didn't. I didn't think to ask why or how my mother managed to pull enough strings to get me that internship in Bella Terra that summer, or why she was willing to leave Mrs. Walters and come here to live with me."

"She was afraid she was going to die, and she wanted to give you a good start in life and spend as much time with you as possible."

Not quite. But close enough. "That's right. At the end of the summer, we left here. I finished college. I went to work. I got married. I lost my husband." She dropped her gaze. She'd said enough. "When Mama came to help me get through it, this time I knew there was something wrong. They'd told her the cancer was gone. Actually, it had metastasized to her lungs. I quit my job. I sold our house. I went to Portland to take care of her." Penelope recited the story steadily, but an unexpected wave of emotion caught her by the throat.

"How long ago?" Noah asked.

Had Mama died, he meant. "Five months."

"What about her family in L.A.? Have you seen them?"

"I let them know when she died. Her mother is dead. Her father never forgave her for getting knocked up. Then he never forgave her for moving out of L.A."

"But you said he washed his hands of you."

"After I got arrested, he wanted Mama to put me in a correctional facility. Said it would teach me a lesson. She said no and we moved. He blames me. Which is true. So he told me I shouldn't expect anything from him. As far as he was concerned, I was no grandchild of his." Not that Penelope expected anything different, but what a bitter conversation that had been!

Now Noah turned to her. "You're alone in the world."

"Mrs. Walters is still alive. She is very old, ninety-seven and feeble. When Mama got really sick, Mrs. Walters finally had to concede defeat and go into an assisted-living facility. She hates it, of course, and she's starting to fail, and she told me . . . well. She told me stuff. Stuff that might be true, but her mind is wandering." And for all that Penelope had not loved the old tyrant, she found that to be another almost unbearable loss. "She thinks I'm my mother."

"Oh, Penelope. You've had such a tough time." Before she realized what Noah intended and could move to take countermeasures, he grasped her hand again, holding it in both of his, warming her cold fingers between his palms.

She cleared her throat. "The last couple of years have been a challenge. But things are on the upswing." She was so uncomfortable. Uncertain and uncomfortable and . . . Why was he doing this? Why was he being nice? The last time she'd seen Noah, he certainly hadn't been *nice*. He had taken her youthful, fragile heart and crushed it with all the focused cruelty of a man who'd had his pleasure and wanted to move on.

She had loved him.

He hadn't loved her.

She had thought he wanted to marry her.

He had dumped her in the cruelest way possible.

It had taken years for her to recover confidence in her own judgment, years to grow an ego large enough to believe a man could truly love her. It had taken Keith, kind and gentle, before she'd been willing to wade into the marital waters.

So what was Noah up to? Did he think she was just going to forget what a jackass he was?

If she was mature, she would.

She was never going to be that mature.

She pulled her hand away and scrambled to her feet. "No, really. I'm fine. Living the usual boring life. *I* don't carry a knife. Or a gun. Or any weapon at all. So tell me, Noah—what's going on here in Bella Terra?"

Chapter 14

Noah hesitated, apparently wanting to extend the moment of connection between them.

But Penelope pointedly rejected him, rising, turning, and walking away from the shadows of the parlor and into the foyer, where the westering sun splashed light across the walls.

Noah followed. "It's a long story." He glanced at the ceiling as if weighing the chances that Rafe and Brooke would return, then gestured Penelope toward the entry and the stairway. "Have a seat. I'll try to make it brief. Over eighty years ago—"

She laughed as she seated herself on the hard step. "It really *is* a long story."

"I wouldn't kid you." But he wasn't amused. He watched her closely as he said, "Less than three months ago, Nonna was attacked in her home."

Penelope's amusement died an abrupt death. "Is she okay?"

"She walked in on a robbery in progress. He hit her with a tire iron, broke her arm, and knocked her out." Noah paced in front of her, the diffused light from the high windows in the entry brushing his dark hair and broad shoulders with a loving hand. "She had a concussion and was in the hospital for more than a week. We sent her home with a bodyguard and a nurse to ensure her safety and health."

Penelope's dismay subsided, and her anger rose. "Did you catch the mugger?"

"Eventually we did, but it turned out he was the harbinger of something much larger. It goes back to an old family feud. Over eighty years ago—"

She didn't laugh this time, but intently leaned forward.

"—my grandfather Anthony Di Luca was born, and on the same day across the valley, the Bianchin family also had a son."

She knew who. "Joseph."

"Yes!" He looked startled. Stared questioningly at her.

"I'm in town because I've got business with him."

"Design business?" He shot the question at her. "But he's not here."

"I know that."

"Is he coming back soon?"

"I don't know. I hope so."

"I hope not. He's the one who initiated the attack on Nonna."

Noah's sharp tone, the harsh words, made her lean back away from him. "What? Why? How do you know that?"

"Over eighty years ago," he began again, "there was a man, unmarried and with no family, named Massimo Bruno. He lived in Bella Valley and he made fine wines. World-class wines."

"I'm listening." Although she wished Noah would get to the point.

"On the occasion of a son's birth, he would give a bottle of wine to the family, to be opened at the child's twenty-first birthday. It was tradition, but this was Prohibition, and that year the revenuers found Massimo's wine cellar. They broke all the casks and spilled the wine into the street. The gutters ran red, and Massimo managed to save enough wine for one bottle only. One bottle. Two sons. Two rival families."

"Uh-oh." She was starting to comprehend.

"Massimo gave the bottle of wine to the child who had been born first, my grandfather, Anthony Di Luca. To Joseph and the Bianchins, he gave an antique silver rattle." Noah looked down, heavy lidded with satisfaction. "As it should have been."

She wouldn't dream of disagreeing. "Yes, of course."

"The Bianchins swore vengeance." Noah managed to convey cruelty in the wave of a hand. "For twenty-one years, they brooded on the perceived wrong—we Italians know how to wait, letting the anger fester year by year."

Penelope's heart clutched in anticipation and anguish.

Had she imagined that she knew this man?

She did not. Her heritage was Mexican: Mayan, Spanish, and French, and in those

American and European heritages she shared the same heated Mediterranean blood as the Di Lucas. But she knew without a doubt that her grandfather's petty grudges were nothing like this.

"On my grandfather's twenty-first birthday, which was also his wedding day, Joseph led the Bianchin family on the attack. They came with guns and knives. They destroyed the gifts, the food, the wine—and they shot my grandfather." The grim lines around Noah's mobile mouth deepened. "He almost died."

No. No. It wasn't true. But she didn't say a word. She didn't want Noah to realize how much this meant to her . . . or why.

"Unfortunately for them, they attacked too soon. Massimo's wine had not been opened. The bottle was still hidden. My grandfather survived, but he never forgave them—"

Please tell me this is not true. Not true. Because if it is . . .

"As long as Nonno lived, he would bring out that bottle of wine and show it off to his friends and his family . . . and put it away again. Because he knew that, across town, Joseph Bianchin would hear about it. He knew Joseph was stewing in his own bile, envying that bottle, coveting it."

When Penelope came to Bella Terra to meet with Joseph Bianchin, she had never anticipated anything like this. How could she? To sit here and watch Noah gesture animatedly, to watch his face change from that of an amiable, civilized man into that of a brutal barbarian moved to violence by old vendettas . . . it was a revelation that both frightened and fascinated her. "Then what happened?"

"About a dozen years ago, my grandfather was diagnosed with Alzheimer's. He slid slowly into dementia and died." Noah stopped for a moment, his head bowed. Taking a breath, he finally continued. "When Nonna went looking for the bottle of wine—it was gone."

"Gone?" She straightened up. "Gone where?"

"Wouldn't we like to know?" Noah flashed a smile. "Nonno hid it, and hid it well. We've looked and looked, but it's gone. And yet the trouble remains."

Chapter 15

Your grandfather could have put that bottle of wine anywhere," Penelope whispered.

"No." Noah shook his head with assurance. "The hiding places are limited. It's wine. Wine has to be properly cared for or it disintegrates, and a bottle of that age . . . Well, there's a chance—a good chance—that no matter how well tended it was, the wine has soured. But the bottle was precious to Nonno, his heritage, the reason he was wounded and almost killed. He would have put it somewhere it would be preserved. He would have put it somewhere dark and cool."

She had to object. "But he had Alzheimer's. Maybe—"

"For Nonno, the proper care of wine wasn't a function of his mind. It was like his hair color or the sound of his voice. The proper care of wine was bred into him by a thousand generations of Di Lucas, and he would never have abused that bottle."

She didn't know whether she believed Noah or not, but it didn't matter. He believed it. His family believed it. But she saw a flaw in the logic. "So the person who broke into your grandmother's house was someone hired by Joseph Bianchin to grab the bottle of wine?"

"That's right."

"You know this for a fact?"

"I do."

"How?" She leaned forward, making her point. "Because frankly, if Joseph Bianchin had wanted that bottle of wine so badly he's willing to resort to violence, he should have come for it sooner."

Noah nodded at her. "Exactly our thoughts. But we knew it was Joseph who started the trouble, because we found the Internet ad looking for someone to do the job."

"He put up an ad for criminals to beat up an

elderly lady and put his name on it?" She made her disbelief plain in her voice.

"No, he put up an Internet ad saying someone would pay to recover a precious possession, and the sly old bastard covered his tracks very well. He's smart enough to make sure nothing he does is prosecutable." Noah's face grew cold again. "But while Nonna was in the hospital, he visited her. He threatened her."

Penelope dropped her gaze, watching as Noah's athletic shoes moved across the faded, worn-to-nubs carpet. She didn't want to hear this. She couldn't bear the impact this had on her stay in Bella Terra. It made her purpose here . . . impossible. Horrible.

But Noah's relentless voice continued. "He told my grandmother he wanted the bottle *now*."

Slowly, Penelope lifted her gaze to him once more, and watched Noah with unwilling compulsion. His family had lived in the United States for over a century, yet he was Italian in looks and demeanor, using his hands to punctuate his sentences, to convey excitement or sorrow. His face, too, was mobile, his expressions so vivid she could almost see the generations of men, the malice, the danger.

"Later, once we realized what was going on, I told Bianchin to get the hell out of town, so he tried to convince *me* to hand it over. Like I would do anything for that mean old bastard."

Noah didn't know—couldn't know—that each word made them enemies. "So Bianchin left town?"

"Nonna's well liked here. We three brothers love her dearly." Noah's deep voice grew silky soft and dangerous. "If he hadn't, I would have worried about his health."

"You wouldn't hurt an old man!" *Would he?*

"He hurt my grandmother—she might have died, and he wouldn't have cared—so in fact, I would have done whatever was necessary to send him into exile." Noah had grown out of the last softness of youth. He was all man now, and he smiled the kind of menacing, toothy smile she had never imagined on his face.

All right. She supposed he had the right to defend his grandmother with every resource available to him. She knew Nonna had raised him. But . . . "It doesn't make sense. Why did Joseph Bianchin decide to resort to violence at this stage?"

"We figured that one out almost too late—and by we, I mean Eli and his new wife, Chloë. She's an author; she writes suspense. Eli, too, did his part." Noah shook his head in wonder. "Who knew he had it in him to defend himself against a crooked FBI agent?"

"Eli?" Penelope remembered him as a large, quiet man, intent on wines and wary of people in general.

"Former FBI, but it took Eli and Chloë both to defeat him, and they look like they've been used as battering rams." Noah sat on his haunches in front of Penelope and looked right into her eyes. "The whole thing is about diamonds."

"Diamonds?"

"Massimo was stealing diamonds, hiding them in the wine bottles he gave as gifts; then, when the coast was clear, he'd steal the bottle and replace it with one that looked identical but didn't have the contraband."

Penelope realized her mouth was hanging open. She snapped it shut and asked, "He was doing this during Prohibition?"

"Apparently Nonna's mother always said he was a gangster. Apparently Nonna's mother was right."

"Whoa. How did Joseph Bianchin find out?"

"Bottles of Massimo's wine are still around; Bianchin's been a collector for years, pathetically trying to be my grandfather, I guess." Noah's eyes flashed with irritation. "We *think* he opened a bottle, poured it, and found jewels in the bottom."

"Jewels Massimo hadn't collected?"

"Jewels he hadn't collected because he disappeared not long after giving his last bottle to my grandfather."

"What happened to him?"

"No one knows. Or rather . . . no one knew

until Eli and Chloë found his body in an old water tower. He'd been tortured. Up there beside the body, Eli found a small diamond—and not just any diamond. It was a pink diamond, so Chloë looked up jewel robberies for that year before my grandfather was born." Noah's mouth twisted in distaste. "In Amsterdam, a priceless set of pink diamonds was stolen and never retrieved."

The whole story was fascinating, horrifying, unlikely . . . and all too obviously, everyone in the Di Luca family believed it was true. Penelope breathed in and out, in and out, slow, heavy breaths as she tried to contain her anguish. "Joseph Bianchin figured that out, too, and he wants those diamonds."

"I think we can assume that." Putting one knee on the step beside her, the other on the floor, Noah took her hand *again*. The light danced on each strand of his short black hair with fevered grace. "Here in Bella Terra, in the last two and a half months, we've had three murders, a related death, and as much violence as we've had in the last fifty years put together. The resort's on high alert, and the press is starting to take an interest. We Di Lucas have managed to distract them, but the reporters will catch on eventually. If that happens, every thug and opportunist in the world will arrive on our doorstep looking for that bottle of wine."

"You truly don't know where it is?" Her life would be so much easier if he knew and for some nefarious reason was hiding the truth.

But it almost seemed that he read her mind and repeated her thoughts back at her. "How much easier it would be for all of us if we knew, and poured it, and found out whether the bottle contained diamonds—or merely sediment."

"Yes. I can see that." She *could* see it.

"That's why Rafe was acting like a jerk, questioning you as if you were a person of suspicion. And that's why I'd consider it a favor if you'd come and see Nonna."

He made Penelope feel as if she were standing at the edge of a swamp filled with old affection and lost love, and sinking in the quicksand. And in her experience, if she were caught by him, really trapped, she would suffer for it.

He looked into her eyes. Looked into her soul. Appealed to her better nature. "Nonna was hurt badly; Rafe and Brooke were traumatized; Eli and Chloë were horribly injured. Then this week, Nonna found out that someone she loved was a liar and a cheat. Seeing you would take her mind off her troubles. Would you go visit her?" When she hesitated, he said, "I promise . . . I promise not to be there."

He seemed to think that mattered.

Chapter 16

Penelope put her hand on Noah's chest, and in a move that surprised him—although why it should, he didn't know—she pushed him so hard he sprawled backward on the hardwood floor.

She stood. "As appealing as that sounds, Noah, it's impossible. I've realized . . . I can't stay in Bella Terra. This criminal activity is too much for me! I'm a coward. I'm going back to Portland tomorrow."

He got slowly to his feet, rubbing his aching butt. A coward? After all she'd been through? "You're not a coward."

"Don't tell me what I am or am not. In the past few years of my life, I have seen enough death. I cannot bear to see any more." She looked fierce and proud, demanding that he respect who she was and what she could endure.

"Okay . . ." he said slowly, thinking hard, thinking fast. "But you've got a job here that you were looking forward to. Or at least, you seemed to be. You could do the design, work with Brooke, without being involved in the, um—"

"Murders?" Her voice rose. "I have to *survive* to work at a job, and survival seems to be a little iffy here in Bella Terra."

From the top of the stairs, Noah heard a small,

high shriek. He turned in time to see Brooke bound down the stairs.

Rafe ran after her, his arms outstretched as if to catch her.

“Damn it, Noah!” she said. “I was depending on you to convince Penelope to stay, not to scare her into leaving.”

“Woman, would you please be careful?” Rafe roared.

She brushed him aside and confronted Noah, fists on her hips. “Did you have to tell her all the gory details? Couldn’t you have glossed over some stuff?”

“I *did* gloss over some stuff,” he said.

Brooke swung her back to him.

“That’s helpful, Noah.” Rafe put his hands on her shoulders.

Noah turned to Penelope. “I didn’t mention that my relatives eavesdrop without compunction or shame.”

She nodded. “You didn’t, but I see it’s true.”

She looked so different from the way she had the last time he’d seen her; she was now so confident, sophisticated—and distant.

Those brown eyes had once adored him. Her hands had once caressed him. He knew her scent, the weight of her breasts in his palms, and when she spoke, he recalled the husky sound of her voice in his ear as she cried out her pleasure.

She was his. No matter how much time passed,

no matter how much distance had separated them . . . she was always and eternally meant for him.

And he couldn't have her.

Yet, selfish bastard that he was, he didn't want her to leave. As his time on earth ticked down, he wanted her near.

"You don't have to go. We could avoid each other whenever possible," Noah said.

"That might work," Rafe said.

Noah raised his eyebrows at his brother. When had Rafe decided it would be better if Penelope stayed?

Rafe nodded toward Brooke, a brief, short movement that clearly told Noah he was a lot more concerned with keeping his wife happy than worried about Penelope's security clearance.

"No. Because it doesn't matter to me whether I see Noah. Our former relationship is of no importance here. That was then. This is now."

Rafe smirked at Noah. "She put you in your place."

Going to Brooke, Penelope said, "I'm sorry. I would really love to do this job. I love the house and I enjoyed talking with you, but I just . . . I don't want to die for it."

Brooke's smile tried to be kind and understanding. "I'm sorry, too. We could really work well together."

"I know." Penelope sounded wistful.

She really did want the job. Noah could tell. "Let me drive you back to wherever you're staying. Give me a chance to talk you out of leaving." He tried a winsome smile.

"No." She gathered up her purse from the corner of the entry. "I've got my car."

So much for winsome. "Your leaving is not necessary. You will never be drawn into our troubles. You're not involved with us."

She turned on him. "I don't have to be involved with you. But I've already been scared by a cop showing up out of the blue and accusing you of breaking some guy's fingers. Nobody seemed too worried about the violence. I've already seen every one of you pull a weapon with such expertise I would have sprinted out of here—but I was afraid to move."

He grinned.

"It's not funny!" she snapped.

He sobered. "No, of course not."

"I'm already involved enough that you told me the whole"—she flung her arms around her head—"background story."

She was upset. He didn't blame her. "At least tell me where you're staying."

"At the Sweet Dreams Hotel."

Soundlessly, he mouthed the words. *The Sweet Dreams Hotel.*

She faced off with him. "Yeah? Did you have something to say?"

She thought he was a snob. She thought he was casting aspersions on her background. On where she was staying. "Nothing," he said softly.

"Good." She started to turn away.

He couldn't stand it. "I could get you a room at Bella Terra resort."

She swung back on him. "I can't afford it."

"I know the manager." Winsome smile. "I could get you a good rate."

"I can't afford you, Noah," she said flatly.

Damn it. His winsomeness worked on every woman in the world—except for the one woman who mattered. He supposed it was justice. But he didn't have to like it.

After nine years, she was back in his territory, and he couldn't have her. Didn't dare even try. "If you moved into the resort, I'd stay far, far away from you."

"I like where I am."

The Sweet Dreams Hotel. "Sure."

"Anyway, I'm leaving tomorrow." She put her fist to her mouth and bit her knuckles, once, hard, as if thinking. "Or maybe the next day. I've got that business with—"

"Joseph Bianchin. Yeah. I remember." Noah did remember, and he wondered what she could want with the coldhearted old bastard. "Listen, I've got to get back, talk to some contractors, find out how quickly they can get out here. Penelope, promise me one thing."

She looked up warily.

"Promise me you'll visit Nonna. If she found out you'd been here and she hadn't seen you, she'd feel bad. I'm not pulling anything on you." A little artfully applied guilt always worked wonders on women. "She really would wonder what she'd done to make you dislike her."

Penelope pushed her hair off her forehead. He could see the shame twisting her insides until she had no possible answer except one. "All right. I'll do it. But what you said before. You have to promise. I don't want you there."

"Great." He'd won one battle. Maybe he'd win the next one, too. "I promise, if I see you coming, I'll run away."

She smiled faintly. "Good."

"If you need me to send a car to fetch you to Nonna's, let me know." Knowing her fiercely independent nature, he knew she would reject him, so didn't wait to hear her answer, ducking out the door as soon as he finished speaking.

Penelope hurried to the door and called after him, "I can drive myself, thank you."

And from inside the house, Rafe shouted, "Hey! Noah! You rode with me, remember?"

Chapter 17

Rafe caught up with Noah as he reached the sidewalk. “I’ll drive you back to the resort.”

“It’s not far. I gotta get a coffee. I can walk.”

Rafe grabbed his arm and swung him toward the car. “I want to talk.”

“Of course you do.” It was the price Noah paid for being the youngest; his brothers could not stop thinking of him as a dumb kid. So he figured he might as well get it over with.

Rafe was speaking even before they got in the car. “Noah, what are you doing? Talking to that woman, flirting with her—after she left Bella Terra, you made it clear you thought you had barely escaped marriage and bondage to a social climber.”

“Nice house.” Noah looked back to see whether he could catch another glimpse of Penelope. “You’ve got a lot of work ahead of you, but the infrastructure is good and you paid a good price. You and Brooke will be very happy there.”

“You are the biggest pain in the ass. Okay, I get it; you’re not going to tell me what you know about the bottle of wine and the diamonds.”

“It’s for the best.”

It said a lot for Rafe’s restraint that he didn’t jump Noah about that. “Can’t you at least give me a clue about your former girlfriend?”

Noah chose his words carefully. "All those years ago, when I said she was a social climber, I might have overstated the situation."

Rafe unlocked the car. "So now you claim she's a nice girl and you're a ruthless schmuck who dumped her so you could screw around with the rest of the world?"

Noah climbed into the passenger seat, and as soon as Rafe got in, Noah said, "If I had it all to do over again, she would have never left Bella Terra. I was a fool." Rafe didn't even understand how big a fool Noah had been. And if it were up to Noah, he wouldn't find out until Noah had redeemed himself.

"I know that feeling. So many years wasted when Brooke and I could have been together . . ." Rafe always turned to mush when he started talking about Brooke.

Good time to change the subject. "Hey!" Noah said. "Everything turned out okay, and now you're having a baby."

Rafe gave Noah a crooked smile and put the car in gear. "Is that not the greatest news ever?"

Noah crowed with laughter. "I knew there was a reason you and Brooke didn't move to Sweden. Congratulations, you old daddy."

"Thanks." Rafe got serious again. "But listen, that's why I've got a thing about who Penelope Alonso Caldwell really is and why she's here."

Noah rubbed the back of his neck. “Don’t you *ever* give up?”

“No. No, I don’t. We’ve got people—strangers, crazy people—hunting for Nonno’s bottle of wine because, right or wrong, everyone thinks the bottle holds a stash of priceless pink diamonds. You know something about somebody who’s after the diamonds, and you won’t tell us.”

“Don’t worry. I’m handling it.”

Rafe turned for one second and glared.

“Watch the road,” Noah said.

“And now, out of the clear blue sky, your old lover shows up for no good reason that she can give. Brooke says I’m paranoid. I say I’m smart.”

“Penelope is not an opportunist.”

Rafe slapped the steering wheel with the flat of his hand. “How do you know? Have you seen her in the last nine years?”

“No. But I know her.”

“Deep in your soul, you know her?”

“Something like that.”

“Did she tell you why she came to Bella Terra in the first place?”

“Something about business.”

“So you don’t know.”

Actually, Noah did. She was here to speak to Joseph Bianchin about something. But telling Rafe that wasn’t going to help clear up any suspicions.

"*I'll* ask her," Rafe said.

"Good luck. When you're acting like a tyrannical ass, she's not going to tell you anything." Noah didn't want Rafe picking on Penelope.

"That's convenient. May I point out that when you're acting like she's your lost love, I'm not going to believe a damned word you say about her."

"Yeah. Well." She *was* his lost love. It made him laugh when he remembered that moment today when he'd realized he was selling himself to Penelope like a rock star on the make.

Rafe turned onto Main, still raging about Penelope and her effect on Noah. "I am running all her references."

"Why bother? She's leaving town." It was better that way. Seeing her today had given Noah hope where there had been none, and hope was a commodity he didn't dare cultivate. It was dangerous for him to think he could find the kind of love his brothers now enjoyed.

"She *says* she's leaving town. But look at what happened with Olivia."

Remembering Olivia was like a bucket of ice water dumped down Noah's neck. He wanted Penelope to stay, but she was right: Death stalked this town. Death stalked him. And he feared for everyone who stood too close.

Rafe sighed. "I don't believe anybody anymore."

Noah snorted. "I didn't know that you suffered from an overabundance of trust, anyway."

"I failed to protect Nonna. I failed to protect Brooke. I'm not letting some female from *your* past wander into town and get hired by *my* wife—"

"Penelope's not taking the job," Noah repeated.

"—without making damned good and sure she is who she says she is. *Especially* since you talked her into visiting Nonna."

"I agree. Investigate Penelope. Makes sense." Investigate her, even though the sight of her calmed his mind, her scent lingered in his senses, and the desire for her burned as strongly as ever . . . not that he could do anything about that desire. Last time he'd been too weak to turn away from his feelings for her. This time he was older, wiser, no longer a boy half out of his mind with rage and hormones. This time, he was in control.

Although, when it came to Penelope, he didn't care to be tested.

"If you would tell me what you know about the diamonds and the people who are after them . . ." Rafe slowed down for the light, glanced at Noah, and his plea was sincere and warm. "If you tell me what you know, I could help you. No matter what it is, I have the expertise either through my employees or myself to handle this."

"Interestingly enough, there's no one who can handle this except me. I know it goes against your grain, Rafe, but this time, you're going to have to trust your baby brother." Noah pointed to an empty space at the curb. "Drop me off there by the Black Bean."

Rafe whipped his car into the tight spot with an expertise that clearly showed he'd learned at a rigorous technical driving school. "Noah," he said sternly. "It's not that we don't trust you. It's that this thing is too big for any one of us."

Noah popped the door open without saying another word.

Rafe caught his arm. Again. "Noah, listen to me."

Noah turned to him in exasperation. "Figure it out. I'm not telling you."

"I know. I got that. But listen." Rafe tried to smile, tried to sound light, but his blue eyes were earnest, anxious . . . affectionate. "No matter what it is. No matter how much trouble you're in. You're my brother, and I love you. Just promise . . . promise that if I can do anything, you'll call me. I'm on your side, man, no matter what."

Noah stared at his bossy, annoying, pigheaded older sibling, and a warmth uncoiled in his gut. "I know. I love you, too."

"Promise." Rafe couldn't stand to have Noah keep secrets from him.

But those secrets would kill them all . . . if Noah didn't choose the right course.

If Noah did choose the right course . . . then only he would die.

That was the good news.

So Noah lied. "Sure. If I think you can help me, I will call. Now, Rafe—I gotta get my coffee and get back to work."

"Okay. See you around." Rafe lifted his hand in farewell.

Noah slammed the door, waved him off, and, when he was sure Rafe was really gone, he strolled through the open courtyard, past the cast-iron patio tables filled with people using the free Wi-Fi and sipping from massive paper cups, past a tall blond older woman who sat waiting for someone, and into the Black Bean's open door. He walked up to the counter and smiled winsomely at Mandy. "I'll take the usual. And . . . a spare. To go."

Mandy smiled back.

How come *winsome* worked on her and not on Penelope?

"You're late today," she said as she prepared two lattes.

"Rafe and Brooke wanted me to look over their house." He glanced out the door as two of the tables emptied. "You're busy today."

"We've got tourists in for the vine-grafting festival."

"The city fathers should be proud of thinking that one up," Noah muttered.

"Don't I know it. But it's good for business, and it's not as if any of the tourists actually want to graft vines."

The two of them chuckled softly.

Mandy put the cups on the counter. "So Rafe and Brooke bought the old gold-digger place?"

"That's it. It's going to take some work to get it ready in time."

"Before Brooke has her baby, you mean?"

He paused, hand halfway to his wallet. "What, am I the only person in town who didn't know?"

Mandy laughed. "No, I wasn't sure until just now, but my sister-in-law Brittany is Dr. Jacobs's receptionist, and when Brooke called in for the exam she figured something was up. We were speculating what the likely choices were, and since she was just married . . ."

"The grapevine in this town is the stuff of legend," Noah said wryly.

"Just among us old-timers. I can't keep track of all the new people moving in and out."

"Me, neither." Noah picked up his cups. "Thanks, Mandy. See you tomorrow."

"You bet, Noah."

Turning away from the counter, he strolled out the door and into the courtyard, up to the table occupied by the tall, fit blond woman in her sixties. Pulling up a chair, he sat down, placed one cup in front of her, popped the top on his, and said, "I was wondering when I'd see you again . . . Mother."

Chapter 18

The first time Noah met his mother, he was fifteen years old, going into the Black Bean for one of their iced mocha cappuccinos.

As he passed the woman sitting at one of the patio tables, he noticed her. How could he not? She was the kind of female everyone noticed: tall, blond, glowing with good health, not pretty, but handsome in an older-woman, strong-faced way. She was the kind of female people remembered, too, so he knew he'd never seen her around town. But that didn't mean anything. As Bella Valley's reputation for fine wines grew, so did the tourist industry and the number of visitors who came to taste the wines and stayed to enjoy the heat, the orchards, the vines, and the gently changing seasons.

What was different about this woman was that she watched him with a half smile. Like she knew him. Like she was proud of him. And that was just weird.

When he got inside the Black Bean,

Jennifer Brisquet was working behind the counter, and as he flirted with the barista, he forgot the tall woman. For any guy of fifteen, an old woman of fifty lost out to an eighteen-year-old with perky tits every time.

But when he came out of the coffee shop, walking backward and smiling at Jennifer, the older woman spoke. "Noah."

That was all. Just his name, but at the sound of her voice, the hair rose on the back of his neck. He didn't know how to define that eerie feeling, but it felt like he should never turn his back on that female. He spun to face her. "Do I know you?"

"No, but I know you. I've watched you for years."

Watched him for years? What was she, a generation-jumping sexual predator? A white slaver?

Warily, he looked around.

It was broad daylight. The Black Bean was located on Bella Terra's busy Main Street. Tourists and people he'd known since he was a kid were walking past. A couple of them waved. He glanced back into the door of the Black Bean. Jennifer wiggled her fingers and smiled.

So if the tall woman was a white slaver, she'd picked a lousy time for her kidnapping attempt.

Besides . . . what kind of weirdo would watch him for years?

He should have relaxed, but still that prickly sensation made him think something horrible was about to happen. "I've never seen you before."

"I observed from a distance." She leaned forward, put her elbow on the table, cupped her chin in her hand, and stared insistently into his eyes. "Don't you know who I am, Noah?"

That voice . . . her voice did seem familiar, although he didn't know why. It was like all his life he'd been hearing it in his head. And her eyes . . . such a strange color. Green with flecks of—

Oh, God.

He saw those eyes every morning in the mirror.

His mother. This was his mother.

She was older than he thought she would be. Not as beautiful as his father's other women. But she had strength and presence, and everyone knew—*everyone* knew—how easily his dad was seduced. . . .

Who else could she be but his mother?

And if she was, he wanted nothing to do with her.

Without a word, he turned and walked away.

And at every step, he felt the gaze from those unique green eyes burning a hole into his spine.

Noah said nothing to Nonno and Nonna about the encounter. Nonna was anxious enough; Nonno had been diagnosed with Alzheimer's and was slowly, inexorably slipping away. She didn't need anything else to worry about.

Noah briefly considered telling his brothers, but . . . his brothers had always known who their mothers were: two different beautiful, exotic women who were lousy parents. But at least their mothers had cared enough to hang around more than five minutes after the umbilical cord was cut. Noah's mother couldn't wait to get away from him. It was humiliating.

So he didn't tell his family. He didn't want them to know.

He didn't even want it to be true. All this time, his mother had ignored his existence, and now, when he was an adult, or damned near, she thought she could stroll in and create a relationship?

Not even.

Probably she wasn't really his mother. She didn't look like him at all.

Well, except for her eyes.

No one in the family had ever had eyes the color of Noah's, a peculiar clear green with yellow flecks that his brothers said looked like mashed peas with butternut squash, and Jennifer said looked like a clear, still, shaded mountain lake. These eyes had come from somewhere, and since asking his father for information made Gavino snap like a junkyard dog, everyone tacitly agreed they probably came from his mother, whoever she was.

Noah put the incident at the Black Bean out of his mind. After all, he'd made himself clear, hadn't he?

He should have known the woman wasn't going to drop her pursuit; she had that kind of aggressive look to her. But he never thought to hear her voice four days later, when he was at home, flat on his back under his grandmother's Mustang, in the parking area, changing the oil.

He never heard that woman's arrival. Just, "Hello, son."

He jumped so hard he smacked his head on the exhaust pipe. He flopped back, saw stars, cursed, and slithered out so fast his T-shirt crawled up his spine and gravel scraped his skin.

She stood over him, smiling, as he scrambled to his feet, rubbing his bruised forehead.

"What are you doing here?" he demanded harshly. He was furious, but he kept his voice down and glanced toward the house in a series of desperate, guilty checks.

She was calm. She was cool. The way she acted, she didn't care whether she met the whole family. "You wouldn't talk to me in public, so I came here to see you. You know who I am, don't you?"

"Since you called me 'son,' I guess I do." She was exactly his height, which he hated. Her shoulders were broad—not as broad as his, thank God—her arms were long; her hands were big. Yet she had a woman's figure, which she displayed in expensive boot-cut jeans, a crisp white shirt belted at the waist, and a hot-shit pair of Italian loafers.

He didn't know what she did for a living, but apparently she had managed to accumulate some bucks.

Yeah, he could see his father getting into the challenge of making her fall for him. What he couldn't see was her putting up with Gavino without a damned good reason. "What do you want?" He yanked the rag off his belt and wiped his greasy hands.

"To get to know you. I've watched you from a distance for a long time and—"

"You've watched me from a distance?

Wow, there's an unwanted benefit to having you for a mother. I've got a stalker."

In a patient, aggrieved voice, she said, "It isn't possible for us to be together. With my job, I couldn't have a child at my side. It would make me vulnerable to outside influences and—"

"Let me make myself clear. I don't want to know you. Why would I? You abandoned me. And I don't care what excuses you have about why you abandoned me. You've never cared for me. What kind of mother abandons her newborn son?" The words came rolling out as if he'd rehearsed them his whole life, yet if anyone had ever asked, he would have sworn he never thought about his mother, never cared one way or another whether she was alive or dead.

Apparently he did.

"It's not like that. There are forces larger than us both, and I had to be careful not to let anyone know that I could care for someone as much as I care for you." She clasped her fist to her chest.

"What, you're like a spy?"

"Something like that."

She must really consider him an idiot. "Oh, for shit's sake, Mother, give me a break."

"Why else would I be here now? You're old enough—barely old enough—to take care of yourself. Son, come and talk to me. You're my closest living relative and I . . . If you don't like me, you can tell me to go away. But give me a chance to explain who I am and what I do and . . ." She started toward the house. "I was trying to keep them out of this, but I could introduce myself to your grandparents if that makes it better."

"No!" He leaped toward her and grabbed her arm.

"I won't hurt them," she said, and she sounded hurt, as if he'd accused her of dreadful crimes.

"I know. There are troubles in the family now, and I don't want to add to them." He took a breath. Another. Thinking frantically, trying to figure out why she was here now. His adolescent brain could figure out no reason she would have arrived now at all, and so reluctantly he said, "Okay. We can talk. Tomorrow at the Black Bean. After school. Figure three thirty. But don't expect anything. I'm not stupid, you know."

The sad thing was . . . it turned out Noah was stupid. And innocent. And credulous.

Innocence was no excuse.

He never allowed himself to forget that.

So everything that happened after that . . . he knew it was all his fault.

Chapter 19

Now, today, at the Black Bean, Liesbeth smiled as if she were genuinely happy to see Noah. "I can't surprise you at all, can I, son?"

"As soon as the cops accuse me of breaking some thug's fingers with a tire iron, I know my mother and her family are in town." He sipped his espresso. The familiar dark-roasted flavor slid down his throat, followed by the pale, cool touch of cream.

"Oh, come. You're not being fair. You've lived your whole life in your beloved Bella Terra without a single sign of trouble. What more could you want?"

"That you should have dropped dead?" The caffeine percolated in his blood, keeping his mind alert, his body trembling on the edge of action.

"Now, dear." She used the chiding tone of a falsely fond parent. "What good would that have done? Your cousins are as interested in recovering the legendary pink diamonds as I am."

With great precision, he said, "No, Mother, they're not." He spun his cup on the table. "These particular pink diamonds—the ones you love so much—hold no special place in their hearts except as something they can sell for cash. A lot of cash."

She seemed genuinely surprised and offended. “That’s not true, dear. Your cousins are Propovs. Just like you.”

“Maybe like you. Most definitely not like me.”

“Accept it or not, you’re my beloved son. Flesh of my flesh, bone of my bone.” She took the cup out of his fingers and took a sip, then pushed her cup toward him.

His gaze flicked between his coffee, now cradled in her hands, and the coffee he had originally given her, and he knew why she had switched cups. “If you really believed that I was your beloved son, you wouldn’t suspect me of poisoning your coffee.”

“That’s simply caution and good sense.”

Yeah, right. “Your family is different from mine. We don’t poison each other.”

“My family is your family. I conceived you, I pushed you from my loins, and as you drew your first breath, I held you in my arms. The same aristocratic Russian blood that flows in my veins flows in yours.”

The shadows from the trees along the street dappled the glass tabletop. The metal chair was cool against his back. Yet the heat of anger—at her, at himself—set fire to his mind. “The same aristocratic, thieving blood.”

“We Propovs have not always been thieves. We were forced into it by poverty and hunger.” From the earnest tone in her voice and from her wide, green-eyed, intense gaze, it was obvious she believed what she said.

"The Propovs could always have tried to get a *job,*" he said.

Again she gave him that uncomprehending stare.

Helpfully he explained, "A job. It's where you work for yourself, or even other people, and get paid by the hour. The government takes taxes; with what remains you buy a home and raise a family—"

She slashed the air with her hand. "A life for serfs!"

He thought of the way his family had worked the soil, here and in Italy, for generations. "Yes. But a life of honor."

"Honest labor." She almost spit the words. "It's an oxymoron. There is no honor in toil from dawn to dusk until you die with a hoe in your hand."

A reluctant grin split his face. "We modern serfs use machinery to do our labor. Eli is our vintner; he uses a harvester. Rafe is our warrior; he uses an automatic weapon. I run the resort; I use a vacuum cleaner." He cackled at the revulsion that crossed her face.

But he knew she understood what he meant. What she didn't understand was the idea of becoming a part of the country that had welcomed her family when they fled the Russian

Revolution, while at the same time being proud of her heritage. She didn't understand moving on. Almost a hundred years after the revolution, Liesbeth considered herself to be an exile from her home in Russia, a home where she had never lived, where all traces of her family had been erased, where even the regime that had overthrown them had been overthrown.

"I'm American," he said. "This is my country. Not the home of my ancestors, but this country I live in *now*."

"I'm Dutch, and a few other nationalities. None of the rest of them matter." She dismissed her current home, the place she'd been born, with a disdainful expression. "I'm Russian. I trace my ancestry directly back to Ivan the Terrible. For giving him a child, the czar gave my many-times-great-grandmother a noble husband, an estate, an exalted title—and the pink diamond necklace."

"And eighty-one years ago, when your ancestor tried to hock the necklace, Massimo stole the diamonds, and your family has been searching for them ever since. Yeah. I got it."

Her eyes glowed green, the color of money. "The pink diamonds are my heritage, and yours."

Noah laughed, a twisted, bitter sound. "A heritage in which I will have no share."

"You could—if you came with us. Stayed with us." Every word was an enticement.

"What would I get from that? A chance to wear the pink diamond necklace to the Propov Sunday-night dance? I mean really, Mother."

"You're my son. I could train you to take my place—"

Noah threw back his head and laughed out loud. "How many of my cousins would I have to kill before they accepted me?"

"Some loss of life is inevitable in a change of leadership."

Her words were so simply, flatly stated, he knew she had killed to take the lead. Killed one of the relatives she claimed to support. He answered just as simply. "No. I have no desire to constantly live a life on the razor's edge of catastrophe. I'm happier running my vacuum cleaner."

Contempt twisted her mouth. What an incredible disappointment he must be to her . . . her son whom she had so easily conned into doing her bidding.

"What are you going to do with the diamonds when you retrieve them?" he asked.

Her face grew taut with hunger, and she gazed over his shoulder into the clear air. "I'm going to have them reset in rose gold in a re-creation of the original setting. I'll keep it in my house under the tightest security. Those diamonds will represent the pride of the Propov family restored."

Noah snorted. “You’re kidding yourself. Hendrik will sell the diamonds as soon as you’re dead. And you’ll be dead as soon as you recover the diamonds.”

She leaned back in her chair and watched him with a lethal gaze. “You don’t understand the ties of blood.”

He thought of Nonna, of his brothers, even of his father. He remembered the threats she had made against their lives. Looking into her eyes, he said, “You’re using the Di Luca family to blackmail me. Can you really claim I don’t understand the ties of blood?”

Her gaze fell beneath his, and he counted that a victory.

Then she looked up again, those green eyes cool and measuring. “So you remember what I told you. That if you ever tell your family about us, who we are and what we do, we will have to kill them.” She kept her voice low and lethal.

“I’m not likely to forget.” Nor was he likely to discount her claim.

He had seen her kill before.

“Good.” She brightened. “I have a gift for you.”

“Do you?” A chill ran up his spine; he had experience with her gifts.

Leaning over, she dug through her capacious Italian leather purse and brought forth something that looked like an expensive leather dog collar. Two strips of black leather had been stitched together. A silver clasp would join the two ends. At every inch, a silver stud protruded, and at the end of each stud, a rhinestone sparkled.

Noah was aghast. "This looks like something the Goth youth in Germany wear."

"That's right," she said encouragingly. "It's a necklace."

"You're giving me a necklace." It was a statement, not a question. "A hideous necklace."

Liesbeth appeared honestly surprised. "I thought it was quite handsome, and as you said, many European men wear such jewelry."

"Too bad I don't live in Europe," he said flatly.

She cocked her head as if trying to ascertain whether he was joking. "Hm. Well. Anyway, Brigetta made it for you with Grieta's help. There's a camera hidden in this stud." She pointed to the stud that would sit at the front. "The lens is one of the jewels."

"So I wear it around my neck and you see what I see. You see where I search for the bottle."

"Exactly."

He didn't really want to know, but the question had to be asked, and as he did, fear tasted like dry sweat socks in his mouth. "Brigetta is your munitions specialist. Why do you need her to help make a necklace with a camera?"

"Ah!" Liesbeth leaned back and waved an apologetic hand. "I told the children you would realize the trap. You're very astute."

"I am now. You trained me, after all."

"You were very good. If you had stayed with us—"

"That wasn't an option. You wanted me here."

"If you had proposed such a course, I would have agreed with vigor."

He leaned toward her and lowered his voice to a furious whisper. "Why would I propose to stay with the people who hated me so much, they spent three months setting a snare that would ruin my life?"

She leaned toward him, and she, too, kept her voice quiet. But she sounded totally reasonable. "We do not hate you. How can you think that? Every plan can be altered when another, more profitable plan is presented."

"So what is the plan for *this,* Mother?" He gestured toward the dog collar sitting flat on the table.

She sat back, clearly disappointed, wanting to resurrect the old memories. But she was a patient woman; after all, she'd been waiting since the day he was born to retrieve her diamonds. "Hendrik is getting impatient with the time we've invested keeping track of you as you search for the bottle, and all with no payback, no reward in sight."

"Poor Hendrik."

"So to appease him, we made a plan to hurry this along. In addition to the camera, this little stud"—she tapped it—"contains a timer. It's set for two weeks from the time the clasp is locked. The collar, by the way, is impossible to remove without the key."

"I suspected that."

"The timer is connected to an explosive powerful enough to blow your throat open." She beamed as if expecting praise.

"I see. Very clever." He closely examined the studs that held the camera and the explosive. "So if I don't find the bottle before fourteen days are up, I lose my life in a bloody and disgusting manner."

"It will be a discreet explosion. At such a sensitive part of the body, it doesn't take much to cause death. But I don't think we need to dwell on that. This will add incentive to your search, and I'm sure that will result in success. Now, if you'll put on the—"

"Give me your tapestry needle."

"What?"

"You still do tapestry work, don't you? Give me your needle."

She stared at him; this was obviously not the reaction she had anticipated. With a shrug, she dug through her purse, pulled out a task bag, and found a three-inch-long stainless-steel needle and handed it over.

He examined it carefully. "In the past, your tapestry needles were always blunt to go through the canvas that you worked." He lightly touched the gleaming point. "This is quite sharp."

She shrugged. "I am older now, increasingly likely to be viewed as a victim, and so I'm more wary than I used to be."

"You hold your weapons in secret. Very clever, although I pity the man who imagines he can take you down." With a flick of his wrist, he popped the jewel out of one of the studs.

She caught his hand. "What did you do that for?"

"I disabled the camera." He examined each stud, found one without a rhinestone, rammed the needle into the small hole.

Liesbeth placed her hand on her own throat and looked into his eyes. "That bomb is real, you know. If you had calculated incorrectly and shoved that needle into the wrong place, you could have blown off your hand."

"Then Grieta would have had to build me another one for my neck, hm?"

He broke off the needle and handed it back to her. "That takes care of the microphone." Picking up the dog collar, he showed it to his mother, front and back, like a stage magician displaying his wares before his next trick. Putting it around his throat, Noah clicked the lock.

Even here, with voices buzzing around them, with the sound of the traffic on the street, the snap was loud, solid, final.

He looked at his watch. "Thursday, three thirty-seven p.m."

She looked at her watch, too, then back up at him. "You don't seem to comprehend. By putting the necklace on and clicking the lock, you started the timer."

"I never doubted it for a minute. If I haven't found the bottle in two weeks, you can kill me, Mother dear, but in the meantime, damned if I'm going to be a walking video camera for you." Leaning forward, Noah caught Liesbeth's wrist. "Did you really think I was going to allow my goon cousins to force me to don this?" He indicated the bench across the street where Hendrik, Klaas, and Rutger loitered, waiting for the signal to carry him off and force him into the collar like a rabid dog.

"I . . . thought . . . Yes, I suppose I thought your cousins would have to coerce you."

"Every day, I am searching the cellars below the resort, looking through every cubbyhole, behind every rafter, in every secret room." His blood churned in fury. "You imagine I don't care, that even if I look, it is to find the bottle for *me*. You are so stupid."

She tossed her head and tried to free herself.

He tightened his grip. "All I want is for you to take the bottle and go. I want my home back, some peace of mind returned to me and my family."

She curled her hand into a fist. "You don't have to search by yourself. Let your cousins help."

"I'm not letting them anywhere near my resort guests."

"Your cousins would behave if I told them to."

"You're overestimating your influence. They're beasts unfit for civilization. They break people's fingers as if they were crushing potato chips." He thrust his face into hers. "No, Mother, and if I find them poking around my resort, I'll kill them, bury them in the tunnels, and no one will never find them. No one."

"But do you understand what will happen if you don't find the bottle . . . ?"

"What? I'll die? Since the day I realized that my mother"—he shook her wrist hard—"*my mother* traced her family's diamonds to Bella Terra and the Di Luca family, and cold-bloodedly conceived me with the intention of someday using me to retrieve those diamonds . . . I have been resigned to dying a violent death. Be proud. That's the heritage you have given me." He let her go and stood. "But never fear. I will work to find that bottle of wine. I will not die and leave Bella Terra with a future filled with ferocity and murder."

Chapter 20

At five o'clock on Thursday afternoon, on her first full day in Bella Terra, Penelope got out of her car in the parking lot of the Sweet Dreams Hotel to find the sun had baked heat into the asphalt. It burned through the bottom of her sneakers and made her wonder why she'd come to Bella Terra in the first place. She could be in Portland, where it was cool and rainy . . . and where there was no one for her, only a simple gravestone in a shady cemetery, and an old lady whose mind was slowly slipping into the next world. Or she could be in Cincinnati, where . . . where Keith's parents hated her for marrying Keith, and Keith had died.

She needed to find a place where no memories haunted her, where she could see a future unmarred by sadness and death.

She stood there, squeezing the car door handle, letting the sun incinerate the day's jumble of emotions into a pile of ash.

But like a phoenix, Noah Di Luca rose from the ashes.

How was it possible that she had met him before she'd even been in Bella Terra for twenty-four hours? How was it possible that she allowed him to hold her hand? Smile at her? Act as if his brutal rejection of her and her earnest young love had never happened?

He was an ass.

Worse, she was an *idiot*.

She didn't want to see him. She thought she'd made herself clear without rancor; no point in having him think she still had a thing for him . . . an awareness . . . a craving for his touch.

Nope. None of that.

But every woman would have recognized the danger of hanging around Bella Terra, with its memories and its obligations. And any woman worth her salt would have run like a rabbit.

Instead, Penelope had committed herself to visiting Mrs. Di Luca.

Not like she didn't want to see the old lady, but . . . With a groan, she thumped her forehead against the door. Then rubbed the place where she'd hit. That *hurt*.

Mrs. Di Luca. Her house, packed full of memories of that summer.

Why couldn't Penelope do the smart thing and leave? What stupid remnant of old-fashioned courtesy and caring made her stay to express her creaking affection for Mrs. Di Luca . . . who had made her so welcome that summer nine years ago?

Why couldn't Penelope turn her back and run away?

Cowardly? Sure. But in the end, all that

mattered was saving herself. Hadn't she learned that lesson yet?

"Hey! You! Number fourteen. Come here."

Penelope glanced up to see a woman, five feet tall and two hundred pounds, sweeping the walk in front of the office and eyeing her with stern attention.

"Oh, no," Penelope muttered.

She was looking at Arianna Marino, in a dark blue dress with a white collar and a black belt and shabby black leather ballet flats. She exuded all the authority of a bulldozer. That was to say . . . a lot of authority. She wielded the broom like a lance, and when she beckoned to Penelope, Penelope went, marching up toward the office as if on official business. She fingered her room key, though, hoping to insinuate that she needed to leave soon on some important matter.

If Arianna Marino was impressed by Penelope's air of efficiency, she hid it well. Instead, she held open the door to the motel office, commanding Penelope to enter. "Number fourteen. Penelope Alonso."

Crap. Had she recognized Penelope? Or did everyone in this town know everything?

"I'm Penelope Caldwell now." Penelope walked into the chilly office, where it smelled musty and damp.

"You're widowed," Mrs. Marino said. "Your husband was killed in a car wreck."

"True." The phone call had been wrenching, a life-changing moment of horror and grief all too soon supplanted by other horrors, greater griefs. "How do you know?"

Mrs. Marino gave the expected answer. "The Internet."

"Why do you care?"

Mrs. Marino went to the tiny, old, chipped refrigerator that hummed in the corner behind the counter. "I liked your mother."

That was an answer of a sort. "So did I."

"Glad to hear it. I had hoped to see her again one day." Mrs. Marino sighed with a gust that made a mockery of that feeble window air conditioner.

"She would have liked that." Penelope knew that was true; her mother admired Arianna Marino, said she was a power to be reckoned with.

Mrs. Marino pulled out two beers, popped the tops, and presented one to Penelope. "Sit," she said, and pointed at the black metal-and-vinyl straight-backed dining chair behind the counter.

Interestingly enough, the presentation of the beer and the directive to sit made Penelope realize how far she'd come in Mrs. Marino's estimation. When she was here with her mom, Mrs. Marino had barely noted her existence, and never had she been allowed behind the counter.

She walked around, and she sat.

"When she came here, when you were a kid," Mrs. Marino said, "your mother wasn't well."

Penelope, who didn't much care for beer, rubbed the icy bottle on her forehead. "I didn't know that then. I wish I had. I would have done things differently." But she'd been so selfish, so self-involved, she hadn't seen what was right before her face. That her mother had suffered from breast cancer. That she was still recovering from chemo and radiation.

"She didn't want you to know." Mrs. Marino patted Penelope's shoulder with a heavy hand. "She wanted you to be young and carefree."

With a bitter smile, Penelope remembered Noah. "Oh, I was that."

"She was a worker, your mother was, cleaning rooms for me, tending bar when she had to." Mrs. Marino seated herself in the chair at the check-in desk. It creaked beneath her weight, but didn't dare collapse. "The customers liked her. She was smart, didn't put up with any shit, yet she was friendly and she listened when they talked. A lot of them were illegals, from Mexico and beyond, here without their families, and they liked showing her pictures of their kids. Not that they didn't like it when we had a bimbo in the bar. But they liked your mother for different reasons."

"She was a great mother." Except for that one big matter that had made Penelope stand before her mother's gravestone and sob out accusations.

That had not been one of her stellar moments.

She tipped up the bottle and took a long, cold drink. "What a hell of a day," she muttered.

"That's what happens when you come back poking your nose in stuff that's none of your business."

Penelope lowered the bottle with a bang onto the counter. "What do you mean? What do you know?"

"I know you met Brooke Di Luca in the Rhodes Café today and went off with her to her new house." Mrs. Marino's chair swung back and forth, back and forth, creaking and begging for lubricant. "Gossip says you're her new interior decorator."

"Interior designer," Penelope corrected automatically. "Did you have someone spying on me?"

"That's not necessary. I have connections." The twist of Mrs. Marino's mouth looked like wisdom. "People tell me things."

Penelope believed her. The iron gray that mixed with her dark hair seemed indicative of her character, and those black eyes ruthlessly surveyed her world.

"But your connections aren't right this time." Penelope felt almost gleeful at correcting her. "I'm not staying."

"Not staying?" Looking thoughtful, Mrs.

Marino sipped her beer and examined Penelope like a bug under a microscope. "You're not taking the job for the Di Lucas?"

"No."

"They're good people. A little snooty, but good people. We're related, of course."

That figured. "Of course."

"Sarah Di Luca was born a Marino."

"Really?" Penelope had never suspected that. "I am going to see her before I leave."

"So why aren't you staying?"

"A person could get killed in this town."

Mrs. Marino nodded, lips pursed. "Especially when a person—like you—has connections with Joseph Bianchin."

The woman took Penelope's breath away. "What do you know about me and Joseph Bianchin?"

"I know you went to his house this morning."

"How do you know that?" Penelope could not believe this depth of knowledge. "How do you know these things?"

"Look." Mrs. Marino sounded practical and brisk. "We Marinos have lived here for a long time. We work all over the county. Did you see a gardener at Bianchin's? That was my husband, Daichi."

"The Asian guy? That skinny little . . . ?" Penelope abruptly shut her mouth. She could not say with any amount of political correctness that broad Italian Arianna Marino and the tall, thin, Asian gardener were an odd match.

But they were.

Mrs. Marino seemed to understand and, for all intents and purposes, she didn't give a damn about political correctness. "Daichi is my second husband. The first one was a good Italian Catholic boy. He got me pregnant when I was sixteen, married me, and made sure I knew he was doing me a favor, beat me when he was sober. Luckily for me, that wasn't often. I beat *him* when he slapped our daughter and knocked her into the wall. Three kids and he was out the door. Died in an accidental gas explosion in his home while he was sleeping. Good riddance." She smiled, a square smile that scared the hell out of Penelope and made her wonder whether that gas explosion was really an accident. "After that, Daichi worked hard to convince me to live with him. After about twenty years I finally gave in and married him. Glad I did. Contrary to most of the evidence, not all men are bums."

"I know. Keith was such a good guy. We would have been married . . . forever." Penelope's voice sounded wistful, even to her.

"Anyway, Daichi is how I knew you visited Bianchin's estate and didn't get in."

"I couldn't get in. Joseph Bianchin is not home."

"He is," Mrs. Marino said flatly.

Penelope took a long breath. She didn't doubt her. Only a fool would doubt Arianna Marino. So that flash of light at the house . . . Penelope hadn't been imagining it. Someone had been watching her. "Then why didn't he let me through the gate?"

"I don't know. A few days ago, Daichi saw him drive up in a limo with a bunch of guests. Possibly Bianchin was busy entertaining them. Probably he didn't think you looked important enough to bother with. That's the kind of man he is." Mrs. Marino scratched her chin. "You want to see him?"

"I do."

"My cleaning crew goes in every week and cleans that old pile of rock Bianchin loves so much, dusts and washes the toilets and the floors. You could go in with them. I'm not going to say he'll welcome you. I'll almost guarantee he won't be pleasant." Mrs. Marino stood, threw her beer bottle into the trash can hard enough to make the white plastic smack against the wall. Turning, she looked Penelope in the eyes. "But at least you'll get your chance to tell him he's your father."

Chapter 21

Penelope froze. Her heart stopped.

This wasn't possible. Someone knew the truth? "What do you mean, m-my father? What do you know about my father?"

Mrs. Marino smiled that scary square smile again. "I know what your mother told me."

"My mother told you stuff?" She thought the whole truth had died with her mother, but here was someone alive today who knew the story about her birth? "My God. I know nothing about what happened. I don't know why my mother wouldn't tell me who he was. And you . . . know. . . ." Penelope couldn't quite say it. "Did Mom tell you how it happened and . . . why she never told me the truth?"

"She worked for me. Remember? We had a lot in common. Crappy life choices. Sacrificed for our children. Had to make our own ways." Mrs. Marino stood tall. "We *talked*."

Penelope could hardly breathe. She didn't know how to proceed.

That Joseph Bianchin was her father . . . that was her deepest, darkest secret. For good or evil, this was the truth her mother had hidden from her all these years. She had barely discovered her father's identity, and now . . . now this woman she hardly knew, this woman whom she suspected of every kind of ruthlessness, could perhaps fill in the details.

How to proceed? How to convince Mrs. Marino to break her mother's confidence?

Putting her beer down, Penelope leaned forward, elbows on her knees, and looked up at Mrs. Marino. "Mom never told me. She refused. Right up until the end, she refused. But the lady she worked for all those years—she knew. Since Mom's gone, the old lady is slipping into dementia. Mrs. Walters thought I was my mother, and she told me I needed to tell my daughter—tell Penelope—the truth. Apparently she'd told my mother that more than once, and Mom never would. Once I realized Mrs. Walters knew my father's identity, I questioned her. It wasn't fair, probably, to ask a lady so lost in senility to betray a confidence, but I had to know, and it was my last chance. Could you . . . Do you know what happened? How my mother came to be involved with him? Why she wouldn't tell me even his name?"

"It's the usual story. She was young. She loved him. He seduced her. She got pregnant and then . . ." Mrs. Marino audibly ground her teeth. "Then she discovered what a pig he was."

"But she was only eighteen. Why would she get involved with a man in his fifties? I mean—ick."

"Honey, you lived with your mother's father."

Mrs. Marino pulled another bottle of beer out of the refrigerator and popped the top. "He was an abusive, nasty jerk. Your mother wanted out, she was beautiful, she worked as a singer in L.A., and Joseph targeted her. He was charming, rich, and flattering. She saw what she wanted to see, believed what he wanted her to believe."

"What did he want her to believe?"

"That he would rescue her from the squalor and desperation of her life." Mrs. Marino seated herself in that squeaky desk chair again. "That he'd marry her and keep her in luxury forever."

"God. How heartbreaking." Penelope's eyes filled with tears for the innocent that her mother had been.

"He kept her in his hotel suite while he did business in L.A., and when his business was concluded, he left. But before he walked out, he told her she could keep the clothes he had bought her."

"Nice," Penelope said sarcastically.

"He said that if she was pregnant, she should come to Bella Terra and give him the child, and *if* he *was* the father, he'd make sure the boy was raised with all the privileges he could offer."

"Wow. What an asshole."

"Your mother had her reasons for not wanting you to have anything to do with him." Mrs. Marino rocked and drank. "But give her credit—the reason she got you an internship with Fiasco

Designs and brought you here to Bella Terra was so she could check him out, see if he'd changed, and if he had, introduce you so that in case her cancer proved fatal you wouldn't be alone."

Penelope's smile twisted with pain. "He failed the test? He wasn't nice to her?"

"Nice to her?" Mrs. Marino brayed with laughter. "He never noticed her."

"What? He didn't recognize her?"

"She went in with the cleaning crew. She saw him. He saw her. But he never *looked* at her. Joseph Bianchin does not look at the people who work for him. They are below him, and therefore of no interest."

Penelope could not imagine what it must have been like for her mother to see the man she had once loved and have him ignore her. "He never recognized her? He slept with her and he *never* recognized her?"

"No."

"They never *spoke?*"

"On the contrary. She spoke to him every week. He would be in his office. She would ask him if he would like it cleaned. He would get up and leave." Mrs. Marino smiled. "She knew then she would not tell him about you, or you about him. She said you were better off alone in the world than being forced to face that sour old face every day lamenting the fact you weren't a boy, raised by him to be like him."

"There's probably justice in that, and I do understand why she wanted to protect me. In those days, I was a fragile flower. I've got some calluses now, and I know how to handle the jerks of this world." Penelope drank another swallow from her bottle, and the beer was not as bitter as the taste in her mouth. "You should have met my mother-in-law."

Mrs. Marino looked grim. "One of *those,* hm?"

"When Keith was killed, you would have thought she was the widow." Penelope paused for a long breath, remembering. "So I can handle Bianchin. He didn't get a son, and according to the research I did, I'm his only offspring."

"Unless some other intelligent woman did the same as your mother and refused to tell him about her baby."

Penelope nodded jerkily. Yes. She might have a sibling or two somewhere.

So what? She had a father to meet first.

"But I think it's doubtful." Mrs. Marino cackled. "If there's one thing about Joseph Bianchin that the whole town has relished, it's the fact that he never could father a child. He tried hard enough, too. In his youth, lots of innocent girls fell to him." Her tone changed from reminiscent to sharp. "You really want to meet him?"

"I've got nobody else. I would like to at least speak to him. I could do as you suggested, as my mother did, and go in with your cleaning crew and meet"—what should Penelope call him?—"meet Joseph."

"It's the best plan."

"When?" The sooner the better.

Mrs. Marino went over to a grubby desk calendar and flipped through the pages. "We clean his house on Monday."

"Monday?" This was Thursday. In that amount of time, Penelope could run into Noah countless times. "But I was going to leave."

"You pays your money, you takes your chances." Mrs. Marino shook her finger at Penelope. "You already got the motel room for seven days, and I don't give refunds." At Penelope's openmouthed surprise, Mrs. Marino said, "Honey, I'm running a business here! I'm bringing you in, doing you a favor. You talk to Bianchin and he could get mad and fire me, and that's a big account. I'd say I'm doing plenty for the cause."

"Yes, but I . . . If I have to stay for a while, I mean, if in the end it's going to take more than seven days . . . I don't have much of a budget. I wasn't exactly flush when I came to Portland, and my mom's illness pretty much drained the bank account."

Mrs. Marino shrugged her massive shoulders. "I can get you an actual job on the housekeeping team."

That summer nine years ago, Penelope had occasionally helped her mother clean motel rooms. The memory made her shudder.

"Or you could get something on your own," Mrs. Marino said.

Penelope didn't really need to get anything on her own. Just this morning, she had found a job.

And this afternoon she had quit.

She glanced up at Arianna Marino.

Mrs. Marino wore a slight smile, like she wanted Penelope to be stuck here in Bella Terra.

But why? That didn't make sense. Why would she care what Penelope did?

Maybe she wanted to make trouble for Joseph?

Of course. That was it.

Everyone in this town hated Joseph Bianchin. Mrs. Marino wanted him to be uncomfortable, unhappy, uncongenial, upset—and what better way to accomplish her dream than to present him with a daughter when he wanted a son, a daughter who was guaranteed to make trouble for him, a daughter who had not been raised in the manner he would deem appropriate? Penelope would be nothing but a horrible surprise and a complete disappointment to him.

Mrs. Marino waited and watched Penelope work through the ramifications, and when Penelope looked up, Mrs. Marino smiled that square smile again. "I can give you a good monthly rate on the room."

• • •

With a sigh of mingled relief and dismay, Penelope put down the phone and turned into the dim hotel room.

Brooke had welcomed Penelope back on the job with open arms.

Once more, Penelope was temporarily employed in Bella Terra. Once more, she would be judged on her creativity and her craft.

Employment was a good thing, especially considering the state of her finances, but now that she'd committed to the job, she was stuck here until it was finished.

Going to the bed, she flung back the bedspread and flopped onto the sheets.

The motel room hadn't really changed from the first time she'd stayed here. Different thin carpet, different ugly flowered bedspread—Mrs. Marino's way of making sure no one stole it, Penelope supposed—and free Internet. But direct light never touched this motel room. The window at the front opened onto the asphalt parking lot and faced the Beaver Inn. The window at the back opened onto a gravel expanse, where a huge blue Dumpster rusted and the garbage stank. Beyond that, a fence surrounded cars and car parts that alternately baked and disintegrated.

No one in her right mind would open the stiff, off-white, plastic-lined curtains. That would expose her to drunks reeling out of the Beaver

Inn and toward their vehicles, or to the psychoses of the madmen who made their homes in the junkyard.

Today she had been so proud of herself for deciding to run away from Bella Terra. Only a fool would remain in a place where violence happened far too often. Only a fool would stay where she had to fight loneliness and sorrow so deep that it made her long for a relationship with Joseph Bianchin. Only a fool stuck where she was sure to see her former lover on a frequent basis and remember that he had once broken her heart . . . as he could, oh, so easily, do again. . . .

But she would learn from the past. Had learned from the past.

She was so much wiser now.

Chapter 22

Penelope stood in the great room of Bella Terra resort, pen in hand, her notebook tucked into the crook of her arm, writing frantically while Storm Fiasco shouted out his thoughts for the redesign of the hotel. She'd been on the job only one day, and already she could see he was a genius. An eccentric genius, but a genius, for as he spoke, he created the new space in her mind: a native stone fireplace that rose all the way to the twenty-foot-high ceiling, with a series of three gas fire inserts created to look like fairy lights. A gathering of low seats and tables around it. A long leather-and-mahogany bar in the corner to serve breakfast in the morning and drinks in the evening.

For all intents and purposes, she thought he paid her no heed. But when he announced they would take out that—he waved an airy hand at the brick wall between the great room and the courtyard—and replace it with tall windows, her eyes narrowed.

He turned on her, his long blond hair swirling around his broad shoulders. "What? You don't agree?"

"No. I . . . No, I think it's a wonderful idea." She realized her voice was squeaking like a mouse, and lowered it to a more reasonable level. "But how is that possible? Isn't that a bearing wall?"

"My dear intern," he said with exaggerated patience, "this is your first day, so I'll make an exception this once. In the world of design, there are three tiers. The top, of course, is the interior designer. We take crude space and make it glorious or comfortable or a showcase—or all three. Next are the architects. They usually have some artistic talent, although I find all too often their understanding of interior space is limited by practicalities. And then"—his Mick Jagger lips sneered—"there are the engineers. They are peasants. They have no creativity, no appreciation, no soul. They are bound by the realities of life." He paused as if he expected a response.

She nodded vigorously.

"I am Storm Fiasco of Fiasco Designs." He straightened his long leather duster. "I do not bother myself with such pedestrian matters as the laws of gravity. Let the peasants meet the challenge and figure that out. It makes them so happy when they do. Now." He waved a long-fingered hand toward the wall once more. "Small bistro tables will sit close against the windows for a view into the arboretum."

The plants were pretty out there, but she would have never called it an arboretum. Yet already she'd learned—someone else would handle those practicalities. Right now, as an intern, that someone was her. On her page, she noted, *Arboretum—call a landscape architect*.

The great room opened into the lobby, and Storm paced into that space and stared fixedly at the desk clerk until she blanched and backed away from the counter; then, with a swirl of his duster, he paced back into the great room and stood where the fireplace would rise in all its glory.

He was silent for so long Penelope sidled close to him and tried to do what he was doing—create the finished product in her mind.

A young man, tall and handsome, and a petite elderly woman stepped in the door.

Penelope barely glanced at them, all her attention on the room.

In a sudden flurry of urgency, Storm said, "All the furniture will have to go, of course."

"Not all," she said thoughtlessly.

Storm was tall, commanding, built like an Oklahoma linebacker, but his voice was soft. "I beg your pardon?"

The two people still watched, but if Storm could ignore them, so could Penelope.

"The rocking chair." Penelope walked slowly toward the simple piece of furniture that sat close to the wall. "It's handcrafted." She ran her fingers over the curved sweep of the back. "Figured maple, I think. Someone took a lot of time to build this piece. You can see the loving care in each piece of wood." She turned back to Storm. "Think of it tucked into the corner by the fireplace, next to it a small table piled with books and an old-fashioned reading lamp. It would tie the new great room to the roots of the hotel. Weary guests would relax and read. Mothers would rock their cranky children. . . ." Too late she saw Storm's narrowing eyes, and her fantasy skidded to a stop.

"That is an idea," he said, each word like an ice cube rattling into a silver bucket.

"It is." The elderly woman hurried forward. "Mr. Fiasco, my grandson Noah brought me down to meet you. I'm Sarah Di Luca, and I confess, I was worried when the boys insisted it was time to freshen the look of our public areas. But to know that you're going to open the room to the grandeur of our gorgeous California outdoors and at the same time provide an anchor to our wonderful family history . . ." She offered him her hand.

For Mrs. Di Luca, it seemed he was bathed in charm. Taking her hand, he kissed her fingers. "Call me Storm," he murmured.

"Before his death, my husband did so much around the resort, and when he could no longer remember how to do the wiring or where all the plumbing ran through the walls, he could still craft pieces like this." She gestured to the rocking chair. "To know you recognized the love that went into the creation . . . You are a man of discernment as well as an artist."

The young man, Noah, turned toward Penelope.

But she was too terrified by Storm's impending rage to pay him any heed.

Still Noah grinned and winked, then went to Storm and shook his hand. “We spoke on the phone. I’m Noah Di Luca.”

“Good to meet you at last, and to know the family is so closely involved is a delight indeed,” Storm said.

Penelope swallowed. She could hear the sliver of frozen sarcasm in Storm’s voice. Couldn’t the Di Lucas hear it, too?

Mrs. Di Luca could, for she laughed and said, “I promise I don’t intend to be here every day checking on your progress. In fact, the only time you’ll see me at all is when you come up for Sunday dinner. We start about three. The meal is about seven. There’s always an incredible lot of people, but we have wonderful times. You will come, won’t you?”

Now Storm melted like a snow cone on a hot sidewalk, and all sign of his displeasure vanished. “Mrs. Di Luca, I would be delighted. And you may boss me around anytime you like.”

In slow increments, Penelope began to relax.

“You come, too, child.” Mrs. Di Luca smiled kindly at her.

“I, um, my mother is here in Bella Terra with me and—”

“Bring her, too. Company is a blessing I

enjoy." Mrs. Di Luca could not have sounded more sincere.

A few more congenial words, and Noah and Mrs. Di Luca backed out of the room.

Storm started shouting instructions again.

Penelope took notes, chastened, and resolved not to contradict Storm Fiasco ever again as long as she lived.

Then she found out it didn't matter, because two hours later, he fired her.

Chapter 23

In all her life, Penelope had never been so humiliated as when Noah found her crying in the supply closet of the unoccupied resort office. Sure, it was a stupid place to hide, but where else was she supposed to go? She didn't have a car. Her mother wasn't scheduled to pick her up for three hours. And the tears wouldn't wait any longer.

So when he opened the door and flicked on the light, Penelope did the only sensible thing to do—she scrunched further into the corner and tried to disappear into the wall.

Most guys—normal guys—would have taken one look at her splotchy face and runny nose and fled. Instead, he came and squatted down in front of her. "Hey, what's wrong?"

She didn't answer. She couldn't. She was

right in the middle of the first full-fledged paroxysm of despair and humiliation of her design life. Which was over. Her career was over before it even began.

So she put her head on her knees and continued to cry, long, wrenching sobs that tore at her throat and shook her whole body. She'd stolen a roll of toilet paper off one of the shelves, and occasionally she used it to wipe her eyes and blow her nose. Violently.

And still Noah stayed, kneeling there, patient and calm.

What a dumb-ass.

She controlled her sobbing long enough to say, "Go away."

He studied her for a moment. "Okay." He left the closet.

"Shut the door!" she wailed.

He didn't. Instead he was back in a minute with a bottle of cold water and can of cold Coke. He thrust them both under her downturned face. "Drink?"

"N . . . no. Th . . . thank you."

But he didn't withdraw them.

So she took the water. Of course, she couldn't get the cap unscrewed—because she really was the incompetent, interfering, ignorant half-wit that Storm Fiasco said she was.

So the Di Luca guy took the bottle away

from her, unscrewed the top, and handed it back.

She took a slurp and cried a little more, then took another slurp. She heard him pop the top of the can. He took the water away from her and put the Coke in her hand. "Drink it. The sugar will make you feel better."

"No, it won't. I'll never feel better as long as I live." And she started crying again.

"Did he fire you?" he asked.

"What? Yes! How did you know? Did he tell you?" Mortification twisted like a snake in her belly.

"I did the research on who we should hire to redesign the facility, so I know a lot about Storm Fiasco." Noah sat down on the floor, leaning against the wall that was at a ninety-degree angle from hers. "Storm Fiasco is famous for firing his interns. Although I think you may have set the new record for least time served."

"Oh, God." She shut her eyes and thumped her head against the wall. "I contradicted him. As soon as I did it, I knew I was in trouble, but I thought Mrs. Di Luca smoothed it over."

"Yeah, not so much. He's known for carrying a grudge and for magnificent temper tantrums."

"He threw his phone at me." She showed Noah the bruise on her shoulder.

Noah placed the lid back on the bottle of water. "Here, put this on it. It's cold. It'll help."

She did as he suggested. "What am I going to tell my mother? She moved mountains to get me this position. She took a leave from her job in Portland to bring me here. She got a job cleaning rooms at the Sweet Dreams Hotel to pay for our stay." Her voice wobbled again. "And now, after uprooting her completely . . . I'm fired."

"No, you're not."

Was he deaf? "Yes, I am!"

"Look. Storm Fiasco is known for his fits. He's also known for getting over them. He desperately needs an intern. You're talented, or your mother could have moved Mount Everest and Fiasco wouldn't have cared. He took you because you're the best." As he praised her, Noah sounded absolutely prosaic. "Let's face it: He's screwed if he doesn't have you. The only interns left for him to hire at this late date are the B-grade students."

"Oh."

"You know what I'd do?"

"What?"

"I'd wait a couple of hours, get my notebook, join him like nothing happened, and do the work."

She stopped thinking about avoiding Noah's gaze, and she looked at him. Really looked at him.

He was about her age, maybe a year or two older, built like a gladiator, with broad shoulders, a fully muscled chest, long arms, long legs, and big hands. He wore ironed khakis and a blue polo shirt with the Bella Terra logo on his left shoulder. He was Brad Pitt handsome, with a facial structure so sculpted as to be almost austere. Yet there was nothing monkish about his lips, sensual and inviting, or his eyes, alight with kindness. Those eyes . . . They were the oddest green she'd ever seen, with flecks of gold clustered around the pupil, and set into his face with an exotic slant made him look almost Asian.

And although he was part of the family that owned this resort, he seemed sensible and mature and down-to-earth.

His advice made her waver between hope and disbelief. "Do you think that would really work?"

"If it doesn't, what are you out? To the persistent go the spoils."

"That's not the saying."

"Isn't it?" He smiled.

For the first time, she saw all the Di Luca charm in full Noah-size bloom.

And for the first time, she realized she looked like hell.

Not that it mattered; he was leagues above her when it came to money and class. But here she was, alone in a supply closet with the best-looking man she'd ever met, and her eyes were swollen almost shut, she held a soggy wad of toilet paper in her hand, and she needed to blow her nose.

He misunderstood her whimper of despair. "You can do it. You were totally handling him. You'll figure him out, you'll keep the internship, and when you graduate, having Storm Fiasco on your résumé will be big-time influential."

"You're right." More important, she wouldn't have to tell her mother she'd been fired.

"Come on." He stood and offered his hand. "I've got the key to the Di Luca family private restroom. You can go in there, splash your face with cold water, drink your Coke, and when you feel better, come out and proceed as if the whole firing thing never happened."

She used her nontissue hand to take his, let him help her to her feet, and dusted off her seat. "What if he doesn't go for it? What if he throws his phone at me again?"

"Duck faster."

She laughed. She wouldn't have thought it possible, but she laughed. "You're so understanding. You must have sisters," she said.

"Nope. Two handsome, talented older brothers. Talk about tough to grow up in their shadows!" As he led her to the spa-luxurious private bathroom, he chatted about Eli and Rafe, his grandmother and his recently deceased grandfather. Then he handed her the key, patted her shoulder, and disappeared down the hall.

She went in, gasped at the sight of her reflection, soaked towels in cold water, and pressed them on her face. She got herself into halfway decent shape, so she no longer looked like an animated Disney gargoyle, gave herself a pep talk, retrieved her notebook and pen from the closet where she'd left them, and went back to the great room.

She hesitated at the entrance.

Storm Fiasco was pacing off the length of the room, and when he turned and caught sight of her, he snapped, "Where the hell have you been? Where's the tape measure? I need you to hold the other end and write down these dimensions."

"Right." She walked over to him, pulled the tape measure off his belt, and offered it to him. "What are we measuring first?"

Chapter 24

In the next week, Storm Fiasco fired Penelope twice. He also skipped his phone across her ribs with a sideways flick of his wrist, and later the same day broke his phone when he flung it at her and she followed Noah's advice and ducked.

He fired her for that, too.

She went and got him a new phone and returned to work.

She saw Noah from a distance, but they were both too busy to speak.

But mentally she hugged Mrs. Di Luca's invitation to her bosom, and waited anxiously for Sunday evening, when she would see Noah again.

When she and her mother drove up, they found the small house filled to bursting with neighbors, friends, and family. The party reached from the kitchen, where half a dozen poker players sat at the round kitchen table and argued loudly over chips valued at no more than a quarter apiece, to the living room, where sports enthusiasts shouted at the baseball game, and finally spilled out onto the porch and the front lawn, where Chinese lanterns hung from the gnarled, wide-armed live oak trees.

Storm Fiasco brought his wife, a plain, quiet, gentle woman, the mother of his four children, and he showed none of his temperament while she was around.

Mrs. Di Luca welcomed Penelope and her mother, introduced them to everyone, and made sure they were comfortable among the crowd of strangers. She made them feel special, like the only guests who truly mattered to her, and the thing was . . . she did that with everyone, and she cooked and she served the food. . . . She never stopped moving, her eyes sparkling with pleasure at the rollicking party.

Penelope wanted to be her when she grew up.

Mrs. Di Luca's meal was rich and filling, better than any restaurant food Penelope had ever had. Penelope's mother allowed her a glass of wine with the meal, and it must have gone to Penelope's head, for when Noah's brother Rafe got out an antique squeeze-box accordion and squeaked out a few songs, she sang along, even when the songs were in Italian.

At eight thirty, her mother gestured her over to her chair at the long dining room table. "Honey, I'm sorry, but we've got to go. I'm pooped."

Penelope felt her joy wilt. "But, Mom. It's not even nine o'clock."

"I'm sorry, dear." Her mother really did seem sorry. "I'm enjoying myself, too, but I can't stay up any longer."

"But you didn't work today." Penelope was whining. She knew she was, but the words grumbled out of her.

"It's been a rough week. I'm not used to cleaning motel rooms." Her mother smiled apologetically and turned to Mrs. Di Luca and began the task of thanking her for a wonderful time.

Penelope sulked, wishing she could stay, wishing her mother didn't work so much, but she always had worked too much; she liked it, Penelope guessed, and why didn't she remember they were dining at the Di Lucas' tonight and not work so hard yesterday . . . when all of a sudden, Penelope realized that her mom truly did look tired, yellowish and waxy. Without thinking, she interrupted the conversation between Mrs. Di Luca and her mother. "Mom, are you sick?"

Her mother's eyes got wide and sort of alarmed. "Just truly tired. But listen—Sarah says she can get Noah to bring you back to the motel. Would you like that?"

"Yes!" Penelope actually hopped a little, then settled down, glancing around, hoping no one had seen her. "Oh, but are you going to be okay going back by yourself?"

Her mother chuckled. "Honey, I survived the whole school year without you. I can get back to the motel on my own." She used her hands to push herself to her feet. She kissed Penelope on the cheek. She thanked Mrs. Di Luca again. Mrs. Di Luca invited her back next week, then summoned her grandson Eli to walk her to the car. Her mom waved good-bye, and Penelope stood and watched her, thinking her mother looked old. . . .

But she wasn't really, really old. She had had Penelope when she was eighteen, and she wasn't yet forty, so why did she look like she need a cane?

Noah appeared at Penelope's side. He tucked his hand into her arm and smiled down at her. "So when the party winds down, I get to take you home."

She realized maybe he felt stuck with her, and she blushed hotly.

"You don't mind if I make sure none of the other guys here swoop in?" he asked. "They've been watching you all evening."

"Why?" she asked.

"Because you're the prettiest girl here." Then he stuck close to her for the rest of the evening.

Penelope was so thrilled, she forgot all about her mom, and she expected she glowed like a lightning bug.

Nonna shut down the party at eleven, and Noah drove Penelope home in his grandmother's classic Mustang, and the best part was . . . there were no awkward silences, no moments when they groped for words. They chatted like old friends.

He told her his brother Rafe's leave was over tomorrow and he flew back to Germany to join his unit.

She confessed she had thought Storm Fiasco was gay, and she was never going to judge people by their career and flamboyance again. They laughed about the moment on the front porch when Mrs. Fiasco had shivered and Storm had rushed to get her sweater and used it as an excuse to wrap it around her and hold her in his arms.

Noah told her that after his grandfather's death, his grandmother hadn't wanted to start up the Sunday-night parties, but his great-aunts Annie and June had visited and asked to see the whole family, and every Sunday night since, Nonna had hosted anywhere from half a dozen people to half the population of Bella Terra and beyond.

Noah and Penelope pulled up to the Sweet Dreams Hotel. She directed him to number eleven. He parked and turned off the motor.

A bare lightbulb glowed above each motel room door. Behind them and across the parking lot, the Beaver Inn blared with music and raucous laughter.

She looked across the console to put her hand on Noah's arm. "That was so wonderful. Thank you again."

He turned to face her and grinned. "You've thanked me about a dozen times. What's the big deal? It was just an evening at Nonna's."

"You don't know how lucky you are to have a family like that."

His grin disappeared. "Actually, I do."

She didn't pay any attention. She charged right on. "My mother's family is the biggest bunch of patoots you've ever met. They fight all the time."

"We Di Lucas fight."

"I suppose you do." She didn't want to think about that. "But not like my mother's family. They're mean. They look for your weak spot and stab a knife into it. Nasty people. My grandfather is still mad at my mom because she got pregnant with me. When I was fourteen and got in trouble with the law, he tried to force her to put me into a juvenile detention center. Then he tried to get her to put me in foster care. Then he turned her in to child protective services and lied and said she was abusing me. He was the abusive one—he used to swing that belt of his, and even his adult sons ran away."

"Whoa." The white light from the porch bulbs and the fluorescent red light from the bar divided his face in half, giving his green eyes an eerie intensity. "Kudos to your mom for getting you away."

"I know." She looked at the motel room where, through the crack in the curtains, she could see that a single light burned. "She's amazing."

"So you don't have contact with your father?"

"I don't even know who he is. She won't tell me. She says he's a creep." Suddenly she realized she was doing all the talking, and felt sick with embarrassment. "I, um . . . What about your parents?"

"My father is Gavino Di Luca."

It took her about three beats to assimilate that and blurt, "Oh, my God. No wonder you're so handsome!"

Throwing back his head, he burst into laughter.

She sank down in the seat as low as she could go. Crossing her arms over her belly, she said, "I didn't mean it like that."

"No! Please! I told you, growing up in the shadow of my brothers has left me with no ego at all. Let me treasure your compliment."

"No ego at all," she scoffed. "You're oozing with ego."

He slid his arm around her shoulders. “Do you think I’m handsomer than my brothers?”

“Of course you are,” she said sullenly.

“There’s no ‘of course’ about it.” He still sounded delighted. “Everyone thinks Rafe is the handsome one. He was a child movie star, too. And Eli’s the tall one with the gift for wines. I’m usually the shorter, younger, okay-looking one with the weird-colored eyes.”

“Your eyes are very . . . unusual. Not just the color, but the shape, almost Asian. Do they run in the family?”

His arm stiffened, he took a breath, and finally he answered, “No one knows where I got them. From my mother, I guess.”

“You guess? You don’t know your mother?”

Another hesitation. “My father has no more told me who my mother is than your mother has told you . . . you know.”

Penelope faced him straight on, more excited than she had any right to be. “Really? You don’t know who your mother is? I’ve never met another person who didn’t know even the name of their parent.”

“We’ve got a lot in common, don’t we?”

She thought about his loving family, his position in the community, his looks, his confidence, his wealth. . . .

“Not really.”

“I think we do. We’re both smart,

ambitious, determined to make something more of ourselves than we were born to be." He was watching her lips.

"Yeah." He made her feel good about herself. He made her feel normal.

He slid his hands over her shoulders, up to cup her face, to slide his fingers into her hair. Leaning in close, he inhaled as if absorbing her scent. His lips parted, and he whispered, "I shouldn't."

Made bold by his hesitation, she asked, "Why not? It's just a kiss."

"No. Not with you. With you, it will never be just a kiss." He started to let her go.

She pressed her hand over his, holding it to her face.

And he started trembling. Just the slightest, finest tremor in his fingers, but . . .

She was young, but she wasn't stupid.

It occurred to her he was feeding her a line. *With you, it will never be just a kiss.* It was a good line. Original. Interesting. Flattering. But still, nothing but a line served with the clear intentions of separating her from her panties.

But she didn't think he could fake the trembling. Or that he would. This kind of emotion displayed over a simple kiss seemed . . . well, sort of unmanly.

"Noah, it's just a kiss," she said again.

His fingers flexed beneath hers. He leaned forward, feathered his lips across hers, and for one moment, she tasted regret. And restraint. And then . . . all the complexities were swept away by a rush of passion: pure, raw, undiluted. She'd never been kissed like this before, as if he wanted her, needed her to hold him, to heal him.

She slid her arms around his neck, trying to get closer. The console got in the way. He hit the horn with his elbow, then banged his knee, hard, on the steering wheel.

They pulled apart, laughing, but when their eyes met, the laughter died. He pushed the seats back as far as they would go. They twisted and turned, trying to touch their bodies together and finally giving up and allowing only their lips to touch.

And for that moment, that was enough.

So much hunger. So much heat. The smooth taste of Noah infused with cool vanilla custard drizzled with warm chocolate. He caressed her cheeks, her chin, her throat. He pushed her hair back off her face, moaning as he sank his fingers into the thick, warm mass.

He hadn't wanted to kiss her, but now that he'd given in to temptation, he offered her himself, generously allowing her to take what she needed.

• • •

After that night, there wasn't a day when they weren't together.

Before the summer was half over, she had given him her virginity.

By the time it was time to go back to school, he had broken her heart, and never again did she feel young.

Chapter 25

On Sunday afternoon, Noah arrived late at Nonna's house carrying a glass bowl of bacon-spinach salad created by his chef at the Bella Terra resort restaurant, and he smiled because today was special. He had a present for Nonna, and he wanted to be here to see her receive it.

Oh, and he smiled because he was pissed. Pissed at the situation. Pissed at fate for bringing Penelope back into his life just to watch him die. Mostly pissed at himself for being such an idiot. At least if he was going to be here wearing an ugly, murderous dog collar, it would be nice if he could blame someone else. He strolled into the kitchen and waved a hand toward the big round wood table where Eli, Rafe, Brooke, Bao, Nonna, and Bryan DuPey sat in chairs culled from various ancient family dining sets, holding playing cards with piles of poker chips at their elbows.

Chloë sat off to the side, her legs propped up on a second chair, a netbook on her lap, an intent frown on her face as she typed and stared, typed and stared.

A chorus of welcomes greeted him.

"I've decided not to arrest you, Noah." DuPey flung a chip into the pot in the middle of the table. "Turns out Eli had a decent alibi and you Di Lucas are *not* the ones who broke the dumb thief's fingers."

"Told you so." Noah stuck the glass salad bowl in the refrigerator, then turned to face the crowd.

Chloë looked up. "Who *did* break the guy's fingers?"

"I've had my officers watching for a pack of three guys." DuPey shook his head. "We had a report that they were sighted near the town square, but when we checked it out, we got nada. That's the trouble with packs. If they separate, they're not a pack anymore."

Noah heaved a private sigh of relief. He did not want DuPey and his officers tangling with Liesbeth and her merry band of criminals. Someone would get hurt, and it wouldn't be the Propovs.

"Shall we deal you in, Noah?" Brooke shuffled the cards enticingly.

"Do it," he told Brooke.

She started to shuffle again, then straightened as if surprised by something, and handed the deck to Nonna. "Please, Nonna, you do it. I have to visit the little girls' room."

"Let's take a break." Eli stood and limped over to rub Chloë's shoulders with his good hand. The other hand, the one in the cast, he leaned against the high back of her chair.

She moaned softly and rolled her head.

He leaned down and kissed the bare nape of her neck. "Do you want to go lie down?" Because of her injuries, he meant. Because she still wore the light body cast that still felt cumbersome and uncomfortable.

"Probably after dinner." She patted his broken arm. "It does get uncomfortable in this thing."

"Don't overdo," he admonished. Then he straightened and asked, "Anybody need something to drink?"

"Iced tea." "Iced tea." "Wine." "Wine." "Coke." "Bottle of water." "Wine."

Eli clomped over to the door that led down to the wine cellar. He swung it wide, looked down the narrow, steep stairs—and sighed. "Noah?"

Noah chuckled at Eli's frustrated expression. His brother, usually so active in the vineyards and at the winery, hated wearing a cast on his arm and doubly hated the cast on his leg. "Tell me what you want," Noah said, "and I'll get the bottles."

Eli looked over the crew around the table. The traits that made him such an expert vintner, the knowledge and instincts that helped him develop and blend wines, made him the undisputed master of predicting their guests' preferences. An almost reverent silence descended while the family waited to see what he would pull from the cellar for their enjoyment. "Before dinner," he said, "for the white wine drinkers, I think a pinot grigio, and for the red wine drinkers, a smooth blend . . . the Dragon's Eye, I think. For dinner, I want a couple of bottles of nice, older vintage barberas."

"Got it." Noah started down the stairs.

"Be careful of those stairs!" Nonna said.

He waved a reassuring hand and descended into the large, dim cellar.

Nonna had raised her son and grandsons in this house, and never said a word, but now that they were grown, she admitted the stairs had always terrified her. Constructed when the house was built, the steps were steep and narrow, with open risers and a rickety banister, and the stairs ended at the bottom on an unforgiving concrete floor that could have broken little skulls if anyone took a fall.

The irony, of course, was that now that Nonna was older, the stairs terrified her grandsons, because she lived alone. She kept her vegetables down here, as well as her wines. If she fell going down for carrots or potatoes, she could lie at the bottom of the stairs for a day before someone came to find her.

Thank God for Bao—she relieved the worst of their current worries, but before she went on to another assignment, Noah and his brothers had to tear these stairs apart and construct them with deeper treads and a sturdy railing, and they'd build a closet underneath with shelves inside, to be used as a pantry. They'd been talking about it for years, urging first Nonno and then Nonna to let them handle the matter.

Nonno, a crotchety old fart to the very end, had scorned their concern.

Nonna had agreed it needed to be done, but she had insisted on getting a new oven first, and her Wolf stovetop, and well . . . Noah's mouth quirked. He and his brothers were givers. If Nonna wanted new appliances so she could cook for them, they made sure she got them.

Noah stepped on the last step; the board gave a tiny, mouselike squeak; then, as he stepped onto the concrete floor, the whole stair groaned as if relieved to be rid of his weight.

No more delaying. One experience of seeing Nonna injured in a hospital bed was enough for Noah. He'd better have a serious talk with his brothers about rebuilding the stairs ASAP, set up a date to get down here and . . . and what?

Noah stood at the bottom and looked up.

Three days had passed since he'd clicked the lock on the dog collar. Bloody death awaited him if he failed to find Massimo's bottle of wine. On the last day, if he hadn't located the bottle, he'd call one of his contractor connections and set up the schedule to have the stair rebuilt. That way at least he'd go to his grave knowing his grandmother would not soon join him.

Windows high on the wall, up at ground level, provided a little bit of natural light, but far corners and the area beneath the steps were rich with shadows.

Noah flipped on the fluorescent fixture.

A wine rack covered the long wall; built at the same time as the house, it was sturdy, but rustic and unfinished, a suitable frame for the bottles, old and new, that filled the slots. Noah searched for the wine Eli required, and stacked it on the bottom step.

Then he did what he and his brothers always did when they visited the cellar.

He looked around, trying to see where his grandfather could have hidden a green glass bottle of wine.

Motes of dust floated in the still air. Sturdy oak beams supported the floor above; Noah craned his neck up and paced the cellar, twenty feet one way, thirty feet the other, looking for a long, slender package cleverly placed against the ceiling that could conceal the old-fashioned bottle.

Nothing. Of course not.

The stairway was quickly eliminated; the

construction was so basic, just two long, thick boards on each side ascending from the floor of the basement to the floor of the main level, cut with jagged teeth that supported the narrow steps.

Nonno had told Noah once that wine wanted to stay close to the earth, to remember the rich soil that grew the grapes that made the wine.

Noah didn't know whether it was true or not, but he liked the sentiment, and his grandfather believed it, for he had always kept his precious bottle of wine down here, tucked into a cubbyhole near the floor in the concrete wall. But when he died and Nonna went to get the bottle, it was gone. All that was left was an ambiguous note written in an old man's shaky handwriting.

So when Noah and his brothers heard the story of the missing wine, they had searched. They had pulled every bottle out of its slot and read the label. They had moved the wine rack—no small accomplishment—and had tapped every inch of the walls. They had examined the floor to see whether their grandfather had somehow sawed through the concrete and placed the bottle in a secret little grave.

Their search had been fruitless, but now Noah wandered the walls again, his fingertips sweeping the rough cement as if the earth that created the grapes would call out to him and give him the answer.

He smelled the scents of wine maturing in its bottles. He felt the chill of the dirt pressing against the walls. He heard plenty of creaking and moaning from the kitchen above. But the earth remained stubbornly silent, and the bottle elusive.

From above, Eli called, “Anything interesting down there?”

Noah walked to the stairway and looked ruefully up at his brother. “No. Damn it.”

“Bring the wine up. Take a day off from your search. You’re going to end up like a mole, blinking at the sunshine.”

“Sure.” Noah took one last look around, collected his bottles, and ascended the stairs.

Chapter 26

While Eli poured wine, Noah shed his jacket. He nodded toward the table where DuPey and Brooke had accumulated twice as many chips as anyone else. “Looks like it’s business as usual.”

“They are lucky,” Rafe said.

“No, they’re not.” Bao looked at him incredulously. “They count cards. We should change decks every hand.”

At once, everyone at the table started bickering.

Typical Sunday. Noah soaked in the familiar

banter and long-standing affection and was glad he had come.

He rolled up his sleeves. In the normal run of matters, he would now strip away his tie and unbutton his shirt. But not today. Today, he loosened his tie and hoped everyone was too focused on the game to pay any attention to his attire.

From the way they snapped at one another and laughed and chatted, he thought he was pretty safe.

He joined Eli at the kitchen counter, and after gathering and distributing drinks, he poured himself iced tea and added two teaspoons of sugar.

Normally, he went a little lighter on the sweetener, but hey, when a man knew the day of his death, he could live it up with a few more calories.

Pulling up a chair, he wedged it between DuPey and Bao and seated himself.

From here he could hear Nonna's gift arrive. He intended to be the first one to the door when it was delivered.

Brooke walked in and slid into her chair. "Thanks for waiting. This baby is sitting on my bladder. I wish I could get through more than one hand without having to go."

Nonna finished shuffling.

DuPey cut the deck.

"Five-card stud, deuces are wild," Nonna announced, and shot the cards across the table with narrow-eyed precision.

Elaborately casual, Eli sorted his hand. "So, Noah—how's the search going?"

Noah looked at his cards. A full house, nines high.

Figured. Of course he'd get his best hand as his time ran out.

Could have been worse. Could have been two pairs, aces and eights—the dead man's hand.

Everyone tossed money in the pot, hummed or sneered, plucking out one or two or three cards and discarding them as Nonna dealt replacements from the deck.

They glanced at their new cards, but the primary focus was on Noah.

"I'll play these." He threw his stake into the center of the table. "Great. The search is going great." He smiled toothily. "Do you know how many miles of corridors there are under that resort?"

Rafe tapped the table. "I'll take two." When he had his cards, he tossed his chips in. "Come on. *Miles* is an exaggeration."

In the 1930s, during Prohibition, the basement had been dug below the original resort building as a root cellar, a space to run plumbing and electrical wiring, and maybe, just maybe, as a secret wine cellar hidden from the revenuers.

Recently, Rafe and Noah—and Brooke—had spent more than a few ghastly hours down there.

Had their grandfather hidden Massimo's jewel-laden bottle of wine in those cellars? Noah had believed the possibility was good. But his hopes were fading. "I have looked in every cubbyhole, every mouse hole, every rat hole, plus I've lifted the cushions and opened the drawers on every cobweb-covered, abandoned piece of furniture." He shook his head. "I used a portable ultrasound to find cavities in the walls, and have unearthed a dozen secret rooms with wine racks and pot paraphernalia and one that was built for—apparently—some long-ago Di Luca and his mistress."

Chloë's head popped up, her attention caught. "How do you figure? Is there only a bed in there?"

"That's right," Noah answered.

Everyone in the room went, "Ooh."

Chloë's eyes sparkled, and she went back to typing.

"I have had my fingers crushed by mousetraps. I have stared into the empty eyes of rodent skulls, cat skulls, snake skulls"—he shuddered at one memory—"and seen one live snake that had somehow found its way down there specifically to scare the crap out of me. I have washed cobwebs out of my hair every damned night."

"No bottle?" DuPey knew about the bottle of

wine, but he thought it was just that—a bottle of wine. He hadn't heard about the diamonds. The family had managed to keep that information to themselves.

"Lots of bottles. Beer bottles. Root beer bottles. Coke bottles. Wine bottles. Empty. Full. With spiders or without. But no bottle of wine made by Massimo Bruno." Chips flew. Players folded or stuck. Noah laid down his hand.

Amid many groans, he scraped the pot out of the center of the table and sorted the chips.

Brooke collected the cards and shuffled like a Las Vegas dealer. "Five-card draw, jacks or better to open."

Noah grinned at her. "Fours, whores, and one-eyed jacks wild?"

"We're playing poker, not Go Fish," she said, and dealt.

Brooke was serious about her poker.

Rafe pulled in his cards. "You could use some help, Noah. That's a lot of ground to cover."

"I've only got about a couple of hundred more feet to go. You're welcome to come behind me and check to see if I've missed anything, but frankly, I've done a thorough search." Noah wouldn't have trusted this task to anyone else.

"Where else would your grandfather have hidden the bottle?" DuPey asked.

All cards were slapped, facedown, on the table. Everyone leaned forward, intense and still.

Chapter 27

I still say the bottle is in the house." Brooke waved a hand around her.

"We've searched. And searched. Everywhere." Rafe's blue eyes burned with ferocity. "There's nothing."

"What if he buried it in the yard?" DuPey asked. "That would be cool and dark."

"If he buried it, it could be buried anywhere," Eli said.

"He left a note in the cubbyhole where the wine was stored," Chloë reminded them.

"He had lousy handwriting, especially at the end. Maybe we're reading it wrong." Noah liked the idea that Nonno had fooled them so easily—except that it got them nowhere.

"It's clear enough." Rafe reached across and ruffled Noah's hair. "It says, 'up.' "

Noah yanked his head away. "What's it say if you turn it upside down?"

Chloë had apparently already thought of that, for she said promptly, " 'dn.' "

"Down?" Brooke sat up straight.

"That doesn't help," Chloë said patiently. "That gets us back to—did he bury it somewhere?"

"If he did, we're screwed. He's been gone nine years." Rafe glanced worriedly at his grandmother. He continued, “Any sign of his work would be grown over.”

“I can’t sit here on my hands and not do anything.” That was an exaggeration. It was late spring. Eli worked all day in the vineyards and in the cellars blending the wines. Yet he couldn’t contain his impatience. “Is there something that detects objects buried in the ground? I could get my field guys together and have them search the grounds—”

“First of all, how well ground-penetrating radar works depends on the type of soil and how much electrical conductivity is in it. Also, I don’t think we want your vineyard workers looking for a precious object like that bottle—the chances that we’d actually receive it from their hands is not good.” Rafe lifted one shoulder in a half shrug.

Eli gave a half shrug back.

Brooke picked up where Rafe left off. “What happens when you start looking at a highly developed site like the resort is you find chunks of pipe, chunks of concrete, nails, two-by-fours, ceramic tile, rolls of insulation, all from the original construction and the construction since.”

Noah nodded. “And bottles, lots of bottles, from the drinks the workers enjoyed after work and then tossed into a slag pit and buried. Every time we build a new cottage, what do you think we find?”

"Bottles?" Bao ventured.

"Right. Plus the resort includes part of the vineyard. Include that, and we've got more than forty acres. Searching the grounds of the resort is a waste of time unless we have something more to go on." Too bad Noah's Propov cousins were such thugs. He could put them on the job.

He half smiled. Maybe he could stick them at the far end of the vineyard and tell them to work their way forward. *That* would keep them busy.

Having Hendrik and the lovable gang o' thugs in town with nothing to do was making Noah extremely nervous.

"I don't think Nonno would have buried the bottle there, anyway. He worked at the resort, but he loved the vineyard, and he loved his home." One by one Eli stacked his chips into one tall pile, sorted by colors. "I think the bottle has to be here, somewhere on the home ranch."

"How about searching Sarah's yard with your ground-penetrating radar?" DuPey said.

Nonna and Bao exchanged glances.

Nonna shrugged and nodded.

Bao spoke up. "We already did it."

Everyone turned to face her.

"You did?" Rafe asked. "When?"

"We needed a distraction. And I'm sorry, but I'm here, a highly trained killing machine"—Bao held up her hands, callused from years of martial arts—"and mostly nothing happens. After a few weeks of peace and tranquility—broken by the occasional murder—even breaking boards with my forehead loses its hint of fun. Sarah and I decided a search was a good idea. So I rented a ground-penetrating radar detector and we combed the yard. We found some interesting stuff, mostly dead pets, buried toys, some used condoms. . . ."

Noah pretended he knew nothing.

His brothers did the same.

Bao continued. "But no bottle of wine. And no one has been digging in the yard recently, either."

"Does it look like anything special?" Chloë asked. When everyone looked at her in puzzlement, she said, "It's old, made during Prohibition *and* the Depression. Didn't they clean and reuse bottles then?"

"Yes, and in those days, when wine was illegal, it was sometimes bottled to disguise the contents," Nonna said.

Eli's mouth kicked up in a half grin. "You're right; this bottle would not resemble the modern red wine bottle. For one thing, it's more than seven hundred and fifty milliliters. That size is a relatively recent development. They used to bottle wine in fifths, like liquor. So Nonno's bottle is thin and tall—"

"More like a white wine bottle?" Chloë clarified.

"Yes, but taller." Eli gestured with his hands. "Twenty-four inches, perhaps? Straight-sided, with slender shoulders. It's heavy for its size. The glass is green and I think thick, although I can't tell that until I decant it."

"Here's to the day that you do." DuPey lifted his glass in salute.

Eli inclined his head. "God grant it be soon."

"Amen," Noah said fervently.

Nonna sat biting her lip and looking worried.

Noah had to ask. "You don't know where it is, do you, Nonna?"

She shook her head. "I wish that I did."

"Because lives depend on finding that bottle," he said.

Nonna turned on him, her usually gentle brown eyes flashing. "Dear. I realize I'm a befuddled old woman who couldn't possibly comprehend the seriousness of the situation, but since I've been attacked, my personal nurse has robbed me and been killed, and Joseph Bianchin himself threatened me. . . . I think I have as good a grip on what is happening as you young people do."

"I know, Nonna. I'm stupid. I'm sorry." He was, and he was.

But she was having none of it. She stood, quivering with anger. "I need to get the dining room ready for company."

Brooke and Chloë came to their feet. "We'll help you, Nonna."

"No!" She pointed a finger at each one. "I want to be alone for a minute." Because they all knew she didn't lose her temper very often, but when she did, it took time and patience for her to bring it under control.

Both girls sank back into their chairs.

As soon as Nonna left the room, Chloë said, "Good going, Noah."

"What happened to the usual smooth charm, Noah?" Brooke taunted. "Got something on your mind?"

Even the girls wanted him to confess his part in this ongoing crime.

But he couldn't dare.

When he remembered last month's outburst, admitting he knew about the pink diamonds and who sought them, he wanted to smack himself. All these years, he had been so careful to keep his mouth shut. Apparently the strain had finally breached his good sense, and this was the result: He had slipped, causing his brothers and his sisters-in-law, and most of all Nonna, aggravation and worry.

Right now, he didn't need them trying to pry his secrets from him. His family couldn't imagine how much danger it would put them in if he shared what he knew. He needed them on their guards, but ignorant. Because with every heartbeat, the leather dog collar seemed to tighten around his neck, and every time it tightened, a tiny bit of his discipline slipped away.

He didn't dare lose control again. He would say too much, and with his mother and her family in town, Noah feared an indiscretion would lead to deaths—Di Luca deaths. As much as he loved his brothers, they couldn't overpower Liesbeth and her gang.

Ignoring Brooke and Chloë, Noah said, "I feel as if the bottle has to be in plain sight, or someplace painfully obvious, and somehow we're just missing it."

Nods all around the table.

He leveled a look at his brothers. "Nonno did so much work in the shed and in the garage, and both of those places are dark and cool. If you want to help, empty them, pull out everything—"

"We already did that," Eli said.

"Do it again. Run your radar detectors over every inch of the dirt floor and any patches in the concrete . . . that would help." Noah must have looked grim. Or determined. Or scared. Or something.

Because Eli said, "Damn it, Noah, tell us what you know!" And in an unexpected move from the usually stoic Eli, his long arm reached around and slapped Noah hard on the back of the head.

An unexpected flash of pain.

A piercing fear.

A single thought.

He was dead.

Noah found himself on his feet, heart pounding, clutching at his throat and the studs that would ignite and end his life, facing a tableful of puzzled, worried faces.

No. Not dead. He was still alive. Still alive . . .

"Noah?" Rafe stood slowly. "C'mon, man. Nothing can be that bad. Tell us."

With an effort, Noah loosened his grip from around his neck. He flexed his hand and cleared his throat.

Yes. *Tell them.* They were his kin and perhaps they could think of something he had not. Maybe they could help—

"Noah, you darling boy." Nonna bustled into the kitchen, laughing and crying.

Noah looked around, dazed and confused.

Nonna threw her arms around him. "I never could stay mad at you long, but this—this stunt exceeds all your other shenanigans."

He looked at her uncomprehendingly.

Then he realized—his present had arrived.

Behind Nonna, his great-aunt Annie rolled down the hall in her electric wheelchair, holding the leash to her assistance dog. Walking behind was his great-aunt June, tall, brisk, white haired. He had flown them in, Annie from Washington State and June from Far Island off the coast of California, to let them reassure themselves that

Nonna was well—and to be with her after she suffered another loss.

They didn't know that part, of course.

Their arrival brought the family to their feet, laughing and calling out, rushing forward to hug and exclaim.

Noah laughed, too, and hugged, and exclaimed, and preened. He explained to DuPey and his brothers that Annie was ready to show up on Nonna's doorstep to see for herself that she was okay, and he had simply made it easier for her.

Annie explained that in three days, they were off to visit June's place off the coast of California, and they wanted Sarah to come with them.

Sarah shot Noah an annoyed, knowing glance and gently refused, saying she couldn't leave until the kids had cleared up a few things. When her grandsons all urged her to go, she promised to visit in the autumn.

Everyone was happy at this unexpected family reunion.

Noah pressed his hand to the dog collar hidden under his shirt.

The impulse for confession had passed.

It was better that way.

Chapter 28

Penelope decided that if she was going to stay in Bella Terra for employment and to work out her personal problems, she had to make her life here bearable.

After Friday, her first full day of working with Brooke Di Luca, she searched out the best Mexican restaurant in town. She discovered it across the river, housed in a crummy little building where plastic tablecloths printed with parrots and hibiscus covered the tables, and the dining chairs all had torn vinyl seats. Yes, the Taquería Guadalajara might look like a greasy spoon, but the seared pork *tortas* tasted so good they brought tears to her eyes.

On Saturday night, while sitting alone in her motel room listening to the ruckus that was the Beaver Inn, she decided to screw up her courage and go to the Di Lucas' the next evening for their weekly dinner party.

Maybe it wasn't the brightest idea. After all, Noah would be there.

But the coming week would be difficult for her, not because of what faced her in the future—she was very aware that in a couple of days she would be meeting her father—but because of what had happened in her past.

Tears filled her eyes, and hastily she wiped them away.

She needed diversion. She needed people around her. She needed kindness and family, and she knew she could find it all in Sarah Di Luca's home.

So Sunday afternoon, she returned to Taquería Guadalajara, and for an extra fee and a lot of flattery, the cook cut the *tortas* into appetizer-size pieces and put them in a to-go box.

Lovingly she placed the *tortas* in the passenger seat and drove to the Di Luca ranch, her stomach growling all the way. That was good, a distraction that kept her from remembering the last time she'd driven up here googly-eyed with a love she thought would last forever.

She snorted.

Ah, youth. Wild, lighthearted, optimistic . . . stupid.

She turned off the main road and onto the long driveway that wove first through vineyards filled with old, well-tended grapevines, then through a large, well-tended yard with grass and flowers and dotted with sprawling old valley oaks spreading their shade across California's heartland.

Penelope slowed as she passed the house to examine it; the Di Luca home looked the same: American farmhouse traditional, square and white, with flowers blooming around the edges and the open windows breathing in the fresh air. The only change she could see was a new coat of white paint and a handicapped ramp that came straight off the left side, took a corner, and came back to the sidewalk. The sameness gave her a feeling of continuity and was at the same time a little disorienting, as if she'd stepped back in time.

She swung into the parking space between a green extended-cab F-250 with massive tires and a gleaming black BMW 650 with an engine so massive she could almost hear it humming—and the car was off.

She knew, without being told, that both vehicles belonged to Di Lucas.

She hoped her mother's conservative old Volvo C70 didn't get a complex.

A police cruiser was parked there, and Brooke's car, and a Porsche Panamera 4-S, and, incongruously, a new red MINI Cooper.

It looked as if the Di Lucas had a good crowd for the evening.

Good. Penelope would blend right in.

She grabbed the *tortas*, got out, and turned to look around.

The summer solstice was only two weeks away, and at five o'clock the sun leaned toward the west, filtering through the massive oaks on the long stretch of lawn and giving the three women moving up the driveway a patina of agelessness.

Penelope recognized them. She had met them all that summer nine years ago: Noah's great-aunts Annie and June and, most important, Noah's beloved grandmother, Sarah. They wore sun hats; obviously they'd been for their daily walk along the paths in Nonna's capacious yard. Now they hurried toward her, Annie's dog in a vest and on a leash, June's hand resting on Annie's mechanical wheelchair, while Sarah smiled broadly and waved at Penelope.

Penelope waved back, deposited her *tortas* on the steps, and hurried to greet them.

"Dear girl, I had hoped to see you!" Sarah embraced her, looked into her face as if rememorizing her features, then embraced her again.

Why had Penelope ever hesitated for a moment to call or visit? Immediately she knew Sarah would never reproach her or pile on the guilt. "It's been too long."

"Don't be a stranger, no matter what is happening with my reprehensible grandson—who is here, by the way." Sarah glanced toward the house. "That's why I hardly dared hope that you would come to our Sunday-night dinner."

Faint alarm stirred in Penelope. "I hope I'm not intruding. I was trying to decide when to come out, and Brooke and Rafe urged me to come tonight—"

Annie laughed. "Intruding! We Di Lucas live for your kind of intrusion. Do you remember me, Penelope?"

"Indeed I do, Mrs. Di Luca." Penelope shook her hand, and then when Annie tugged, she leaned over and hugged her.

"You can't call us *all* Mrs. Di Luca." June kept one hand on the handle of the wheelchair and offered her cheek. As Penelope kissed her, she pointed and said, "June, Annie, and Sarah. Those are our names. We married the Di Luca brothers, which worked out well, since we knew and liked one another in high school—although I'm the youngest—"

"Yeah, yeah," Sarah said.

"—by three years," June continued.

"Only two years for me!" Annie said.

"And in the Di Luca family, we are collectively known as 'the girls.' " Sarah smiled at her friends.

They smiled back.

"This is Ritter." Annie indicated her dog. "He's half yellow Lab, half golden retriever, trained by Canine Companions for Independence, and he's been with me for six years. Ritter, sit!"

Ritter sat lopsided, as if the rocks in the driveway pushed him off-kilter.

"Penelope, offer your hand," Annie said. "And you, Penelope, you say, 'Ritter, shake!' "

Penelope did as she was told, and when he offered his paw, she laughed into his big brown eyes. "He smiled at me."

"He loves everybody. People who don't know him say, 'It must make you feel safe to have a dog with you all the time.' But this dog would help the burglar carry out the family silver." Ritter looked at Annie as if he understood her lament, and she rubbed his head. "Yes, you're a good boy."

"He's not with Annie to protect her; he's here to assist her, and he does that very well." Sarah hooked her arm through Penelope's. "Pretend you're an assistance dog, and help this old woman into the house. My younger friends have worn me out."

"I told you to let us know when you got tired," Annie scolded. "You're barely out of the hospital."

"I'm fine," Sarah said, then admitted, "My arm still aches from the break, and sometimes I get a lingering headache." She pressed her fingertips to her forehead. "I don't heal as quickly as I used to."

"You've never had a concussion and a broken arm at the same time before." June directed Annie toward the handicapped ramp.

"The girls had been chomping at the bit to visit, but we told them no, it was still too dangerous." Sarah glanced at Penelope questioningly. "Noah said he'd told you of our troubles?"

"Yes, and I'm sorry to hear of them." And not just because she was a coward. She hated to think of Sarah injured and her lovely, pleasant world blighted.

"The girls don't listen worth a darn." Sarah glared at the other two *girls*.

Annie craned to look behind her and around June at Sarah and Penelope. "You scared us half to death, Sarah!"

"I'm a tough old bird." Sarah and Penelope followed Annie and June up the ramp.

"The operative word being the *old* part," June said.

"You girls are *mean*. Now stop before you scare Penelope." At the top of the ramp, Sarah turned Penelope to face the valley. "Whenever I need a dose of courage, I come out here and ask myself, How many eons has the river carved the rock? How long have the oaks dug their roots into the rocky soil? How many years have men and women loved, laughed, lived, and died in this place?"

Penelope took a breath. Sarah had divined that she was nervous about going in, meeting the family, being drawn into the relationships she enjoyed before . . . seeing Noah again. So Sarah had given her the strength she needed to go on.

Penelope's doubts were nothing but a momentary shift in the winds, and if she kept her composure, behaved with dignity, treated these Di Lucas like the friends they were . . . her time here would be another layer of serenity and warmth added to the long Bella Valley years.

That was why she was here now, tonight. To

face the Di Luca family, to join the human race again, to prove that she had the strength to move on with her life. It only made sense to do it here, in the place where she had tumbled from foolish girlhood onto the long, rocky road to maturity.

Penelope ran down the steps, picked up the box of *tortas*, and ran back up. "Shall we go in?" she asked.

Sarah pressed her arm. "Let's do it."

Chapter 29

Penelope held the screen door open as Annie, June, and Sarah went in. She followed them down the hall to the kitchen at the back, past the living room where the muted television played a baseball game no one watched, past the dining room where the long table groaned under the weight of salads, wraps, and casseroles. From the kitchen, they heard the steady hum of conversation punctuated by the occasional loud argument or metallic slam of a pan.

When Penelope had visited Nonna's house all those years ago, the party always started in the kitchen. Apparently nothing had changed.

Everyone looked up and greeted Penelope when she and the girls walked in. She recognized Eli, Rafe, and Police Chief DuPey. Sarah introduced Penelope to Chloë as a dear friend of the family, and Eli's young wife examined Penelope as if she didn't quite see her.

"She's writing a book," Eli explained. "She checks in and out of reality at her own convenience."

"It's a good trick if you can do it," Penelope said.

Chloë's eyes widened; she nodded. "Good line." And she typed briskly for a moment.

Sarah's kitchen looked different, updated with new appliances. And the same, with the big round wooden table where the enthusiastic group was gathered around a pile of red, white, and blue chips in the center of the table.

The general feeling was of ramshackle goodwill and impending fun, except . . .

Penelope's gaze zeroed in on Noah.

Damn it.

He looked back, his eyes narrowed, noting her casual wine red button-down shirt, chosen for comfort and for the message it sent—*I'm a woman at ease with myself.* He skimmed her formfitting blue jeans, noted her red cork wedge sandals and the sheer gloss polish on her toes. He looked at her clothes, but what he saw was . . . her, naked and vulnerable.

He saw, and she responded with that familiar breathlessness that came from being flung high into the atmosphere.

And he didn't even have to touch her.

She had told herself that coming to this

gathering would serve as a signal to the others—and herself—that she had moved beyond her old fears and desires. That as a mature adult, she could face whatever life threw at her.

Perhaps what she should have remembered was that in less than two years she had suffered great losses. Time was slowly returning her strength and confidence. She was no longer as fragile—but she was still desperately lonely. And a sizzling chemistry still existed between her and Noah. Loneliness around him created a danger to her peace of mind, and maybe her sanity.

How long had they stared at each other? Too long.

The others were watching.

Penelope tore her gaze away from his.

An awkward silence reigned in the kitchen.

Then, to her surprise, Rafe came to the rescue. "Hey, Penelope, I forgot to tell you. Your security check was clean."

His reassurance was so completely unexpected, she blinked at him in confusion. She snapped into the moment and in a sarcastic voice said, "Imagine my surprise."

He laughed.

Like a spring, the tension in the kitchen was released.

"You know how it is—Rafe likes his security checks," Eli said. "Girls scare him."

"Girls scare any intelligent man," Rafe said.

He got a heartfelt, "Amen," from DuPey, and Penelope relaxed as conversation began to rumble along at a normal level.

The poker game seemed to be down to two players—Brooke, holding her cards open and smiling faintly, confidently. And Noah, sprawled in his chair, five cards in his hand, a bottle of beer at his elbow, handsome as hell and just as likely to incite Penelope to sin. If she wasn't careful. Which she would be.

Luckily for her, he seemed faintly . . . hostile.

Good. *Hostile* she could handle.

A thin, delicate-looking young Asian woman slipped silently into the kitchen.

Rafe went on alert. "How're things out there, Bao?"

"Quiet, but . . ." Bao spread her hands in a helpless gesture. "Someone's watching. I can feel it."

"You can *feel* it?" Brooke sounded surprised.

"Like a rifle aimed at the middle of my forehead," Bao said.

Concerned glances were exchanged.

"Bao is my bodyguard," Sarah said quietly to Penelope. "When I go outside, she watches over me."

Bao acknowledged Penelope, then seated herself in an empty chair.

"Bao is not inclined to be fanciful," Sarah told Penelope.

"Oh." Thus the heightened sense of tension.

Rafe stood, went to the window, and looked out. "No one in sight?"

"I spoke to the men on the perimeter. No. All quiet. No alarm has been tripped." Bao bit her lip. "Maybe I'm imagining things? Maybe I've been on duty too long?"

"Maybe." Rafe pulled out his cell phone and stepped out onto the back porch. "But just to be safe, I'll call in more personnel."

Sarah sat beside Bao, and Bao returned her smile. Yet Bao did look pale and tired, as if the strain of constant vigilance had worn her down.

Penelope recognized a sense of closeness between Sarah and Bao, like soldiers who every day faced the possibility of combat. She didn't want to share in that possibility, but she had made the decision to stay—she was committed. She rattled her to-go box. "Does anybody want some of the best pork *tortas* I've ever had in my life?"

"*Tortas*?" Chloë shut her computer with a distinct click. "Eli and I found this little place across the river called Taquería Guadalajara—"

"I found it, too." Penelope opened the box.

The tension in the kitchen slowly, quietly slid to a more manageable level.

Groans of pleasure greeted the heavenly smell of meat and cumin, onions and jalapeños, beans and guacamole.

Noah, the jerk, didn't react in any way. He sat unmoving, unsmiling, staring at his hand as Nonna got a serving plate. He didn't stir as Penelope unpacked the *tortas*. He didn't glance up, didn't acknowledge Penelope as she passed them around.

He didn't eat the food she had brought.

Penelope wanted to smack him. He had asked her to visit his grandmother. She had managed to defuse the tension in the kitchen, and he was thoughtlessly, rudely making everyone uncomfortable.

Or at least . . . he was making *her* uncomfortable.

Chapter 30

"Those went fast!" Sarah disregarded Noah as if he were a sulky boy under her care.

That seemed like an intelligent plan, and Penelope resolved to ignore the big spoilsport, too.

Annie laughed. "Sarah likes to see people eat."

"What? Like you don't?" Sarah stood and pulled salad makings out of the refrigerator.

Noah probably was mad about something that had nothing to do with Penelope. She needed to remember that the whole world didn't revolve around her and her feelings.

"Brooke and Noah, we need you out of the way while we get dinner ready," Nonna said firmly.

Good. Sarah was shooing Noah out of the kitchen. Penelope would stay right here and help the cooks. She wouldn't have to look at his bad-tempered face anymore.

"We're almost done, Nonna. Noah's stalling because he doesn't want to lose this luscious big poker pot to me." Brooke curved her arm around the pile of poker chips in the middle of the table and smiled at Noah.

An alarm went off on his watch.

He looked at the face.

"What's that for?" Brooke asked.

"It's three thirty-seven p.m.," he said. Like that mattered to anyone.

Confused glances around the room.

"What's three thirty-seven p.m.?" Eli asked.

"Another day gone." Noah shut off the alarm. He ignored Brooke, ignored everyone, and looked up into Penelope's eyes. "I thought we agreed to avoid each other."

So he was angry at her for being here?

Last time they'd met, at Rafe and Brooke's home, he had been charming. Interested. Conversational. He had insisted she promise to come and see his grandmother. The fact that she was here was *his fault.*

Her own antagonism rose to greet his.

Because really, wasn't that always the way with Noah? First he loved her; then he hated her. He never knew what he wanted.

With a shrug that rudely dismissed him, she said, “I figured we were both mature adults who could behave in a civilized manner—as long as the group was large enough.”

DuPey laughed, then with a glance at Noah’s expression cut off his amusement.

Noah sat quietly, absorbing her words.

Penelope’s hostility hardened into hatred. Hatred that he had challenged her. Hatred that he dominated the room so that everyone, *everyone,* watched them as if riveted by this Tin Pan Alley drama he had stirred up.

At last, as she shifted, meaning to turn away, he slid the fan of his cards closed. Put them facedown on the table. “I fold,” he said to Brooke. He stood up. Chips rattled as he pushed the huge pot toward her.

“I knew you were bluffing,” Eli said.

“Then why didn’t you stay in, Eli?” Chloë asked.

“Wait. Look! I’ve got a good hand.” Brooke laid down her cards. “Four of a kind. Sixes! Look!”

Noah paid no heed to his family or to Brooke’s cards. Instead, he fixed his green gaze on Penelope’s face, and like a great hunting cat, he paced toward her.

She refused to back up.

This was stupid. Why antagonize him? He was angry.

About what?

And so what? She was mad, too. Moreover, if his grandmother chose to welcome Penelope to her house, he had no right to behave like the visitor police. . . .

No, she wasn't going to retreat.

Although he got very close very quickly, and what from a distance had looked like hostility now looked more like some kind of smoky sexuality, directed at her.

And he *loomed* in an alarming way. . . .

About the time he got within three steps, she decided she was being stupidly valiant. She'd taken one large step backward when, with a move so swift she never saw it coming, he took hold of her wrist in one powerful hand.

That grip. Hot. Strong. Sure. Familiar. Intoxicating, despite the defense she tried to put up against him, leaving her breathless.

"Come on." He turned and led her toward the front door. "Let's talk about how many people we need around us to behave in a civilized manner."

"What? No!" She set her heels.

He turned back to her, moved close, way too close, and in a voice pitched only to her ears, he said, "I *will* pick you up and carry you, Penelope."

She stared at him, teeth gritted, angry and . . . and a little afraid.

At least, she thought it was fear. Her heart pounded hard in her chest, her fingers curled into fists, she heard a roaring in her ears, and her eyes hurt from holding them wide. She realized she was holding her breath, and gasped in some much-needed air.

Did she believe him? Did she believe he would pick her up and carry her out of here?

He surrounded her with angry heat. His green eyes sparked with gold.

Oh, yes. She believed him. And how much humiliation could she stand?

"All right. I'll go." She let him pull her out of the kitchen, down the hall, and out the front door.

Their exit left a stunned silence in the kitchen.

"Wow," Chloë whispered.

Annie stirred, turning her wheelchair. "Well. I don't know about you girls, but I'm going to go watch." She put the wheelchair in full roll down the hallway.

The rest of the women—and Ritter—galloped toward the front of the house after her.

Rafe, Eli, and DuPey sat around the empty table and shook their heads in manly disdain.

"Honestly," Eli said. "Women."

"I know it," DuPey said.

"They are so nosy," Rafe said.

"Really. What do they think they'll see that they haven't seen before?" Eli asked.

They sat, staring into space, thinking about it.

DuPey looked from Eli to Rafe. "Why do you think Noah's so buttoned up today?"

"He definitely had a stick up his butt, especially once Penelope walked in," Rafe said.

The other two nodded.

DuPey morosely shoved the rest of the chips out of the center of the table toward Brooke's place. "That's one big pot the little lady won."

Rafe preened. "What can I tell you? She's smart."

"Hey, Eli, look at Noah's hand." DuPey gestured toward the little pile of cards sitting before Noah's place. "Because you're right. He must have been bluffing."

Eli picked up the cards and looked—and his jaw dropped.

The other two men went on alert.

"What is it?" DuPey asked urgently.

"What's he got, a pair of twos?" Rafe asked.

One by one, Eli placed the cards on the table.

King of diamonds. Queen of diamonds. Ten, nine, eight of diamonds.

The guys stared at those cards. At the hand that could have taken every chip, that came along once in ten lifetimes.

Finally Rafe whispered, "Noah folded on a straight flush, king high? To make a grab at

Penelope?" He shoved his chair back. "I'm going to watch."

The other men stood.

They rushed toward the door and headed down the hall.

Chapter 31

Noah didn't pause, didn't slow.

Penelope's heart pounded as he dragged her down the steps, across the driveway, and into the front yard. They passed the first tree and moved to the second, a broad, towering valley oak, an oak that lazily rested its longest branches on the ground. He stopped, whirled to face her.

"Not this tree," she said.

"Yes, this tree. For nine years, every time I walked across Nonna's yard, I saw you here, your long hair tangled in the branches, your brown eyes staring at me, soft and warm. . . ." His eyes blazed with heat, anger, and a long, slow unfurling of sweet reminiscences. "The memories are always here, so yes. Most definitely. This tree."

It was early August, California hot and Bella Terra dry. The summer had almost vanished, each day slipping away before Noah could grasp it in his eager hands. Now he stood on the porch, watched Penelope walk across

Nonna's lawn, and marveled at her figure, her grace, the marvelous way her jeans fit her curvaceous behind, the flow of her straight, dark hair down her back. . . .

Eli sat on the swing, idly rocking, observing him. "You've got it bad."

"No, I don't." Noah knew it sounded like a young man's pride, that instinctive denial that a young woman could rope him in so easily.

Eli snorted.

That was fine. Better Eli be amused by Noah's self-deception than for him to suspect the truth—that Noah was violently, wildly in love with Penelope, and soon, too soon, he would send her away.

He had so little time left. . . . He ran down the steps, across the driveway, and toward Penelope.

He was a fool for falling in love.

He was an ass for making love to her.

For her sake, he should wish he had never met her.

And yet for his own sake, he would rather spend this summer with Penelope and live off the memories forever.

She heard him running toward her and turned, smiling, open, her brown eyes shining with trust.

Never pausing, he picked her up by the waist, lifted her high, and swung her around.

She shrieked and laughed.

He placed her on a low branch of one of the huge oaks on guard on Nonna's lawn, the second one from the porch, the one with leaves that mostly hid them from the house.

She put her hands on his shoulders and looked down at him. "I knew you'd come to find me."

"I can't stay away," he told her, and hoped that wasn't true. Once he had sent her away, he had to avoid her.

She had an uncanny knack of knowing when his thoughts wandered into the dark places, and now she frowned. "What's wrong?"

"Nothing!" He smiled widely. "I was wondering if you would like to go on an adventure."

"Yes?" She was smart enough to be unsure.

"Turn around. Straddle the limb, and I'll take you on a trip around the world."

She slanted her head and looked at him sideways in disbelief.

"No, really!" Was he distracting her? He couldn't tell. "When Eli and Rafe and I were boys, we used to come out here and mount up our trusty steeds, and we'd ride off to find gold or chase down some rustlers, and one year Nonna showed me *Robin Hood*, the one with Errol Flynn, and I galloped all over England robbing the rich."

"And giving to the poor?"

"Of course. All the maidens kissed me in gratitude." Bitterly, he said, "I've always had a thing about being a hero." And look how well that had turned out.

Once again, she saw too much, for she cupped his cheek and said, "You're my hero."

"No. I'm really not."

She reproved him with a shake of her head. "Such modesty. Your brothers didn't want to play Robin Hood?"

"They didn't live here then. They lived with their mothers." He remembered those lonely days.

She knew, of course. Leaning down, she pressed her lips to his, and in her kiss he tasted sweet, warm comfort and the assurance that she would be here for him forever.

That was the kind of promise he could not make, and he pulled away. "Well. Turn around, straddle that beast, and tell me where you want to go!"

For a second, she looked both bewildered and hurt.

But he grinned and did his best imitation of boyish excitement, so she flung her leg over the wide branch, placed her hands flat on the rough bark, and ordered, "Take me to medieval England to meet this Robin Hood you speak of!"

"Hang on," he warned, and pushed the branch up, then down, then settled it into a steady, rhythmic swaying like a horse's trot. He waved an arm around. "Here we are in Sherwood Forest."

"It's beautiful." She pointed. "Look at yon castle!"

"Ride quickly!" He picked up the pace. "That's the castle of evil Prince John."

She booed.

"Now here we are among Robin Hood's merry men." He let go of the branch, and it swayed to a stop. Putting his fists on his hips, he struck a pose. "And I am Robin Hood. You are Maid Marian?"

"No." Penelope sounded absolutely disgusted. "Maid Marian always needed to be rescued. I don't need to be rescued! I ride with you, for justice and freedom."

Noah looked around. "My merry men don't know what to think about that. What qualifications does such a weak little woman have to ride with my stalwart band?"

Breaking a narrow, leafy branch off the tree, she pointed it right between his eyes. "I come from the future, and I brought a light saber!"

Surprised, he started laughing, a little at

first, then so hard he fell down on the lawn and rocked and held his belly.

She jumped off the branch and whacked him on the stomach with the branch. “Hey, if I want to bring a light saber on my trip, I can!”

He nodded and wheezed. “Yes, of course you can. And because of your forethought, you are henceforth one of Robin Hood’s men.”

She knelt beside him and grabbed his arms, and he let her push them over his head. “Robin Hood’s woman,” she said, “or no deal.”

He looked into her eyes and his laughter faded. “That is exactly who you are—Robin Hood’s woman.”

“And Robin Hood had better be careful or his woman will overthrow him and take control of his band of merry men.”

He snapped his arms down and around her, and rolled her beneath him. “I’d like to see you try, my maiden warrior.”

She struggled, giggling.

He watched her and laughed, too, and all the time his heart ached, because . . . never in his life would he find another woman like this one, and all too soon they would be parted. . . .

Chapter 32

Now Noah backed Penelope against the same tree, against the same trunk . . . but everything was different. She had lived through sorrow and the destruction of her life, both at his hands and at the hands of fate. And nothing she had believed about Noah was the truth . . . was it?

"Civilized?" He used the word like an obscenity. "You say we're civilized?"

"*I* can be civilized." He smelled good, like bergamot orange. Yes, and he smelled of brimstone, too. Of temptation irresistible.

"*I* know better." His voice vibrated through her, all heat and depth and not very hidden message.

"What do you mean by that?"

His face was flushed, his features taut and intense. "I mean you might walk the walk and talk the talk, but you can't deny there's something between us. And I know what you're like when I—" He didn't even finish the sentence. Before her brain could work out what was coming next, he was leaning against her, trapping her between the sturdy strength of the oak and his own warm, living, muscled power, and he pressed his lips on hers. And for all that his body threw off anger like heat from a furnace, the pressure was perfect. She remembered *this*.

And then his kiss changed. Became persuasive. Needy. Unrelenting. Different from any kiss she'd ever enjoyed. Different from any kiss they'd ever exchanged. Different from any kiss in the history of the world.

This was seduction, pure and simple, a rage of passion, a glory of touch, a distraction from anything outside of this moment, anything that was not *him*. Tongues. Teeth. Lips. Raw emotion.

Longing.

That was it. She recognized it. *Longing*. He longed for her, desired her, wanted her.

He wanted to be one with her. To kiss, touch, be inside her.

She opened her lips wider, wishing for a lasting taste of him, and at once he filled her mouth with the flavor of his emotions: fury, determination, anguish. . . .

Anguish?

She pulled away just far enough to murmur, "Why anguish?"

He jerked back as if she'd slapped him.

Then his eyes flashed. "You're too smart for your own good. That's why I've missed you every damned second since the day I was a complete and total ass . . . and drove you away." The memory of his own actions seemed to infuriate him more, and whatever subtlety he had used in the previous kiss vanished. He wrapped his arms around her waist, gathered her so she was leaning against him, teetering and off balance—and he *kissed* her.

All her senses opened to him, taken by storm. She could almost hear the crackle of hell's fire as it enveloped her, enveloped them, shrouding them from the breeze, from the whisper of the trees, from the scent of grass. The world narrowed down to Penelope and Noah, and nothing else existed.

Stupidly, she opened her arms to him, reaching her hands up to his shoulders, gripping him, glorying in the muscles that rippled beneath her fingers. She opened her lips to him. Opened her body to him. And she *longed* every bit as fiercely as he did.

He finished the kiss to her mouth, but he wasn't through with her. His fingers dug into her bottom; he lifted her.

She needed no urging, for instinct and desire drove her now. She wrapped her legs around his waist, her arms around his shoulders.

He walked to the most massive oak branch, one that draped the ground, and placed her into a fork where the mighty branch split into two.

It was a leafy nest, a promise of green privacy in the midst of nature. She was secure, the tree holding most of her weight, the bark rough against her jeans, and at the same time she was wedged against him, against his erection and that was exactly where she wanted to be.

He kissed her eyelids, her cheeks, the lobes of her ears.

He rocked his hips against her.

He feasted on her throat all the way down to the first closed button on her shirt.

Lower down, he moved rhythmically, with precision, pressing himself into the cleft of her body. He kissed her lips again, caressed her breasts through her bra, ran his thumb over her nipples.

And that rhythm went on and on, relentless, taunting her.

He looked into her eyes. “If we were naked, you would come, right out here beneath the blue skies.” He smiled, a buccaneer’s slash of amusement. “Oh, wait . . . we don’t have to be naked. You’re going to come anyway.”

“No.”

“Yes, Penelope. I promise. You’ll come.”

“No.” She didn’t want to. That kind of orgasm, here in his arms, outdoors where anyone could walk up and see them; it was embarrassing. And while he maintained control? No. She did not want to yield that power to him.

“No,” she said again.

But not only her heart was lonely; her body was lonely, too. She had neglected it, ignored its needs, and now . . . He was so precise, targeting exactly the right spot, whispering in her ear,

"Yes, Penelope. Do it. Now. I need you to come for me. I know you're so close." He opened two more buttons on her shirt. He fingered the front catch on her bra, popped it open, used his fingers to spread it wide.

She had forgotten how long his fingers were, how efficient his big hands were when it came to giving her pleasure.

She had forgotten that his erection could be so hard, so hot, so present beneath too many layers of clothes.

She had never had the occasion to realize she could say, "No," and at the same time use her legs to hold him tightly, or that she would rub herself on him without a thought to anything except achieving sex. With him.

She knew only that when he cupped her bare breast, lifted it to his mouth, and sucked hard on her nipple—she came. Hell's flames enveloped her, burning her to cinders. She dug her fingers into his back. She gasped, her body pulsing against his. She cried out. *At last.*

And he lifted his mouth from her breast, pressed her face to his chest, muffled her sounds of completion in the folds of his shirt.

She smelled starch. Cotton. Noah.

Bergamot orange. And brimstone.

Vaguely in some corner of her mind she knew that later she would be embarrassed. Right now, there was only complete and utter satisfaction.

And the mighty tide of his longing washing over her.

He longed, yes. He wanted to be inside her. But right now he was taking care of her, holding her, encouraging her, touching her, stroking her.

Yes, her pleasure gave him pleasure, too.

When she had finished, when the orgasm eased and Penelope was limp in Noah's arms, he tilted her back until she was dependent on him for balance. He slid his hand up to her throat, held her until she lifted her eyes to meet his.

"Civilized?" He nudged his still-strong erection against her. "All I want is to sleep with you, screw you, come with you, come in you, make you mine until you can't remember any man, any life except me and mine."

She whimpered, his words creating a brief aftershock of climax.

He waited until she had finished, then said, "So don't talk to me about civilized. There is nothing civilized about you and me."

She heard him, looked at him, absorbed him. Wanted everything he wanted. Finally, she whispered, "Why can't we have all those things? Why can't we have sex?"

He smiled.

It wasn't cheerful. "Because there isn't time." He helped her slide off the branch. He supported her while he fastened her bra, buttoned her shirt.

He held her. . . . "Don't look at me like that," he whispered. "Your eyes are so big and brown, pleading with me, and you make me want more than I dare grasp." He wet his lips. "I brought you out here to vanquish memories, not build them. And . . . there's no time," he repeated, and he touched the closed top button on his shirt as if he had taken a vow of celibacy.

"Noah . . ." She brushed the soft strands of hair off his forehead, feathered the tips of her fingers across his cheek, tenderly outlined his lips . . . and smiled a wanton's smile. "Actually, it wouldn't take very long."

He gave a bark of laughter, then sobered. Once again, he was intense, burning her with his gaze. "Not the first time. But once I got you underneath me, the rest of the world could go to hell. And I would go to hell for forgetting." Catching her hand, he pressed a kiss into her palm, folded her fingers over it. "No, Penelope. You've already distracted me and challenged me. Time vanishes even while I race to catch it."

She didn't know what he meant. His eyes were wild, and his words seemed to ramble. "Noah, what's wrong?"

"Nothing. I've had ten years to prepare for this. There's no use whining about the way it's playing out." He held her elbow. "Are you steady enough to stand?"

She nodded.

"I've got to go for a walk." He gestured down at himself. "I'm not fit for *civilized* company."

Just like that, he walked away, down the driveway and out of sight.

She didn't know why she was surprised. Walking away was, after all, what he was good at.

Sarah, June, Annie, Brooke, Chloë, and Bao—and Ritter—walked out of the living room, where they'd been clustered around the big window.

Eli, Rafe, and DuPey walked out of Sarah's bedroom, where they'd been clustered around that window.

They met in the hall.

"Now, *that's* the way it's done," Annie pronounced.

"Um-hmm," June agreed.

"Nonna, you've got too many leaves on that tree," Rafe said. "We couldn't *see*."

"My front yard is not a peep show," Sarah said primly.

"No. Damn it." Eli laughed and tucked his hand in Chloë's arm. "I'd say that fire in Noah never got put out."

"No," Sarah said thoughtfully. "Which leads me to wonder—again—why did he ever let her go?"

Chloë took it to the next logical level. "And why is he leaving her now?"

Chapter 33

Noah walked down Nonna's winding driveway like a man fleeing his demons. But there was no leaving them behind.

He touched the collar that held his doom.

What was he thinking, kidnapping Penelope like a pirate on the prowl? He couldn't blame alcohol—he'd had one beer, and he hadn't finished it. Yet as soon as he'd seen her stroll into his family's kitchen, he had been intoxicated with desire. Not just for sex. That was too easy. But for the years they had lived apart when they could have been together, for the meals they'd missed sharing at Nonna's, for the children they would have had, for fights and reconciliations and laughter and love.

He had a brain. He had never needed to use it more than he needed to use it now.

Unfortunately, he also had a dick.

And he had only enough blood in his body to supply one or the other.

He could *think*. Or he could *lust*. Not both. Not at the same time.

And he desperately needed to think. As soon as dinner was over and he could escape, he was going back home to work on his project. It was delicate. It took every ounce of his attention. His two weeks were flying past. He'd told

Penelope there was no time. He meant it.

Liesbeth didn't know him. She didn't understand him. She imagined that because he'd been raised in a loving environment surrounded by honorable people, he was not like her.

Yet given the right circumstances, he *was* like her. The blood of the czars ran in his veins. Could he be cruel? Could he be ruthless? Oh, yes.

Liesbeth didn't realize that if he didn't find that bottle, if fourteen days passed and his time was up, he wasn't going alone. He wasn't dying and leaving his wacko criminal of a mother and her depraved family to threaten Nonna, and Rafe and Brooke, and Eli and Chloë. And Penelope, who had found a job with Rafe and Brooke.

Noah might go to hell.

But by God, he would have company.

The walk in the late-afternoon sunshine, up and down the hills, past the lawn and the trees of Nonna's yard, past the vines planted by the original Di Lucas at the start of the twentieth century . . . it should have soothed him.

Yet frustration sizzled in his veins, and he couldn't take it in. He couldn't reminisce about his boyhood spent here in the sunshine. He couldn't remember the hours spent tagging along after his grandfather, learning to trim the vines. He couldn't remember days spent with his brothers, climbing trees and playing baseball. He remembered the happy moments of his boyhood through a gray veil of grief: grief that he had taken them for granted, that he hadn't understood how rare and brief those days would be.

How was it possible that Penelope was here, no longer the girl who had ignited his desire, but a woman, confident and intelligent?

Damn it.

Damn it.

He wanted, he lusted, he longed . . . and he could not have.

Nine years ago, he had had no right to involve her in his doleful fate, yet he'd been young and impetuous, and he hadn't been able to resist her.

Since then, she'd lost a husband and a mother. What kind of ass would jump her bones now, use the solace of her love to smooth the edge of his fear, and then in a violent, bloody display, abandon her to loneliness again?

He couldn't. He wouldn't.

Yet he had been in the same room with her for less than five minutes and he'd dragged her outside because she'd made a single snarky remark.

Civilized. *Civilized*. Not in a million years.

He'd kissed her with all the ferocious desire that was in him, and after a moment's resistance, she had yielded with grace and passion.

Then . . . *Anguish,* she had whispered. She had recognized his anguish.

How was that possible? How could she read him so ably?

Because she was his soul mate, of course. He'd figured that out the first time around. But what cruel destiny had sent her here again now?

Had her husband tapped that hidden reserve of spirit within her? She buried her emotions so deep, this girl who had been raised in the Los Angeles ghettos. She had suffered early under her grandfather's rule, where only he was allowed to rage or shout. Then she'd escaped, she and her mother, to a different place, where she could be what she wanted . . . if she fit in.

She'd learned her lesson, and now she pretended the fire of her Latin heritage didn't exist, and she did fit in.

But her passions called to him, loosed his own fire, until he was crazy to touch her, to have her, to love her in every way a man could love a woman. If he could have stripped off her clothes right there in that tree—in a damned tree!—he would have done it. Done her.

And now he wouldn't be walking along with a woody the size of that tree trunk.

Except that he would, because once he had her . . . he wanted her again.

He needed to remember he was out here walking the two miles down to the road in an effort to distract himself. He needed to stop thinking of

Penelope, of her soft, dark hair, her olive skin, and those eyes that spoke to his soul. . . .

Absorbed as he was in the memories of Penelope, he paid no attention to his surroundings . . . until Hendrik stepped out from behind a tree.

Chapter 34

Noah stopped. Lust vanished. His blood rushed to his brain, and he used the weapon he possessed in abundance—intelligence. "Wow. I was just thinking of a dick, and here you are."

Hendrik's face crinkled in confusion.

"It's like God knew I needed a punching bag and threw you into my path."

Hendrik understood that, and grinned. "You want to fight, little cousin?"

Yeah, the big guy still thought Noah was the feeble, gullible weenie he had been the first time around. "Not yet. What are you doing here?"

"Watching for you. Wanted to make sure you are wearing the pretty necklace Brigetta made for you." In the ten years since Noah had last seen him, Hendrik had grown thicker, his green eyes smaller, his fists meatier. Sometime in the last three days, he'd dyed the tips of his short black hair blond. He wore black from head to toe: black shirt, black jeans, big black boots that concealed weapons Hendrik knew all too well how to handle. The meanness . . . that was the same. Hendrik was mean through and through, and ten years ago Noah hated him as he had never hated another person.

He saw no reason to change his mind now. "If I weren't wearing the necklace, I would not be wearing my head. Isn't that right?"

"That's right," Hendrik said in his singsong Scandinavian accent. "I never know when *Tante* Liesbeth talks to people whether she fully explains matters." Like a soldier on a mission, he had smeared dirt on his face and neck and on the back of his hands. "She's getting on, you know. Not as sharp as she used to be."

"I think you should express your concerns to her," Noah advised. "Perhaps she could reassure you."

Hendrik's smile changed to a scowl, and he stepped up chest-to-chest with Noah. He was two inches taller and a full thirty pounds heavier. "I never liked you. I never could tell whether you were stupid or sarcastic."

"Anyone who is sarcastic to you would have to be stupid." *But only if you understood.*

Hendrik tried to work that out, and when he couldn't, he bumped Noah's chest with his.

Noah stumbled backward. "Some of that muscle you used to throw around . . . isn't muscle anymore." In a voice rife with phony concern, he asked, "Hendrik, have you let yourself go?"

"I can still crush you with one fist." Hendrik lifted his hand, and right in front of Noah's face, he closed his fingers. He shoved his knuckles under Noah's nose.

We'll see . . . but not today. "How did you get on the property?"

"The security is good." Hendrik nodded in approval. "Expertly done. But Grieta's taught me a few tricks for disarming security alarms."

"So it was you at my brother's house."

Hendrik grinned, his white teeth big in his mouth. "Me and the others, we were bored."

"I figured." Noah looked around. None of Rafe's people were in sight. "What about the security detail we have patrolling the grounds?" His voice sharpened. "You didn't kill anybody, did you?"

"No. That would be fun, but not conducive to the success of our mission." Hendrik sneered; obviously those were Liesbeth's words. "The visuals are only as good as the people who watch. A little diversion, and they're off on the wrong scent."

"So you broke the alarms, and you screwed with the guards. Nice." Something to tell Rafe. "Why? Why bother? Not just for fun. What are you really doing here?"

Satisfied he'd made his point, Hendrik said,

"You used to talk. When you thought we were your friends. Remember? About your Nonna's Sunday parties with all her friends. I wanted to see. There are some pretty girls in that house."

A chill swept through Noah. Hendrik bullied anyone who was weaker, but with women . . . mentally, physically, he loved to abuse them.

Brooke. Chloë. Bao.

Penelope.

"Next week you could invite me," Hendrik continued. "Introduce me as your friend."

"*My mother* wouldn't like that," Noah said, spacing each word.

"*Your mother* doesn't need to know." Hendrik imitated him.

Sneaking around behind Liesbeth's back, was he?

Yes, Noah had been right to be nervous with Hendrik and the gang in town.

In a split-second decision, Noah locked eyes with Hendrik and reached around for the back of his necklace.

"What are you doing?" Hendrik grabbed Noah's hand.

"I'm going to cut off the necklace. Better to blow my head off than to bring a Dutch pig like *you* into my family's home."

Hendrik crushed Noah's fingers. "I am not Dutch. I am noble. I am Russian. And I'm going to kill you. I can't wait to kill you. Before this is over, I'm going to tear you to pieces."

As the hard bones of his knuckles ground together, Noah fought a groan. "Let me take off the collar and save you the trouble."

Hendrik squeezed harder, then flung Noah's hand away. "Liesbeth would think I forced you."

Yes. Hendrik might scorn Liesbeth aloud, but he was still afraid of her.

Noah cradled his rapidly swelling hand. "In Holland, afterward . . . Mother would have put me in charge. If I'd stayed with the gang, I'd be in. And you'd be out."

Hendrik's voice rose. "That's not true."

Noah hammered at him. "I'm Liesbeth's son. That summer, I learned a lot. In a year or less, I could have learned everything it took *you* a lifetime to learn. Because I'm smarter. I could have the job in a minute."

Hendrik lunged, and he was fast.

Noah blocked Hendrik's fist with an upraised arm, then smacked him backward with a blow to the throat.

Hendrik's head snapped back, and he staggered away, choking.

Someone shouted.

Noah glanced down the road to see two men rounding the curve, running up the hill toward them: Gary Shoemaker, one of Rafe's employees, a security guard patrolling the perimeter of Nonna's property, and an older man who looked . . . familiar.

Hendrik recovered. “Kill you now,” he said hoarsely, and prepared to charge.

“Witnesses, Hendrik. Witnesses.” Noah pointed.

Hendrik stopped. Looked. Saw the younger of the two men picking up speed, reaching into his jacket, pulling a gun. Hendrik stood with his chest heaving, his reddened eyes fixed on Noah. “Kill you,” he repeated.

“But then there’s no chance for me to get my head blown off,” Noah mocked.

Gary Shoemaker was getting closer, shouting, pointing the pistol.

“I’ll tear your head off.” Hendrik turned and raced into the vineyard.

Gary stopped. Spoke into the walkie-talkie pinned on his shoulder. Then ran after Hendrik, shouting, and when Hendrik picked up speed, Gary shot.

Hendrik staggered.

Damn. He was wearing a bulletproof vest.

Noah watched as he took evasive action: ducked low and wove through the vines.

Every job has the potential to go bad, Noah. Always have more than one escape route planned. His mother’s voice echoed in Noah’s mind as he watched Hendrik drop into a ravine that wound its way through the landscape and eventually into the river.

Gary followed.

Noah glanced down the road at the older man. He had slowed to a walk.

Noah shouldn't have blocked Hendrik's blow. He shouldn't have punched back. He should have let his foul cousin believe he had lost all his fighting skills. But the truth was, Hendrik was in a rage. He could have killed Noah. Better that Hendrik realize Noah still sparred than to die too soon.

Noah's mistake was taunting Hendrik in the first place. Normally he held himself in exquisite control, but ever since he'd clicked the clasp on this damnable collar, ever since he'd heard his watch strike three thirty-seven p.m. three different times . . . he had been very aware he had inherited those uncivilized Propov genes.

He wanted to kill Hendrik.

He wanted to bring his mother and her gang to justice.

He wanted to have long, slow, leisurely sex with Penelope.

And he wanted to do it all before the tiny bomb at his throat exploded.

He intended to succeed in two of his three goals.

But right now . . . as he watched the older man puff up the hill toward him, tall, handsome, and putting on his best act of concern, Noah knew they had other problems.

What timing. Just who they didn't need here now.

"Noah!" the older guy shouted. "Are you all right?"

"Shit," Noah said with deep feeling, and hurried toward him. "Dad, what the hell are you doing here?"

Chapter 35

Penelope made her wobbly way from the oak tree in Sarah's yard up the steps to the porch, and sank down on the swing.

Oh, sure. She could go inside and face a dozen pairs of eyes that had seen Noah drag her out like a caveman dragging his mate. They would be wondering what had happened between her and Noah. They would speculate and chuckle, imagining a mating ritual between two consenting adults that should turn out well.

But she and Noah were doomed. She'd been willing to sleep with him—not just willing, but orgasmically eager. He'd refused. She'd even suggested a quickie. And he'd walked away, saying there was no time.

He had time to play a game of poker, but not to play around.

Really. She didn't need a house to fall on her. She got the message: He didn't want her.

But—she sighed—he said he did. And he

sounded so sincere, so full of that seductive *longing,* and she'd seen such anguish in him. . . .

She'd yielded easily. She knew that. She was embarrassed by that. All her noble intentions washed away by one man's seemingly genuine feelings. Conflicting feelings, at that.

Anguish.

And longing.

Those feelings . . . they made her want to comfort him, hold him, love him until he was the confident, arrogant, conceited Noah she adored.

With a groan, she leaned forward, put her elbows on her knees, and cradled her head in her hands.

Orgasms were funny things. They left a woman tearful, trembling, unsure, needing more emotion and wanting it to be real. Being alone afterward . . . that sucked.

The orgasm Noah had forced on her had left Penelope feeling more isolated than ever before, and very glad that tomorrow she would go with Mrs. Marino into Joseph Bianchin's house to confront the man who was her father.

Penelope lifted her head and half laughed.

Only another round with Mr. Wonderful, Noah Di Luca, could make her consider confronting her unsuspecting ass of a father to be stress-free. On the other hand, maybe Noah had done her a favor—she wasn't going to take any shit from the old man, either.

Once she'd spoken with Bianchin, she would know better how to proceed with her life. Yes, she had committed to finishing the project for Brooke Di Luca, but if Bianchin embraced Penelope and her claim as his daughter, she would consider putting down roots in this town and dealing with Noah as needed.

If Bianchin rejected her, as she fully expected he would, she would view this visitation as temporary and be oh, so careful not to make friends, join in this community, look for a home.

That was a good plan, for this week of all weeks, she needed to have a care for herself.

She recognized the irony of seeing her father now. She realized that the timing could blast away the thin veil of her composure and expose feelings still new and unhealed.

She whimpered softly.

She straightened and, with her toe against the floor, she gave the swing a push. As it rocked her, she gave herself the lecture she had been reciting more and more frequently.

It had happened a year ago Wednesday, but she should not consider it an anniversary. One commemorated an anniversary. This Wednesday was not a commemoration. It was . . . a moment to remember, and then she needed to move on.

Yet nothing convinced her that when the day came, she wouldn't crumple. She didn't want to face the heartache that lay in wait. She didn't believe that this was just a week, just a day, an hour, a moment . . . because that moment had changed her forever, broken her on the rack of grief.

She needed to remember where she was, find a way to stop the parade of painful memories, practice self-control and tranquillity, because . . . through the screen door, she heard the sound of running footsteps.

The screen door swung open. Bao dashed out of the house. The door slammed behind her.

Penelope watched in astonishment as Bao hit two of the steps on the way off the porch and raced down the driveway.

What was happening?

Penelope waited.

Nothing more occurred.

She relaxed back into the chair. *Self-control . . . Tranquillity . . .*

Then—more footsteps running down the hall. Rafe blasted out of the house. He cleared the steps in one leap and raced after Bao.

Penelope stood and stared after them.

What *was* happening?

The shadows were lengthening; evening threw its first shadows across the yard. Penelope saw two men walking up the driveway. She saw Bao and Rafe meet them. They stopped and talked; then Rafe and Bao ran on.

The men continued toward her.

One was an older man. She couldn't see him well, but he seemed somehow familiar.

The other . . . was Noah.

She didn't want him to see her like this. She didn't want him prying into her past. This pain did not need to be shared. And if she could recognize his anguish, he might recognize hers.

The people inside would surely be more concerned about whatever emergency had sent Bao and Rafe flying out of the house than with Penelope's tearstained face. And any angst she felt about facing them was nothing compared to facing Noah.

She reached for the screen door.

Once again it swung open, and DuPey stepped through, looking stern and talking on his phone. He barely glanced at her, but headed down the stairs toward the police cruiser.

The word *murder* floated unbidden through her mind, and she glanced behind her again.

Noah and the older man strode toward her like men on a mission.

She caught the screen door and hurried through it.

She rushed past the living room, where Chloë and Annie were tensely pretending to watch the ball game, past the dining room, where Eli was setting the table and watching the hall, past the bathroom, where Penelope met Brooke coming out.

"What happened?" Brooke asked in a low voice.

"I don't know, but I guess it's not good." Penelope stepped into the kitchen.

Sarah and June greeted her calmly enough, but Sarah pulled food out of the refrigerator and handed it to June, and June carried it into the dining room and put it on the table in silence. They seemed to be straining to listen for voices, for shots outside, for a calming voice. Like everyone in the house, they were doing one thing while anxious about another.

Sarah focused on Penelope. "Are you all right, dear?"

"I'm fine."

Penelope must not have sounded too convincing, for Brooke patted her shoulder. "Don't let Noah get to you," she said absently; then with sharpened apprehension she asked Sarah, "What happened?"

Sarah said, "Bao was right. There's an intruder on the grounds. They're searching now."

"There's a stranger walking up with Noah," Penelope told them.

The front screen door slammed. Footsteps traveled toward the kitchen.

"Anyone who's with Noah is surely not the intruder," June said.

They heard the rumble of voices from the living room, then from the dining room.

Sarah and June, Brooke and Penelope faced the entrance.

Penelope continued. "He's an older man, blue golf shirt, khakis, tall, great physique, dark hair streaked with gray . . ." Again some hint of memory niggled at her. "I really feel like I should know him. . . ."

Noah and the older man stepped into the kitchen.

Sarah's face lit up.

Brooke gasped.

Penelope wanted to sink through the floor.

She felt like she knew him?

Of course she did. She had paid money to see him in movie theaters and watched him on television.

He was famous. He was a movie star. He was Gavino Di Luca, handsome, gracefully aging, much-sought-after Gavino Di Luca, son of Sarah, father of Eli, Rafe, and Noah, and possibly the sexiest man alive.

Chapter 36

Nonna's eyes lit up. She opened her arms. "My darling boy!"

She and Gavino met in the middle of the kitchen and shared a hug that seemed genuinely full of affection.

Noah supposed it was. Certainly Nonna loved

her son. And Gavino was as shallow as a kiddie pool, but as much as he could love, he loved his mother.

Gavino kissed her cheeks, smiled, and said, "Did I surprise you?"

"So much! Why didn't you tell us you were coming?"

"I didn't want you to go to any extra trouble. You've barely recovered." His face sobered. "You are recovered, yes?"

"I'm fine," she said.

Gavino cocked his head inquiringly.

"Really," she said. "I'm fine. Don't worry, Gavino."

Eli wandered in from the dining room, scowling. He seemed to consider their father's arrival as suspicious as Noah did.

Chloë tagged along behind, her eyes as big as saucers and fixed on Gavino.

Penelope hadn't taken her gaze off him since he walked in the room.

Because Gavino was everything a woman wanted a movie star to be: handsome, personable, charming.

Even Noah had to admit Gavino had cornered the market on charming.

On the screen, Gavino projected charisma.

Yet film muted the range of his personality. In person, when he smiled, the air around him grew warm. When he frowned, the clouds covered the sun. When he hugged his mother, all the women sighed at the evidence of his filial devotion—and never mind that he stayed on location while Nonna recuperated from a broken arm and a concussion, too dedicated to his career to abandon his current film to stand vigil at his mother's bedside.

"I should have come home when you were attacked." Gavino frowned and put on his best guilty expression.

Noah and Eli nodded in agreement.

Nonna frowned fiercely. "Nonsense. What could you have done? You're not a doctor. And you had a movie to finish. It would have cost the production a fortune if you'd come home. Did you finish your film?"

"It's in the can," Gavino said with apparent satisfaction. "Number thirty-eight, and I've been the top talent in thirty of them. It's a body of work to be proud of!"

Noah slumped against the wall and rolled his eyes. Thank heavens his father didn't spend *too* much time inquiring after Nonna's health. Obviously, it was more important to boast of his worldly accomplishments.

"We are all proud of you." Nonna turned Gavino to face the rest of the people in the kitchen. "Look, you came home at the right time. Your aunt Annie and aunt June are visiting!"

Gavino released Nonna and hugged his aunts,

then went around the room to greet the others.

He met Chloë and hugged her, exclaiming about his new young daughter-in-law. He promised he would bring her mysteries to the attention of important people in the movie business; then he poked Eli in the ribs and teased him about his hurried marriage.

As usual, Eli did not crack a smile.

But then, none of Gavino's sons ever thought he was funny.

He met Brooke, and when she told him she was having a baby, he pretended to be delighted by the idea of being a grandfather. He insisted she sit at the table, telling her he knew from experience that she needed to sit while she could, because after the baby arrived rest would be in short supply.

Like he'd ever done a damned thing to care for any of his children.

And he met Penelope.

Noah watched her fall in love with Gavino Di Luca.

She blushed. She smiled. She fluttered her lashes.

Every female always did.

When Gavino looked into Penelope's eyes and listened to her stammer out her favorites of his roles, he acted as if he were hearing it for the first time. And he didn't seem to notice her tense jaw and stiff smile.

She was upset. Over Noah? And the way he had swept her off her feet and into a colossal orgasm, then walked away?

He hated to admit it, but he had one thing in common with his father: He was a jerk.

When Gavino had met everyone, and charmed the ones who didn't know him for the jerk-off he really was, Eli asked, "What are you really doing here, Dad?"

"Weren't you listening? I told you. I finished my movie. I came to see that my darling mother was okay." Gavino took Sarah's hand and kissed it.

Sarah beamed.

Penelope watched, hand on her chest as if trying to contain her sentiment.

Usually Noah managed not to care what his father said or did or where he said or did it.

But today . . . by God, today he wanted to shake Gavino until his teeth rattled.

"Don't have another role lined up? Getting a little too old for the screen?" Eli projected hostility and impatience in a way he saved for lazy farmhands—and Gavino.

"Dear." One word, one look from Sarah, and Eli subsided.

"It's no big deal, Mama. I know my boys have issues." Gavino kept his arm around Sarah and said to Eli, "I've auditioned for a couple of roles. Nothing's come through yet. But don't worry.

I've saved my money. I won't have to move in with you and Chloë . . . yet."

Eli couldn't have hidden his horror if he tried.

Gavino laughed out loud. "Don't worry, boy. If I never work again, I've got enough money to support myself." His amusement subsided only a little. "Of course, if I never worked again, I'd want to move back to Bella Terra."

Now Noah felt himself turn pale. Just what he needed was another parent from hell in town. His mother and his father, here together . . .

Gavino had a lot to answer for—and as always, he would escape unscathed, because when the going got tough, Gavino pulled a magician's trick and vanished every time.

The sooner, the better.

Noah's eyes narrowed at the thought.

"You're such a wonderful actor, Mr. Di Luca," Penelope said.

"Acting's not hard. You know what Spencer Tracy said—'Just memorize your lines, and don't bump into the furniture.' " Gavino laughed heartily.

So did everyone else . . . except Eli and Noah. They'd heard it before.

"What kind of roles are you up for, Mr. Di Luca?" Chloë asked.

"One for a forty-year-old with a family. One for a seventy-year-old estranged from his family." Gavino took a breath that expanded his impressive chest. "I have a broad range I can play. The trick is convincing the directors."

"I think you could play 'estranged from your family' like you were born to it," Noah said.

Annie rolled her wheelchair past him.

He jumped. "Ow!"

"I'm sorry, dear." Annie looked meaningfully at him. "Did I run over your foot?"

Stop upsetting your grandmother, she meant.

Penelope glared at him as if he were a hardened criminal. Because she was already infatuated with his father. He wanted to tell her, *You would be better off in love with me.*

But probably not, because . . . He touched his tightly buttoned shirt collar.

Gavino's gaze followed his gesture. "Auditioning for a role as the Amish farmer?" he asked.

Noah smiled tightly and took his hand away. The death he carried gnawed at his mind. He couldn't forget; every moment he was edgy, as if the silver studs of the dog collar were stealing bits of his sanity.

His gaze sliced to Penelope.

Every moment his need to live one last, grand celebration of life grew greater, his scruples less firm.

She must have felt his eyes on her, for she looked at him, and for a long moment, her gaze clung.

Then she looked away.

And he remembered her offer again. A quickie . . .

No, never. Long, slow, desperate hours of lovemaking, on a bed, on a chair, on a desk, in a tree. Wherever they were, that was the place they should love . . . but never quickly. He wanted to spend days getting to know her body again.

He *had* to think of something else.

"Gavino, I didn't hear your car pull up," Nonna said.

"I had the driver drop me off at the end of the driveway so I could walk up. I've been on a plane all day. I needed my exercise"—he patted his flat belly—"and I wanted to see the place. I almost didn't get to. Since when do we have guards stopping visitors and demanding ID?" Apparently that rankled; Gavino didn't like not being recognized.

"Since Nonna was attacked and people in Bella Terra started getting murdered," Eli answered.

"Murder." Gavino's eyes narrowed the way they did when he played a police detective. "Really. No wonder the guard ran after that guy who was talking to Noah."

That did it. The tension in the house rose to break-a-sweat level.

"The intruder was talking to you?" Eli asked. "Who is he? What was he doing here?"

Noah heard voices from outside. He held up his hand and listened.

Every head turned toward the back door.

Rafe and Bao came in, both covered with dirt, both scowling.

Brooke sighed in relief and went to hug her husband.

As Rafe hugged her back, Nonna asked, "Are you both all right?"

"We're fine." Bao wiped furiously at her face. "But we didn't get him. The bastard disappeared like a rat down a hole."

Rafe looked over the top of Brooke's head. "Bao was right. Someone was watching. Someone with impressive professional skills. He used them to get onto the property, and when he was sighted, he used those skills to get off the property without a trace." Whipping his head around, he glared at Noah. "You were talking to him. Shoemaker said you two were *talking* like you knew each other. Shoemaker said this thug raised his fist to you. Is this it? Is this what you know?"

Chapter 37

Noah looked around the kitchen. Every eye was focused on him: Nonna and the aunts were anxious, Brooke and Chloë inquisitive, Gavino puzzled, but his brothers . . . they were accusatory.

So Noah told the truth. Not all of the truth, but

the truth. "The intruder—he accosted me as I walked down the driveway. He's one of the gang that smashed that one guy's hands." He looked directly at Rafe. "He's one of the gang who broke into your home. He's fast, he's trained, he's dangerous"—and now Noah decided to see what he could find out from his father—"and he's after something we hold that he cannot have."

"I'd say that was obvious!" Rafe snapped.

Noah sliced his gaze toward their father, then back to Rafe.

Rafe looked startled, as if the idea that their father might be involved had never occurred to him.

But Noah could easily make a case to his brothers that Gavino's arrival at this particular time signaled a reason to be suspicious.

The moment dangled like a shiny bauble, enticing Rafe to grab at it.

But before he could, June said in a soothing tone, "My polenta casserole is ready to come out of the oven."

"I brought a fresh strawberry pie." Chloë walked to the refrigerator, opened it, and removed the decadent red dessert.

"I can't wait!" Annie said brightly. "Let's all sit down to eat. We can talk then."

Ah, yes. The women thought to ease the tension with food.

Well, why not? It always worked.

"Wash up, dears," Nonna said to Rafe and Bao.

They nodded and went to the kitchen sink.

Nonna shooed the company toward the dining room.

Noah waited until Penelope walked past, then joined her, his hand resting lightly on the small of her back. It was an instinct, a claiming, and one he noted his brothers also utilized with their wives. Not that Penelope was his wife, but . . . if life was fair, she would be.

His chair was on the back side of the table against the cabinets. He led her there, then held out the chair next to his.

She looked at him, and the memory of his forceful claiming was in her resentful eyes.

"Please." He indicated the seat, and tried to look trustworthy and not at all insane.

He didn't have his father's acting skills, but he must have pulled it off, because she seated herself next to him, although she turned her face away from him.

June brought the yellow ceramic casserole dish and with a flourish placed it on the table. Steam rose in the air, and the fragrance of tomatoes, mushrooms, Italian sausage, and Parmesan rose like the memory of good times past.

Everyone relaxed, and sighed, and exclaimed; then June served spoonfuls of heaven and Nonna passed the salads.

For a few minutes, all was quiet as Annie said a brief grace thanking God that the whole family could be together again; then the silence was broken by the clatter of forks and the muffled exclamations of pleasure.

Noah waited until the first pangs of hunger had been eased before he said, “Dad, we’ve had some problems since you last checked in.”

“Which is why you should leave,” Eli said. “You don’t want to be involved in any problems.”

Shut up. But Noah didn’t say a word.

“I know someone attacked Mama. How much worse could the problems get?” Gavino leaned back in his chair and steepled his fingers, a move he’d learned while playing a judge in one of his most popular movies, a remake of an old Tracy/Hepburn romance.

“It’s all about Nonno’s bottle of wine,” Noah said.

Gavino stopped faking concern and got real. His hands dropped to the arms of his chair. He gripped them tightly and leaned forward. “Papa’s wine? Someone’s looking for Papa’s wine?”

“That’s right. Several someones,” Noah said.

“Joseph Bianchin, for one,” Rafe said.

Noah wanted to tell Eli and Rafe to let him handle this. But they had as much right to disdain their father as he did. In addition, Noah was their baby brother, and they didn’t trust him to handle anything. And, of course . . . they had no idea who his mother was.

If they knew that, they'd have more respect.

But his father knew who his mother was, so Noah said, "It seems the bottle of wine probably contains a fortune in lost pink diamonds."

"Son of a bitch," Gavino whispered. "Is that what it was all about?"

Noah thought that was probably the first unrehearsed line his father had given since the day he turned three. In an innocent tone, he asked, "What was *what* all about, Dad?"

Noah saw him snap back into actor mode. "The attack on your grandmother, of course."

Liar.

"How did you find out about the diamonds?" Gavino asked.

"The Internet," Chloë said.

"How did *she* . . . ?" Gavino whispered.

"She looked it up on the Internet," Eli repeated. "You know, the Internet? Where your fan club is based?"

Only Noah understood what his father meant. He wasn't questioning Chloë's abilities to do the research. He was wondering how, twenty-nine years ago, Liesbeth figured out where the diamonds had disappeared. "The information was always available, Dad," Noah said. "It might not have been easy, but as long as you were willing to do research in newspaper archives and old travel records, it was possible to connect the famous winemaker Massimo Bruno to the thief who was always hanging around when the jewels vanished."

Penelope faced Noah now. "Eighty years is a long time to remember lost diamonds exist, much less search for them."

"Throughout history, stolen treasure has captivated the imagination. People become obsessed. They search for ships' treasures and buried treasure and lost gold mines." Chloë spoke with the assurance of a writer who studied the human psyche and used it in her novels.

"In this case, where the diamonds that vanished are from one extremely valuable necklace owned by dispossessed Russian nobles who fled the 1917 revolution . . . the diamonds are inherently romantic. And when they're big . . ." Brooke tempted them with the concept.

"Big diamonds definitely command attention," Chloë said, "and the diamonds in the Propov necklace ranged in size from one-half carat to a six-point-eight-carat pink diamond, the Beating Heart, which has an inclusion that when viewed through a jeweler's loupe looks like a red heart that appears to pulse."

Noah pressed his fingers to the artery that pulsed in his throat.

How appropriate that the Beating Heart should be the death of him.

Turning, he caught Penelope's gaze on him, on the way he took his own pulse, and once again he thought she saw him all too clearly, for he appeared to puzzle her. . . .

He smiled and used his hand to pick up his knife and smear a roasted garlic clove on a piece of Parmesan-pepper bread. He offered it to her. "In this family, if you don't eat enough garlic, the rumor goes around that you're a vampire."

"We can't have that. Thank you." She took it, but she didn't smile back, leaving him to wonder whether she was still angry or if his absentminded gesture had given her food for thought when he preferred to keep her firmly in the dark . . . with everyone else.

Eli lifted Chloë's left hand.

Chloë wiggled her fingers. An impressive pink diamond flashed in its platinum setting.

Penelope did a double take. "Wow," she said in an awestruck voice.

"This is not quite a two-carat diamond," Eli said.

Now Gavino said, "Wow . . ." He nodded slowly. "So this Beating Heart diamond is more than three times that size?"

"Even without the history attached to it, with its clarity and size, it's worth probably"—as he thought, Eli screwed up his forehead—"probably five million. In an auction with rabid buyers interested in such a unique stone, and with the other stones associated with it sold at the same time, I bet the price could go as high as fifteen or twenty million."

"Dollars?" Rafe asked.

"No, clamshells. Of course, dollars!" Eli said.

"I can't even imagine such a stone—or such an amount of money." Penelope shook her head. "It's haunting to think that that bottle of wine containing those stones could be somewhere in this house."

"I wish the location of Anthony's bottle would haunt me," Nonna said. "Then this whole terrible situation would be finished."

"If you find the bottle, what will you do with it?" Penelope asked.

A silence fell over the table.

Then the argument broke out.

Everyone wanted to open the bottle and see if the diamonds were inside.

Nonna thought they should give the diamonds to a museum.

Rafe and Brooke agreed.

Chloë wanted to examine the big diamond through a jeweler's loupe and see whether the heart really did beat.

Eli wanted to taste the wine.

Throughout the quarrel, Noah smiled benignly, and covertly observed his father.

Gavino's actor's face was a showcase for false emotion, but now, while he thought no one was watching . . . he showed the real thing. In his expression, Noah saw the memory of Liesbeth's seduction and the lies she had told, all with the intention of getting pregnant and placing her spy into Anthony Di Luca's home. Gavino could not countenance what had happened in his past, yet there was no other explanation: He had been set up, enticed, his sperm taken and used for procreation. He had been a fool of incredible proportions.

More important for Noah—Gavino believed Noah knew nothing about Liesbeth.

Now was the time to enlighten him. With a smile, Noah leaned across the table toward his father and said, "Seems as if there should have been an easier way, doesn't it, Dad?"

For the space of five heartbeats, Gavino didn't comprehend.

Then he turned to Noah so quickly his neck popped. He saw the knowledge in Noah's eyes, and the accusation. And Gavino did what he always did when facing a personal crisis.

He ran.

Pulling his phone out of his pocket, he glanced at it, then pushed back his chair. "Excuse me. This is a very important phone call, and I've got to take it." He moved quickly toward the hall, turning back only to say with a smile, "Mama, I think maybe I have nailed one of those roles!"

Chapter 38

Noah watched his father walk away from him the way he'd always walked away from him and, in a single violent gesture, threw his napkin on the table. "Excuse me for a minute." He shoved his chair back and headed after him. As Gavino swung open the front screen door, Noah grabbed his shoulder. "Oh, no, Dad. Not this time. You know stuff I need to hear."

Gavino twisted out of Noah's grasp. "She's in town, isn't she?" His brown eyes were narrowed, intent . . . scared.

"My mother?"

"Liesbeth."

"Oh, yeah."

"Then I'm getting the hell out." Gavino shoved his way out the door and onto the porch.

Night had fallen. The porch lamp was on. The windows cast squares of light into the shadows, but ultimately . . . the shadows won.

It seemed to Noah they always did.

Grasping Gavino by the shirtfront, he shoved him against the wall. "Tell me all about your affair, Dad. I need to know the truth—or at least your version of the truth."

Gavino glared into Noah's eyes, but he didn't struggle. "I don't know anything."

Noah tightened his grip. "Look at me. I'm your

son. And I'm her son. She's in Bella Terra for me." Taking his hands off his father, he unbuttoned his collar and bared his throat. "And I've got a bomb waiting to blow off my head."

Gavino's outraged gaze dropped to the dog collar, then lifted to Noah's face, and his horror seemed genuine.

In this case, it probably was.

"When does it explode?" Gavino asked.

"Not yet," Noah assured him. "If I don't find that damned bottle, I'll be dead in eleven days, at exactly three thirty-seven p.m. So tell me what you know."

Gavino sucked in a long breath; then, like a tortured prisoner, he gave up the information. "She planned everything. Our meeting. The story she fed me, of how she was an international spy. My seduction. She played me, and then . . . she talked about Dad's bottle of wine. I couldn't figure out how she knew, or why she cared. Why would a spy give a damn about my father's bottle of wine? The glamour was wearing off, nothing was adding up, and I got the hell out right before I was supposed to help her pull off a job."

"You . . . left her hanging?" Gavino's foolishness made Noah breathless.

"Yes." Gavino looked both frightened and defiant.

"Why?"

"Come on, son. I'm famous." Gavino tapped

his nose. "I've got a good instinct for when someone wants to use me."

"You're not as stupid as you would like us to believe." It was a revelation to Noah.

Gavino puffed his chest. "No one stays on top in Hollywood by being stupid." Then his pride collapsed. "I guess I am, though, because nine months later, there she was, her and an infant—you—and two of her goons in the middle of the night, standing in my trailer on a movie set on studio grounds." Gavino thrust his face back at Noah. "Do you know what movie studio security is like? We were filming the last scene of the Wilder series. It was a closed set. We couldn't leave. No one got on without a pass. And there she was, handing you over to me." Gavino shoved back at Noah.

Noah let him go.

"I took you. Of course I did. I didn't know if you were mine, but I wasn't about to argue, not with those two black-haired boys of hers grinning at me." Anger and humiliation fought for supremacy on Gavino's face. "But they weren't done. She pulled out a metal rod and plugged it in. She got the end of it red-hot—and while those two bastards held me down and smothered my screams, she branded me."

"She *branded* you?" Noah could hardly believe it.

"With the Poopon coat of arms."

"Propov," Noah corrected.

"Whatever. She branded me on the front of my hip, right on the bone." Gavino touched the spot as if it still hurt. "Ever since, I haven't been able to do a nude scene without body makeup."

Noah bit down on a reluctant grin. Trust his father to find the real tragedy of the matter.

Gavino had given up his information. Now it was his turn to ask questions. "How did *you* find out about her?"

"She came for me."

"Of course she did." Gavino pushed his hands through his head of salt-and-pepper hair in a gesture reminiscent of his despair in the remake of *Death Takes a Holiday*. "So she got pregnant on purpose. To plant her child in the middle of my family and get her hands on that bottle of wine. That's Machiavellian! I mean, it makes a little more sense now, with the diamonds in play, but—why not just come to the house and steal it? Her gang is a bunch of what?"

"Expert thieves."

"Right! They could have done it years ago. They could have been in and out and no one would have ever known. No one would have been hurt. Dad would have blamed the Bianchins."

"So why didn't they steal the bottle?" Noah wondered.

Chapter 39

For the first time, Noah really put his mind to the matter of *why*. "I know Liesbeth has lusted after those diamonds her whole life, looked on their recovery as the restoration of Propov honor. This spring, Bianchin tried to get his hands on the bottle, and that put things in motion. But I think perhaps she took his involvement as a sign." Noah tried to follow all the threads of logic to their rational conclusion. "She's old enough. Considerably older than you, Dad, which makes the whole affair even more revolting."

"Yes, yes, everyone knows I'm easy."

Noah wanted to heartily agree, but no matter how much satisfaction he got, he didn't have time to wrangle with his father. The clock was ticking. He *had* to get this figured out. "I wonder if she's retiring."

"How in the hell does a woman with a family like that retire?"

"She disappears off the face of the earth—with the diamonds. In fact, I wonder"—Noah looked down in to the valley where the lights of Bella Terra twinkled—"if she has told her people what's really in that bottle?"

Gavino started laughing, low at first, then with increasing volume and delight. "You've nailed it, son. The rest of them are after a valuable bottle of wine. She's after the diamonds. Not to sell—to restore her family's rightful honor. No one else knows about the diamonds—or at least she hopes they don't—and as soon as the Beating Heart is in her hands, she is gone and the others have to fend for themselves."

"Yes. Which, if they put her training to use, they should do very well." Every time Noah had mentioned the diamonds, told Liesbeth that the rest of the family wanted to recover them merely to sell them, she had denied that with remarkable tranquillity. Noah had assumed her pride and affection for the gang blinded her to their greed.

But no. Liesbeth was far too astute for that. Years ago, she had figured out where the Propov diamonds were hidden. She had kept that information to herself, and she'd been biding her time. She was taking those diamonds with her into retirement. "No wonder she wants me to take over the gang. She makes the plans. She's the brains of the operation. Without her, they'll dwindle to a petty band of thieves, get caught, and go to jail."

"That's it." Gavino glanced at his Rolex, then clapped Noah on the shoulder. "I've got to call for my car and get a plane ticket, because I am getting the hell out of Dodge. Wish you could come with me."

"I could, but how would you explain it when my head blew off my shoulders?"

Gavino cocked his head and studied Noah's collar. "Liesbeth really put a bomb in there?"

"So she said. She included a camera and a microphone, too."

Gavino's start of terror provided Noah a great deal of amusement. "She can see me? She heard everything we said?"

"I disabled the camera and the microphone before I put it on."

"Damn it, son! You scared me to death." Gavino put his hand over his heart. "I was about to sprint down the driveway. But I suppose *you* wouldn't say all that stuff in front of her, either."

"No. She doesn't need to know what I know. I probably don't have a chance of surviving, but I'm still going to try my damnedest." Because if he did, if somehow this whole mess turned out and his life suddenly became normal . . . he would court Penelope; he would build her a house; he would shower her with jewels and possessions; he would give her children; he would grovel at her feet.

Most of all, he would love her for all the rest of their days.

He wished he could see beyond the bleak days he now lived, but he had so long lived with death that he couldn't even glimpse that shining future.

Gavino pulled out his phone. "I wish I could

tell you what Dad did with his wine, but I haven't got the foggiest idea. Have you looked in the house?"

Noah thought about the endless searches they'd conducted. "Gee, Dad, no. We didn't think of that."

Absently, Gavino said, "It's worth a try." Into the phone, he said, "Stephanie, darling, I need my car now, and get me on a plane out of here. I don't care where. First plane out. Yes. Yes. Good. Thank you, darling." He hung up and saw Noah looking at him. "Oh, stop glaring at me. Stephanie is my assistant, and she's about a hundred years old. I'm going in to say my good-byes. Coming?"

"No, I don't want to listen to all the ladies weeping over your departure." He didn't want to see Penelope's disappointment. Feeling jealous of the woman he loved and his father was just too awkward. Besides, for once in his life his father had done him some good, and now Noah wanted to sit here and think about how he could bring this new information into play.

In less than fifteen minutes, a black Town Car with darkly tinted windows pulled up to the bottom of the steps, and Gavino came out of the house whistling. When he saw Noah leaning against the porch post, he composed his expression into one that was suitably grave. He flung an arm around Noah's shoulders and hugged him. "Take care of yourself, son."

It was not like Gavino Di Luca could help being vain, feckless, and irresponsible, and as long as Noah expected nothing from him, he was never disappointed. So he flung an arm around Gavino and hugged him back. "I'll do my best."

"Okay, I'm leaving." Gavino pulled away, then stood at the top of the stairs, unmoving. "Son, when Liesbeth made contact with you—how did she know she would be able to use you?"

"I was young. I was stupid. I wasn't suspicious like you, Dad. I made it easy for her."

Gavino turned to face him. "She's not going to let you die."

Noah was surprised that Gavino allowed himself to think about the disagreeable possibility of death. "I would beg to disagree."

"No. I not only am good at sensing when people want to use me. I'm also good at reading people. In my profession, jobs depend on that ability. Your mother is fanatically loyal to her family." Gavino sounded very sure of himself.

And Noah wanted to believe him. He really did. But he knew too much. "She killed to take over as the head of the gang."

"Sure. If someone isn't good for the Poopon family—"

Noah started to correct him, then figured Gavino knew his lines well enough to deliberately make the mistake.

Gavino continued. "—she'll weed him out without conscience. But she doesn't kill indiscriminately, and you're her son. That means something to her."

"I doubt that." What she saw when she looked at him was the same thing she saw when she looked at Gavino all those years ago—a tool to be used.

"I glimpse a lot of her in you. When you look at me, you've got a cold, clear gaze. You evaluate ruthlessly. Your will is formidable, and while you hide your intelligence, it's there for anyone with eyes to see." Gavino nodded curtly. "Yes. Your outer shell might for the most part look Di Luca, but scratch the surface, and you're her son. She won't kill you—but she will try to bend you to her will."

"I'm bent. I'm doing exactly what she wants. I'm trying to find that bottle."

"What else does she want from you? That's the question you need to ask yourself."

Noah was silent. He knew what else his mother wanted from him. But even to save his life, he wasn't going to take over her gang.

To do that, he would have to kill Hendrik, and once he walked down Murder Road, there was no turning back.

"One more thing," Gavino said. "If Liesbeth is in town—get my mother out of here."

Noah knew the right answer for that. "I brought

in June and Annie to do just that. She says no, but I have hopes."

"Good. If anyone can pry her out of this house, they can. All right." Gavino saluted as he ran down the stairs to his car. "Until next time."

Noah watched his father greet his driver, get in, and, with a wave of the hand, drive off.

Noah lifted a hand in farewell.

Would he ever see his father again? Only God knew that.

God. And Liesbeth.

He wrapped his hand around the killer dog collar and wondered—did he wear a time bomb wrapped around his neck? Or was his father right? Was this a ruse?

Behind him, the screen door creaked open.

Noah turned a little too fast—he was jumpy, on edge—and saw Penelope silhouetted against the light.

Her purse strap crossed her chest. She held her car keys in her hand. "I'm sneaking out early."

No.

She continued. "I've got a long day tomorrow."

No, please. "Surely Rafe and Brooke aren't such slave drivers that you have to go home at"—he glanced at his watch—"eight?"

"I'm not working for them tomorrow. I've got other stuff to take care of." She smiled politely, not a real smile at all, and she didn't look him in the eyes.

Was that the expression he'd been wearing lately? Pained and lonely, as if human contact created more trouble than it was worth?

Or was she furious at him over his caveman drag-her-out-of-the-house-by-the-hair routine?

He waited until she was even with him at the top of the stairs, and put out his hand to hold her arm. "You know you can call on me anytime. I'm here for you."

"Oh, can I?" She turned to face him. "And what happens when I do? Do we talk? No. You get offended by having me around. Do we avoid talk and simply indulge in mindless sex? No. You don't have time. No, Noah, you are not here for me! So don't lie to make yourself feel better. I'm not in the flattering mood."

Chapter 40

Joseph Bianchin sat in his bedroom, his laptop on a tray before him, studying the material he'd uncovered on Liesbeth and her gang. Not that he was absolutely sure he had uncovered them—Liesbeth hadn't been exaggerating when she said they could change appearances at will.

But he'd used the information she'd given him as a starting point, looking up robberies of expensive jewels, exquisite art, and bottles of fine wine, and he thought he had positive identification in at least five different thefts over the last ten years. He started his investigation with the Smit family's body type—they were all tall, strong framed, and that physical ID was hard to disguise. He examined eyewitness accounts of suspects and hacked into security videos.

It appeared Liesbeth's gang struck infrequently and without warning. Their usual modus operandi consisted of stealing valuables as they were moved. But occasionally they robbed the châteaux of France, the fortresses of Morocco, the mansions of South Africa. He hadn't found any evidence of their working in the Far East—again, they were tall, a trait difficult to disguise—nor had he uncovered any of their jobs in the United States.

Was their attack on him and his treasure their first foray into the country?

What a privilege, indeed.

He didn't know what he could do with this information. They gave him no freedom, allowed no phone calls, and if he was forced to admit the truth, he had no friends he could summon for help.

But in Bella Terra, that idiot chief of police ran the station downtown. Joseph didn't think Bryan DuPey could do a thing against Liesbeth's gang, except probably get himself killed, but he had sent out e-mails demanding to be rescued.

He got answers, too. Police Chief DuPey said he would look into Joseph's allegations that he had been kidnapped, while at the same time politely indicating that Joseph should go for a psychiatric evaluation. The FBI sent him a letter with a form for him to fill out and promised him that once he had done that, they would jump on the case in a mere six to eight weeks.

He was Joseph Bianchin, damn it. He was rich and important, and he needed help. The law enforcement agencies were required to pay attention to him.

He had sent further, more sternly worded e-mail listing the important people he knew and acidly suggesting DuPey and the FBI check his references and mount a rescue immediately.

He awaited their response, and he made his plans.

He knew Liesbeth's gang of hoodlums hadn't found his bottle of wine yet. That was the one bright spot in his current existence: that Massimo's wine had evaded her as thoroughly as it had evaded Joseph. Not that he didn't want them to find it. He did, for when they got their grubby mitts on that precious bottle, he would take it from under their noses and make his break. That bottle rightfully belonged to him.

At the same time . . . to know that Anthony Di Luca had made an international gang of accomplished thieves look like fools . . . that was grand.

Not that Joseph remembered that damned

Anthony Di Luca with any fondness, but in the end Joseph would cheer on a local rustic before that mob of sophisticated louts.

Lifting his head, he listened to the new noises within the house.

Even when he was gone, his team of housekeepers arrived to clean. He recognized the sounds of their industry now: the vacuum cleaner, the flush of toilets, the occasional sharp tone of that low-class Marino woman.

With their usual disregard for those who they considered lesser beings, Liesbeth's gang had apparently decided the housekeepers were no threat, for they locked him in his room, then allowed the housekeepers into his mansion. He thought about throwing a fit to alert them to his presence, but the housekeepers *were* no threat—if he managed a moment alone to tell that Marino woman he was being held hostage, she'd tell him he deserved worse. He had made enemies in this town; no one would put a hand out to get him out of this situation.

She had the attitude of a woman whose high opinion of herself far outweighed her station in life. But housekeeping services in this town were expensive and seldom reliable, and Marino always handled everything without bothering him about it. And really, what did he care about Marino and her attitude? She was a servant.

No, the real reason he didn't try to get the

attention of the housekeepers was because he remembered Hendrik's big fist smashing through the canvas painting and into the wall, and he hadn't a doubt Hendrik would love to do the same to Joseph's face.

Surely his last round of e-mail to the authorities would bear fruit soon.

With a wary glance toward the closed door, he moved from his investigation of Liesbeth's gang to an Internet site he had bookmarked: Pressure Points for Self-Defense. Every time he was alone, he studied the moves, because the first time he used a pressure point on Liesbeth, he'd better get it right.

The sound of the key in the lock made him start. He slammed his computer shut as a petite young female, dark haired and dark eyed, opened the door and sidled in. Quietly she shut it behind her, and cleared her throat. "Mr. Bianchin? If I could speak to you for a minute?"

She'd startled him, and he snapped, "What the hell do you want?"

She took a few steps, just far enough to come across the threshold. Her forehead puckered with anxiety. "I . . . I . . . I just need to talk to you, to tell you—"

He recognized her. "Aren't you that girl who was at the gate?"

She looked relieved. "That's right."

"How the hell did you get in here?" God, he

was sick and tired of people showing up when they wanted, doing what they wanted, without his permission or his consent.

"I came in with the housekeeping crew." She wore worn jeans, a dark T-shirt, and a light and careful application of makeup.

"You work for that Marino woman?"

"Not . . . really."

"Then why the hell are you here?"

She walked over to stand before him, and in an aggravated voice said, "Because I need to talk to you."

Another smart-mouthed woman. He didn't have to put up with this. "Don't take that tone with me. I pay your wages!"

Her spine snapped upright. Her eyes narrowed. She said coolly, "Actually, you don't. I am not part of the cleaning crew. My name is Penelope Caldwell, and I came in with them so I could *talk* to you—since you wouldn't let me in, in any normal way."

He should have yelled at her, slapped her down for her insolence, thrown her out the door. Hell, he could have practiced one of those pressure-point moves on her to see how well it worked. But . . . there was something about this girl. She had power, she knew he was here, and she wanted something. Perhaps she was his ticket out. If he could strike a bargain . . . "What do you want?"

Reaching into the pocket of her apron, she pulled out a photo and placed it on the tray in front of him. "Do you recognize her?"

He barely glanced at it. "Of course I do. I'm not senile. That's the Alonso woman."

"Yes. My mother." The girl waited like that was supposed to mean something to him.

"Yes. So?" This girl held his attention. In her, he caught glimpses of someone in his past. Not the Alonso woman, though. Someone else . . .

"She had an affair with you when she was eighteen, Penelope said. "I'm the result."

He stared at her without comprehension.

"I'm your daughter," she clarified.

Rage rose in him, the same rage that had accompanied him every time he thought of his childlessness—and how much the people of Bella Terra sneered at him. Did this girl imagine she could pull off this scam? He was far too canny for that. Throwing back his head, he burst into derisive laughter. "Pull the other leg. I've never fathered a child in my life. Slow sperm, they told me."

She flushed, a gradual build from beneath her collar up over her cheeks and up to her hairline. "Slow sperm doesn't mean no sperm. I'm your daughter."

He glanced down at the photograph, then up at the girl's distinctive features. "What's your name again?"

"Penelope Caldwell."

"What happened to Alonso?"

"I've been married."

"Divorced already?"

"Widowed."

"That's a shame." He didn't really care. "You don't look like your mother."

"Yes, I do."

"Not the way I remember her."

"I'm now ten years older than she was when you seduced her." Clearly, this Penelope had judged him and found him wanting.

The rage rose hotter, higher. "You don't need to make it sound like she was unwilling."

"You were over fifty. She was eighteen. That's . . . disgusting." Her lip curled in scorn. For him.

She had quite the attitude, considering who and what she was—illegitimate, the daughter of an easily seduced whore, and a scam artist trying to get in his pocket. "The whole thing is bullshit. I told the Alonso woman that if she was pregnant, she was to bring the child to me and I would raise it." Although . . . when he'd seen this girl at the gate, he had thought she looked familiar.

"She didn't like you," Penelope said. "She didn't want you to raise her child."

"Don't be stupid." It was a great line, but—"I'm rich!"

"I know. For all the good it's done you."

He didn't like the contemptuous tone in her

voice. “Don’t pretend that my money isn’t the reason you’re here.”

“I don’t have to pretend anything. I’ve got a degree in interior design and a good job. I don’t *need* you. And from the look of the folks downstairs in your study, I’d say you don’t need any more hangers-on.”

He’d forgotten. He wanted to bargain with her to get out of here.

Yes. He should say something about his uninvited guests. He meant to . . . but it stuck in his craw to be the focus of her pity—especially since she really *did* look eerily familiar.

“You’re my only surviving relative, and unless I’m much mistaken, I’m your only surviving relative, so”—Penelope pulled a padded envelope out of her other pocket and handed it to him—“here.”

“What’s this?” He viewed the envelope with suspicion. It was addressed to him.

“It’s a DNA test. You and I scrape the inside lining of our mouths with the cotton swab, seal it in a plastic tube, and send it to the lab.” She saw the expression on his face and smiled kindly, as if he were senile and she felt sorry for him. Or something. “You don’t have to do it,” she said. “You can pretend I don’t exist. You can pretend we never had this conversation. But”—taking the swab out of her sealed package, she ran it over the inside of her mouth, put it into the tube, sealed it, and held it out to him—"here's my DNA."

He sat there, gripping the arms of his chair, and stared at her, captured by a memory so old and precious he barely recognized it. In Penelope, he had caught a glimpse of someone else. Not her mother, but his. His mother, dead for seventy-two years.

The poor woman had been abused by his father, treated like a beast who had failed in her primary function, for despite repeated pregnancies, she had borne only one child who lived, and that was Joseph.

He had been cherished by her, loved and cosseted, her little boy. Her baby. She had stepped between him and his father when his father got too free with the belt; she had told off his bigger cousins when they teased so much they made him cry; she had been his bulwark against the world. And when she died . . .

He had forgotten her.

He had to. His father told him to. Told him life was tough and only the tough survived.

And he did survive. In fact, he thrived.

But now he was looking into this girl's face . . . and his mother's eyes stared back at him.

In slow motion, he reached out and took the tube she offered.

"Okay. I wrote a check to pay for the lab work. So fill out the forms. It takes two days after the lab receives the package to get an answer one way or another. You can access the results online, and the lab will send you something official through the mail, too. I'll wait to hear from you. Or not." She tossed her head, turned away from him, and headed toward the door.

"Wait!" he called. Damn it. He should tell her about Liesbeth's gang. But to do that was to admit he had lost control of his life, and that humiliation he could not bear. It was worse than being kept captive in his own house. Because he thought . . . Well, perhaps she was . . . his daughter. "Where will you be?"

"My job is in town."

"Doing what?"

"I told you. I'm an interior designer." She seemed very proud of that fact. "I'm redesigning one of the old Victorian houses for Rafe and Brooke Di Luca."

"What?" He came to his feet. His computer slid off his lap, but he didn't care. All he cared about was halting this outrage. "You can't work for the Di Lucas."

She swiveled slowly to face him. "I beg your pardon?"

He shook his gnarled finger at her. "If you are my child, you'll have nothing to do with those thieves, those—"

She laughed. "It's a little late for that kind of discipline . . . Father." She laughed again—

laughed at *him*—and walked out, leaving Joseph shaking with rage and something else. Shock, perhaps.

Or perhaps . . . an old hope resurrected.

Chapter 41

Downstairs in the den, Grieta sat staring at her computer screen. "Liesbeth, we're going to have to kill the old man."

Liesbeth looked up from the panel of her tapestry. "Why's that, dear?"

"Every so often, I check what he's been up to." Grieta swiveled her desk chair and faced the room. "He's found us."

"What do you mean, he's found us?" Hendrik paused his latest computer game, Zombie Zombat.

"He went poking around the Internet, looking for unsolved robberies of note, and by God, he managed to isolate a few of our jobs. The old fox is smart." Grieta sounded admiring. "Smarter than the police, that's for sure."

"Not that smart if he didn't realize you'd put a worm on his hard drive and are diverting his e-mail." Klaas's voice was slurred by the foam inserts he had stuffed in his cheeks.

"All that means is, he doesn't realize what I'm capable of," Grieta said.

"I'll be glad to get rid of him. His wrinkled,

sour face always looks like he bit into a bug." Hendrik tossed his computer tablet aside and headed for the door. "I'll do him now."

"No!" Liesbeth slashed him with the single word. "Bodies smell."

Hendrik didn't so much as turn back. It was more of an off-kilter swivel fueled by sampling too much of Joseph's fine wine cellar. "He already smells."

Liesbeth recognized the danger signs. The boy was bored by his enforced leisure and resentful of her continued dominance over their little family. She wanted to pat his pudgy cheeks and tell him it was all right, that soon he'd see action aplenty and have his chance to prove himself worthy of the name Propov.

She looked around.

The once mighty Propov family had dwindled to so few, and none of them were concerned about this all too common struggle between Liesbeth and Hendrik.

Twenty-two-year-old Brigetta was calibrating the gunpowder to load into hollow-point bullets just in case they got into a gun battle with law enforcement wearing bulletproof vests. She was intense, a proper Propov, who said the family needed to be prepared at all times.

Forty-five-year-old Grieta worked the computer, a faint smile on her lips. "I'm erasing all the evidence Bianchin found. If the old man could figure it out, so could Interpol. I mean, they're incompetent, but let's not make their job any easier."

Thirty-two-year-old Klaas stood in front of a gold-framed, full-length mirror and stuffed small buckwheat pillows on his shoulders under his shirt, giving him a hunched appearance that worked well with his puffed cheeks.

Fifty-year-old Rutger relaxed in a chair and read a book taken from Joseph's library on famous historical robberies, occasionally putting down the book and using his tablet computer to do research. Catching Liesbeth's gaze on him, he shrugged. "A bottle of wine is nice, but I think the next job should be something more exciting." He lifted the book. "Maybe a private art collection stocked with stolen art. Then they can hardly complain to the authorities, can they?"

Liesbeth smiled at him.

They were good children, intelligent and practical, visionaries in their own way, and each of them knew he or she didn't have the chops to be the leader.

For so many years, she had pinned her hopes on Hendrik. She had believed he would mature, observe her as she planned their jobs and learn from her skills, and move into the position of director without undue upheaval.

Hendrik was now forty-two, and more and more she had begun to suspect he would be their ruin.

Yet . . . she had done her time. She had brought them this far. The little group either flew or they faltered, and she would not be around to see whether they fell. "With a little twist of the arm, I can get information out of Joseph about the Di Lucas. He's not very brave."

"I thought that was what your son was for." Hendrik strolled closer to Liesbeth and wiggled his fingers and his eyebrows. "Information was the reason you spread your legs for the actor, you said, and gave birth to his child who we trapped so neatly."

"Noah will be useful soon enough. The timer is ticking, and I think that sooner or later, he'll surrender the bottle. Its value is worth our time. But for now, we have to take care with him." She smoothed the tapestry in her lap. She had created the glorious golden story of the Propov family in canvas and thread, and this was the last of eight panels to be carefully folded and stored in a trunk, and transported to her new home in the Crimea. "He has morals."

In unison, her entire family said, "Ooh, morals."

Liesbeth plunged her long, sharp needle once more into the tapestry. "He'll die rather than betray his family."

Hendrik swaggered forward. "We are his family, too."

"He doesn't see it that way," Liesbeth said with

a smile. "His loyalty is to the people who are loyal to him."

"Are you sure he hasn't told them?" Hendrik didn't like her son. Probably he suspected she preferred her son.

Probably he was right. "Noah is mortified by his behavior when he lived with us," she said coolly. "He doesn't want the Di Lucas to know. And he made a proposal—if he can find the bottle and pass it to me, we'll make sure the world knows it has passed out of Bella Terra and beyond their grasp." She laughed contemptuously. "He wants his little town back to its safe, humble self."

"How do you know he's not lying?" Hendrik asked. "That bottle of wine is worth hundreds of thousands of dollars."

Liesbeth heard the greed in his voice. She understood it—she felt a similar greed, although her avarice was fired by a different motive.

He wanted to auction the wine, to drive the price up by revealing its intriguing history.

She wanted the rock-solid proof of the Propov family legend.

Years ago, she had done the research. She had spent hours and days and weeks in libraries and in newspaper archives. She knew what was inside that bottle. She yearned for the pink diamonds that had been stolen from her family. She lusted after them. And after all these years, she was close. So close. Her plans were coming to fruition at last. She would soon see the Beating Heart, and hold it in her hand.

"Why won't Noah take the prize and run?" Hendrik repeated.

"I told you. He has morals."

"You depend on his morals?" Hendrik scowled, leaned forward, and, leaning his hand on her knee, he squeezed hard with his strong fingers. "You're getting soft, Liesbeth."

"And you are a bad judge of character." Hendrik bruised her, a bruise for each one of his five fingers, but she didn't flinch. "I know Noah. I've watched him grow up in this safe environment. I've watched his Di Luca family coddle him. I know his loyalty to his family is rock-solid." She smiled as she drew the long silk thread through the canvas. "Just in case I am wrong about his morals, last week I watched him click the lock on the necklace Grieta made him."

Grieta looked up with a grin and gave Liesbeth a thumbs-up. "I'm working on fixing the microphone. I mean, if scientists can repair the Hubble telescope from earth, then I can repair a microphone from a few miles away."

"Fix the camera while you're at it," Hendrik said.

Grieta scowled at him. "Forget that. The camera works fine, but he popped off the lens, and I can't replace it without getting my hands on the collar."

Hendrik grunted.

"If Noah doesn't come through, he's going to die. He knows it. You know it." Liesbeth smiled now without humor, smiled full into Hendrik's face, teeth bared, eyes savage. "I, too, am loyal to my family, Hendrik, as long as they are loyal to me." She clamped her hand over his, holding it in place on her knee. "But please remember—I am the descendant of Ivan the Terrible, and I would not hesitate to destroy anyone who tried to overthrow me." So saying, she drove her bright, sharp needle through his hand.

He screamed in surprise and pain, and jerked away. Lifting his hand before his eyes, he stared at the needle protruding from his palm, at the long strand of mustard gold thread that dangled from the back of his hand, and screamed again, this time in rage.

"Back it out of the wound," she advised. "Otherwise you'll have to pull the thread through your flesh."

He stared at her, poised on the razor-thin edge of violence.

Calmly, she indicated the small but widening pool of blood on her knee. "The needle went all the way through. I am wounded, too. When I hurt you, I hurt myself. We bleed together. We rise together. We fall together. Remember that, Hendrik, as you plot to replace me as the head of this family."

Chapter 42

When Wednesday morning came around, Penelope rose at seven, showered and dressed, and headed downtown to the Rhodes Café for breakfast.

She felt fine. Today was just another day.

She met Brooke, who was nibbling on a bagel.

Penelope ordered only toast and tea, not because this day signified any momentous occasion in her life, but because she didn't feel as hungry as usual, and because she'd found the runner she wanted to use on the grand stairway that led from the entry to the upstairs landing. She showed it to Brooke on the new computer tablet she'd purchased with her advance on her design fee.

Penelope was pleased when Brooke clasped her hands and sighed in delight. The runner was plain, almost Spartan in design, but rich with reds and golds. Brooke declared it was exactly what she had envisioned.

Then she had to run to the ladies' room.

Morning sickness.

Being with Brooke during her first trimester was difficult, but only because Penelope considered Brooke a friend, and seeing her suffer like this, even in such a joyous pursuit, was difficult to watch. Other than that, Penelope felt fine.

When Brooke returned, Penelope suggested they go to the house.

Noise assaulted them as soon as they stepped in the door.

The contractor had three men working in the kitchen to strip it bare; linoleum, appliances, cabinets, wallpaper, and plaster were coming down, and the screech of power tools drove Penelope and Brooke upstairs to the master bedroom. There Rafe had installed a desk and two chairs, and a recliner for those moments when Brooke needed to put her feet up.

He was a devoted husband. Penelope admired him for that.

Brooke wanted to talk about the design for the baby's room.

Not that it mattered to Penelope whether they talked about the baby's room—she felt fine—but they needed to finish the kitchen design ASAP. They'd already ordered the cabinets, in bird's-eye maple, and picked out the tile for the floor. Now they used a bare-bones room drawn with the correct dimensions to arrange and rearrange the six-burner stovetop, the microwave, the two ovens, and the huge refrigerator. Penelope suggested that rather than a kitchen island, Brooke might consider a family-size table in the middle of the room, pointing out that Nonna's family practically lived in the kitchen, and Penelope guessed that Brooke's family would, too.

Brooke agreed ecstatically.

The two women went to lunch.

Brooke ate heartily; her morning sickness seemed to be easing.

Penelope ordered a salad, but although she felt fine, she only picked at it. Too much dressing, she told Brooke.

Then they drove to the massive design warehouse in Santa Rosa and picked out appliances. Penelope felt competent doing that; discussing the merits of convection versus regular-bake, gas versus electric, and, most important, stainless steel versus a colored enamel . . . that was so real, so prosaic, so *solid,* she really did feel fine.

Then, while she was collecting stats sheets from the salesman, Brooke wandered away, and when Penelope went in search of her friend, she found Brooke looking at wallpaper and fabric swatches . . . for the baby's room.

Of course. It only made sense. This was Brooke's first child, and she was obsessed with getting the baby's room finished.

Penelope felt fine. She breathed deeply, and she felt fine. And she stared fixedly at Brooke's hands as she fondled the wallpaper.

"We aren't going to find out the baby's sex," Brooke said, "so I think something like this in a cheerful yellow would be perfect."

"Perfect," Penelope repeated.

"I know it's possibly a little masculine, but girls like cars, too, right? I know it's not politically correct to be concerned with gender issues, but I'm pregnant and you have to give me a pass." Brooke laughed.

Penelope smiled, but her lips seemed stiff.

"I like this material for the curtains, very plain, and I was thinking of using something like this"—Brooke slid a soft chenille out from under the pile of fabric—"for a throw. I want a nice, snuggly comforter to fling over the back of the rocking chair, so I can wrap my baby up and sing to him." She laughed again. "Listen to me; I've already decided it's a him!"

A low buzzing started in Penelope's ears.

"Mostly I want the room to be a happy place." Brooke slid her hand across her tummy. "A place where he can play and sleep and learn and love."

Black and red splotches swarmed over Penelope's vision, and she couldn't quite see the table, or the wallpaper, or the fabric. . . . In some safe, distant part of her mind, she knew she should go and find some carpet samples to match Brooke's design, but she couldn't move; she couldn't breathe; she couldn't—

Brooke grabbed Penelope's arm in a firm grasp.

The contact made Penelope look up. Her vision cleared.

She was here. She was here now. She had to pull herself together.

Brooke's face was distressed, her eyes anxious. "Penelope, you look awful. Are you all right?"

Penelope wanted to be. But—

"No. No. I'm not. I'm *not* fine." She pulled away from Brooke and stood in the middle of the huge room, her hands clasped in her hair. "I'm not fine," she repeated. "I'm going home."

She walked fast, away from Brooke calling her name, seeking refuge, going home. . . .

But when she got out to her car, she realized she didn't have a home to go to.

So she just . . . drove.

Chapter 43

Liesbeth sat at the desk in the study, doing what she did every day: going through Joseph Bianchin's mail. Bills, a few catalogs, an offer from some old-people's organization . . . but nothing personal. No notes from friends, no birthday cards, no females expressing their sincere desire to meet him for a cup of coffee. With his age and his money, Liesbeth knew women should be swarming around, trying to get into his pants and into his wallet. So her first assessment of him was correct: He was a very unpleasant man, so unpleasant that not even desperate widows would have anything to do with him.

She almost didn't open the brown manila envelope; it looked like junk mail. But the return address caught her eye. Either this was a scam, or Joseph Bianchin was receiving information from a genetic testing laboratory.

Interesting.

She used Bianchin's letter opener to slice open the envelope and viewed the contents.

Even more interesting.

According to the lab, Bianchin had screwed up somewhere along the line, because he had a daughter.

But whom?

The answer came easily enough.

The girl who had arrived at the gate and stood there for ten minutes, waiting for someone to allow her in.

Why, the old fox. He must have known all along why the girl was visiting, and he'd lied to protect her.

Of course, he'd insisted on a paternity test, too, so he didn't trust her.

Could this new wrinkle in the scheme of things be turned to Liesbeth's advantage?

Perhaps. And perhaps it could be used to keep an ever-more restless Hendrik busy.

She put her head out of the study and called him.

He didn't respond.

So she walked to the library and found him, alone and looking bored, playing Zombie Zombat on his computer.

Yes. Of course. He was trying to regain his masculine pride after she had used her tapestry needle to stab him.

But to see him lolling around, defying her . . . she wanted to stab him again, with something larger.

She had to face facts: Hendrik was too old to take over the successful direction of the gang. He had been under her management for too long. He had no drive and little ambition. And he was out of shape and cared nothing for improvement.

It was time to once again make her offer to Noah. Hendrik had left her no choice.

Keeping her voice even, she asked, "Didn't you hear me call, Hendrik?"

"Yeah, I heard you." He remained slumped in his chair.

"Where are the others?"

"Working out in the gym."

"Good. You should try that."

He didn't even glance up. He only sighed, deeply, like a teenager taken to task by his parent.

He tested her patience, for he was not her son. Her son was better than this. "Come on. I have a task for you."

"Doing what? What am I going to do with a hole in my hand?" He held up his bandaged left hand.

"That tiny thing!" Then she reined herself in.

She needed him . . . for now. "I was stabbed, too, and I'm not complaining. You'll enjoy this job. Come to the study. I want you to follow someone for me."

"Who?"

"A girl."

He looked up at last, and his green eyes gleamed. "Is she pretty?"

"I think you'll like her."

He tossed his tablet aside. "Sounds like fun."

Chapter 44

Death visited some men in the whistle of a bullet.

Death visited some men in the slow drip of an IV.

Death visited some men in the creaking loneliness of old age.

Noah stared death in the face on a Wednesday, almost halfway through his two allotted weeks, at the end of a tunnel beneath Bella Terra resort . . . for nowhere in the cellars was Massimo's jewel-laden bottle of wine.

Turning, he walked along the wide, dim corridor lit by the occasional bare lightbulb toward the stairs that would take him up to sunshine and fresh air, to his resort full of happy tourists and busy staff.

He told himself he wasn't disappointed about

the bottle, or even surprised. After all, his optimism had faded as, day after day, he searched in the dim, dusty graveyard of hopes.

He almost hated to climb the stairs—these days, someone who cared for him always lingered nearby, waiting to ask him how the search was going and give encouraging reports of the still-futile exploration of the shed and garage. He hated having to smile, to nod, to pretend he had faith in their chances of success when they didn't have a clue where to search next.

At the bottom of the stairs, he turned and looked down the long, dark hallways, and in grim humor, he told himself that spending time in the underworld had prepared him for the next stage of his existence.

Gad, he was getting too depressing for even him to be around.

He trudged up the stairs.

After the trouble Rafe and Brooke had down here, Noah had had the huge old-fashioned wooden door replaced with a self-closing steel door with digital locks, one on each side, and different codes for getting in and getting out. That way if someone managed to get in—say, Hendrik—he wouldn't easily leave.

Noah punched in the code to pop the lock. The door issued a quiet click as the latch released, then sighed quietly as he shoved it wide.

He blinked at the light in the hallway. He shut

the door behind him, listened until the lock set, then headed for his office.

He stepped inside to find Chloë sitting in his chair behind the desk, her feet propped up, reading a book. "What's the matter?" he said. "Did you get tired of pacing up and down outside the basement door waiting for me to come up?"

"No!" She smiled brightly. "I came to the resort to do research for one of my mysteries and I just happened to—"

He looked at her, head cocked, eyes knowing.

She sighed. She was a writer. She told lies for a living. But she told them well only on paper. "Yes, this body cast is driving me nuts, and I didn't expect you would be up for at least another hour."

"I finished."

"You searched the whole basement?" She perked up. She glanced at the map he had stuck on a corkboard over his desk, then back at him. "No luck?"

"None."

She stuck her finger in her place in the book. "What's next?"

"Good question." He'd been thinking hard about that. "With my brothers dealing with the search up at Nonna's, I need to consider more possibilities here at the resort. So I'm going to take my grandfather's workroom apart right down to the studs."

"Good strategy." The mystery author nodded her head in approval. "How come you didn't do that sooner?"

"Because there's no way to keep wine cool in there—it's just a bare room full of tools and shelves—and in my heart I still believe he would have preserved the bottle's contents." Although, despite his assertion, he was beginning to get a horrible churning in the pit of his stomach.

"Then why look?"

"Nonno was good with his hands." Helping his grandfather with his work was one of Noah's fondest childhood memories. "He could fix everything around the house, around the resort." Noah looked around, remembering how much his grandfather had done here even after the dementia had taken so many of his memories. "If Nonno wanted to install and wire a small wine cooler inside the wall under the Sheetrock, the voltage would be tough to trace."

"Seems unlikely he would do that."

"Seems unlikely he would hide the damned bottle."

"True enough."

"But first"—he turned toward the door—"I'm going to go do my job and check on the running of the resort."

"I wouldn't do that if I were you." She turned down the page on her book and stuck it in her bag.

"Why not?"

"Have you looked at yourself lately?"

He stared down at his filthy hands, then pulled his shirt away from his stomach and examined it. Dust and cobwebs.

"The rest of you looks just as bad." She tried to launch herself out of the chair, failed, then used the desk to help her stand and wiggled, trying to settle her abbreviated body cast into a comfortable position. With a sigh, she gave up.

"How much longer do you have to wear that thing?" he asked.

"The doctor promised me he'd remove it next week. On Thursday. In eight days. Not that I'm counting." She sounded petulant. "I shouldn't even have to wear it. If I had healed correctly, and if my surgeon wasn't so old-fashioned . . ."

"But he's the best, right?"

"So Eli says. But if I go in next week and have X-rays, and that doctor says he can't remove the cast yet, I swear I will take a can opener and cut it off myself."

He hoped he would be alive to see her released from her body prison.

"Why don't you go home and catch a shower?" she asked. "Have some lunch? Maybe take a nap? You look so worn-out you'll scare the tourists if they see you."

He tried to smile, but didn't think it worked too well.

She scrutinized him, her gaze clear and knowledgeable. “You know, when it comes to actual walking, talking, real live human beings, I don’t always pay much attention. But I think you look like a man with something on his mind, and it’s not good. Sometimes it helps to tell other people your problems. Sometimes those other people can help.”

He didn’t dare tell her, but the truth was, no one could help him. Not if they wanted to live. He had to carry this burden alone. “I’ll go home,” he said. “A shower and a few minutes of rest would do me good.”

She nodded. “Remember, if you want to talk, I’m your sister-in-law, and I’m on your autodial.”

“Thanks.” He touched her arm, then strode down the hall toward the parking lot.

He stepped outside into the afternoon’s dry, comfortable heat. This time of year, the sun shone, the clouds pretended they had never heard of Bella Valley except for a few discreet nighttime showers, and summer made promises on the wind.

Noah stopped and stretched, and thought about how much he loved his home, and how much he would miss it. Perhaps that was hell, looking back at a life spent in the Di Luca family home and knowing he would never step foot there again. . . .

His car was parked in the sun, and heat whooshed out as he opened the door. The leather was hot under his butt. The steering wheel burned his hands. But a few minutes running with the windows wide-open brought the temp down to bearable levels, and the breeze blew the cobwebs out of his mind, if not his hair.

He drove in the opposite direction from Rafe and Brooke's fancy Victorian, toward the small bungalows built in the 1950s. His home was smaller than most in the neighborhood: one bedroom, one bath, eight hundred square feet on the main level, with a tiny, bare, concrete basement underneath built for God knew what reason. Perhaps it was supposed to eventually become a rumpus room, but no one had ever even tried to finish it, and so he kept his projects down there.

Or rather, his project—a decent-size bomb built to strap around his waist and detonate at the same time as the necklace around his throat. The plans for such a contraption were easy to find on the Internet, and he intended to be close to Liesbeth and her gang at the moment of explosion, so they could all descend into hell together.

For Noah, that was heaven enough.

He parked in the tumbledown single-car garage and headed toward the back door. He got out his key, reached out to put it in the lock—and saw that the door was already open about an inch. He hesitated, then pushed it wide.

The scent of fresh-brewed coffee wafted out.

That figured.

He walked into the kitchen. "Hello, Mother."

Chapter 45

Liesbeth turned away from Noah's coffeemaker and smiled fondly. "I can't surprise you, can I?"

"Nothing you do surprises me." He strolled into the tiny kitchen.

But apparently he had surprised her, for she viewed him with a frown and said, "Son, you look like a coal miner."

"That's what happens when I spend days underground searching for Nonno's bottle of wine with the aim of giving it to you . . . and saving my miserable, puny, vacuum cleaner–filled life."

"You and your vacuum cleaners!" she huffed. "I can offer you a better life than that."

"Goody. A proposition. Give me a minute. I need to wash up. And then . . . we can talk." He smiled unpleasantly and headed into the bathroom.

It took him fifteen minutes to shower, change into jeans, his favorite old shrunken white turtleneck T-shirt—he thought it would annoy

Liesbeth—and a shabby pair of running shoes, and wander back out to the kitchen.

He caught his mother rummaging through the cupboards as if searching for something, anything of interest. "Find what you're looking for?" he asked.

Had she been in his basement?

The stairway down, and the door, were outside, as worn as the rest of the house, and although Noah had been working down there every night, he had taken care to assure it looked unused.

Yet Liesbeth noticed everything.

"Why do you live in such a tiny, unkempt hovel?" She gestured around at the worn countertops, the aging appliances. "If you don't want to care for a home, why not live at your resort? Or at your grandmother's?"

Would Liesbeth believe every inch of his home was worth investigating?

Or did she believe he was so scared of dying he would do her bidding . . . and no more?

"Nonna deserves to live as she wishes in her own home. I have to get away from the resort occasionally or I am always working. And ever since I visited you in Europe, I have known that my days on earth were limited. So why should I marry?" he asked. "Why have children? Why waste my time on creating a beautiful home when I know I'll leave it too soon?"

"You are a practical man. That is much to be admired. I despise my prey all the more when it begs. It's so dispiriting." She spread her hands as if helpless. "I hated to invade your privacy by searching your cupboards, but have you got sugar? And cream?"

"I can see digging through my personal belongings would offend your code of ethics," he said with fine-tuned irony. He fetched the sugar canister off the counter and the skim milk out of the refrigerator, and two spoons. He placed them on his tiny, drop-leaf table, and gestured. "Have a seat?"

As Liesbeth walked toward him, he noted that she listed a little to one side. "You're hurt?" he asked.

She rubbed her leg right above her knee. "I had a run-in with a tapestry needle."

Hendrik must be challenging her more and more. "Be careful. A woman your age doesn't always heal well."

"Yes. That's why I came to you." She sank down in the chair.

He looked her over. Liesbeth was still tall, fit, healthy. She dressed neatly, and her blond hair was coiled at the nape of her neck. But for the first time in his memory, she had bags beneath her eyes, a sallow tint to her skin, and she too plainly watched the window over the sink and the door. "Not sleeping well, Mother? Afraid to close your eyes for fear one of your beloved family will take you out?" he asked.

"Don't be ridiculous, dear; it's *you* that I'm worried about. Half of your allotted time is gone."

"I promise you, no one knows that more than me." He sat down opposite her.

"You look haggard." Reaching across the table, she grasped his hand. "I'm fond of you. You're my son, and I have my hopes pinned on you."

"You're fond of me as long as I do what you wish."

"I'm fond of you regardless. If I weren't, would I bother to come here to urge you to save your own life?"

He didn't relax, didn't indicate in any way that she had relieved his mind. But if she had seen the makings of the bomb downstairs, she would have flaunted her knowledge. His mother enjoyed nothing so much as being a know-it-all.

No, she hadn't been in the basement . . . yet. "If I knew how to save my own life, do you think I wouldn't?"

"But you can." She squeezed his hand. "I want to talk to you about just that."

"About killing Hendrik and taking over his position as heir apparent?"

She withdrew her hand. She ladled two teaspoons of sugar into her mug, then topped off the coffee with milk until it was a smooth, pale tan.

"It would take a bit of ruthlessness to step into my place. But without the ruthlessness, you're not capable of filling my shoes." She sipped.

Reaching across the table, he pulled her mug toward him and pushed his toward her. When she looked startled, he said, "Yes, Mother, you taught me to be cautious of any cup you give me."

"I would not poison you." Her indignation sounded real. "That would be counterproductive to my goals."

"Poison me? No. Drug me? I think so." He took a sip of her sweet brew, then with a shudder pushed it back toward her. "Such a shame Hendrik doesn't know the real reason you brought the gang to town."

Liesbeth lifted her brows with assumed innocence. "I don't know what you mean."

"I've been trying to remember how and when I discovered you had traced the Propov diamonds to Bella Terra."

She played with her spoon. "It was while you visited us in Europe."

"I know *that*. But at first, I don't think anyone said anything about the diamonds. At first, you had told me I was to watch my grandfather's bottle of wine, to make sure it was safe." He remembered her sitting while he stood, making clear for the first time the inescapable control she now exerted over his life. "You said when it was time, you would come and get the wine."

"Give me the wine and I'll go."

"My grandfather hid it."

"So you say."

"You believe me, I think."

"I don't know if I believe you," she admitted. "I do know if you'd watched over the bottle as you should, we wouldn't be in this mess." She smacked her spoon on the table, then used it to scoop more sugar into her coffee. Or rather . . . his coffee.

"Very true," he said patiently. "I never anticipated my grandfather would hide the bottle before he died. But, Mother—I feel as if you don't want to discuss how I came to realize there were diamonds in that bottle. I don't think you told me. I seem to remember an *aha* moment when I realized your devotion to the legend of the Propov pink diamonds was exactly the same devotion you paid to Nonno's wine."

Liesbeth stared at him, her mouth pursed. Then she relaxed back in her chair and chuckled. "Yes. Yes." She nodded repeatedly, proudly. "You are a fit heir to me. To observe me so closely, to draw that conclusion with accuracy—such cunning, such intelligence!"

"I also seem to remember you hustling me away from my cousins before I could say anything in front of them."

Liesbeth stopped chuckling, stopped nodding.

Noah now reached across and clasped her hand,

holding her in place. "My cousins do *not* know the truth, do they? Hendrik knows you're here after a rare and expensive bottle of wine, he knows you're using me, but he doesn't know what treasure is in the bottle. He thinks it's all about the wine. He thinks he's going to make a fortune auctioning off the wine."

"Hendrik is a boy." Liesbeth smiled scornfully. "He doesn't need to know everything."

"You don't trust him. Wise move, Mother."

And for the first time, Liesbeth eyed Noah with some trepidation. As she should. If he chose to talk, he could make a bargain with his cousins, a bargain to save his own life and end hers or, at the very least, end her dream of owning an important part of her heritage—the Beating Heart.

The balance of power had shifted. "So when you get your hands on the diamonds, what do you intend to do?"

"I told you. I will have them reset in platinum and keep them in a safe location, where I can see them whenever I want." Her eyes softened in longing.

"Yes, you told me. But I think the reason you aren't worried about Hendrik killing you is because . . . you don't intend to stay with the family."

Her shocked gaze flew to Noah's.

"This is your last job, Mother," he said. "You're retiring."

"You really are very smart." It was no compliment.

"And *you* are not as smart as you imagined." Noah weighed his bomb, then dropped it. "Did you know that on Sunday, Hendrik came to visit my grandmother's property?"

Her smile disappeared. "*Stupid* boy. He could ruin everything."

"The cops are looking for him. My brothers know about him now."

With a scornful wave of her hand, she dismissed law enforcement and Noah's brothers. "What did Hendrik want?"

"He wanted me to introduce him to my family."

Liesbeth grew pale with terror, then red with rage. "I will kill him."

"I'm fine with that."

She clenched her fist, visibly struggled for control. "But not yet. Not—"

"Until you have the diamonds? You're skating on thin ice. He wants to oust you anyway, and when he discovers the truth about the bottle, he'll kill you and claim he was justified. And who will debate his claim?"

She leaned toward him, her green eyes aflame. "Make sure he doesn't discover the truth about the bottle. Take his place as my successor, and I will personally take the bomb off your neck and you'll live."

"As attractive as that sounds—" Noah's phone

rang. He pulled it from his pocket and looked at it in puzzlement.

The Beaver Inn. What was the Beaver Inn doing calling him?

"As attractive as that sounds, I've got to take this call," he said, and answered.

Primo's deep voice rumbled in his ear. "Listen, Noah, I've got a situation at the bar."

What the hell . . . ? "And you need me because . . . ?"

"It's Penelope. She's in here, getting drunk, and she's scaring me to death."

Noah clicked the phone shut.

"What is it?" Liesbeth asked.

"I've got to go." He headed out the door.

Chapter 46

The Beaver Inn smelled like disinfectant, which meant one of two things—last night someone had tossed his cookies (and there were unexplained splotches on the linoleum), or there had been a fight with a lot of blood spilled (and there were unexplained splotches on the walls). So probably a little of both.

But for all the bar's raucous reputation, tonight the atmosphere was subdued, the vineyard workers staring into their beers rather than at the slender female figure sitting on a barstool, arguing with the bartender.

Probably the customers were frightened; no one argued with Primo, or at least no one who wanted to remain in one piece. Primo was notorious for his extraordinary strength and fearsome fighting skills, and speaking as someone who'd been on the receiving end of his punches, Noah could attest that Primo's fame was well deserved.

In fact, Noah knew the sound and the sight and the smell of the Beaver Inn—in his time, he had tipped back more than a few shots and kicked more than a little ass there. And had his ass kicked, too.

Which was why having Primo look so desperately relieved to see him was more than a little funny. Penelope had the big guy terrified.

As Noah slipped into the seat next to Penelope, he nodded at Primo. "I'll have a banana daiquiri," he said.

Primo put his elbows on the bar and glared.

Hey, just because Noah was here to rescue Primo didn't mean he had to make it easy. "A nice light chardonnay?" he questioned. "Maybe a frozen strawberry margarita with a little sombrero on top?"

Now Penelope turned and glared, too, through brown eyes so deep and pooled with sorrow that Noah's breath caught on a shared shard of pain.

Had something terrible happened since he'd seen her at Nonna's? What had occurred to make her look as if she viewed the world from behind a dark veil, where no light or happiness could penetrate? Was it the loss of her husband? The loss of her mother? Or did she hide secrets that shredded the fabric of her soul . . . ?

Was she more like him than he had ever imagined?

He must have stared too long, seen too much, for she lifted her chin and turned away.

No wonder Primo was rattled. No wonder the customers were quiet. No one wanted to see that kind of anguish staring out from the mirror over the bar. Her pain, so palpably obvious, reminded a man of his own mortality.

Noah glanced at Primo, his eyebrows raised.

PMS? Primo mouthed silently.

Noah shook his head.

Primo shook his, too.

Primo tilted his head toward the door.

Noah nodded.

He had to get Penelope out of here.

He scrambled to get back to his lighthearted teasing, to change the mood, to ease her away from the gaping darkness. "What?" He punched her lightly on the arm. "Can't a man order a drink around here?"

"You *can,* but the big oaf across the bar doesn't put any liquor in the drinks, so what difference does it make?" Her voice sounded absolutely normal. Snappish, but normal.

"Look." Primo took her glass away. "I'll make you a whole new drink. You can watch me. Ice and straight gin. How's that?"

"How about straight gin, no ice?" she countered.

"I'm telling you, we don't serve your fancy-ass girly gin in here. The only kind of gin we have is pure rotgut. It doesn't taste like juniper; it tastes like the whole pine forest." Primo pulled a steaming-hot glass out of the under-the-counter dishwasher. "Just let me put a little ice in the glass to take the edge off. Your ulcer will thank me for it."

"You never care about my ulcer like that," Noah said.

"I don't care if *you* suffer." Primo ladled ice into the glass and swirled it around. The ice was melting, pooling at the bottom. "The sooner the crap you drink *kills you,* the happier I am."

Penelope made a whimpering sound.

Both men turned in time to see her cover her mouth for a telling moment.

They froze. What was wrong? What had they said?

Kills you. It was death that made her cringe.

"He didn't mean it," Noah said comfortingly. "We're frenemies."

"Yeah," Primo said. "We've known each other our whole lives, and we take care of our own. The stuff we say to each other—it's just talk."

They waited on tenterhooks to see whether she

would cry or collapse or . . . or tell them what was wrong.

Instead she pulled her hand away from her face and tapped the bar. “Hurry up with the drink.” She was finished with that brief, revealing moment.

“All right.” Primo pulled a bottle of gin out of the freezer, slapped the glass in front of her, and poured. “Straight gin with a little ice mixer. That’ll get you properly toasted.”

She sat up straight, said, “Thanks,” and took a long swallow.

Noah and Primo exchanged glances. Even with the melted ice, it was powerful stuff, and she sucked it right down.

“For me—tequila. Salt. Lime.” Noah turned to look over the big, cavernous room, where fluorescent beer signs turned the peeling paint orange and pink and bilious green. “So how’s business here at the Beaver Inn?”

“We’re busy. It’s a good night when the farmworkers leave their knives at home.” Primo lined up the ingredients on the bar. “How’s business at the resort?”

“Okay. We spend more time screening the guests, trying to figure out whether they’re media or tourists or cold-blooded murderers.” From the corner of his eyes, Noah kept track of Penelope. For a self-professed coward, she didn’t flinch or even seem to notice his talk of crime. She simply kept drinking.

Noah had to get her alone, to a place where she could cry or scream or . . . just tell him *what had happened.*

"Any luck with that famous bottle of wine?" Primo asked.

Noah swung to face him. "What do you know about the bottle of wine?"

"Exactly what my aunt told me I could know," Primo answered. "Did you think you could keep info like that away from Aunt Arianna?"

"No. Of course not." Noah glanced at his watch.

It was almost time.

He was getting so he knew without even looking.

His watch alarm went off. Three thirty-seven p.m.

Eight days left.

He licked the salt, shot the tequila, and bit the lime. And shuddered. To Penelope he said, "Arianna Marino knows everything that goes on in this valley."

Penelope nodded. "I know. I came here to stay because it was cheap, and I knew the place, and I knew I would be safe." She laughed, and her laughter cracked in the middle. "But wherever I go, there I am."

Chapter 47

Noah didn't know how Primo did it, but somehow, without moving from behind the bar, he stage-directed a fight between the vineyard workers and the orchard workers. The ruckus began quietly, and Penelope paid no attention to anything but her liquor. The argument became an uproar; then, with the suddenness of a summer storm, fists and chairs were flying. A single punch sent one worker slamming into Penelope's barstool as she hunched over the bar.

She turned, and for a moment, Noah thought she was going to launch herself into the fight.

Primo gave a roar, vaulted the bar, lowered his head, and rushed the crowd.

Drinkers fled before him.

Noah grabbed Penelope's arm and hustled her out the door.

They stepped out into late-afternoon sunshine.

Penelope blinked and staggered.

Noah caught her, steadied her. "Come on; I'll walk you to your room."

She looked at him sideways. "What's the matter? Afraid if you don't I'll go back to the bar?"

"Afraid you'll fall on your face."

"Did you not see how Primo was watering my

drinks? I'm only tipsy." Her mouth twisted bitterly. "And I wanted to be roaring drunk. Number fourteen." She pointed at the grimy white door not far from the office.

"Why?" He guided her across the parking lot.

"Why number fourteen? Because Primo put me in . . . Oh. Why do I want to be drunk?" She concentrated on putting one foot in front of the other. "It's an anniversary."

"Your anniversary." Her wedding anniversary.

Noah hadn't realized her grief for her husband was so fresh. So real. Sunday, when he'd dragged her out of Nonna's house and enjoyed her body, and she had responded . . . she'd been using him as a substitute.

Wow. That would teach him to imagine stuff about soul mates and eternal love.

"Which anniversary?" he asked.

"The first."

He thought he'd misunderstood her. Or she'd misunderstood him. Or . . . something. "That doesn't make sense."

"Tell me about it."

As Penelope used her key card to open the door, he followed her inside. The minuscule room contained a dresser and a queen-size bed, and two of the ugliest lamps he'd ever had the bad fortune to see. But at least the furniture covered most of the hideous carpet.

He'd been inside a room at the Sweet Dreams

Hotel one time, the same day he'd told Penelope he no longer wanted her and she'd left with her mother. He'd come to the Beaver Inn looking for a fight, and when the bartender refused to serve him—he was still underage—he'd gotten belligerent. By the time the bouncers hauled him out of there, he was covered with bruises and contusions, and Arianna Marino said she wasn't sending him back to his grandmother in such disgraceful shape. She'd slapped a steak on his swollen-shut eye, shoved him in a motel room, and told him no one would ever know if he cried.

No one ever did.

Now he barely stopped himself from saying, again, that he would get Penelope a room at the Bella Terra resort.

She must have known what he was thinking, because she said, "I can afford this. Okay?"

"Right. I understand." He did. She had her pride.

He had his pride, too. Or at least, he *should* have his pride. He *should* care if she used him as a sexual substitute for her beloved husband.

One lousy shot of tequila, and the sleazy motel room was looking good . . . because Penelope was in it.

He had to get out of here. "Are you going to be all right now?"

"All right?" She stood swaying, staring at

nothing. "No. I don't think I'll ever be all right again."

Uh-oh.

In a sudden movement, she stepped to the bed, gripped the comforter, and threw it down on the floor. "As long as you had to come and interfere with my well-deserved drinking binge, why don't you make yourself useful?"

"Like . . . how?" He could think of only one way: using the bed. But he was a guy with a one-track mind. When it came to women, he was usually wrong about . . . well, everything.

But when she grabbed his shirtfront, he knew he wasn't wrong about this.

"Make me forget," she said. Her wide brown eyes were sorrowful, but mostly . . . they were angry. Angry at him? No, angry at life for dealing her such a lousy hand.

He understood that all too well. "I can't. I shouldn't." God, he sounded *coy*.

But he really shouldn't.

"What? You shouldn't take advantage of a woman who's been drinking? You shouldn't take advantage of a woman in mourning? Or you just don't want to start it up between us again?" She dug her fingernails into his shirt, into his flesh. "Because I'll tell you, Noah, the thing I remember best about you is that you were good in bed. And the other thing I remember is . . . after dumping me like that, you owe me. And you know it."

He did owe her. Nine years ago he had treated her like hell.

But this . . . this was wrong. She was tipsy. She was in pain. If they had sex, tomorrow she would be sorry. . . .

Maybe.

But worse . . . he would enjoy it. He would revel in it. Whatever he did with her now would be the most wonderful moment—*moments*—of his lousy, worthless, miserable life. Sex with Penelope would be no sacrifice, and that was the only way he could justify rolling around on the bed naked. . . .

He had to think of something else.

Her pleading eyes? Her rosy cheeks? Her luscious body pressed so tightly against his?

He was hard, ready, and in agony.

And apparently, she decided he had thought about it long enough. Standing on her tiptoes, she took his lower lip between her teeth and bit. Hard.

Chapter 48

Restraint shattered. Well-intentioned thoughts died. The only emotions left were lust and need, and they took command.

Noah picked Penelope up and tossed her on the bed.

The hard, cheap mattress bounced beneath her.

She smiled, her objective achieved.

She kicked off her sandals. They arched through the air and smacked the wall.

He reached for his belt.

She sat up and pulled her shirt over her head.

He saw the warm, soft swell of her breasts above the constriction of her bra and his damned zipper couldn't open fast enough.

Penelope seemed to be having no trouble with *her* zipper. It slid right down. She kicked off her pants.

Her rose cotton bikini panties wrapped her lush hips, her waist so tiny he could span it with his hands. And he forgot about his jeans, still clinging to his hips. He forgot about his shirt, his shoes, the removal of which were necessary for normal, naked sex.

Instead, he reached out with wondering fingers to stroke her hourglass profile. Then, like a boy, he grabbed the front clasp of her bra and popped it open.

Her breasts sprang free, beautifully round, creamy, and full, with taut brown nipples that pointed at him. Beckoned him. He cupped the richness, marveling at the velvety texture. . . .

She shoved his greedy hands out of the way. She pushed his jeans and underwear down to drop around his ankles.

His dick stood at attention, erect and ready to serve.

"Perfect," she whispered.

Vaguely the idea floated through his mind that this was too fast, too violent.

Then she cupped his balls with one hand, held his erection at the base, leaned forward, and took him into her mouth.

One flick of her wet tongue zapped hot lightning on the tip of his dick. Electricity arced through him. For one mindless moment, he almost . . . *almost* came. Then he caught a strand of her hair and tugged.

She let him go and looked up, her big eyes wild and hungry.

"If you want satisfaction, you'd better stop *now*."

She slid backward on the mattress and opened her arms—and legs.

He didn't fling himself on her. Not quite.

He didn't devour her. Not quite.

But he was on top of her immediately, mouth open, licking, tasting, kissing, sucking. . . .

She was as frantic as he, as needy, as voracious. She kissed his shoulder, then his chest. She ran her hands down his spine. She caressed his butt before pulling him closer to her, so his dick pressed against her belly, and she undulated against him in an ordeal of pleasure.

They were sideways on the bed. Her bra still hung off her shoulders. He still wore his turtleneck T-shirt, and his jeans and underwear hung off his ankles.

Neither of them cared.

His blood thundered in his veins.

Her breath panted against his skin.

They grappled in absolute silence, as if every ounce of energy needed to be spent in this living moment, this *now*.

Now.

He reached between her legs, opened her. She was damp, ready.

And he needed a condom. *He needed a condom.* Where was his condom?

He carried a condom. Always.

But . . . the condom was in his wallet. His wallet was in his jeans. His jeans were around his ankles.

Like a teenage boy taking his first shot at sex, he writhed, groped, and fumbled, located the wallet, opened it.

The condom's gold plastic package and the black leather of his wallet had formed some kind of bond, and he had to wrestle the package out, furious with the delay and growing more desperate by the moment.

While his trembling hands worked feverishly, Penelope stroked his hip, slid her fingers across his stomach, explored his balls with her cupped hand.

She was not helping. And she knew it.

At last the condom popped free.

He forcefully tore the package open.

She helped him don the sheath.

Finally . . . he slowed down. For just a second. He didn't want to hurt her. He wanted to ease inside. . . .

Ease . . . inside . . .

As he slid home, they groaned in unison.

Nothing in his life had ever felt as good as being joined with Penelope. It was desire incarnate. It was a reunion. It was a love story fulfilled.

He looked into her face.

Her long lashes were damp, her brown eyes swimming with tears.

Anxiously, he smoothed her hair back from her face.

She whispered, "Have you ever had something feel so good it makes you cry?"

He nodded. *Right now.* But he couldn't speak.

"Please." She flexed her muscles inside. "Hurry."

That was all he needed.

He moved out and in. Out and in. And then—they were thrusting together, fierce with need. Lust rioted along his nerves. He held her tightly, trying to meld the two into one. Her scent mixed with his, forming a perfume heady and rich.

She wrapped her legs around him, digging her heels into his thighs, demanding more.

He slid his hands under her bottom, lifting her higher, getting farther inside her. All the way inside her . . . and it would never be far enough.

Every primitive instinct in him insisted that he possess her, imprint himself on her.

She yielded, softened, gave him everything she had.

Their sex was brilliant, swift, powerful, bright, primal.

As she climaxed, her hoarse cries echoed in his ears. Her body bonded with his. She demanded.

And he gave, a violent orgasm totally out of his control, come spurting from him in hot jolts as he drove inside her again and again.

This was mating, a bondage for them both. Forever. An eternity.

Slowly, the agony of pleasure eased.

Little by little, the ferocious tumult came to a stop.

He was gasping, sweating, collapsing with exhaustion. He eased his weight on top of her, pressing her into the mattress, wanting never to let the moment end.

Still totally attuned to her, he listened to her breathing. Heard the first hitch. He embraced her, held her, remembering those tears as they joined. Heard another hitch. Felt her body shake beneath his. He slid his hands under her head. The sheet beneath her head was damp . . . with her tears.

"I know I'm a selfish shit and maybe I'm flattering myself," he said, "but this isn't about what just happened between you and me, is it?"

She shook her head.

Thank God. Still cradling her, he said, "Then you need someone to talk to, and you know you can trust me. Please, Penelope. Tell me what's wrong."

She was crying now in earnest. "Today's the first anniversary of my baby's death."

Chapter 49

Noah's heart stopped. He slowly came up on his elbow.

No wonder Penelope had fallen apart today.

Her husband. Her mother. And her baby?

Penelope didn't seem to be crying, yet tears slid down her cheeks in a soft, steady stream, as if so many tears had gone before they knew the way.

He toed his shoes off, kicked his pants off his ankles, strove to be less a beast of instinct and more a man with a modicum of sensitivity. Leaning over her, he stroked the hair back from her fragile face. "Tell me."

"When Keith was killed, I was pregnant, six months along. His death . . . It was a shock." She put her hand over her heart as if to contain the ache. "Some poor trucker had a heart attack, crossed the white line, hit him head-on. The trucker survived. Sent me flowers and a letter of apology from his hospital bed." She shivered.

"Reading that was the most awful . . . He felt horrible. He said if he could do it over, he'd rather be the one who died than my young husband."

"I'm sure he meant it."

"I'm sure he did." She stared fixedly at the ceiling, not acknowledging Noah at all. But she didn't move away from him, either. "My father-in-law is a lawyer. He wanted to sue the trucker, said it would give the baby security. I talked him out of it. Keith had some life insurance; we had a house; I had a job. . . . Suing was just Ronald's knee-jerk reaction, some kind of male power-trip need to do something."

Since Noah was experiencing a male power-trip need to do something to help her, he could understand.

"Keith was a good guy. He had gone against his parents' wishes to marry me. Me, a girl from the L.A. ghettos, part Hispanic, illegitimate, with no lengthy family history that reached back to the first settlers of Cincinnati. We were happy. His parents were not, although once I got pregnant they settled down a little. We were eager to have a family. Mind you, Keith and I weren't violently in love, but I'd done that once before and—" She stopped in midsentence.

"Once was enough?" Noah suggested.

"Exactly."

Noah thought that while Penelope might not

have been violently in love, any guy who married someone so different from him probably had it bad for her. But he wasn't going to say that. "You got the bad news about Keith and . . . ?"

She shivered. "I was afraid for the baby. I mean, how does such a fragile being survive the storm of grief and shock I experienced? But my ob-gyn reassured me, and showed me that the baby was fine, safe inside me. I arranged Keith's funeral, dealt with my mother-in-law's hysteria—"

"He was an only child?"

"Yes, and Barbara's grief far overwhelmed mine." Penelope's mouth twitched in what could have been an ironic smile. "My mother . . . my mother couldn't come to the funeral. She said it was because Mrs. Walters was ill and demanding. I should have realized. . . . She knew I needed her. She was always there when I needed her. I should have realized . . . But it never occurred to me how wrong it was that she didn't come." Penelope shivered again, and goose bumps sprang up on her skin. "I hadn't ever found out about the first occurrence of breast cancer. Still . . ."

"You were in shock." Noah helped Penelope to sit up, turned her so the head of the bed was at her back, put pillows under her for support. "There was no way for you to know, and anyway, what could you have done differently?"

"Nothing." Her skin was chilled. "I guess nothing."

Noah brought the covers up from the foot of the bed, pulled them over her, brought her close to give her warmth.

"We made it, my baby and me, through almost another two months. I could feel her move every day. I worried about stuff, mostly about Barbara obsessively trying to take over my child. I planned ways to combat her influence. I talked to my mom about moving to Portland, but she didn't sound too enthused." A frown knit Penelope's forehead into little wrinkles that looked partially like unhappiness, but more like bewilderment. "She sort of hurt my feelings."

"You didn't know what was happening in her life." He cradled Penelope's head in his arm, watching her, gauging her distress as if he could do something to assist.

There was nothing. In the face of such grief, he was powerless.

"I don't know what she was thinking." Even now, Penelope sounded baffled. "Things were going badly with her treatment. I was going to find out soon enough, so why not tell me?"

"Because you'd suffered a horrible shock and you were pregnant. And maybe she hoped for a miracle?"

"Yes. That sounds like my mother. After all, she'd managed to raise me and put me through college, and fight cancer one other time. She believed in miracles." Penelope paused as if remembering her mother. "She said—and she was right—that financially I couldn't make it if I moved to Portland. The housing market was bad and getting worse every day. If I sold, I was going to lose money, a lot of money. Plus, it would have been a gamble to give up the security I had with my firm. And let's not even talk about the nightmare with insurance. Without Keith, I was on my own. I had to support myself and the baby. I mean . . . on my own unless I wanted to take money from my in-laws, which I did not, because—"

"You didn't want to give your mother-in-law that kind of influence over your lives."

"Right. And a baby is expensive. The crib and the car seat and the little, tiny shoes . . ." She half smiled at the memory of the little tiny shoes. "The baby kept me looking to the future, planning ahead. I was reading books on raising a child. Searching for the best care facilities. Working really hard at my job, because while I was on maternity leave, I didn't want to be a casualty of some downsizing scheme."

He took her hand, entwined their fingers, held his palm against hers in some futile attempt to take the weight of her grief.

"She was such an active baby. I suppose they all are, but I felt her move a month early, and in a couple of weeks, I joked to Keith, she would play soccer for the pros. She'd get her fist in my hip and her foot in my ribs, and she'd push." Penelope writhed as if she could recall the pain. "I thought she was doing isometric exercises."

"So she was healthy?"

"She looked great in the ultrasounds. The doctor was so pleased."

What happened?

Penelope continued. "One of the reasons I handled Keith's death as well as I did was because . . . I knew I was never alone. I had to get past the grief and focus on our child. She was there, rolling and twisting, alive inside me. Even now, it's amazing to me how much connection I felt. She took over my body, and everything from that moment was animal instinct. So primal and so . . . She controlled my life. My every thought was for her." Penelope's tears dripped onto his arm. "My every thought . . . even in my sleep . . ."

She paused so long he wondered whether she had decided she couldn't stand it, couldn't tell him the whole story.

But at last she resumed talking, her voice weaker, quieter. "That morning, a year ago today, I woke up really early, and my first instinct was . . . 'There's something wrong.' I didn't even have to think. I knew that sometime in the night, she had stopped moving."

He imagined Penelope waking alone in the big bed she had shared with her husband, and knowing . . . knowing her baby was dead. "What did you do?"

"I called the doctor. Told her she had to help us. She told me late-term babies stopped moving because they were cramped. I knew better. I got hysterical—which I'm not the type. I insisted on coming in. She listened, thank God. She met me at her office, put the fetal stethoscope on my belly. . . ." Penelope shook her head over and over, her eyes dull with remembrance.

"How . . . ? What . . . caused . . . ?"

"The cord slipped around the baby's neck. It happens. Not often. But sometimes. I went into the hospital. They induced me, and I delivered my beautiful infant." Penelope shivered and shivered.

Noah rubbed her, held her, tried to convey comfort where no comfort was to be had.

In a low voice, Penelope said, "She was so beautiful, Noah. Perfect in every way, fingers and toes, a beautiful, still face . . . I delivered her knowing she was gone. I held her, just held her. . . . I gave her her name—Keith and I agreed on Mia, pretty and simple and then . . . I let them take her." Again, Penelope broke down, turning away from him into the pillow, sobbing without restraint.

He rubbed her back, smoothed the hair out of

her face, felt ineffectual and stricken with grief for a child lost before she lived.

He faced his own death, and hated that he would die so soon. But he had at least *lived*. He had drawn breath, walked and talked, had a family who loved him, made an impression on this world.

No one remembered Mia . . . except her mother. That was the tragedy that broke his heart. And Penelope's.

After what seemed like an eternity, Penelope's crying began to calm.

He disengaged himself, grabbed a bottle of water off the desk, the box of Kleenex out of the bathroom. He came back to see her watching him, her hand tucked under her cheek, her brown eyes wide pools of endless sorrow. And now . . . a kind of peace.

He sat back down, opened the bottle, handed it to her. "What happened next?"

She sat up and drank, then slid back on the pillows and huddled under the blankets. "The day I delivered Mia, my mother arrived in Cincinnati. I was ready to leave the hospital when she walked in, and I almost didn't recognize her. She was wearing a wig. She was bloated from the steroids and pale from the shots they had given her to build her bone marrow—her blood count was down—and she had trouble breathing when she exerted herself. I don't know how she made the trip, but I'd been waiting for her to arrive to cry, really cry." Penelope rubbed the center of her forehead as if it ached. "And you know what? When I saw her . . . all my tears dried up. There was no point in breaking down. She couldn't help me. She had death written on her bones."

The picture rose in Noah's mind: the stark hospital room, the two women parted for too long, and soon to be parted forever.

"She knew it. I knew it. We signed me out. I took her to my home and put her to bed—she was exhausted. I called a real estate agent to come and look at the house, and I started packing. The next afternoon, we buried Mia in the same grave as her father." Penelope set her chin. "It was awful. Barbara said . . . unforgivable things."

Noah did not like the sound of that. "What do you mean, she said unforgivable things?"

"She blamed me for Mia's death, said she died because I worked too hard after Keith's death, said I had destroyed the last piece of her son left on earth."

Noah wanted to reach across the stretch of time and slap the woman.

"My mother went feral." Penelope did not seem surprised. "I thought she was going to kill Barbara right there in the cemetery."

"Good for your mother."

"Yes, but she didn't have the strength to get to

the car afterward. I sold the house at a huge loss. Within the month, I moved to Portland. My mother lived another seven months." Penelope sat up, gathered half of a box of Kleenex, and blew her nose. Hard. She threw them in the trash, then blew again. "I just . . . as soon as I saw my mother, I couldn't mourn my baby. She reminded me I still had family. I had other priorities, pressing commitments to the woman who gave me birth and who sacrificed everything for me. My mother knew it was wrong; she urged me to take the time to grieve, but my emotions directed differently."

"You'd been through too much." He ached for her.

She shrugged wearily. "How much is too much? That which doesn't kill you makes you stronger." She slid out of bed, grabbed her pajamas out of her suitcase, and disappeared into the bathroom. She called, "I just don't see why I need to be so strong."

He heard water running, some splashing, and when she came back, dressed in a comfortable-looking cream cotton tank-and-boxer combo, her face was damp and a little less red.

She climbed back in bed with him, moved close, and let him take her in his arms—and he felt a fierce pride that she turned to him for comfort.

"Today . . . I was determined to get through

today. I mean, it's just another day, right?" She pressed her head against his chest as if listening to his heartbeat. "But Brooke wanted to talk about decorating the baby's room. I tried to head her off, but"—Penelope sighed—"she's got one thing on her mind, the baby she's carrying, and what could I say? I remember. I know how much that life within you means. So without meaning to, Brooke reminded me of all I had lost."

"In a way, I think it would have been more awful if you'd managed to get through the day without breaking down." He was out of his comfort zone, not sure he was right, but he struggled on. "Mia deserved for her mother to cry for her, and you wouldn't be the woman I"—*love*—"admire if you never gave her her due."

"That's . . . that's right. You're right, I think." He was afraid she was going to cry again, but instead she nodded as if he had comforted her.

Thank God, because right now he felt like a big, dumb, clumsy guy.

She snuggled closer again. "How did you know I was at the Beaver Inn?"

"Primo called."

"He's like an old lady."

"Primo's a good guy." Noah rocked her a little. "If I'd known about the baby, I wouldn't have jumped you like that."

"It was what I wanted. If the liquor wasn't going to erase the memories, I thought sex might.

But it worked a little differently than I thought. It broke open my emotions. . . . I've never told anyone. Ever. I've never had the chance to talk about it." She looked up at him, red eyed and anxious. "Thank you for listening."

He almost said something then. Something stupid like, *I'll love you forever.*

But by a stroke of good luck that made him so happy he wanted to slam his fist through the wall, he was saved by some piece-of-shit bastard who knocked once, hard, on the door.

Chapter 50

Penelope jumped, clutching the blankets to her chest. She'd been spilling her guts to the one guy she should distrust, and that intrusion from the outside world made her feel more naked than she had ever been in her whole life.

Noah glanced around. "Were you expecting someone?"

"Who do you suppose . . . ? It wouldn't be Mrs. Marino, would it? She doesn't police the rooms and eject anyone who's having sex, does she?" At the thought of Arianna, Penelope sat up and finger-combed her hair, as if that would erase any sign of their fabulous, wanton lovemaking.

There wasn't much she could do about the tears.

"Heaven forbid." Noah's voice sounded deep

and fervent. "If it's her, I'm hiding in the bathroom. The woman terrifies me."

Penelope grinned at the thought of this big, strong man cowering at the thought of meeting Arianna Marino. She grinned, too, at the sight of him wearing nothing but a worn white turtleneck T-shirt, the material so thin she could almost see through it. The impulse to amusement felt odd. But good, too, and natural, as if this were what should come next in her life.

"I'm serious." He rolled over and sat up on the side of the bed. "I suppose I have to look and see who it is."

"I can."

He glanced at her, and she must have still looked like she'd been dragged through a keyhole, because he said, "No. You stay where you are. For you, I will joust the fearsome Marino dragon."

Penelope laughed, low and warm, then stopped, surprised at herself. The day had started with a distant dread that had grown closer until it covered her gaze with a murky gray mist, separating her from human contact. At the time, that seemed good; better to be removed from life than broken on the rack of sorrow.

Then Brooke had picked out those wallpaper samples, had talked about using yellow for the baby's room and wrapping her baby in the softest cloth and holding it close while she rocked and sang . . . and all Penelope's dreams of Mia came rushing back, shattering at her feet like small treasures dropped by careless fate.

That afternoon, Penelope got into her car to drive and drive, trying to outrun the pain, until at last, not knowing what else to do, she had gone back to the motel and there it was—the Beaver Inn. Anesthesia in a bottle.

"Where's your robe?" Noah asked, like he knew she had to own a robe, like every woman kept a robe nearby and he knew every woman in the world.

Of course he was right. She did have one. "On the hook on the back of the bathroom door."

But getting drunk hadn't worked, either. Despite the fact that she didn't have to drive anywhere afterward, Primo was absolutely resistant to allowing her to get plastered. He acted as if he were her big brother or something.

So she got mad. And she welcomed that feeling, because anger held off the agony. Maybe she would escape the mourning she feared. . . .

Noah showed up, and that was even better. She had practice being mad at him.

Noah grabbed the white cotton wrap, tied the tie around his waist his shoulders strained at the seams, the hem reached his midthigh, and his T-shirt covered his chest and hid his neck.

She reclined on the pillow, her arm under her head, and watched him walk toward the door.

He looked silly.

He didn't seem to care.

He didn't seem to care about a lot of things. This afternoon at the Beaver Inn, when she turned her hostility on him, he had been unfazed. A little reluctant to give her the sex she demanded, but his wavering morals didn't stand a chance against a determined woman.

And she had been determined. The anguish that had grown sharper and more real throughout the day was vanquished by sensations of first warmth, then pleasure, then . . . passion. And somewhere in the middle of all that raw sex, her chalice of sorrow shattered, leaving her broken by memories.

Closing her eyes, she remembered Mia's sweet, small face, and tears swarmed up again.

"No one's there," he reported.

She opened her eyes to see him looking out the peephole.

Stepping around to the side of the door, he opened it an inch and squinted out. "Huh."

His voice was so full of suspicion, she sat up. "What is it?"

"A bag hanging on the knob. And a pizza box on the mat." He reached out, unhooked the bag, brought it inside. His eyebrows rose. He looked at her, his mouth quirking. "It's a box of a dozen condoms. Someone has a lot of faith in me."

She nodded. Nine years ago, she'd had sex with him. Probably he had a reputation.

But . . . *was* she going to have sex with him again?

Yes, they'd just enjoyed the best, most explosive, most mutually orgasmic sex imaginable, and yes, he'd been incredibly good about her breakdown afterward. She couldn't imagine another man who would let her cry all over him without fleeing in terror.

But when they'd had sex tonight, it had been impulse and heat and need. She couldn't call a second time, and a third time, *compulsion*.

She and Noah had a history, and not a good one. She should be cautious. She should be smart. She should think about tomorrow.

Yeah. She needed to think about tomorrow.

Soon.

He opened the door the rest of the way, stepped out, and came back with a large pizza box. In case she wasn't sure what was in the box, the smell of Italian sausage, pepperoni, onions, peppers, garlic, marinara, and crispy crust filled the room.

She moaned, but it had nothing to do with sex.

"You look more turned on about the pizza than you've ever been about me," he said.

"I'm sure that's not true." She thought she was going to faint with hunger. "I'm not really drooling over a pizza; I . . . I haven't had a lot to eat today."

"I suppose you haven't." He shut the door and flipped the lock. He latched the chain and then, in some excess of caution, he stuck a chair under the door handle. "Let me call Primo and make sure this is from him."

Noah was acting, and sounding, paranoid. "Who else would it be from? He's the only one who knows we're here."

"You never know." Noah found his pants on the floor, dug out his phone. "Someone might want to poison us."

Sometimes he said the oddest things. "I can't decide if you're being funny or not."

"Or not." He made the call. "Primo. Was that you, man? Did you bring the stuff and put it at the door?" He nodded, pleased, then shook his head and frowned. "Oh, Primo. I didn't want to know that."

"What don't you want to know?" she asked.

He held up one finger and listened again to the voice on the other end of his call. "Okay. I appreciate it. I owe you." He hung up.

"What don't you want to know?" she asked again.

"Arianna Marino called and told him to get us, um . . ." Noah gestured with the bag.

Penelope didn't want to know that, either. "Why did she do that?"

"There are a lot of boys in the Marino family. She probably knows guys all carry one condom in our wallet for emergencies, and after that, it's a matter of self-control."

"A dozen condoms? She doesn't think much of *your* control."

He looked at Penelope, making her self-conscious about her messy, dark hair, her prosaic pajamas, her red face and eyes. "Arianna Marino is one smart woman."

And suddenly, Penelope was flushed and basking in warmth. Noah made her feel . . . beautiful.

Noah wiggled the pizza box. "Primo, being Primo, figured we would need sustenance, too."

Surprise caught her. She flung herself back onto the pillows, and she chortled. "I love this place!"

"*This* place?" He looked around.

"Bella Valley. I could live here forever." She sat up again, alarmed at what she'd so carelessly said. "I mean, not with you. I just meant . . ."

"I know what you mean. I love this place, too." Something in his voice made her wonder . . . why was he yearning over Bella Valley as if he were in exile, when he had everything here at his fingertips?

But when she looked more closely at him, he seemed relaxed and amused. "So." He stood over the bed and lifted first the pizza box, then the condoms. "EF, or FF?"

She shook her head. "I don't understand."

"Eat first, or . . . ?"

She sat there and looked at him—intelligent and handsome; at his magnificent body, wrapped in a woman's robe and yet not womanly at all; most of all, at his green eyes. In them, she saw an aching loneliness that called to her across the vast gap between one human being and another, and the upsurge of love was almost more than she could contain.

Why she loved him, she didn't know, but no matter what she had done, no matter where she had gone, no matter where she would go, that love was alive, constant, eternal. Why run from it right now, when she needed the human contact?

She took his hand and tugged. "I like cold pizza," she said. "How about you?"

Chapter 51

Help me forget," Penelope said as she had said once before. But this time she added, "Make love to me until all that's in the world is me and you."

Noah's eyes changed from stark pain to warm delight. "Yes. Let me love you." He placed the pizza on the desk and stripped off the robe.

Her heart started a slow, thunderous beat.

The first time, she hadn't looked at him. She'd been too busy trying to get her own clothes off. But now . . . here he was, powerful, muscular, compelling. As he put one knee on the bed, his body flexed and moved with a fighter's grace. Her gaze danced over him, appreciating the broad shoulders, the narrow waist, the thighs that looked as if he could ride her forever. . . . "Take off your shirt." She tugged on the hem, shrunk by too many washings and slightly yellowed by bleach. "I want to see the whole"—she looked from his toes to his hairline—"package."

He hesitated as if . . . as if he had something to hide. Then, quickly, he reached down and stripped off his shirt.

The black studded collar he wore made her stop and stare. "What's *that?*"

"I have to wear it. I lost a bet."

"You're someone's bitch?"

"Only yours, darling." He lowered his face to hers and kissed her lips. "If you want me."

He was so relaxed, so leisurely . . . every touch of his mouth was a lifetime.

That was why she had always taken care not to remember Noah and the past. Because Noah was the kind of lover every woman dreamed of. He behaved as if he lived to kiss her long, slowly, and passionately. He lingered over her body as if he had never tasted anything so delectable. He touched her as if he couldn't get enough. He loved her as if he never wanted this moment to end.

When he lifted his lips from hers, she was limp

with desire. With her lids half-open, she trailed her fingers along the edge of his foolish dog collar. "As long as you perform like that, Fido, I'll keep you."

He opened a condom, started to don it . . . and she helped him by making sure he was as hard as a man could be.

"Keep it up. The second time's going to be faster than the first." But he was smiling, a smile so saturated with sex that Penelope could have used it to scent candles.

"I don't know." Even to her, her voice sounded vibrant and seductive, and she smiled up at him as she placed her palm flat on his thigh and stroked upward. "I think last time we set a land speed record."

He caught her wrist and pulled it away. "You are asking for trouble."

"And here you are."

He laughed and tumbled her back onto the pillows. "Stop that. I have things I want to do to you."

"What kind of things?"

"Slow things. Naughty things. Things that shouldn't be said out loud, like . . ." His lips came close to her ear.

She thought he was going to murmur something . . . wicked.

Instead his tongue slid around in a slow, wet, sensuous glide.

Such a small thing, yet his action acted as a cue to her body. Suddenly she was airborne once more, chilled by the heights, warmed by the sun, barely able to breathe at such a high altitude.

His hand slid under her tank to caress her ribs, to hold her breasts, and then to turn the tank inside out as he pulled it over her head. "Pretty," he said.

"You, too," she whispered.

His laughter vibrated through her. He kissed her eyes shut and whispered, "Concentrate on nothing but the feeling."

Without her vision, each of his movements was a surprise: the soft touch of his lips against her mouth, his thumbs circling the sensitive shells of her ears, his wet, warm mouth against first one nipple, then the other. She slid her hands through his hair and experienced his vitality as it curled around her fingers. And experienced, too, a growing delight as he took her hand and kissed her palm, then each finger, and finally her wrist, pressing his lips hard against the pulse that beat with ever-increasing excitement. Still holding her hand, he nuzzled the soft, sensitive skin where her belly and her thigh met.

She whimpered, an open admission of the passion that grew and flourished in the darkness behind her eyelids. Her legs moved restlessly, wanting more, wanting it soon, but contrary to his threat of speed, he was relaxed as he explored her, admiring her with his fingertips, his lips, his tongue, his teeth.

When she was with Noah, the past was gone; the future did not exist. She had his complete attention for this moment.

He turned her onto her stomach, moved her hair aside, and feasted on the nape of her neck. He massaged her shoulders until she purred, kissed his way down her spine, explored . . . everywhere. He rubbed her thighs, praising their taut shape, suggesting in his dark velvet voice that he could not wait until she crushed him in her ecstasy. He tickled the backs of her knees, kissed her toes until she squirmed.

When she could no longer contain her pleasure, and muffled her whimpers in the pillows, he eased her onto her back.

Now he focused all his attention between her legs. He opened her, tasted her, and made a sound of pleasure that matched her own. With his mouth, he took her apart and put her back together, until she slid smoothly out of time, out of place, held suspended by Noah's lips on her clit, his hands stroking her skin.

When she was trembling on the edge of climax, he slid up and into her. He was big and bold, and as he moved, so demanding, she knew then he'd been lying with his unhurried caresses.

He wanted her. He wanted this. *Now*.

Yet he held himself back, taking his time,

thrusting surely, steadily, increasing the speed by slow increments until she squirmed beneath him, flushed and frantic, wondering whether she would survive this long, continuous roll of climax that built and built. . . .

He murmured her name over and over, his voice caressing the syllables, encouraging her. He gathered her closer, holding her legs around him, lifting her up to meet him, going so fabulously deep she shuddered and begged, on the verge of something so powerful she didn't dare let herself go.

Then . . . he kissed her. Just kissed her, a simple smoothing of his lips against hers . . .

And she broke. She came. She spasmed around him, wild and primitive, demanding and giving.

And he broke, too, thrusting, providing, his voice a deep groan against her chest, his hands clutching her as if he would never let her go.

What they had between them wasn't sex.

It was a glimpse of heaven.

Chapter 52

Late that night, when Noah and Penelope sat on the rumpled bed, half-dressed, the open pizza box between them, napkins draped all over the mattress—because neither of them was willing to take a chance of getting pizza sauce on Mrs. Marino's sheets—he asked, "I was wondering . . .

That is, it seems to me that you may have come to Bella Valley so you wouldn't be alone on your baby's birthday?" He watched her almost as if he hoped she had run to him for comfort.

She didn't, although for a moment, it was a near thing. Should she tell him? Would he turn away from her? She cleared her throat. "Not really. That was more serendipity than anything. I came to Bella Valley now because I finally discovered why my mother brought me here that summer."

Clearly Noah did not expect that answer. With a frown, he lowered his slice of pizza. "Why?"

"Knowing how you feel, I shouldn't tell you." She really shouldn't. "But no one understands my need to know my father more than you. Because you don't know your mother, and it's such a hole in your life, always wondering . . ."

"You found out who your father is?" His voice rose enthusiastically. "That's great!"

Probably not. But—"He lives here. This is his home."

"So I know him?"

"My father, Noah—he's Joseph Bianchin."

Noah froze in shock. He stared, jaw dropped, eyes wide and unblinking.

She was right. She shouldn't have told him.

But they'd been so close, so connected, and foolishly she'd returned to that time nine years ago when they confided everything in each other. "Noah?" she said tentatively.

He shook himself lightly. He seemed to breathe again. Took a bite of pizza. Chewed and swallowed. And he said, "So the old fart did one thing right in his life."

She half laughed, startled and more thrilled than she had any business being. "I wouldn't go so far as to say that. I talked to him."

"He's really in town?"

"I saw him myself. I took a DNA test in front of him; then I gave him a DNA kit and told him to use it if he wanted to know the truth. I don't know whether he sent it to the lab or not." She shrugged. "If he did, the results should be back. But I haven't heard, and honestly, I don't expect anything to come of it. He really is a weird old crank, and he did not welcome me with open arms."

"It's Joseph Bianchin." Noah sneered quite effectively. "He accused you of being after his money, right?"

"On the nose." She pointed at her nose.

"Actually"—Noah started clearing away the napkins—"no one's seen him around town. We didn't know he was back. I wonder what he's up to?"

"He has company staying with him."

"Who?"

"Friends, I guess."

"Friends? He doesn't have any friends." Noah dismissed Bianchin with an indifferent wave of his hand. "Are you about done eating?"

"I suppose." She flicked her gaze over him from head to toe, noted that he had satisfied one hunger and now another stirred . . . again. "Do you have something on your mind?"

He picked up the pizza box. "It is *not* on my mind."

Lifting her hands, she rumpled her hair, then smoothed it back and smiled.

He dropped everything on the desk and moved with glorious speed to her side, and once more they started the erotic mating dance they performed together so well.

When Noah looked at Penelope, when he loved her, she felt beautiful, as if she shone from within. She was no longer merely human, but a goddess, worshiped and adored.

This was why she loved to be with him.

That was why she loved him.

The next morning, when Penelope's alarm went off . . . Noah was gone. No note. No evidence he'd ever been there. Just crumpled sheets and her own satiated body.

She'd been dumped by Noah Di Luca again.

Chapter 53

On Thursday morning, eight days later, Penelope stood in the attic of the Victorian with Brooke Di Luca, discussing whether or not they could knock out walls and turn the whole, capacious space into a playroom.

"The walls are merely partitions flung up to give the servants a little privacy." Penelope moved between one small cubicle to another, opening windows to allow the morning's cool breeze to sweep away the stale air. "The bathroom is nothing but a toilet and a sink, which is perfect for children at play—"

"Makes you wonder where the servants bathed, doesn't it?" Brooke said.

"Or *if* they bathed," Penelope said.

Both women shuddered.

But nothing could stop the onslaught of Penelope's decorating vision. "We could make this bright and airy, with a cupboard color-coded for each child. We could install an intercom with a monitor so you could periodically check on the kids and make sure there's no blood flowing, and as the kids grow, you could change the environment from lots o' toys to stuff like a foosball table. You'd be the coolest parents in town."

"All the kids would practically live here." Brooke looked horrified.

Penelope grinned. "Yes, but at least you'd know where *your* kids were."

Brooke nodded; she could comprehend that logic. "It's a trade-off, I guess."

"Good thing we're getting the whole house rewired, because you can bet the owners did the cheapest job possible up here. We've got the potential for asbestos, but we knew that, and it has to be dealt with before you can move in, anyway. The floor and the walls are the biggest decorating problems. I'd suggest a bamboo floor, something renewable, not too expensive for you to replace, easy to clean, and there's a little give for when the little ones fall down." Penelope was in full swing, envisioning the playroom as it could be.

It wasn't until Brooke mumbled, " 'Scuse me," and ran for the bathroom that Penelope realized she had missed the telltale signs of Brooke's distress, and morning sickness had struck again.

Poor Brooke. Her first trimester ranged from difficult to horrendous, and Penelope felt for her.

For Penelope, the last week had been an interesting roller coaster of emotions. She had been devastated by the anniversary of Mia's death, then angry, then aroused, then comforted by Noah's gentle kindness. And then . . . she'd been dumped. Again.

It had taken her about an hour before she realized—she didn't care. She liked that her time with Noah had been a walk on the wild side, where respectability vanished and her dream of settling down and raising a family had been . . . not replaced, but dismissed, at least for the moment. For the first time in her life, she had no ties, no responsibilities except the ones she chose for herself. If she wished, she could work abroad, live where she wanted, learn to ride a horse, and travel back in time to visit Robin Hood.

She chuckled. How wonderful to realize Noah had done her a favor.

When Brooke reappeared, Penelope was making notes and sketches. Penelope gave her a sympathetic grimace. "I'm sorry. I won't talk about injuries anymore."

"I think what you said was the icing on the cake." Brooke put her hand on her stomach and shook her head at the same time. "I can't seem to get through one morning without worshiping at the foot of the porcelain god."

"I'm so sorry." Penelope meant it. "It breaks my heart to see what you're going through."

"Everyone's different, so they tell me." Brooke clearly wished she were different. "Before this, I hadn't been sick since I was twenty and got the Asian flu. Or the chicken flu. Or whatever it was called that year."

"I don't like to brag"—Penelope loved to brag—"but when I was pregnant I never felt so good in my life. Right away I knew I had conceived, because all of a sudden I was full of energy. My hair grew inches an hour, and my fingernails were so strong I could hardly trim them. I was running a couple of miles a day, and my work was *good*. It was like being pregnant turned my mind on, and I was so fabulously creative that—" Penelope stopped in mid-sentence.

Without even thinking, she was talking about her pregnancy.

Since the day she'd held Mia in her arms, she had never mentioned the experience to anyone until Noah. It had been a private tragedy, a time to be remembered only during the darkest hours of the night, when she cried for what she had lost.

She waited for long seconds. Waited for that grief that tore her apart . . .

But while Mia's small, sweet ghost passed through her memories, Penelope was not in tears.

She sighed in relief and an odd kind of regret.

That night with Noah had given her this, too, a kind of peace to cherish.

One week ago, she had passed through a portal into the next stage of her life.

Her sorrow at Mia's death was part of her. It would always be a part of her.

But it wasn't all of her, not anymore.

"You lost your baby?" Brooke asked, then rushed on before Penelope could do more than nod. “Last week when you raced out of the design center, I guessed something like that. I should never have dragged you over to decorate the baby’s room.”

“It was the anniversary of Mia’s death. You didn’t know. Anyway, I’m better now.” Although Penelope wasn’t about to tell Brooke the reasons why. “I think that having this job and working with you has helped bring me back to life, because actually, I’m overflowing with ideas for decorating. I feel really good, too. Healthier than I’ve felt for . . .” She stopped.

She really did feel good. Amazingly good. No . . . it couldn’t . . .

“I haven’t felt this healthy since . . .” Since the last time she was pregnant.

The words reverberated in her mind.

The last time she was pregnant.

She was pregnant.

The shock made her stand tall, frozen in place, unmoving, not breathing.

“Penelope, are you okay?” Brooke grabbed her arm.

The world faded to black.

Penelope stumbled backward into the wall, slid down until her butt hit the floor, put her head between her legs.

Breathe. She had to *breathe*.

She was pregnant.

Brooke knelt beside her. “It was the shock of

talking about your ordeal, wasn't it? I'll bet you haven't been to counseling, have you? You should talk to someone who could help you through your grief."

Numbly, Penelope nodded.

Brooke put her arm around Penelope. "Why don't you get in my recliner and rest for a couple of hours? I'd send you home, but as long as you stay in that awful Sweet Dreams Hotel, that's more of a punishment."

"It's cheap. Safe," Penelope mumbled. "Got a monthly rate."

"I think you should buy a house right here in Bella Terra and stay." Brooke sounded as if she were on a crusade. "Prices are down, loan rates are good, you'd have plenty of work, and I know it's silly, but I keep hoping you and Noah could get back together."

"A house in Bella Terra. Might have to do that." Although not for any reason Brooke could imagine. Slowly, Penelope lifted her head and stared, dazed, into the future. "I have to go to the drugstore."

"Now? Why? Oh . . ." Brooke thought she understood. "You've started your period."

"Something like that." It had been seven days—no, eight—since Penelope had been with Noah. A week was the minimal time for a pregnancy test to be accurate. She could buy the test, do the test, find out the results, stare at the stick, and try to comprehend how this could have happened. . . .

Not that *she* needed a positive test.

She already knew the truth. She was pregnant.

And Noah, untrustworthy, constantly inconstant Noah, was the father.

She had been grateful to him for abandoning her, and now . . . this!

"No wonder you fainted. I'm sorry. I don't have supplies here." Brooke was sympathetic—and clueless.

Noah couldn't even stick around until morning.

With a kid, they were looking at a minimum of eighteen years.

All because Penelope had wanted sex to forget the pain caused by the hurtful end of her last pregnancy.

Some kind of cosmic justice was at work here.

But *why?*

"I wouldn't expect you to." Penelope got slowly to her feet.

What was she going to do about Noah? What was she going to say to him?

Brooke said, "I can run to the drugstore for you—"

"No!" *God forbid.* More calmly, Penelope said, "I mean, no, I can do it. I'd like the fresh air. In the meantime . . ." How to keep Brooke from volunteering to accompany her? "In the meantime, maybe you could rest and get over your morning sickness, and when you feel better . . . I brought samples for the master bedroom curtains and comforter."

Brooke clasped her hands. "Oh. I can't wait to see them!"

"You sit in the recliner and I'll put them on the table at your elbow. We'll talk about them as soon as I get back. Sound good?" Penelope thought she was talking too brightly and too fast, as if she were distracting a preschooler with a shiny toy.

But she could be allowed her awkward moments caused by surprise and . . . well, she didn't know what else she was feeling. But surprise for sure. And alarm, because really, a baby with Noah, the king of the vanishing lovers, could create all kinds of difficult situations.

But inside herself, underneath all the clutter of emotions, she spotted the tiniest, iridescent bubble of expanding joy.

Because . . . she was pregnant.

She was going to have a baby.

Perhaps her luck had turned at last.

Chapter 54

Dear Penelope, I know you hate me, but please read this. The last eight days have been a pure hell of loneliness. I treated you shabbily—again—and I am ashamed, but I promise you I have my reasons. . . .

Someone knocked on the door.

Noah stopped typing.

He had specifically instructed everybody at the resort that he was going to work in his office and he was not to be disturbed. And he meant it. He had so little time to get these letters written to Nonna and his brothers . . . and Penelope.

Hours, in fact.

He glanced at his watch.

Four hours and two minutes until three thirty-seven p.m.

He'd put his will in order. He'd done his best to prepare the resort to run without him until a new manager could be hired. He'd prepared a list of possible candidates.

Annie and June had left for Far Island, driving down the coast and taking the commuter plane across to the resort. Noah had booked their flights back to Bella Terra for tonight, knowing they would be making the journey and wanting them here for Nonna as soon as possible.

He'd put off writing the letters until the last minute, hoping against hope that he would find the bottle and free the Di Lucas from the constant threat of murder, and himself from a bloody and violent fate.

But this afternoon, the bomb at his throat would detonate.

So whoever was knocking at the door would

have to ask for help from someone else at the resort.

He started typing again.

I've been searching through the resort with ever-increasing desperation, trying to locate my grandfather's bottle of wine. The stakes are higher than you know. My brothers have been searching, too, starting at Nonna's house and working in ever-increasing circles outward. . . .

Another knock, harder this time.

Did no one at this resort believe Noah when he said, "Leave me alone"?

Actually, they did. Almost everyone who worked at the resort respected his orders, especially for the last two weeks, when he'd been a little, should he say, obsessive and irritable.

And since Brooke had retired from being his right-hand man and they'd hired a new assistant manager, problems had inevitably popped up.

So actually, if someone was knocking at his door, there was a good chance some kind of emergency had occurred and they really *did* need his help.

But he had no time.

The deathwatch had started.

The next knock on his office door made him want to snarl like a wolverine.

Yes, he had descended to some of kind animal being who snarled and slathered rather than swore like a man.

"Come in," he yelled.

No one did.

He sighed. Whoever it was had probably fled at the sound of his impatience.

Or not, because whoever it was now drummed at the door with his fingertips.

Fine. Noah would take a few precious minutes to deal with one more emergency. He wouldn't mind performing a last act that the staff could remember him by: soothe an irate guest, find some lost luggage, straighten out a security glitch.

Going to the door, he opened it.

What. A. Mistake.

Hendrik stood there. Hendrik, grinning, dressed in shiny black leather like some tough biker dude with a fashion disability.

Noah looked him over, insulting him without saying a word. But it was Hendrik, so he had to say the words or the guy wouldn't get it. "Nice threads. Afraid when I blew up, you'd get brains on yourself?"

Hendrik grinned more widely. "*Ja.* I worried. You know I had to go to San Francisco for these?"

"I'll bet."

"The shops here are so provincial!" Hendrik tried to push Noah aside and walk in.

"They really are." Noah blocked the door. "We don't have any jewelry shops with ugly man-necklaces."

Hendrik's gaze went to Noah's neck, to the tie he kept tied around his throat to hide the black band of his dog collar. "Still you cover it up. I helped Grieta and Brigetta design the necklace. I thought it looked good!"

Noah sighed. "All your taste is in your mouth. Now go away. You're not coming in. I'm not spending my last hours on earth with you, Hendrik, so I say this with the Propov familial affection—go to hell."

"You first." Hendrik tried again to bully his way in.

Noah grabbed Hendrik's leather coat and pulled him close, chest-to-chest. "Hang around and I'll take you with me." With a slap under the chin, he shoved Hendrik backward into the hall.

Hendrik flushed. "I don't take that from you, little cousin." Lowering his head like an enraged bull, he started to charge.

Noah plucked the small pistol out of his pocket and aimed it at Hendrik's chest. The click of the safety sounded as loud as a shot.

Hendrik skidded to a stop. The look of surprise on his face made Noah want to laugh out loud . . . if he could have laughed.

"Tell me why I shouldn't kill you right now,

Hendrik. The police might come and arrest me, but I'll be dead at three thirty-seven p.m." Noah couldn't believe it, but he'd just discovered the bright spot to being a walking time bomb. "So really, tell me—why shouldn't I shoot your worthless ass right now?"

"I'm wearing a bulletproof vest."

Noah aimed at Hendrik's head. "Thanks for letting me know."

Confusion and then indignation crossed Hendrik's face, and he sounded affronted when he said, "I came to do you a favor."

"Really? I thought you came to get into trouble." Hendrik had come to torment Noah, and Noah had no time. "And you're doing a fine job of it."

"I came because I thought you needed pointers on how to use a condom," Hendrik said in a patently patient tone.

"What?" *What?*

"Your girlfriend, the pretty, dark-haired one." Hendrik made a curving gesture with his hands. "I followed her this morning."

Noah pulled back the hammer on the pistol. It clicked into place.

"To the drugstore," Hendrik said so quickly he slurred his words.

"So?" Noah waited, within seconds of shooting the bastard.

Hendrik's gaze flicked between the eye of the

pistol and Noah's face. "She was buying a pregnancy test."

Noah froze.

Hendrik waited, and when Noah didn't move, didn't speak, he explained, "You know? A pregnancy test? I've been following her for a week. You're the only one she's fucking." Hendrik laughed his nasty laugh. "She's going to have your baby."

Penelope. *Having a baby.*

Penelope. *Pregnant.*

Penelope, alone in a world that included Hendrik, the abusive, lawless stalker.

In a cold, dead voice, Noah asked, "Why were you watching her?"

"She's pretty." Hendrik grinned, seeing the stillness in Noah, reading him completely wrong. "You like her, and I thought it would be fun to—"

Noah straightened his arm and aimed right between Hendrik's eyes.

"Run."

Chapter 55

Hendrik must have seen something in Noah's expression that convinced him, because he ran. He raced down the hall, looked back once to see Noah had stepped out to aim again, and took a left. Noah heard him hit the outside door. He yelped as the metal didn't yield fast enough. Then the door slammed behind him.

Noah stood, still as a statue, and wished he had killed him.

If he had, he would know right now that Penelope was safe.

But he also knew he had to be free to eliminate the threat of the Propovs and finish them entirely before they killed Nonna, and his brothers, and his sisters-in-law, and terrorized the town even more than they already had.

Noah had made the right decision.

But he didn't like it.

Turning, he walked back into his office and kicked the door closed. Going to his computer, he found a clear shot of Hendrik on the security tape and sent it to all personnel with the notice that if this man was seen on the property, they were to call the authorities and have him removed at once. And take all precautions, because he was dangerous.

Sinking into his chair, Noah stared at the letter he had been writing to Penelope.

Was Hendrik telling the truth?

Noah and Penelope had made love over and over, more times than he could count, but they had used a condom every time. *Every* time.

Of course, Noah knew the stats on condom use weren't perfect. With his casual lovers, he had always insisted on double protection—a contraceptive foam, or pills, or an IUD.

That was the trouble. Nothing about Penelope was casual.

The first time . . . well, the first time. Before he pulled his condom out of his wallet, it had been lodged in there quite a few months. Maybe the heat from his body had affected its strength. Maybe condoms had an expiration date.

Most important, Noah and Penelope had been in a hurry. In fact, they'd been downright violent. Maybe the condom had torn. . . .

Penelope. *Pregnant.*

He wrapped his hand around his stupid dog collar.

Hours left.

His whole life had played like a cosmic joke, but this was the worst. He'd made all the sacrifices, trying to ensure that no one was injured by his death. No wife to mourn him. His family would remain alive. But now . . . he was leaving an innocent child? A child conceived one week from the day her father died?

It couldn't be true.

Penelope would have told him.

But would she?

He'd walked out on her. Walked out because he'd done the wrong thing in loving her again. He didn't want to toy with her. Walked out because he needed to spend his time searching for Massimo's bottle of the damned . . . and failing.

Penelope wasn't going to tell him about the baby. She judged him as her mother had judged Joseph Bianchin: as unworthy of fatherhood.

But no matter what she thought, he had the right to know.

Anger rose in him. He stood.

He needed to know.

He strode toward the door, yanked it open—

Penelope stood on the other side, fist raised to knock.

They looked at each other, both surprised.

Penelope glanced away as if afraid of the coming conversation, or maybe of him. "Hi." She caught herself avoiding his gaze, and looked right at him. "I was wondering if I could talk to you for a moment?"

"Sure." Was it true?

Had they made a baby?

He stepped back and gestured her in.

"I won't bother you for long." She walked inside and stood in the middle of the room.

He shut the door after them. "You could never bother me."

"I guess I could. When I'm around, you disappear fast enough." She caught her breath, shook her head. "No, I'm sorry. I wasn't going to bring that up."

"It's fair."

She flicked him a scornful glance. "Yes, of course it's *fair*. But that's not why I'm here." She paused as if gathering her forces. "I just . . . I don't know how to say this. It's not what we intended—I mean, obviously—but for me it's a miracle, a gift from God. But I do understand you're not going to feel that way."

He didn't dare speak. He didn't dare assume. . . . But it was true. She had a glow about her, and for all that she was nervous, she kept trying to smile; then, intent on being serious, she would wipe away her smile.

"I don't want you to think I'm trying to get into your wallet," she said. "I can take care of myself, and . . . and I thought about this for the last hour or so, what I should do. When it comes to me and our relationship, you've been untrustworthy and irresponsible. But I knew that; I knew I shouldn't have gotten involved with you again; I can't blame you for being who and what you are. It's not like you've changed in the past nine years or anything."

His gaze fell to her hands, hanging at her sides, clenching and unclenching.

She continued. "But last week, you were there at the right time, and I've always loved you, and I'm grateful for the time we spent together. You know, after you got me out of the bar."

"Yes. I know what you mean." The tight ball in the pit of his stomach eased as she spoke, and he began to feel almost . . . giddy. Light-headed. And for a man condemned to die today, that was odd. To him, his voice sounded odd, too, as if it were coming from inside a seashell. "What are you trying to tell me?"

She looked at him, then away, then at him again. She gnawed her lower lip, braced herself, and said, "We're having a baby."

It was true.

It was true.

He took a breath.

It was true.

"Noah? Are you okay?"

He shook his head.

He was going to die. Literally. He was going to die, killed by his mother and her brutal family.

And he was having a baby with the woman he loved.

In the space of three minutes, everything had changed.

What seemed like the right thing to do before, was now wrong.

Three minutes ago, he could say farewell to his family, to Penelope, and know that because they knew him, they would believe the best of him. They would know he was a good man who had given up his life for them. And not without a fight. They might not approve—his brothers most definitely would not—but his choice had been clear-cut.

Now . . . eight days ago, he had created an innocent life. That child would never know him.

That child would blame him for not living and being the father he should be.

Noah had to make a different choice.

He had to gamble with everyone's life . . . for the sake of the child.

He walked like an automaton toward Penelope.

She backed away, her eyes wide, viewing him as if he were a madman.

He supposed he looked that way.

Reaching out to her, he enfolded her in his arms, pulled her close, and whispered, "Thank you. Thank you for giving me a reason to live."

Chapter 56

Fists in the air, Grieta swung her computer chair around in a circle and chortled. "I did it!"

"What did you do, dear?" Liesbeth's hand trembled as she pulled the black thread in and out of her tapestry.

"I reactivated the microphone in Noah's necklace," Grieta said.

"About time," Klaas said. "How about the camera?"

Grieta cast him a look of disgust. "You're welcome."

"That's very good, Grieta," Liesbeth said. "Once again, you've come through for us."

Grieta beamed, pleased with Liesbeth's praise.

They still valued her praise.

Yet they were cruel creatures. She had trained them to be proper Propovs, to despise the meek and the poor. They would kill her for any weakness.

Liesbeth's thoughts shifted to Hendrik. Hendrik especially would kill her. He had enjoyed his time spent stalking Joseph Bianchin's daughter. Every night he talked about how pretty this Penelope was, how vulnerable, how unaware . . . how eight days ago, she had spent all night with Noah and then they had separated and not seen each other since.

Right now, he was after her again, watching her, plotting how he would use her to make Noah's last hours miserable . . . and how he would hunt her after Noah was dead, and hurt her.

After all, this girl didn't matter. She was one of the lesser beings they all despised. But Liesbeth didn't like the way Hendrik gloated, as if he thought his intentions for Noah's woman would disturb Liesbeth. Hendrik seemed to imagine Liesbeth had a fondness for her son. It was as if he could see within Liesbeth's mind, and enjoyed watching her affection wash away her cruelty.

He viewed Noah as a weakness he could use against her.

"Grieta, you've made me happy," Brigetta said. "I want to hear Noah whimpering as his hour of death grows closer."

"You really are a bloodthirsty little thing." Rutger admired that. "But so is our leader."

Everyone faced Liesbeth in awe and admiration.

"Come, now," she said in a steady voice. "You know I abhor violence."

Klaas snorted.

She ignored him. "I thought up the bomb at Noah's throat only because I believed it would never be activated. I imagined he knew the bottle's location and all he needed was the incentive to produce it." How could Liesbeth have so misread her own son?

"If it's true that he knows, he's one cool customer." Brigetta glanced at the clock. "He has four hours to hand it over."

"He's wetting himself," Klaas assured her. "His dampness will probably short-circuit the bomb and he'll die early."

Their cruel laugher echoed in Liesbeth's ears.

"We've got sound. Want to hear our little boy cousin sweating his last day on earth?" Grieta turned back to the computer.

Brigetta, Klaas, and Rutger rushed toward the computer desk.

Liesbeth followed, dragging her feet.

She didn't often give credence to her forebodings, but . . . she had a very bad feeling that today would not turn out well.

• • •

Penelope stood in Noah's embrace, limp with relief. Of all the reactions she'd imagined, that Noah would be glad had never crossed her mind. "You believe me, then?"

"Of course I believe you." He laughed. "Why would you lie?"

"To catch a Di Luca."

"You caught me," he replied with easy amusement.

"I thought you might accuse me of going home from the bar every night with a different guy." She tensed, waiting for an answer.

"If I had thought such a thing—and I hadn't—a quick fact check would have changed my mind. Like, Arianna Marino would have thrown you out. Like, if you had been a regular visitor at the Beaver Inn, Primo wouldn't have called me about you, would he?"

"Right. But do you realize . . . I mean, have you thought about the fact that the baby's grandfather is going to be Joseph Bianchin?"

Picking her up, he sat in one of his office chairs and held her in his lap. "I've got some relatives who aren't so hot, too. You'll meet them at the . . ." He looked suddenly grim. "Well. My current plan is that you will meet them at the wedding."

"Um. Well. I don't think we need to rush into anything." She didn't trust him not to run off as soon as things got tough. She believed in the wedding vows; she wasn't about to have a five-minute marriage. "As I said, I can raise the baby on my own. I *have* done all the research already."

"Hm. We'll talk about it. If we have a girl . . . would you want to call her Mia?"

Ready tears sprang to Penelope's eyes. "No, I couldn't. That's the name of my first child. I was thinking maybe . . . Sarah? For your grandmother, who has always been so good to me."

"And me." He put his forehead against hers and smiled into her eyes. "And me."

"Plus the name is from the Bible, so it will always be in style." She smiled back at him, and thought how very much she liked him when his eyes gleamed green and gold.

"I think Sarah is a wonderful name."

Penelope should have been totally relaxed, sheltered and warm in Noah's arms, but something niggled at her mind, something he'd said. "Noah, what do you mean, I gave you a reason to live?"

He released a breath that sounded like the first gust of an oncoming storm. "I have a story to tell you."

She tensed. "Is it really long and boring, like *Moby-Dick*?"

"No, actually it's incredibly exciting. At least, it was when I lived it. But it *is* long enough that I only have time to tell it once." Standing, he deposited her in the chair, then paced across the room to his phone. He made two quick phone calls, one to Eli and one to Rafe, telling them to meet him at Nonna's, and then he held out his hand to Penelope. "Come on. There's no time. We've got to hurry."

Chapter 57

Noah looked around the table at his brothers. At his sisters-in-law. At Nonna. At Penelope. It had taken all of them two hours to assemble here in Nonna's kitchen, always the setting for the most important moments of his life. How appropriate that here they should all be, together again, while he bared his soul and confessed his shame.

He was out of time, less than two hours left before his head left his shoulders, and yet with all the people he cared about here and all their attention on him, his voice failed him.

No, not his voice. His nerve.

Taking Penelope's hand, he tried to smile.

She squeezed his fingers.

The tension ratcheted up.

Eli said, "C'mon, Noah. Chloë's got an appointment to get her body cast off, and she's been looking forward to this for weeks. If you make her late, you'll be wearing a body cast, instead."

"No kidding," Brooke said. "If you're finally going to tell us who's after Massimo's pink diamonds, do it in a hurry, before I have to go to the bathroom again."

The way they teased him, supported him, made him smile—and hope they would still support him when the story was finished.

Or at least, that they would rescue him from his folly.

Noah's high school graduation present was a year spent trying to find himself, enough money to travel the world, as long as he stayed within his budget, and the freedom to do it alone (as long as he checked in with his grandmother once a week).

He waved good-bye to his family on a sunny day in June, excited and scared, and not realizing that when he returned, he would be a man who had left all remnants of his innocence behind.

He flew directly to Amsterdam, guilty about keeping a secret from his grandparents and thrilled to embark on the adventure his mother had promised him.

She met him at baggage claim. "Darling boy." She kissed him on the cheek. "I'm so glad you could come."

"Of course. Why wouldn't I?"

"I thought perhaps your grandparents

would forbid you from making the trip by yourself. You are so very young."

As he was supposed to, he stiffened resentfully. "I've been abroad before." One other time, when he was nine. He had gone with Nonno and Nonna and met the Di Luca family, a small but gregarious tribe who lived in a Tuscan villa, served so much food, and laughed so often, they reminded Noah of an Olive Garden commercial.

They also pinched his cheek a lot, something he did not recall fondly.

Now Liesbeth patted his cheek. "I know, dear. I was watching you from afar. Remember?"

The thought made him squirm—it seemed so underhanded—so he added resentfully, "And my grandparents don't tell me what to do. They let me make my own decisions."

"As it should be. Why, when Klaas and Hendrik were your age, they had already performed many important missions. . . ." She furtively glanced around. "But this is no place to talk." She led him to a fabulous BMW M3 and drove off even before he had buckled his seat belt. "Let us go home, where you can meet your other family. The Smit family."

"Smit? I thought the family was Russian."

"Yes," she said approvingly. "Our real

name is Propov. Smit is the Dutch name your ancestors had picked so they could blend in. It has worked very well. Our neighbors barely notice us."

The house—old, tall, gloomy, and located on a canal—was also chosen to fit into the Amsterdam landscape. Furniture was minimal and plain, very Scandinavian, and the big rooms were always cold.

Noah told himself he loved it, although he spent most of the first week shivering in corridors and wishing he were home in sunny Bella Terra.

Liesbeth introduced him to his male cousins: an older man named Falco, Klaas, and, of course, Hendrik. "They've just come back from a mission," she told Noah. Then she sat them down and interrogated them.

Noah was impressed, both at their knowledge of how to enter a diplomatic function when they hadn't been invited, and by Liesbeth's absolute mastery over them. They answered her respectfully. When she chided them they groveled. When she praised them, they beamed.

Noah's perception of his mother became filled with awe, and when his male cousins shook his hand and fervently welcomed him home, he felt warm inside, flattered that they would believe he belonged among them.

He met the girls the next day. They were dazzling, too, but clearly their jobs were less dangerous than the guys'. And Noah desperately wanted to be one of the guys.

He told Liesbeth he would like to be trained in the trade.

He wasn't exactly sure what the trade was, but he thought it involved Interpol or spying or something cool.

Later he wondered why he thought that.

Mostly because he couldn't imagine that his mother would work for the bad guys. But also because he was being played by a team of experts.

She laughed and shook her head. "My dear son, these men have been in training their whole lives. They've been on the job since they were seven, risking their lives for all that's right. To train you before our next job . . . in so short a time . . . I just don't believe it's possible."

"I'm in good shape. I'm smart. I'm a fast learner."

Liesbeth chewed her lip thoughtfully. "Let me talk to the others. See what they say. Perhaps they would be willing." She started to walk away, then turned back abruptly. "Even if they are, understand this—if I think you couldn't make it, if I thought you put our mission in danger, I would cut you out."

"Of course." He lifted his chin. "I wouldn't want to drag the family down." And he swore to himself he would succeed.

In fifteen minutes, the family came back to him and with serious faces surrounded him and interrogated him about his life, his loves, his intentions, and why he wanted to do this.

Then they got into a huddle, where they buzzed with conversation, occasionally glancing at him with visible doubt.

Noah wanted to chew his nails, but he stood and waited, only occasionally shifting from foot to foot.

When the family was finished talking, a very serious Hendrik came back to him. "We'll train you for the next three months. But God help you, because you're going to wish you were dead."

Hendrik was right.

They put Noah through the most grueling kind of boot camp, with training in physical defense of every kind. Every day, they battered him until he was exhausted and covered with bruises, and then they put him in the classroom and made him learn. Electronics. Ballistics, disguises, languages. His brain sagged under the weight of the information he took in. And God forbid that he fail to answer a question right—his punishment was more physical exercise.

He slept five hours a night; then he got up and did it all again.

At the end of three months, he was lean and tough, faster than he could have ever imagined, knowledgeable about everything from disabling a security camera to opening a safe to taking on a surprise attack by all three of his male relatives at once. When Liesbeth told him he was ready for his first mission, he was so proud.

He was such a fool.

Chapter 58

Noah and Hendrik traveled by train to the small eastern European country where they would do the job.

Hendrik was in disguise.

Noah was not.

The rest of the team traveled separately, arriving one at a time in an upstairs room at the local inn in the small mountain village. There Liesbeth gave them their mission. "The former dictator of the country lives in the castle on that hill." She pointed out the window.

Noah walked over and looked.

The gray stone castle looked like something out of a Dracula movie. Its roots dug into a high, rocky knoll, its towers reaching six stories into the cloudless sky. The road that wound around and up the rock looked precarious at best.

Noah suffered a disagreeable insight. He did not want to do this.

"Oblak is an evil man," Liesbeth said, "reviled for his cruelties to his country and his countrymen. He tortured. He raped. He killed without compunction and buried his victims in mass graves. He extorted wealth from every family. He is alive only because of his special private militia, whom he pays very well."

Great. An impregnable castle, a tough, well-paid force of bodyguards, and Oblak the monster dictator. Even Noah had heard of him.

"So whatever we do, we are serving justice on a monster," Hendrik said.

Everyone nodded vigorously.

Noah nodded, too, but more cautiously. The knowledge of Oblak's crimes against humanity left him feeling a little dizzy.

Not so the others. When Liesbeth said, "So it is with great pleasure that I say . . . we are to steal a valuable painting from him," they cheered, even the women.

The mission surprised Noah; he had thought they would be doing something more . . . spylike. Retrieving a computer chip or something.

He faced the others and asked the first question he'd asked in weeks. "Are we returning the painting to its rightful owners?"

Everyone froze in place.

Not even Liesbeth spoke.

Only Hendrik answered. "Sure we are."

"Good." Noah hoped it was a small painting. Getting anything big out of that aerie seemed unlikely at best.

As Liesbeth popped up the floor plans of the castle and the photographs taken by some surreptitious means, Noah realized the painting hung high over the fireplace in Oblak's great room, a centerpiece, a thing of pride, so big Noah would barely be able to reach from one side of the frame to the other. Furthermore, he recognized it; the painting was famous for both its seventeenth-century artist and its disappearance thirty years ago from the Hermitage in St. Petersburg, Russia.

Noah tried to tell himself he was proud to rescue the celebrated artwork and see it returned to the Hermitage.

In fact, he broke a sweat wondering what he would be expected to do.

Liesbeth's scheme was intricate, delicate, involving a slow break-in that would go undetected and a fast escape involving a helicopter, and, she announced proudly, the whole mission depended on her son, Noah.

His heart pounded. He couldn't swallow the lump of fear in his throat.

The team seemed to notice nothing wrong. Instead, they patted him on the back and congratulated him, and went to work immediately, not giving him any chance to think things through, to wonder why he was the only one not in disguise, to ask about the plans to return the painting to the Hermitage.

Instead, he concentrated on completing his mission and coming out alive.

And he did.

Only to discover the whole thing, every moment of the last three months, had been nothing but a setup to trap him into doing whatever Liesbeth and her gang ordered him to do.

Chapter 59

Noah had broken the first commandment of Liesbeth's gang: He had betrayed them.

Now Klaas and Grieta, Brigetta and Rutger stared at Liesbeth, waiting for her to take command. And for the first time in her life . . . she didn't want to do what had to be done.

Yes, Noah had ignored their threats and told his other family, the Di Lucas, who they were and what they did. He had put himself firmly on the side of the enemy. But he was her son, her only child. From the time she had first observed him, seen the intelligence in him, the ability to act swiftly, his physical strength and his potential to serve as the gang's leader, she had put her hopes in him.

She had always told herself her interest in naming him her successor was nothing more than a cold assessment of Hendrik's abilities weighed against Noah's abilities. Yet now, facing the decision she knew she had to make, she felt the unlikely and incredible biological tug of motherhood.

She could not speak the command to kill him.

And as she hesitated, the others' gazes grew distant and chilly.

Then the study door slammed open, and Hendrik walked in, smelling of sweat and perfume, with a long scratch on his cheek and lipstick on his collar. "Hey, guess what I've done," he said. Without waiting for an answer, he said, "The girl Noah rammed last week, she's bought a pregnancy kit! And when I told our little Noah, I thought he was going to faint."

No one responded.

Hendrik looked around. "Have you lost your senses of humor? He's going to be a father, and he found out a few hours before that bomb at his throat goes off."

Brigetta faced him. "Grieta got the microphone

on Noah's collar to work. We heard him. He told them about us."

"Noah?" Hendrik looked from one to another. "He told who about us?"

"His family. His *real* family," Klaas mocked with his singsong tone, but Liesbeth could tell he was ugly-angry.

"But he knows better. He knows we'll kill anyone who knows. . . ." Hendrik seemed to exhale pleasure. "So let's go teach that little bastard a lesson."

Everyone turned to Liesbeth and waited. She said, "Yes. We have to kill them all."

But she was too late in responding, too . . . emotional.

This was not what she had planned.

But it was what Hendrik had planned. All his life, he had been waiting for the moment when Liesbeth faltered. Now he slid smoothly into command. "We'll go in teams. Klaas and Grieta, you'll go onto the property through the culvert. They lost me there last time. It's the best way around their feeble security. We'll ride together—I'll drop you off."

Klaas and Grieta stood and started gathering their gear.

"Rutger and Brigetta, you take the Cadillac."

They groaned.

"I know," Hendrik said sympathetically, "but that thing is built like a tank. You can off-road and come in through the back of the property. As for me—I'll stick close to Liesbeth to make sure she hasn't lost the stomach for revenge on the Propov enemies."

Liesbeth dived for her weapon.

But she was too late.

Hendrik's Glock was already in his hand and pointed at her. "You drive, Liesbeth. I'll give you the directions. I wouldn't want you to get lost." With his free hand, he gestured widely. "Come on. Let's go!"

Chapter 60

In less than twenty minutes, Noah finished his story—really, even if he wasn't scheduled to die, why would he dwell on every little humiliating detail?—and when he was done, he discovered he didn't dare look around. He couldn't stand to see Eli and Rafe glaring at him, to have Brooke and Chloë examine him as if they had never met him before, to witness Nonna's disappointment . . . to observe as Penelope realized that the man who was the father of her baby was every bit as corrupt as she had believed.

"All those letters you wrote from Paris . . . you were in Amsterdam?" Nonna sounded stunned.

"Yes, Nonna. I'm sorry." An understatement.

Eli jumped in first. Of course. "Let me get this

straight. You survived this horrendously difficult robbery, and they told you . . . ?"

"They told me I'd been taped by Oblak's security system, and since I was the only one who hadn't been in disguise, I was the only one who could be identified." When Rafe would have spoken, Noah held up his hand for silence. "We're short on time here. Let me finish. Liesbeth and the gang had taken the evidence, not to ensure that I was safe, but so they had me under control. If they decided to release the tapes, Oblak would send his private thugs to kill me. If Oblak didn't get to me, well, we had stolen the painting to be sold to another private collector, so the Russian secret police would take me and torture me until I gave up all the information I knew. Which was nothing. If Russian secret police didn't get me, the CIA and Interpol would put me in prison forever, or until one of my dear relatives assassinated me."

"They're after Nonno's bottle of wine and the diamonds?" Rafe said.

"Exactly." Noah nodded.

Okay, the worst was over. They were still speaking to him. Although everyone was definitely viewing him differently, especially Penelope, who sat with her head cocked, her soft brown eyes watching him as if she couldn't quite comprehend everything he had done.

"How did you not suspect?" Brooke had

known and worked for Noah for years, and that he could have been so gullible clearly astonished her.

"Part of the training was respect for those who had more knowledge than me. That was everybody. So I didn't ask questions. I did as I was told. Frankly, I was so exhausted, I didn't even think of the questions until afterward." Noah's voice faded. *Excuses.* Those were nothing but excuses.

But Rafe nodded. "They brainwashed you."

"Clean as a whistle," Chloë said, and she sounded as if she wanted to take notes.

"I have a question," Penelope said. "All these years, you've told no one. Why are you telling us now?"

Noah knew this wouldn't go over well. "I've been protecting . . . all of you."

Bao and Rafe both snorted.

"I'm serious." This was the critical moment. Noah had to convince them of the truth. "I told you they trained me hard and long. I've trained since, too, and I'm pretty good. Rafe, you know that."

Rafe nodded. "You are."

"In hand-to-hand combat, they're better than I am. In weaponry, they're better than I am. Better than you are, Rafe, and for sure better than Eli."

"Hey!" Eli said.

"I saw you fight, Eli. You saved my life, and I

love you for it." Chloë leaned across the table and put her hand on his arm. "But right now, what would you do in a fight? Club them with your cast?"

Rafe and Noah laughed.

Eli glared at his wife, then shot his brothers a distinctive signal with that cast.

They hastily sobered.

Noah said, "The gang, even Hendrik, physically trains at least three hours a day. They shoot an hour a day. They can engage in close combat and shoot a bull's-eye and change their disguise—all at the same time. And they have rules."

"What kind of rules?" Nonna asked.

"First rule: Family is the only thing that matters. Never betray them. Second rule: No matter what it takes, bring home the treasure. What I'm trying to tell you is"—Noah couldn't say this clearly enough—"they don't care if they kill. Human life means nothing to them." He gritted his teeth, but he had to tell them the whole truth. "During the heist, they killed three of Oblak's servants without even blinking. That was when I realized—as far as they're concerned, the Propovs are at the top of the food chain, and everyone else is inferior and therefore not worthy of consideration."

"They kill for sport?" Eli asked.

"Not even that," Rafe said.

Everyone looked at him, surprised.

"Sorry, but I know what Noah's saying. I've met people like that in special ops and on the other side. Killing is not done for fun; it's just something that happens. Women, children, old men . . . if a murder makes your mission work more smoothly, then murder and never think twice. Those people, they call it collateral damage." Rafe shook his head. "Noah's right. I do think before I pull the trigger."

Convincing Rafe was half the battle. "You can't fight these guys. I can't fight these guys. I can't kill without compunction. I would hesitate to murder another human being, and in that hesitation, I would be dead."

"But why are you telling us *now?*" Penelope spoke clearly, spacing the words, demanding the real response.

Noah didn't want to answer. He really, really didn't want to answer.

And before he could, Rafe said, "You believe you know too much about them. You believe they're not going to let you live."

"I've always known I had two choices. I either take over the gang, or when I've fulfilled the duty for which I was born—to find the bottle of wine—I'd be killed. As you said, I know too much, and if my mother balked at doing the job, my cousins would not. But right now, it's a little more immediate than that." The clock was ticking, and so was the bomb at his throat . . . and the baby in Penelope's womb was growing by the minute. He looked at her, but he spoke to his brothers. "Because unless we do something, I'm going to die in about an hour and a half."

"What?" Eli snapped.

"What?" Rafe came to his feet.

Now Noah spoke only to Penelope. "I know I've proved myself to be the corrupt fool you always believed I was, but I love you. I always have, and as God is my witness, I always will. If I live through this day, will you marry me?"

Her eyes sharpened. "If I say yes, will you live through this day?"

"That is my intention."

"Then, yes. I will." She smiled, but her lips were tight. She grabbed his hand in both of hers and dug her fingernails into his skin, although he didn't think she realized she was doing it. "Why do you think you're going to die?"

Noah eased his hand out of her grasp, loosened his tie, and unbuttoned his shirt. As the dog collar came into view, the reactions almost made him laugh. Almost.

Trained by long years of absurd adolescent fashion, Nonna tilted her head and silently studied it.

"I'd stick with the shirt and tie," Brooke advised.

Eli woofed.

Chloë, the mystery writer, said, "Wow, with those studs, you could wire that thing to do anything. Play music, show videos, shoot off a—" Then she got it, and her eyes got round with horror.

Rafe and Bao got it, too, and came to their feet.

Penelope slowly stood also. She leaned toward him, looked into his eyes as if demanding the truth. "You told me you lost a bet. That's a lie. You're not going to *die*. Those animals tied that around your neck. They're planning to *murder* you—and *now* you propose to me?"

Chapter 61

Joseph Bianchin stood in the window and watched those Smit hoodlums drive away in his cars.

How dared they? They had eaten his food, lived in his house, hacked into his computer—oh, yes! He knew the truth. It took him a long time to realize that was the problem. He'd blamed it on his computer, on the connection, on everything and anything, trying to figure out why the damned thing worked only part-time.

He was indignant until he realized that the Internet was behaving oddly, too. He could get to certain pages—no problem getting to his pressure-points page or researching pink diamonds or reading his news stories. But other pages, pages about the Smit gang and their crimes, pages he'd visited only a few days before—they showed up blank, as if they had been hijacked. He didn't want to believe those thieves downstairs could outsmart him . . . but the suspicion had been growing on him.

Somehow, they had hacked his computer and falsified e-mails.

He hadn't been able to make calls.

He hadn't been able to leave the house.

They had controlled him in every way.

Now they stole his cars, leaving him here alone for the first time in weeks . . . and like an animal caught in a trap, he was afraid to leave.

What if this hurried leaving was nothing more than a trick to lure him outside, where they could slaughter him? Or they'd set an explosive that activated when he opened his door?

But none of that made sense. If they wanted to kill him, they could have done it at any time. As he'd once heard Liesbeth say to her bloodthirsty relatives, *Let the old man live; a body stinks*.

Going to the phone, he lifted it and held it to his ear.

Still no dial tone.

He walked down the stairs. He peered in every room. The study showed signs of their hurried leaving.

He walked toward his desk.

His mail was here, opened, stacked, tossed, violated.

His indignation clawed at his gut.

His *mail*. Was nothing sacred anymore?

A brown manila envelope caught his eye.

For more than a week, he'd been watching for something like this. Not that he expected that that Penelope person was truly his daughter, but he wanted to know for sure. It only made sense to know. . . .

He picked up the already opened envelope, pulled out the report, read it. Then he stood there, stupidly holding it in his hand, staring at the words.

That girl *was* his daughter.

Penelope was his daughter.

He had a child.

He looked out the window.

He'd wanted progeny, but in an abstract way, as Bianchin-DNA-bearing creatures who would take him into the future.

She wasn't what he wanted. Penelope was opinionated, sharp-tongued, without the proper respect for his position and his wealth. She had no patience for his intolerance. She said she had no need of his fortune. Not that he believed her, but . . . she'd so clearly despised him. She hadn't bothered to fawn on him even the slightest bit.

Most important, she failed him because she was a girl. She would not carry the Bianchin name into the future. She'd get married, have children, and those children would bear their father's last name.

Or maybe Joseph could bribe the young couple to do his bidding, get them to take the Bianchin name.

But not if he didn't get out of here *now*.

He quickly moved toward the front door, then hesitated, his hand on the knob.

What if one of those awful goons stood on the other side, waiting with a loaded rifle and an obnoxious grin?

No. He had seen them leave.

Taking a deep breath, Joseph flung the door wide. He stepped out on the porch.

Nothing stirred in his shady, well-groomed, expansive, and expensive front yard.

Nothing except . . . his gardener, that Jap, driving his Ford F-150 down the curving driveway toward the gate, headed out for lunch.

Joseph realized . . . this was his chance. He could get away.

"Hey!" he shouted. "Hey!" He waved his arms.

The Jap kept driving.

"Hey!" Joseph shouted louder, running down the stairs, sprinting across the lawn, trying to cut off the truck before it reached the gate. "Hey. You! I command that you wait for me!"

Chapter 62

Nonna got to her feet, looking agitated. "I've already got a roast out of the freezer, so I'd better get dinner going."

"Get Darren on the phone," Brooke instructed Rafe.

Rafe already had his cell phone out, calling his best computer guru. He explained the situation in terse sentences, then handed the phone to Brooke. "Talk to him. From the information Noah presented, it's my opinion the Propov gang will be coming to watch the Fourth of July—"

Noah supposed that was Rafe's way of saying, *When Noah gets his head blown off.*

Rafe continued. "—and if my security can get the jump on one, we can pull him in here and force him to remove that thing around Noah's neck."

"Quite right. I'll work the team." Bao ran out the door, speaking into her phone.

Rafe put his hand on Noah's shoulder. "One way or another, we'll get this taken care of." His voice was affectionate and reassuring.

Improbably, Noah relaxed. He had confessed his past and his present to his family for exactly this reason. Because these sensible, loving, intelligent, daring people were the only ones in the world who could rescue him, and even better—they would save their reproaches until the collar was off.

Then, he knew, they would kick his ass, individually and collectively.

Turning to Penelope, he said, "I proposed to you because for the first time, I could ask and know you could answer honestly, knowing the truth about me."

Penelope nodded. She stood up. She slapped him on the side of the head.

He swayed back.

"I always knew who you were," she said. "I just didn't know the specific details."

He glanced around.

Smiles all around, hidden or not.

"Thank you for saying yes anyway." He rubbed his skull.

More smiles.

"You're welcome," Penelope said coolly, and sank back down on the chair.

"See you when I get back." With one more squeeze of Noah's shoulder, Rafe raced out after Bao.

Chloë had her netbook on the table and open, her fingers flying on the keys. "I can find no reference to a murder weapon of this type," she said to Brooke, "but surely they didn't invent the device." She shot a worried look at Noah.

"I assure you, they did," Noah said.

Brooke held the phone away from her ear and

asked, “Noah! Is that thing around your neck leather?”

“Yes.” Noah ran a finger around the edge. “The Propovs were very concerned about fashion.”

The Di Lucas frowned at him as if questioning his sanity.

“They have crappy taste,” he added.

Chloë shoved her netbook under Eli’s nose.

Eli studied the screen and nodded. “Great. On the leather, I mean.” Going to Nonna’s junk drawer, he dug around until he found the utility knife. Opening it, he tested the razor blade, then got a fresh razor blade. He changed it, then pointed at the chair closest to the window. “Sit there. We’re going to slice that baby open to see what’s inside.”

Penelope moaned slightly.

Noah hugged her. “Don’t worry. I’d trust Eli with . . .” *My life,* he meant. He decided to leave it unsaid, and sat in the chair indicated.

“Well, you’re gonna.” Eli stared at the open blade with a cold eye, then nodded kindly at Penelope. “Don’t worry. I’m always grafting vines, and it requires a steady hand. I’m the best man for this job.” Eli’s assurance was immutable. “But I would like another pair of eyes. Chloë, can you talk me through this?”

Chloë closed her netbook and stood. “Yes. Let Darren search. Because I’m getting so many hits on explosives, I can’t distinguish a good link from a bad link. Why do so many people want to blow stuff up?" She walked to Noah, put her hand on his shoulder, leaned close, and looked.

He stretched his neck, moving it from side to side to allow her a clear view.

"Put me on video so I can watch," Darren said on speakerphone.

He and Brooke made the connection; then Brooke placed the phone on the counter close to Noah, propped up so Darren could see and hear.

"It's a flat leather band against his skin," Chloë said. "Another leather band is overlaid on that and they're stitched together. The studs cut through the top leather, so it's safe to say there's a wire underneath the top band that connects the studs and controls the mechanism."

Darren's voice came from the phone. "Noah, how are they going to kill you? Bomb or electric charge? Or laser?"

"Explosive," Noah said. "On a timer."

"Primitive, but effective," Darren muttered; then he yelled, "Cut the stitching very carefully."

For a brief, disgusted moment, Eli glared at Darren's face on the phone's screen. "I'm going to do this whole thing very carefully."

"Right," Darren said, a little more subdued.

Chloë moved out of Eli's light.

Nonna turned away from the stove to watch.

Brooke crossed her arms, her gaze narrowed and intent.

Penelope covered her eyes, and then took her hands away; Noah knew she couldn't stand to observe, and couldn't stand not to.

The kitchen was deadly silent as Eli positioned the utility knife at the side of Noah's throat, slid the sharp blade between the two leather bands, and cut the first stitches.

Nothing happened.

It was the best nothing Noah had ever experienced.

Relieved, frightened, angry glances were exchanged; then Eli continued slicing through the stitches, moving slowly, making sure he disturbed nothing lethal, until Noah finally snapped, "I haven't got all day, Eli, and I mean that literally."

"Right." From the corner of Noah's eye, he saw Eli's hand tremble; then he moved swiftly to slash the stitching, top and bottom.

"Now slice the leather up and down so we can peel it back," Darren said.

"Want me to take over, Eli?" Brooke asked. "You're sweating."

"So are you," Eli said.

Brooke pushed her hair off her forehead. "Am I?" she asked distractedly.

Chloë circled Noah, examining the collar again. "Take the slice right there." She pointed toward the middle of his throat.

The profound silence made her look around at

their doubting faces. "Ask Darren if I'm right. Eli can't cut at the back. Everything's connected into the latch, which is the timer and the most wired part of this contraption. The farther away from that we get, the better we are."

"She's absolutely right." Darren's voice got a little wobbly. They could hear him still typing, still searching for some knowledge of how to fix the problem. "Not that there's a good choice."

No one appreciated his adding the last comment, but he was seventeen and a nerd, so Noah tried to sound as prosaic as possible. "This is going to turn out well, or it isn't. So let's get it over with."

Nonna moved in with a kitchen towel and blotted Eli's forehead. "I'd like to give it a try," she said, her voice as bright as if she were offering to take over a sewing project.

"Nonna, thank you, but you've got a bit of a tremor," Eli said.

"That's because I've got eighty-year-old hands." Nonna held them out. "They've got arthritis in the joints. They've been used for a lot of things. I wouldn't miss them much."

Noah tried to smile at Penelope, but he couldn't. His guilt and worry were too profound. Because Nonna expressed what they'd all been thinking: If the collar blew, it wasn't only Noah who would lose. Eli's hands would go, too.

"Nonna, when I get done with this, I'm going to

want a meal. Please cook for me." By that, Eli meant no, and he kept the knife firmly in his grip.

"You boys make me so angry." Nonna stood with her fists on her hips. "I suppose I should be happy you're not fighting anymore, but somehow, that's not cutting it." Turning, she whipped around and started banging pans, hard, on the stove.

She wasn't really mad, Noah knew. She was scared.

Eli sliced at the leather and in a conversational tone said, "Noah, I didn't quite understand why you decided to tell us now rather than fling yourself on a martyr's grave."

"He had no choice." Penelope was chalky with tension, but her voice was firm and strong. "We're having a baby."

"But this morning you started your . . . Oh." Brooke looked startled, then thoughtful. "Ohh."

"Hey! Congratulations, Noah!" Darren's voice was cheerful.

"My dears." Nonna came to hug first Penelope, then Noah. Her brown eyes were bright with joy, and heavy with added fear. Being Nonna, she spoke only of the joy. "You've made me so happy."

"Good job, man!" Eli socked Noah in the shoulder.

"For Pete's sake, don't jostle him!" Chloë admonished.

Eli pulled his hand back. “Sorry!”

“The collar seems very stable. I’ve worn it for two weeks,” Noah said.

“Two weeks!” Eli smacked him again, more lightly. “What the hell? You couldn’t have told us sooner?”

“I was trying to do the right thing.” Noah watched Penelope with such warmth, she flushed, bringing some color to her pallid face. “It’s okay,” he said to her. “We’ll do this.”

She nodded as if she believed him, but her face was bleak.

She was recalling, he knew, the deaths that had previously broken her, and bracing herself for another future alone. She knew too much of sorrow, and his heart ached as he imagined her anxiety now.

Going to the stove, Brooke said, “Darren’s searching the net. Chloë’s helping Eli. I’m not doing anything, and it’s making me jumpy. Want me to peel potatoes or something?”

“Thank you, dear, but you’re supposed to drive Chloë into town to have her cast off,” Nonna said.

Waving a dismissive hand, Chloë said, “I can’t go.”

“Yes, you can,” Noah said. “I appreciate your solicitude, I truly do, but you can go to the doctor’s, get the cast cut off, and be back before anything is scheduled to . . . happen.”

Penelope glanced at her watch, then glanced at the clock above the door. "What time did you say . . . ?"

Noah saw no kindness in keeping her in suspense. "Three thirty-seven p.m."

"Right. You go on, Chloë. My eyes are good. I can examine the collar and give Eli directions." Penelope got to her feet and stood beside Noah, her hand on his shoulder.

He was getting a lot of shoulder action today, but only Penelope stroked him, taking comfort as well as giving it. She seemed steadier with something to do, and he thought they all recognized it.

"See, honey? There's always another female to tell me what to do," Eli said to Chloë. "You've been miserable for six weeks. Get the cast off and come back. I'll have the dog collar off of Rover by then."

"Long-distance worry counts as support, too," Noah assured her, then made a shooing motion.

Brooke pointed her finger at Noah. "I want to know the second Eli gets the bomb defused."

Noah appreciated their certainty. "We'll give you a call."

Brooke and Chloë grabbed their purses and ran down the hall and out the front door, not to escape the situation, but so they could quickly return.

"I can't quite get this vertical cut all the way through this leather," Eli muttered.

Noah tilted his chin back.

Penelope bent down and looked. "The stitching is thicker there."

The blade snagged on something.

Eli yanked it back, hard.

The point caught Noah under his chin, stabbed and slashed.

"Damn it," Eli muttered. And, "Sorry."

"No harm done. I cut myself worse shaving." Noah reached for a napkin, pressed it against the stinging wound, and glanced at Penelope.

She stared at the blood, her eyes wide and despairing, her complexion bleaching to a terrifying white.

He looked to Nonna for help.

Nonna had already seen the trouble. "Penelope," she said, "if I'm going to make a roast, I need carrots and potatoes. They're downstairs in the wine cellar. Would you go get them for me?"

Penelope didn't stir.

"Penelope?" Nonna said sharply.

"What?" Penelope started. "What? Carrots and potatoes. Sure. But I'm the one watching for Eli."

"This'll just take a minute." Nonna rinsed a kitchen towel under cold running water and placed it on Penelope's forehead, then draped it around Penelope's neck. Handing her a wide metal colander, she said. "Fill that up. That should be enough to feed us all. Oh, and bring an onion and a head of garlic."

Penelope nodded. "Potatoes and carrots. Onion and garlic."

As she started down the stairs, Eli put down the knife and peeled back the leather.

"Man. Would you look at those wires," he said.

Chapter 63

"Show me," Penelope heard Darren say. Then, in a horrified tone, "That's awesome!"

Reeling with despair and horror, Penelope stumbled down the last two steps and landed on her hands and knees, then sank onto the floor and rested there, her forehead on the cool concrete.

She took long, deep gulps of air, trying to clear her swimming head.

She had sat in the kitchen, watching and listening, being absolutely ineffective as Brooke talked strategy with Darren, while Eli risked his life, while Chloë summed up the lay of the land with a few well-chosen words, while Nonna offered her hands for her grandson, while Rafe and Bao raced out to counterattack the people who wished to kill Noah and all the rest of the Di Luca family.

Penelope felt useless. She was useless. She wanted to save Noah, but she couldn't even walk down the stairs without collapsing. She knew it wasn't her pregnancy that caused her weak knees. It was a gnawing sense of hopelessness. She had seen so much death, and now, on the day when she realized that life had bloomed anew within her, and Noah had affirmed his love for her, she also discovered the man she loved was doomed.

As she lay there, her cheek on the floor, facing the stairway, she wondered, What could she do to help? She had promised herself she would *live* again, and despite the horror of Noah's revelation, she couldn't hide from it.

A random thought popped into her mind.

The bottom step was built . . . oddly.

Unimportant, Penelope.

She needed to concentrate. There had to be *something* she could do to help Noah in his hour of need.

Her eyes narrowed. Her sense of proportion was offended.

The bottom step was wrong.

Not so wrong that anyone could tell there was a problem if they were standing upright. But for a design professional who was on the ground looking straight at it . . . the bottom step was too thick.

Lifting her head, she looked around, trying to see some other examples of *Alice in Wonderland* construction.

But no. The basement was long and wide, mostly bare except for bins of vegetables and a huge, old wine rack that looked like a wonderful instance of early-American construction.

The white-painted staircase itself was the essence of simplicity—wooden steps supported by two long wooden stringers down the sides. Every step was the same: a single flat two-by-ten. Except the bottom step, which was four sturdy inches thick and probably fourteen inches wide with the extra inches at the back. There, where the step above it cast its shadow, the board had the slightest indent that ran the length of the smooth painted surface.

To Penelope's trained eye, the top of the step looked like two pieces of a jigsaw puzzle carefully fitted together.

But who would create such a thing, and do it with such craftsmanship that no one would notice no matter how hard they were searching . . . ?

Eyes fixed on the step, Penelope walked her hands along the concrete floor, pushed herself into a sitting position.

Noah's grandfather. Nonno. The inveterate builder, fixer, repairman. That was who.

And why would he do that?

To create a space to hide his precious bottle of wine, to keep it cool and in the dark.

Penelope forgot her nausea, her despair.

In a flurry of motion, she crawled to the step

and felt along the barely visible seam between the wide front board and the narrow back board. Yes, they were definitely two pieces sanded and painted to resemble one step.

She dug her fingernails into the seam.

Nothing budged.

She sat back on her heels, her elation dying a little.

She looked again.

Felt the seam again.

No. She was right. Somehow, this came apart.

She walked around to the back, ducked under the stairway, and knelt there. Here she saw more clearly the extra width of the step, and a notch above the step on the inside of the wood stringer. She lifted from the back—and the step shifted. Lifted. She slid it free.

And there, resting in a hollow box that ran the length of the step, was an old, very old, bottle of wine.

The bottle of wine.

She placed her palm on the long, stretched neck and stroked it as if it were a living creature.

It was beautiful: green glass, tall, thin, with a long neck and a small, worn, faded label marked, MASSIMO.

Then reality caught up with her.

She crawled out from under the stairs, jumped to her feet, ran around the stairs, and shouted, "Noah, could I see you?" Too emphatic. She should be calmer. She called, "Noah? I need to see you." A moment. *"Really!"*

Noah appeared at the top of the stairs.

Even from here, she could see the strips of leather Eli had dissected off his dog collar, and the confusion of tiny silver cables that encircled Noah's throat.

But he smiled as if the sight of her gave him pleasure, and his voice sounded easy, cheerful. "Hey, what's up?"

"I need you to look at something." She didn't know why she was being enigmatic, only that today the scent of danger hung around every word, every action.

He hurried down a couple of steps, frowning, his gaze fixed on her face.

Eli called, "Noah, come on; we're almost there."

Noah called back, "In a minute." He ran down another three steps. "Penelope? You look as if you're going to . . . What's happened?"

Above in the kitchen, the phone rang.

Someone answered it.

Distantly, Penelope heard a vague, one-sided conversation. "Hurry," she said in a low voice, and beckoned him as she walked around behind the steps.

"Are you okay?" He ran the rest of the way down, joined her, and with his gaze followed her pointing finger. For a long second, he hung suspended by amazement. Dropping to his knees, he touched the bottle with the same reverence she had shown. "Nonno's bottle of wine. You found Nonno's bottle of wine." He looked at her as if she illuminated his soul.

"I did."

"Look. It has Massimo's name on it. But how . . ." Noah was talking to himself now. "Nonno hid it in the step itself. We looked all over the floor, all over the walls, but we didn't look *in* the steps. And his note said, 'up.' And when it was turned over, it said, 'dn.' " Turning to Penelope, he took her shoulders. "You've saved me." Noah looked into her face, his own features hidden by the shadows of the stairway, and the gleam in his eyes made her heart swell with love.

"Call them," she said urgently. "Tell the Smits, or the Propovs, or whatever they call themselves. Tell them to come and get it, and remove that damned bomb from your throat."

"Noah!" Eli called from the top of the stairs. He sounded tense and angry, in the grip of a crisis that had intensified yet again.

Noah turned his head with a frown. "What's wrong?"

"Chloë called. She and Brooke were on their way down toward town on our narrow little highway. They saw four people in a car headed this direction, trailed by another car with two people."

Noah went on alert.

Eli continued. "Both cars were taking the curves too fast, like they were on a mission. Chloë called Rafe to warn him. Brooke turned back and tracked them."

Noah and Penelope scrambled out from underneath the stairs.

"Damn it!" he said. Those women were going to get themselves killed.

"The car dropped two people off in a wash that leads into the property. The people remaining in the car gunned their way across the lawn and—" Eli turned and looked toward the front door.

Penelope heard it open.

Eli shouted, "They're here!"

Chapter 64

Noah heard a shot.

Nonna screamed.

Eli smacked the side of the upper door, stumbled forward, then tumbled down the stairs.

"Eli!" Noah leaped up the steps, catching Eli halfway down.

Feet thundered above.

Another shot.

Nonna. They'd killed Nonna.

Eli was limp, unconscious, a deadweight in Noah's arms.

Penelope ran toward the stairs to help.

Noah said, "Hide!"

Absurd. She had nowhere to hide. But he couldn't stand to see her just die. . . .

Already he'd lost Nonna.

Nonna, who had loved him his whole life . . .

And Eli, whose crimson chest bore witness to the fact that the Propovs were shooting to kill. Lifting him, Noah swung around and jumped off the stairs. He deposited his brother out of the way at the edge of the stairs.

Penelope jumped, too, landing next to Eli. She ducked and got under the steps.

Thank God she listened to him. Thank God she was hiding.

Noah looked into her eyes, saw the strength and compassion there. Their hands touched, clung; then Noah released her. He straightened. He stepped to the bottom of the stairs, where he faced his death.

Hendrik stood at the top of the stairs, his Glock held at the ready.

Noah held his arms wide, baring his chest, inviting the shot. "Do it!"

"No way. I'm not letting you off that easy. You've got"—Hendrik consulted his watch—"eight minutes before your head blows off. I want to watch you squirm as every second of your life ticks away." His cold, killer eyes took on a cruel sheen. "But look at you. Isn't that cute! You tried to disarm your collar."

Noah took one step up. “How do you know I didn’t succeed?”

“We’ve been listening.” Hendrik laughed with all the pleasure of a man at the height of his powers. “Grieta fixed the microphone. You know she’s good at what she does.”

“Yes. I know.” Noah’s mind raced. When had they fixed the microphone? How much had they heard?

Hendrik took a step down. “You doomed the Di Lucas with your touching confession of your youthful adventures with us. Because of you, we’ll search everyone down, kill them one by one, until we wipe the blot of your existence from this—”

Liesbeth appeared in the doorway behind him and gave an exasperated sigh. “Stop the melodrama, Hendrik, and move. Let me talk to him.”

Hendrik turned on her. “You’re not in charge anymore, old woman.”

With one large, strong hand, Liesbeth gripped Hendrik on the muscle between his neck and his shoulder.

Hendrik twisted and went down on one knee, his pistol drooping in his hand.

“That was dumb,” Noah said. During the robbery of the famed painting, Noah had seen Liesbeth use her pressure points on servants and security people; they always crumpled. But never had he seen her use one on one of her own.

But then, he'd never heard Hendrik speak to her like that, either.

Hendrik believed the power had shifted.

Liesbeth corrected him. Holding Hendrik helpless, she looked reproachfully at Noah. "Why did you do that? Why did you tell the Di Lucas? I warned you what would happen if you did."

Noah didn't know whether she was being deliberately obtuse, or if she put new meaning into the word *clueless*. "I told them because I didn't want my head to blow off, Mother."

"Six more minutes!" Hendrik called out.

Liesbeth gave his neck another twist. He writhed and groaned.

Noah kept his gaze at the top of the stairs. If he could get up there fast enough, remove the pistol from Hendrik's hand, gain control of the situation . . .

Liesbeth's gaze shifted to look over his shoulder.

He half turned to see Penelope rising from under the stairway, the bottle of wine in her hand. "Penelope. No," he said.

Penelope paid no attention to him. Her focus was on Liesbeth and Hendrik. "There's still time to stop the timer," she said to them.

"No," Noah said again. Didn't she see? Those two wouldn't make a deal. Not while they held the power.

But Penelope held the bottle sideways on her

palms, offering it to the two at the top of the stairs as if they were gods. "Disarm the bomb at Noah's neck and this is yours."

Liesbeth let Hendrik go.

Hendrik got to his feet.

Both of them stared at the bottle, eyes agleam with greed.

"That's it?" Liesbeth pushed past Hendrik and clattered halfway down.

"You're shitting." Hendrik's voice was rich with disbelief—and hope.

It was too late to back away from Penelope's offer, so Noah said, "You know it's the right bottle . . . if you were listening in."

"We lost transmission." Hendrik took two steps down. "I guess when you came down to the basement."

"This is it, the genuine article." Penelope spoke in a soothing tone. "It was in the staircase." She retreated, one slow step at a time.

Noah did the same, never looking away from Liesbeth and Hendrik.

As if pulled by a lure, Liesbeth came the rest of the way down to the basement. "Where was it?" she asked. "Where was the bottle?"

"In the bottom step." Noah pointed.

Liesbeth looked at the long, narrow open coffin in the bottom step. She turned on Noah, her green eyes sparking with indignation. "How could you not have found it sooner?"

"I didn't find it at all. Penelope did," he said.

"You can have it if you'll remove the bomb from Noah's neck." Penelope sounded so hopeful . . . when there was no hope.

Hendrik lifted his pistol. "I can have it anyway."

Penelope retreated again, her hands steady, and she spoke to Liesbeth, not Hendrik. "Are you really going to let him kill your son? Your only child?"

Was Penelope playing them one against the other? It wouldn't work, but . . . it was the only chance they had. "Mother, you always said the Propov family was the most important thing in your life. Everything you've done is to advance the standing of the Propovs." Noah injected spirit and strength into his voice. "Penelope is carrying the next generation. She's carrying your grandchild."

"I don't care about Liesbeth's grandchild," Hendrik snarled. "And I'm the one with the firepower here." Yet he didn't shoot. Not yet. He held the Glock steady on Noah as he walked down another three steps.

Beside the stairway, Noah saw movement.

Eli was alive. Noah could suddenly breathe more easily. His brother was alive!

Now . . . to keep him that way.

Liesbeth looked sideways at Eli; so she'd seen the movement, too. She glanced at Hendrik, but said nothing.

So. What Noah had suspected was true.

Liesbeth and Hendrik were no longer a team.

Desperate to distract Hendrik, Noah asked, "How much longer do I have? How soon will I be dead?"

"Not much longer." Hendrik's mouth curved in a cruel smile.

Eli's bloody hand crawled toward the stairway.

"Maybe I won't kill your girlfriend," Hendrik taunted. "Maybe I'll just wound her. There's a real pleasure in screwing a woman while she writhes in pain."

Penelope flinched.

"You're going to die," Noah vowed, and started toward him.

Hendrik lifted the pistol, pulled back the hammer, and pointed it at Noah's forehead. "What was it you said to me this morning? Oh, yes, I remember—run!"

Instead, Noah prepared to pounce.

"Catch it!" Penelope shouted.

Hendrik and Noah turned, surprised, confused.

Penelope tossed Massimo's bottle high in the air. The long green glass rose in a curving arc toward the stairs, toward Hendrik.

Too many things happened at once.

Hendrik lunged for the bottle.

Noah lunged for Hendrik.

Liesbeth shouted, "No!"

Hendrik shot—at Penelope. He caught the bottle in the other outstretched fist.

The two men collided in midair, then hit the concrete floor, the dull thud of flesh against flesh knocking the air out of them both.

Something in Noah's shoulder tore.

Didn't matter.

Hendrik had killed Penelope. Hendrik wanted to kill them all.

The bottle was positioned between Hendrik's body and Noah's body.

Hendrik still held the Glock.

They rolled.

Noah smashed his head into Hendrik's face. Blood spurted. He grappled for Hendrik's ear and yanked. More blood.

Hendrik howled and slammed his pistol into the side of Noah's head. The metal grip made contact.

Noah saw stars.

Hendrik tried to pull his hand back far enough to aim the gun.

Noah moved in close, punching with all his skill and fury and anguish. He used moves Hendrik himself had taught him, moves he'd learned in every self-defense class since he'd left the Propov gang, moves he made up now in the heat of battle.

They rolled into the wine rack.

Hendrik brought his elbow up under Noah's

chin. Noah's head snapped back. Bottles clattered. Fell. Shattered. Glass flew.

Something stung Noah's cheek. A sharp shard sliced him open. Warm blood coursed down his face.

Yet . . . this wasn't right. Noah couldn't figure it out.

He was taking a beating. He was. But Hendrik, faster, more skilled, more practiced, should have already killed him.

Then Noah realized—Hendrik was using one hand. In the other, he held the bottle of wine.

The second Propov rule: Always bring home the treasure.

Noah's ire cooled to the ice-cold reasoning of a condemned man. Without Penelope, without their baby, he didn't give a crap about the pain, about the breaking bones or the blood splattering the floor. He sure as hell didn't give a crap about Nonno's bottle or the diamond contents. He let Hendrik strike again and again with his free hand, and when he saw his chance, he grasped Hendrik's wrist. He used the pressure point that his mother had taught him all those years ago, twisted, and snapped.

Hendrik jerked, kicked, struggled, dropped the pistol.

But he also dropped the bottle. It thunked on the concrete and rolled. Somewhere in the distance, Noah heard someone yelling a protest.

He caught a flash of someone dashing down the stairs. An old man. Grabbing the bottle.

But Noah couldn't take his gaze from Hendrik's bloodshot eyes as the two men rolled on the floor, brutally punching and kicking.

Hendrik no longer cared about watching Noah die from the bomb around his neck. He lived to kill.

But Noah had three minutes left in his life.

And if it was the last thing he did, he was going to protect what was left of his family from this monster.

He owed Nonna.

He owed Penelope.

And one thing he knew without a doubt: He was smarter than Hendrik, and he had more at stake.

This time when Hendrik grabbed for him, Noah whimpered and tried to crawl away, toward the stairway.

Hendrik laughed.

The dumb-ass laughed.

Getting to his feet, he grabbed Noah's ankle in his good hand and dragged him backward.

Noah twisted and begged, rolled and fought, an actor in the role of a lifetime.

They reached Nonna's wine rack against the long wall.

Noah staggered to his feet and faced Hendrik, hands loose at his sides.

Bruised and bloody, Hendrik laughed again and charged.

On one foot, Noah spun in a circle. He used his momentum and his hand on Hendrik's shoulder to propel that brutal, grotesque face into the bottles protruding from the rack.

The rack shuddered from the impact.

Hendrik backed away, staggering, shaking his head, trying to clear his brain.

But Propovs were bred for fighting.

Even before he recovered, he attacked.

Grabbing two of the bottles by the necks, Noah smashed them against the sides of Hendrik's head.

Glass shattered.

For a split second, Hendrik remained on his feet, staring at Noah. But the wide green eyes were vacant, seeing nothing. Then he folded like an accordion and dropped face-first on the concrete.

Noah stood, gasping, waiting for Hendrik to rise again.

Nothing.

He had intended to strap bombs on his body and take out the Propovs in one magnificent explosion. Instead, he had defeated his enemy in a fight that raged between intelligence and brute force.

Noah was victorious. He had saved his family . . . perhaps.

He had failed Penelope . . . totally.

He touched the collar at his throat. Death couldn't come soon enough.

Then . . . he heard the distinctive click of someone drawing back the hammer of a pistol.

Chapter 65

Noah spun.

Penelope stood, covered with blood, pointing Hendrik's pistol at Hendrik's inert body.

Liesbeth sprawled facedown on the floor, unmoving.

Eli sat propped against the stairway, white faced but conscious, holding one of Nonna's clean rags against his bloody shoulder.

"Penelope . . ." Noah whispered. He couldn't believe it.

She was alive.

"I'm fine." Penelope took a sobbing breath. "I'm fine. The blood . . . is your mother's. I'm sorry, Noah." Her hand, the one that held the gun, shook. "She's dead. She saved me. She saved the baby." Penelope shook her head over and over. "But . . . without her . . ."

Without Liesbeth, there was no way to disarm the bomb at his throat.

Penelope was alive.

But Noah was dead, condemned by the death of his mother to a wonderfully inventive, absolutely bloody murder.

He could see the knowledge in Penelope's eyes: the anguish, the dying hope.

Without volition, he glanced at his watch.

Less than a minute left.

Penelope lowered the pistol. She tried to come to him, hold him, hug him.

He gestured her away. "No. We don't know how violent the explosion will be."

"I don't care!" She gave a sob.

"Penelope . . . it's okay." He patted his chest over his heart, overflowing with love for her. "Look at me. I mean, look past all the bruises and the cuts, and really look at me! *You're* alive. That means my baby is alive, and that's more legacy than I ever expected to leave. I'd do anything if I could stay here and be with you and love you every day. If I could watch little Sarah grow up, I would praise God every day in all humility. Instead I'm grateful for the time we had together, and the life we made out of our love." He took a long breath. A last breath. "Wherever I go, I promise I'll watch over you both, and I will always, always guard your happiness. You believe me, right? You can see it in me, right?"

She stared at his anxious, earnest face.

For all of their time together, Noah had pulled a veil over his eyes, never allowing her to see too deeply into his soul. Because always he had been hiding his past, the truth about his mother's family, and his inevitably early death.

Now, however, he had nothing to hide. The veil was down.

She could see him: warm, tender, and so in love with her, her throat closed. "Yes," she whispered. "I believe you."

From the floor came a hideous groan.

Penelope jumped.

Noah turned with a snarl.

Slowly, painfully, Hendrik turned his head and whispered, "I wish the goddamned bomb would go off early so I don't have to listen to that shit."

Penelope lifted the pistol. She wanted to kill Hendrik so badly. . . .

From the stair, Eli said, "Have you ever shot a gun, Penelope?"

She shook her head.

"Then give it to me. I'm conscious; I've got a good aim—"

Penelope hesitated. Eli looked pasty white, but his brown eyes snapped with pain and fury.

Eli continued. "—and one more comment out of the little prick who murdered my grandmother and I'll be glad to kill him."

Yes. Eli hated enough to kill.

Penelope walked over and handed him the pistol.

Noah said, "Twenty seconds. Penelope, why don't you go upstairs and . . . ?"

"No. I'm not leaving you." She went to him,

and although he tried to evade her, she wrapped her arms around his waist. "I love you, and I need to hold you. I *really* need to hold you."

"How brave," Hendrik sneered.

"No, I'm selfish." She buried her anguish in a deep, hidden part of her soul. She smiled up into Noah's face, wanting his last view on earth to be a memory to carry for eternity. "I want to be close to Noah until that far-distant day when we're together again."

Noah seemed to want her here, and yet he wanted to send her away from this scene of impending death. "This explosion is small enough that it won't harm you . . . if you can bear the sight of—"

"It's not about me and what I can bear, is it?" she said fiercely.

"Then stand behind me and hug me—quickly!"

She did as he commanded, pressed herself against his back.

"It's time," he said.

She braced herself to hold him, to hold the sudden weight of his dead body. She braced herself for the pain of his passing, for the grief she knew awaited her. She tried to look ahead to that time when she would hold his child and see his green eyes looking up out of that tiny face . . . but nothing could surpass the barbarity of this moment.

Tensed against him, she waited, every second

crawling into the next second, and the next, and the next. . . .

She started to feel embarrassed. Did they have the wrong time? Had someone set the timer incorrectly? Was she so impatient to get the worst horror of her life over that she felt as if time were crawling?

"Hey, Noah?" Eli said. "It's about a minute past your D-day."

"Hm." Noah pulled away from Penelope and looked around.

He looked very odd, mouth puckered, eyes thoughtful. In a sudden motion, he reached up, pulled the latch free, and flung the necklace as hard as he could into the corner.

The dog collar hit the wall, landed on the floor, and just . . . sat there, innocuous and unexploded.

Hendrik's vile curse made Penelope realize—Hendrik had expected it to blow up.

Why hadn't it exploded?

Picking up a shard of glass, Hendrik focused on the necklace, and, on his hands and knees, he crawled over. Taking the leather in his hands, he started at the left side and counted the studs, and using the glass, he cut one particular stud free. He rolled it in his palm, examined it, then looked at Liesbeth's body with such virulence, Penelope feared for her. "The bitch disarmed the necklace," Hendrik said.

Noah laughed incredulously. He laughed again

in absolute amazement. "My mother—she lied to me. She gave me the collar *knowing* it was a dud. She lied."

"She lied?" Penelope couldn't believe it. "She tried to control you by threatening to kill you? And she lied?" She was indignant. Not about the fact that Liesbeth had sabotaged the bomb at Noah's throat. But that Liesbeth had been willing to destroy Noah to rebuild him in her image.

What a lesson for Penelope, facing all the long years of child raising.

Noah moved toward Eli, his palm extended.

Eli handed over the Glock; then, in slow motion, he slithered down onto the floor, his strength gone.

Noah touched him briefly, a single gesture of reassurance, then moved back toward the middle of the basement.

"She lied." On his hands and knees, Hendrik scratched at the collar, ripping off the studs one by one.

"I never said she was a good mother. More like the witch who tried to bake Hansel and Gretel in the oven." Noah laughed some more, low and deep, as if this moment meant something great to him.

Probably it did. Better to find out your mother didn't try to kill you than to know she did.

Penelope's nerves winched tighter. Something was going to happen. Something so terrible it would play in her nightmares forever.

Noah winced, put his hand on his neck as if it hurt, and winced again. Yet all the while, he kept his gaze on Hendrik. "My mother. God, what a piece of work."

"Liesbeth. She disarmed the necklace before she ever gave it to you. You!" Hendrik rose to a sitting position. He glared at Noah. "You little nancy-boy."

Noah still chuckled. "Poor Hendrik. It must sting to be defeated by a nancy-boy."

Hendrik lumbered to his feet, his malevolent eyes fixed on Noah.

Abruptly, Noah stopped laughing. "My mother tried to convince me to kill you and take over the gang. Did you know that, Hendrik?" Blood smeared his face, dried on his collar, colored his taunts with crimson. "Liesbeth didn't trust you. She didn't think you were good enough to take her place."

Hendrik's swollen features resembled a prize-fighter's. "I'm going to slaughter you." His fat fingers reached out—and he charged at Penelope.

She screamed.

Gunfire roared through the basement.

With her hands over her ears, Penelope dropped to her knees.

Noah had fired the Glock.

But when she opened her eyes and looked . . . on the stairs, Rafe stood, dirty and scraped, holding a large-caliber pistol. And he had fired, too.

It was over.

Hendrik was a crumpled body on the floor, his malice vanished, and he . . . not even a memory.

But Noah . . . was alive.

Chapter 66

By the time Penelope's ears stopped ringing, Rafe was at the bottom of the stairs, lifting the rag Eli held over the wound, looking and talking. "Bao and I caught two of those bastards sneaking toward the house from the vineyard. Caught them by surprise. They didn't expect resistance. They fought. Dead, both of them." He probed Eli's shoulder with his fingertips. "Hey, brother, good news. This gunshot wound—it's a through-and-through. That's good."

"Chloë?" Eli gasped.

Rafe gave a brief laugh. "She's fine. She and Brooke followed two of the others—"

Eli groaned. "The woman is trying to kill me."

Rafe continued. "They drove cross-country in Chloë's Porsche."

"Dragged bottom?"

"Totally. They ran down the guy. He's got critical injuries. The female got away."

"That's six." Noah clicked the safety on the Glock, put it into his belt, and helped Penelope to her feet. "Get her, and you've got them all."

"DuPey has the local police chasing her. They know the area. I've got my people guarding the house." Rafe glanced at Noah. "You look pretty good, kid, for a guy who had his head blown off five minutes ago."

"False alarm," Noah said casually.

Penelope punched his ribs hard enough to make him wince.

But then . . . he was already hurt.

Rafe stopped his bandaging of Eli long enough to critically examine Noah. "I'd say you need some stitches."

"And I think"—Noah flexed his hand, rolled his shoulder, felt his ribs—"maybe a cast and some bandages."

"You have broken bones?" Penelope didn't know why she was surprised. In a lifetime of watching Hollywood movies, she had never seen such a vicious fight in her life.

"Things are broken inside, but compared to how dead I thought I would feel . . . I'm pretty good." Gingerly, Noah pulled her into his arms and looked toward his brothers. "Penelope saved us. She found the bottle and used it to bargain with them."

"No. Really? Good job!" Rafe nodded approvingly at Penelope. "Where was it?"

"Under the stairs," she said.

He glanced toward the bottom step. "Whoa. Where is it now?"

"Hendrik dropped it." She glanced around the floor. "I think . . . someone grabbed it." She tried to remember the details, but the last twenty minutes had been like one snapshot after another, moments frozen in time, all the focus on Noah. Noah. Noah. Stupid to be unsure, yet all of her attention had been fixed on the struggle between Noah and Hendrik.

She hadn't cared about the bottle of wine.

She had cared only about her lover.

In a disgusted tone of voice, Eli said, "It was Joseph Bianchin. He's got the bottle. If Nonna were alive . . ."

"What?" Rafe grabbed Eli's hand. "What about Nonna?"

Bao rushed down a few steps and stood above them, poised to run in any direction. "DuPey got the last one of the gang. The woman killed herself rather than let law enforcement take her. But where's Mrs. Di Luca?"

"They shot her in the kitchen," Noah said.

Bao and Rafe exchanged glances.

"No," Bao said. "No blood. No blood trail. But she's not in the house."

Rafe looked at Bao, at Penelope, at Noah. "Find her."

Sarah stood in her backyard under the wide-spread branches of the oak tree she loved so much, and pointed her cute little handgun, a

Judge Public Defender, at Joseph Bianchin. "Put it down *now*."

"Sarah, you know it's mine." Joseph held Anthony's bottle of wine in his gnarled fingers, caressing it as if it were the woman of his dreams. "Massimo liked the Bianchin family better than the Di Lucas. My father always said so. It's rightfully mine."

"Massimo did not leave you without a gift." Sarah was giving Joseph his last chance to redeem himself.

She considered herself generous.

"A silver rattle!" Joseph's eyes blazed with indignation. "He gave me a silver rattle. Not the priceless bottle of wine he gave to Anthony, but a simple silver rattle."

"It is a beautiful, antique piece of art," Sarah reminded him.

"The wine . . . that was a celebration laid down to be enjoyed on Anthony's twenty-first birthday." Joseph bared his yellowed teeth. "The rattle . . . it's a baby toy."

"Put the bottle down." Sarah's gaze didn't waver. Neither did her aim.

"You wouldn't shoot me. You're a woman, and a sweet woman at that. Stop pretending that you would." Joseph smiled a smile of scorn and false sympathy, and turned away.

Sarah waited until he was about thirty feet away.

She shot him in the butt, a spray of buckshot that pierced his pants and his skin and ripped into the muscle and through the veins. . . .

He screamed in surprise, pain and rage. He dropped the bottle. He fell down and writhed on the ground.

She heard shouts from the house.

The children had found her. But she had a few minutes with Joseph before they got there. A few precious, much-needed moments.

She strolled over to him. She stood well away from his flailing body, and she spoke clearly and coldly. "Any woman whose husband was shot in a family feud and almost killed who doesn't take shooting lessons is a fool." Leaning over, she picked up Anthony's bottle. "It's taken you sixty years, Joseph, but I hope you realize now—I am not a fool."

Chapter 67

Eleven months later . . .

The babies had been christened.

The party had gone on all afternoon and most of the evening. They'd hired a band to play music from the forties, the music that Sarah loved. Caterers set up tables and chairs, and torches and trash cans. Bottles of water and cans of Coke had filled icy tubs. Masses of food had been set out on long tables in Sarah's acres of front yard. Eli tapped a cask of one of his finest wines, and the guests who arrived brought casseroles, salads, cakes, dips. . . .

Sarah had been in her element, directing, placing, greeting, exclaiming. She couldn't remember the last time she'd had so much fun.

All the police department came, of course, and Eli's vine crew, the staff from the tasting room, the staff at the resort, Police Chief DuPey and his wife (no matter how difficult she found the woman and how much she longed to, Sarah could hardly exclude his wife), and everyone who had worked security during last spring's bottle crisis, as Chloë blithely called it.

And the family had come. All the family from Washington, from Far Island off the coast of California, from Italy, and from every other far-flung corner of the world.

Annie and June were here with their families, all charming, as Di Lucas tended to be, all chatting and smiling.

Rafe's mother, Francesca, had taken time off from her Broadway play to be here for her granddaughter's christening.

Brooke's mother, Kathy, looked great in the designer outfit she'd picked up in New York with Francesca's help.

Arianna Marino was here with her whole family.

Sarah had decided it was time to end that feud, especially since Primo Marino had stood as godfather to Anthony Joseph, solemnly promising to take care of the child and guide him through his life.

Sarah liked Primo.

She suspected who he pretended to be and who he actually was . . . were two different things.

But as the sun slid in a golden haze toward the horizon, the first batch of guests, guests with exhausted, grubby children, began to say good-bye. Elderly friends yawned and joked about their wild lives, and thanked the Di Lucas and left.

Finally, as dusk settled among the trees, only the family remained.

Chinese lanterns hung from the great oaks, their light spreading a golden glow, and Sarah stood arm in arm with Bao and smiled benevolently at her dear ones.

"You know," Sarah said to Bao, "you don't have to guard me tonight. It's not your job anymore."

The usually reserved Bao hugged Sarah's waist. "I've missed you."

"I've missed you, too." Sarah hugged her back.

Bao had gone on to other security jobs, but before she left Sarah had made her promise that in between she would regularly check in to assure Sarah she was well. And Bao, who was the most responsible young woman Sarah had ever met, always did. Which was good, because Sarah worried. Bao was strong and brave. She stood on the forefront of the fight between good and evil. Someday . . . she would be hurt, and Sarah would weep.

But for now, Bao was relaxed and smiling, although every time Primo Marino spoke to her she stared at him in alarm.

Sarah found it greatly amusing that Bao, who feared nothing, ran away from Primo.

"I'm glad to see Mr. Joseph Bianchin is walking pretty well." Bao's tone indicated quite the opposite. "For a man who's been shot in the ass."

"Yes." Sarah lowered her voice. "Although they say he occasionally has to visit the doctor to have another piece of buckshot taken out of his posterior."

Bao laughed, a great burst of uncharacteristic amusement. "He will never again challenge another female to shoot him."

"I don't know. He's been a superior swine all his life, and you know how hard it is for old geezers to change." Sarah realized that during all this long day, she hadn't seen him sit down at all.

Good. His butt still hurt.

What a day it had been! Sarah reflected with satisfaction.

Four-month-old Katherine Sarah Di Luca had

been christened first, shrieking loudly as the priest anointed her head.

Two-month-old Anthony Joseph Di Luca stayed awake, placidly sucking his fist through the entire proceedings. He was without a doubt the calmest baby Sarah had ever seen.

Penelope claimed that in the first eight days after his conception, he'd been involved in so much drama he found nothing else worth getting excited about.

Sarah thought Penelope was right.

Now little Anthony slept on his father's shoulder, his chubby, sweet face lax and wrinkled as Noah wandered toward Penelope, smiling as if he'd won life's lottery.

Which he had, and Sarah was glad to see that he knew it.

Eli carried Katherine Sarah upright in the crook of his arm. Katherine Sarah had a grumpier outlook on life than her cousin, but she adored her uncle Eli, and for him she flirted and smiled. Which was fine with Rafe and Brooke, both exhausted from dealing with the biggest diva ever born to the Di Luca family.

Sarah admired her great-granddaughter, and privately agreed with Brooke's mother, Kathy, that she hoped the child gave them both hell.

"For a man who has never before had a child, Mr. Bianchin seems very proud of his grandson," Bao said in a low voice.

"If not so pleased about his grandson's name. Anthony Joseph." Sarah rolled the name off her tongue.

"Mr. Bianchin thought the Joseph should come first?" Bao did not guess so much as make a statement.

"Mm-hm. Dear Joseph is suffering from the ordeal of having a grown daughter he cannot bend to his will."

Sarah and Bao put their heads together and laughed.

Bao said, "He probably imagines he can train his grandson in his image."

"The old fart has never been around a small child. He's in for a shock." Sarah's gaze lingered on Joseph's erect figure as he spoke stiffly to Tom Chan about wines. "Still, he's trying. He polished the antique silver rattle Massimo gave him at his birth and gave it to little Anthony."

In fact, Joseph had had a blue satin-lined wooden box made to display his gift, and now it sat in a place of honor on the table that groaned with christening gifts: receiving blankets, engraved christening cups, silver spoons, booties, handmade afghans, baby-food cookbooks, subscriptions to *National Geographic*, vegan cookbooks, car seats, onesies, cardboard books, mobiles, bottle warmers, boxes of diapers, silver rattles. . . .

Sarah's first great-grandchildren had been

welcomed into the community with prayer, with blessings, with song and wine and joy.

Her life was exactly as it should be.

Bao ran her finger along the box's polished wood, and then along the rattle's smooth silver handle. "It's very beautiful. And valuable, I think?"

"Joseph has never appreciated it, because it wasn't what his family wanted from Massimo, but yes, I suspect it is valuable." Sarah picked it up out of the box. "Look at the workmanship on the bell. Someone spent a lot of time creating little grapes on little grapevines that grow off the handle. . . ." She caught Joseph watching her, and carefully placed the rattle back in the box.

Joseph hadn't been very friendly since she'd shot him.

Imagine that.

With a kiss for them both, Noah handed little Anthony over to Penelope and came to get Sarah. "We're ready, Nonna," he said in a low voice.

She nodded to Bao. "Be careful."

Bao nodded back. "You, too." She moved into position on the porch, overlooking the yard.

Sarah took Noah's arm and they walked slowly toward the house and the most important event of their lives. "How is Eli doing?" she asked in that same low tone.

"He's doing well." Noah's gaze sought out his brother, standing close to the table, one arm around his wife, Rafe's baby girl cradled in the other arm. "The doc told him it would take a year to recover completely, and I'd say he was right on the money. Eli has his moments, but he's almost completely back to normal."

"We were lucky the emergency room doctor had served in the military and realized Eli had been shot twice." When Sarah remembered how close they came to losing him, she felt sick and faint.

"I thought *you'd* taken the second shot." Noah leaned down and gave her a kiss on the cheek. "I thought I had lost you, Nonna."

"I'm tough to kill." For one moment, she leaned her head on his arm. "I wanted to live to see my three grandsons so happy."

"I'm glad I lived to see the day, too," Noah said fervently.

Since the day Noah had faced his mother and his family from hell, since the day he had defeated the fate that had stalked him for so many years . . . he was a changed man. He lived every day as if it were precious, he embraced his family and friends, and most of all, he loved Penelope with all his heart and soul. She was the center of his life, and little Anthony Joseph was the jewel arrived to crown their happiness.

Eli stood holding little Katherine and watching Chloë as she tried desperately to get a smile out of the obstinate baby. He laughed at his wife, but at the same time, the worship in his eyes brought a lump to Sarah's throat.

Chloë with her wild hair, her artistic temperament, her acute mind, and her loving heart had broken through to Sarah's distant, controlled grandson and made him a whole man who lived with no fear and no barriers.

Noah followed Sarah's gaze. "I think he loves her better than his wine. Don't you?"

Sarah nodded. "I really do."

Rafe and Brooke had moved into their beautiful, old, mostly remodeled home barely in time for Katherine's birth. Brooke's mother, Kathy, had stayed with them for the first week and helped out, for which they were both pathetically grateful. Now they learned parenting as they went along, and best of all, they did it together.

"I wish Anthony could have seen how you children have grown," Sarah said.

Noah lightly bumped her shoulder with his. "He knows, Nonna. He knows."

"Yes. You're right. Today . . . I've felt him close. He would approve."

The band was packing up, but on Rafe's request they performed a drumroll.

Sarah clasped Noah's hand. "Here we go!"

The crowd gathered around the bandstand.

In his best radio-announcer voice, Rafe said, "As you know, tonight the Di Luca family celebrates a night unlike any other in our family. Tonight we want to welcome Joseph Bianchin into the family. You all can only imagine our excitement on discovering our beloved sister Penelope is Joseph's long-lost daughter, making Joseph the grandfather of Noah's son, little Anthony." Rafe wickedly did not give the baby's full name.

The small crowd politely clapped.

Joseph limped forward and waved a hand in acknowledgment.

"I don't say it to Penelope, of course"—Noah kept his voice quiet—"but that limp you gave him is small payment for the trouble he started over that bottle of wine."

"And for the years of agony his attack caused Anthony. If I had it all to do again . . . I would have shot between Joseph's legs."

"Nonna!" Noah laughed, startled.

"So there!" She nodded emphatically.

"Tonight we also welcome our former enemies into our family." Rafe gestured. "The Marinos, always our favorite fighting foes, have joined us from our beloved Nonna's side of the family."

Joseph looked sour.

The Marinos cheered.

At the outburst, Katherine Sarah started crying.

"Oh, no." Brooke collapsed into a lawn chair hidden in the shadows.

Chloë took Katherine from Eli and brought her to Brooke.

Brooke tossed a blanket over her shoulder and put baby Katherine to her breast, then waved at Rafe to continue.

He smiled at his wife, then returned to the announcements. "Our father, Gavino Di Luca, is currently filming and was unable to attend. He sends his love."

Nonna looked down and sighed. She wasn't surprised at Gavino's defection. He might be willing to play a grandfather in a movie, but to actually be old enough to be a grandfather . . . he wouldn't acknowledge that.

"So we—Nonna, Eli and Chloë, Noah and Penelope, and Brooke and I—have decided this day, with the joyous celebration of the newest generation and their christenings, is the right and proper time to honor our grandfather, Anthony Di Luca." Rafe paused to clear the emotion from his throat. "To do that, we will open the gift of wine Massimo made and gave to him on the day of his birth, and share it with all of you."

Chapter 68

Clapping. Laughter. A buzz of conversation as the small crowd agreed they were thrilled to be included in this momentous moment in wine history. They surged toward the serving table, set up close to the porch and spread with a white tablecloth.

Sarah hung back and watched Joseph.

He stood tall, his shoulders erect and proud, his nostrils quivering, his eyes narrowed.

"He's been waiting for this moment all his life," Noah said quietly.

"Yes, but now he wants more than merely the taste of the wine," she said.

"He wants a look at those diamonds," Noah said.

"Well, don't we all," she said tartly.

"It's okay, Nonna," Noah said. "We don't expect trouble—but we're ready for it."

The Di Lucas, all of them, were carrying firearms concealed beneath light jackets and bulky cardigans.

Bao was packing, too, and DuPey was in uniform.

Sarah brushed her hand over her pocket and across her Judge Public Defender, loaded with buckshot. "He wouldn't dare."

"I don't think Joseph will do anything, not in this group, but if anyone else realizes what's going on—we could have trouble." Noah scanned the crowd, then nodded to Penelope and the now bright-eyed baby Anthony. "He's awake," Noah said unnecessarily.

"At his age, there's little difference between night and day." Sarah smiled as Anthony blew a bubble.

The Di Lucas had discussed where to place the mothers and babies, and they'd decided two seats in the corner behind the table were safest. As soon as they were finished nursing, Brooke and Katherine would join Penelope and Anthony.

Rafe waved at the crowd to quiet down. "We can give each person only the merest taste, and Eli says I must warn you that after eighty years, it's very likely the wine has turned to vinegar. But let us pour Anthony Di Luca's wine to celebrate the christening of Anthony Di Luca's great-grandchildren. *Salute*!"

The family had had small wine goblets made especially for the occasion, with BELOVED GRANDFATHER ANTHONY DI LUCA etched into the glass, and Chloë placed thirty of them on the table, one for each guest.

The Di Lucas had focused floodlights on the table—it looked like the most narcissistic production ever staged, but they had their reasons, and the reasons had nothing to do with immodesty and everything to do with legendary diamonds and tight security.

A smiling Brooke joined them behind the table, holding the sleeping Katherine Sarah, and seated herself beside Penelope.

Everyone held their breaths as, with steady hands, Eli eased the cork out of the tall, narrow old bottle. He sniffed the cork and said in surprise, "I think . . . I think it's good!"

Quiet applause.

Carefully Eli decanted the wine through a cheesecloth into a glass decanter.

More applause.

But no diamonds.

Sarah observed her family. They showed no reaction at all . . . because they had discussed this as a possibility. As the years passed and a wine aged, a hard red sediment called the lees settled out and clung to the sides of the bottle. The diamonds could very well be stuck in the lees.

But Joseph's eyes narrowed.

Of course. The suspicious old bastard.

Rafe took the cheesecloth and put it into a waiting plastic bag, then took the bottle and placed it on a small stage built behind the table especially for that purpose. The bottle was easy to see—and hard to reach.

Eli poured the wine, drop by drop, into the glasses.

Thank God the bottle was bigger than the modern standard, and he managed to squeak out enough for everyone there.

When the glasses were full, Chloë handed them out.

"Wait for the toast!" Eli called.

When everyone had wine, all eyes turned to Sarah.

She moved into the spotlight. She lifted her

glass. She looked up at the heavens. "For Anthony," she said simply.

"For Anthony!" everyone repeated, and lifted their glasses.

Joseph looked as if he were having an appendicitis attack.

"And!" With a word, Noah stopped the guests. "For our grandmother, Sarah, kind and dear and an example of strength for us all."

"For Sarah!" everyone repeated, and lifted their glasses again, and clicked them together.

Then, in a reverent silence, they drank.

Sarah held the glass for one more moment, breathing in the scent of deep red ripe fruit, spice, and a long-ago California summer sun. "Anthony, I miss you," she whispered. Then she, too, took the wine in her mouth.

It was smooth, rich, with flavors that lingered on the tongue like a kiss on the lips.

Massimo's wine was everything it was reputed to be.

And then . . . it was gone.

In unison, the families sighed in delight. A babble broke out as everyone compared their impressions, sniffed the glasses, tried to eke out another taste.

The Di Lucas remained around the table, accepting thanks, nodding and smiling, saying good night as slowly the guests took their leave.

Finally, only Sarah and Bao, Rafe and Brooke,

Eli and Chloë, Noah and Penelope, and the babies were left.

And Joseph, of course.

Rafe let DuPey go home and shooed his own security people away. Although not Bao. They all insisted she stay. She knew what was in that bottle. Her curiosity was as keen as theirs.

Eli and Noah brought the lights closer and shined them on the table.

In a portentous silence, Eli spread plastic on the table.

Rafe opened the bag and pulled out the cheesecloth and Massimo's glass bottle. He laid out the cheesecloth. "We decided that since Noah has the youngest eyes, he would be best suited to examine the cloth."

No one even smiled.

They were too tense.

Noah used a magnifying glass, going over the stained cloth again and again. Straightening, he shook his head. "No. No diamonds. Not even the tiniest chip."

Eli poured water into the bottle and swished it around, breaking the lees off the sides of the glass. Placing another clean white cheesecloth over the decanter, he strained the water and eighty years' worth of wine sediment through the cloth.

Again, they laid the cheesecloth out, and both brothers stepped back to let Noah examine it.

With great care, he mashed up the lees, smoothing out the flakes and the lumps. He used the magnifying glass. He went over it again and again.

But everyone could see the truth.

Noah looked around at the faces staring at him incredulously. "There's nothing here. There were no diamonds in this bottle."

A babble broke out.

"All that for nothing?" Chloë said.

"People killed for nothing?" Penelope said.

"Shot twice for nothing?" Eli said.

"It wasn't nothing," Rafe reminded him. "The wine was very good."

Eli nodded. "True."

"Maybe somebody stole the diamonds from Massimo?" Brooke suggested. Then, "No, because they never hit the market."

"But where *did* he hide those diamonds?" Nonna's eyes drooped. "Hm."

Joseph leaned across the table and glared at Noah. "This was a trick!"

Penelope leaned back, little Anthony in her arms, and returned the glare. "Don't accuse anyone here of thievery, *Father*. You could live to regret that."

Noah patted her back until she settled down. In a sensible tone, he said, "Joseph, we did it like this for *you*. So *you* could see exactly what we did and how many diamonds came out of the bottle. We didn't expect to come up clean, either. I mean, after all the trouble and pain we had, don't you think we want the diamonds?"

"It's a trick," Joseph repeated.

"How do you think we stole the diamonds out of the bottle?" Rafe asked.

"You changed the bag. . . ." Joseph's voice faded.

Rafe had kept the bag within view the whole time.

Slowly, as cold reality sank into his old brain, the red blotches of anger faded from Joseph's cheeks. But he was still breathing hard, and he muttered, "I know Massimo stole those diamonds."

Laughing softly to herself, Sarah slipped away from the table.

"Perhaps he did," Noah said. "But even if he did, they weren't ours to start with."

"I suppose if they're anybody's, they are Noah's," Penelope said to her father. "*He's* the last remaining Propov."

Noah snorted. "Ah, the legacy of the Propovs. Bitterness, death, and lost diamonds."

Sarah walked to the gift table, where all the babies' presents were displayed. She knew exactly what she wanted: the gift Massimo had given Joseph at his birth.

"I did want to see the Beating Heart," Chloë said wistfully.

"I want to see any six-point-eight-carat diamond," Brooke responded.

All the women nodded in unison.

Picking up the satin-lined box, Sarah carried the antique silver rattle back to the little group that hovered under the lights, reluctant to let this evening end.

"Anyway, all those years ago, before the diamonds were stolen, they were sold to a duchess," Noah said. "If we had found diamonds, they would belong to her, or rather, her descendants."

"Actually, I did the research." Chloë had that instructional tone in her voice, the one she got when she'd found information that excited her. "The insurance company decided the fault for the robbery lay in the Propovs' handling of the security, and they made them pay the money back to the duchess. So in fact, with all known Propovs dead, the diamonds *are* yours, Noah. I mean . . . they would be if there were diamonds."

"Noah is not the last of the Propovs," Sarah pointed out. "Little Anthony is."

"Poor kid." But Noah grinned as he put his arm around Penelope and looked down at the baby in her arms.

"We'll have to make sure he's not the very last of the Propovs," Penelope said. "In a year or two?"

"I would like that," Noah murmured.

Sarah waited until the children had begun to clean up before she approached Joseph.

"It's difficult to imagine Massimo *lost* such valuable pink diamonds," she said to Joseph.

"I don't believe it," he snapped.

"I don't either." Picking up the rattle out of the box, she shook it back and forth, back and forth. The rattle did not so much ring . . . as clatter. "I think Massimo was even craftier than we could have ever imagined."

Joseph stared at her as if she were a batty old woman.

What a thickheaded old fool.

"Noah!" she called sharply.

Noah responded to the tone in her voice, and hurried immediately to her side. "What is it, Nonna?"

"Earlier in the evening, I was admiring the gift Massimo gave the newborn Joseph Bianchin, and I was so pleased to see that today Joseph gave the precious rattle to his first grandchild, little Anthony." Sarah's smile invited Noah to share the joke.

Noah's gaze fell to the silver rattle, and he said uncertainly, "Yes, that was very kind of Joseph."

She shook the rattle again.

Joseph drew in a horrified breath.

Look at that. Comprehension had finally dawned.

"Joseph is very generous," she said, "for this is a *kingly* gift."

Noah looked at Joseph. Looked at the silver baby toy in her hand. Met her gaze. And he, too, realized the truth. In a wondering tone, he said, "I think you're right."

"You should keep this in a safe place. You should guard it with your life." She spoke to Noah, but she kept her gaze on Joseph. "And I think, on Anthony's twenty-first birthday, you should present it to him with all ceremony." As she handed the box to Noah, she shook the despised baby toy once more.

Joseph's hand reached out in appeal.

"Thank you, Nonna." Noah took the box and the rattle, and kissed her forehead. "That is exactly what Penelope and I will do." And he, too, shook the toy.

Joseph stood stricken, staring, listening to the sound that diamonds made as they rolled back and forth, back and forth, inside the rattle.

Center Point Large Print
600 Brooks Road / PO Box 1
Thorndike ME 04986-0001 USA

(207) 568-3717

US & Canada:
1 800 929-9108
www.centerpointlargeprint.com